CROSSING THE LINE

A SINNER AND SAINT NOVEL

LUCY SCORE

Bloom books

ISBN: 978-1-945631-02-3 (ebook)
ISBN: 978-1-7282-8277-0 (paperback)

Published by Bloom Books, an imprint of Sourcebooks
P.O. Box 4410, Naperville, Illinois 60567-4410
(630) 961-3900
sourcebooks.com

lucyscore.com

040921

To Tim,

My real-life romance novel hero inspiration. Without you, none of this would be possible.

I love you to the tropical beach and back.

Love,

Your Eternally Grateful Lucy

1

Waverly Sinner timed her escape perfectly so that the glossy Mercedes slid through the opening security gate at the foot of the driveway with inches to spare. Heart pounding, head aching, she accelerated past the two photographers, one next to a street bike and the other leaning against a dented Toyota the color of the pollution that clung to L.A. like a wool blanket in the summer.

She made it through the gate and down the street before they'd even shifted into drive, feeling like a small victory had been won. The element of surprise was the only way she could get a head start on the photographers that followed her everywhere these days.

She heard the whine of the motorcycle engine and spotted it in her rearview mirror as it came over the crest of the hill. *Damn it.* The Toyota she could lose, but that beat-up bike was going to be a problem.

She shouldn't have taken the car. Ruby red, it was an attention magnet, which is why it usually sat in the garage unless her mother was feeling convertible-ready and took it on a joy ride for the gossip sites. But it was the first set of keys she'd blindly grabbed while trying to unsee the naked bodies sprawled on her couch. The couch that she would now have to burn.

The car handled the corner as if it were a straightaway, and the guy on the street bike behind her leaned into the turn, but she heard the squeal of the Toyota's tires.

Why couldn't they just leave her alone? What was it she had that they needed so desperately?

She snaked her way through the hills, disappointing the photographers when she headed away from town. Away from the chaos that had invaded every aspect of her life. Away from her father and the brunette he'd decided to undress in the pool house where she lived. Away from her mother and her never-empty glass of vodka that fooled no one.

Waverly just wanted to be normal. She wanted a house that didn't need security. A family that didn't spend their entire lives pretending for the cameras. She wanted a job where people didn't follow her around demanding to know what she had for breakfast and who she was sleeping with. Where no one wanted a piece of her or maliciously hoped to witness a very public and humiliating downward spiral.

It was the real Hollywood story. The industry built you up so the audience could gleefully tear you back down.

She'd never had a chance at normal. Not the daughter of two Hollywood legends whose volatile love story was more fascinating than any film. Their partnership had cemented a renown more permanent than their side-by-side stars on the Walk of Fame.

After a conception timed perfectly to coincide with one of her parents' movie premieres, Waverly joined the Sinner clan. She'd inherited her mother's golden looks and her father's acting range. But their desire for the spotlight seemed to have skipped a generation. However, not following in the family footsteps was not an option.

At twenty, she already had twelve movies under her belt. She'd won an Oscar at fifteen, been gifted this very Mercedes from a studio at sixteen, and filed her first lawsuit against tabloids at eighteen. She had her own star on the Walk of Fame. She'd never attended a day of school, instead getting her education crowded around tight tables in trailers with on-set tutors. Prom and Homecoming had been traded for hundreds of red carpets.

She wasn't ungrateful. The opportunities that this life, this career, had provided for her were immeasurable. But they came at a price.

As the rarified air of Bel Air fell away behind her, the wind, dry from the desert with just a hint of salt from the Pacific, whipped over her. Estates and lush, green country clubs gave way to rows of Spanish style houses crowded along congested roads that snaked their way around canyons. She wasn't sure where she was going. Maybe the canyon, maybe the coast? But she knew exactly what she was leaving behind.

All those demands that piled up on her shoulders were beginning to take a toll. She had a family legacy to live up to, her mother liked to remind her. And her success provided for others. She couldn't just walk away from agents and assistants and stylists and attorneys. They depended on her.

An image of her mother flashed into her mind as she squeezed into traffic on Sunset Boulevard. Waverly didn't know whether her father's philandering had spurred her mother's drinking or vice versa. But the two had fed each other's vices for years now. It didn't surprise her to find her father in such a compromising position, however, his decision to bring his date into *her* home did.

A glint in her rear view mirror caught her attention. The

motorcycle was splitting the lanes to get to her while the dented Toyota struggled a few cars behind. They never gave up. She was either going to have to give them what they wanted or lose them. And she was tired of giving.

Waverly swooped off of Sunset and wound her way through a neighborhood of dust-colored townhomes with orange tile roofs. Two careful turns later, she was on a lonely highway that climbed through desert and hills.

The motorcycle stuck with her and, on a straightaway, swerved out around her to speed alongside her car.

"Geez, got a death wish?" Waverly muttered, hugging the edge of the pavement. As much as she hated giving this crap sandwich a shot he could use, it would be worse to see his body splattered all over the road. She gripped the leather wheel a little tighter and slowed down. The idiot shoved his camera at her and snapped away.

He was wearing a half helmet with a scarred visor that looked more appropriate for bicycle use. Stringy brown hair curled limply around his face. His Pantera t-shirt and black denim shorts had both seen better days. He was grinning like the winner at a cock fight.

Reluctantly Waverly slowed to a crawl as they crested another hill.

"Get back in the lane," she yelled, hoping she wasn't about to witness a vehicular homicide up close and personal.

He flipped her the bird and swung his bike in front of her car, cutting her off.

Waverly jammed on the brakes and swerved across the double line narrowly missing him. Her fingers gripped the wheel in a rigor mortis grip. Death Wish wasn't just going for pictures, he was trying to create a story. One where she got hit head-on.

Her heartbeat was thudding in her ears as adrenaline

surged through her system. She made sure the world's stupidest man was still upright before stomping on the accelerator. The second she was clear of the photographer, she cut the wheel to the right, squeaking back into her lane just as a silver Range Rover sped around the turn. The driver laid on the horn as she narrowly avoided his shiny bumper of death.

"Holy shit. Holy shit. Oh my God," Waverly chanted. This guy was trying to get her killed. She hit the Bluetooth button on the steering wheel and, through clenched teeth, called 911.

"Nine-one-one. What is your emergency?"

"I'm on Promontory Road and there's a man on a motorcycle trying to—"

Waverly watched in horror as the motorcycle once again drew alongside her.

"Smile pretty for the camera, sweetheart," he shouted. She saw the glint of a gold tooth.

He didn't see the pick-up truck coming down the hill, but Waverly did.

"Jesus, look out!"

The photographer gunned the bike and swerved in front of her, clipping her bumper. She cut her wheel to the right and hit the brakes as Death Wish lost control of the bike and went into a slide.

She heard the scraping of metal on metal as the Mercedes met guardrail and felt a small sense of relief when there was no sickening thump of a human speed bump.

"Ma'am? "Ma'am?" the 911 operator's dispassionate voice came through her car's audio system.

"There's been an accident," Waverly said, her voice miles calmer than she felt. "We're just south of Mountaingate. Send an ambulance."

She cut her engine and shoved open her door. She hurried around the front of her car, her flip-flops echoing on the asphalt. Death Wish was facedown and motionless. His bike was a tangled mess wrapped around the guardrail.

"Crap," Waverly muttered.

The pick-up truck had come to a harmless stop on the opposite side of the road. "Are you all right?" A man in his fifties decked out for a day on the golf course called out the window.

Waverly nodded. "Yeah. Are you?"

"Better than that asshole on the ground. I'm gonna move my truck back to the other side of the hill to control the traffic," he told her.

Waverly nodded and returned her attention to Death Wish. She tiptoed her way through glass and metal to kneel down next to his unmoving body. Blood trickled from a dozen shallow scrapes on his legs, but it was the nasty gash on his forearm that looked dangerous. Blood was pumping out of the jagged tear at an alarming—and disgusting—rate.

"So gross," Waverly muttered under her breath. They were miles from the closest hospital, which meant Death Wish might just get what he wanted if she didn't do something.

She yanked her tank top off over her head and wrapped it around the wound. When she applied pressure, Death Wish flinched.

At least he wasn't already dead.

When he started to move his legs in a bid to sit up, she shoved him back down. She flipped up the half visor on his helmet. "Stop moving or you'll probably die," she warned.

"Where's my camera?" he whined through gritted teeth.

Waverly glanced around the debris field and then grinned.

"Ah, gee. It looks like your camera went over the cliff."

"Un-fucking-believable. I've got Waverly Sinner involved in a car accident doing first aid with her shirt off and no god damn camera."

"Un-fucking-believable," Waverly agreed and flipped the visor back down.

"Holy shit."

It looked like the driver of the Toyota had finally caught up. A shaggy stick figure in jeans and a camo t-shirt picked his way around Waverly's car, fancy camera in hand.

"You know this guy?" she asked.

"Sure, that's Douchebag Joe," he nodded, still studying the scene with more curiosity than concern.

"Fitting," Waverly muttered under her breath.

"Hey!" Douchebag Joe had apparently taken offense.

"He's not dead?"

"Apparently not."

"Hey, kid. I'll give you a thousand bucks for your camera. Gotta get this bitch doing first aid," Douchebag Joe said, reaching a road-rashed arm toward the other photographer.

"Bet you can't guess how he got his nickname," the guy said, ignoring Joe's charming proposal.

"What's your name?" Waverly asked.

"Arnold. Arnie," he corrected himself, kicking at the bike's front fender.

"Arnie, if I have to take my pick between you and Douchebag Joe here, it's gonna be you. So if you can back your car down around the turn and leave the four ways on so oncoming traffic doesn't turn us into a guardrail sandwich, you can take all the pictures you want."

"Sweet," Arnie said, perking up. "Make sure you smile pretty for the camera, Joe."

Xavier Saint held himself upright on the low, cloud-like sofa that was threatening to swallow him. His friend and partner,

Micah Ross, shifted his rangy, six-foot five-inch frame next to him."I feel like we're in a circus tent," Micah muttered under his breath and Xavier smirked in agreement.

The butler, house manager, majordomo—whatever he was—had stoically led them into *"Mrs. Sinner's private sitting room"* where they had been waiting amongst cream-colored leather, ivory cashmere throws, and dizzying wallpaper that glinted like gold in the late afternoon sun. The ceiling was draped with billowing fabric that gathered above a gilt chandelier decked out with about a thousand crystals.

It was nothing like the tents Xavier and Micah had grown used to. After a long stint in Afghanistan with Army intelligence, Xavier had been recruited by the Defense Clandestine Service. There he met Micah when they spent a week crouched in a frozen ditch watching for a particularly slippery Taliban leader in Tikrit.

Many missions later and Xavier and Micah were disillusioned alumni of the intelligence world with a wealth of security knowledge. They'd put that expertise to work on the West Coast with Invictus Security, a private security firm that provided military-grade protection to those who could afford their services.

Two years out, and Xavier was still getting used to Hollywood mansions and diamond-studded clients. Micah had transitioned to the management side of things, while Xavier continued to chase the adrenaline out in the field and train new personnel. They earned their astronomical fees by offering security services that ran the gamut from protecting high-level executives from kidnapping and ransom threats all the way down to Xavier's personal nightmare, baby-sitting heiresses whose worst enemies were themselves.

Xavier had a feeling about this job. Through training and

experience and well-honed instincts, his gut was practically clairvoyant. And his gut told him this job was trouble.

He glanced out the wall of windows that overlooked a freeform pool bigger than most waterparks and checked his watch. "I thought she said this was an emergency?"

Micah grunted non-commitally. The man's patience knew no bounds at work or home, where a hobby-of-the-month wife and three daughters—each with his dark hair and bronze skin that spoke of their Colombian ancestors—waited for him nightly.

They'd been waiting for twenty-two minutes for the "emergency" that had required them to drop everything and fight their way through mid-day freeway traffic. Xavier didn't trust people who threw around the word emergency.

"A delicate matter" that Sylvia Sinner hoped to discuss in person rather than over the phone.

Finally, one of the ornately carved French doors across the room opened. A woman he'd seen on screens large and small glided in. She was a tiny figure in a billowing kimono over what looked like a silk and lace nightgown. Her blonde hair was pinned up in an artful twist and her face glowed with painted on color and contour. It was four-thirty on a Wednesday, and the woman was lounging in a nighty and fake eyelashes.

His gut was never wrong.

"Gentlemen," she said, floating across the Aubusson rug toward them holding a crystal glass in one hand. "Please forgive me for keeping you waiting. A meeting ran terribly late. Forgive me?" Her voice was a breathy sigh.

Judging from the slick look of her raspberry fingernails and the faint odor of acetone, Xavier was fairly certain what kind of "meeting" it had been.

She was on the early side of forty-five but could easily pass for younger. Even this close, Xavier couldn't tell if it was good genes or the steady hands of a very talented plastic surgeon.

"Mrs. Sinner," Micah said, extending his hand. "I'm Micah Ross, and this is Xavier Saint. We understand you have a delicate situation."

Her laughter, light and airy, trilled through the room. She brought a hand to the swell of her breasts in a practiced flirtation. The woman was used to having an audience.

"Sinner and Saint," she said, with a slow wink. "It can't be a coincidence. And please, both of you call me Sylvia."

Sylvia looked Xavier up and down appreciatively as she held out her hand knuckles up. He wasn't about to start off a business relationship with a kiss. He firmly gripped her hand in both of his and shook.

She shot him a calculating look before offering her hand to Micah.

"Please sit," she said, gesturing toward the couch they'd just pried themselves out of. Sylvia arranged herself on a wingback chair covered in stark white fabric. They sat and waited. The elicitation training Xavier had aced with the DCS served him well in business. The quieter they were, the chattier the clients became.

Sylvia's expression seamlessly transformed from welcoming to distressed, her baby doll blue eyes filled with unshed tears. "I'm afraid my daughter is in danger," she said, wringing her hands together, careful to avoid smudging her fresh paint.

Xavier had done his due diligence in the car on the way over. Waverly Sinner was a twenty-year-old all-American beauty with a list of movie credits that any actress twice her age would envy. He'd actually taken his younger sisters to see one of her movies years ago after losing a bet with them. She'd been a pretty, long-legged teen then and had since grown into a genetic lottery winner.

She was also paparazzi bait, if the accident last week was any indication.

"I'm sure you've seen the news," Sylvia continued.

They both had. The three-vehicle accident in the hills had gotten its fair share of screen time. First with the media outlets' speculation that Sinner was at fault and then again when police released the 911 call and dash cam footage from her Mercedes. This time around, she was labeled a hero.

"The photographer involved in that accident was extremely aggressive," Micah stated. "Is that common?"

"It's not an everyday occurrence," Sylvia said, pulling her feet up under her. "But it's something we've all had to get used to. It goes with the territory." She sipped delicately from her glass.

"What's your main concern about your daughter's safety?" Xavier asked, his curiosity piqued.

Sylvia shifted again, this time from concerned mother to beleaguered parent, her lovely features rearranging themselves effortlessly.

"Honestly, she's going through some sort of willful phase. She's turning down movies, refusing interviews—"

"Mrs.— Sylvia," Micah interrupted. "That isn't the kind of situation that we generally work with."

It was, of course, a service they did reluctantly provide. For a fee.

She waved a slim hand that looked too fragile to hold the cluster of diamond rings she wore. "Of course not. It's just that this little rebellion of Waverly's is putting her in danger. That accident occurred shortly after she and her father had some sort of argument over who knows what? Neither of them tell me anything," she said with a charming eye roll. She took another sip from her glass. "I need someone who can protect Waverly from herself."

"THOUGHTS?" Micah asked as Xavier drove the company Tahoe down the drive.

Xavier waited until they were through the security gate before answering. "She wants a glorified babysitter."

"And?"

"And yet she seems to be painfully unaware that her daughter actually finds herself in dangerous situations. That guy on the bike could have killed her, but she's more concerned that her daughter get used to it and start picking up parts again."

"And?" Micah probed again.

"And that wasn't water in her glass," Xavier concluded.

"Same page. So are you up for a security detail with some babysitting thrown in to appease a very insistent client?" Micah asked, breaking the rules of an operative and rolling down his window to let the early summer air into the car.

"I have no interest in making this my specialty," Xavier warned his friend.

"But you do it so well," Micah said with a grin.

He was referring to Xavier's last princess-sitting job. The daughter of a British business magnate with a trust fund in the eight figures. She'd pranced around in lingerie and sunbathed topless by the pool for two weeks before realizing he wasn't going to bite. Once that realization had set in, she'd thrown a hissy fit and tried to go on a cocaine binge in the bathroom of a club. He'd gotten her out of the club, cleaned up, and dumped in a swanky rehab facility without anyone snapping any embarrassing pictures.

The bonus the grateful father gave them was enough to send an entire kindergarten class to a four-year college.

If Waverly Sinner thought she could get around him, she was going to learn very quickly that no one swayed Xavier Saint from his purpose.

2

Xavier had done a high-level run on the Sinners before his meeting with Sylvia, but now that Invictus had a contract, he would perform a more in-depth scan. Intel helped him anticipate potential threats and problems well before any materialized. He could usually build a fairly accurate snapshot of a client, which gave him a leg up.

Xavier's guard duty started tomorrow, and he needed that leg up immediately.

When Sylvia was walking them to the door, her husband had come home. At fifty, he still pulled down leading roles effortlessly. His hair was streaked with gray, and the lines around his eyes crinkled when he flashed his movie star grin. He was distinguished, polished, and completely checked out.

He'd had no idea that his wife was hiring security for their daughter and wasn't overly concerned with the why. He smiled affably, his tanned hands resting on his wife's thin shoulders. *"Whatever you think, darling,"* Robert had told his wife vaguely. With parents like that, Xavier didn't have high hopes for the daughter.

Feet bare, his evening run in the books, and his hair still

damp from a shower, he cracked open a beer and settled in behind his home workstation. He used the term "home" loosely. Since leaving the DCS, the two-bedroom condo with its bland beige everything had been a place to lay his head and hang his clothes. The workstation in the spare room was the only place he'd bothered to put any personal mementos. Pictures of his parents and his sisters smiled back at him next to his widescreen monitors.

He was getting a picture of Waverly Sinner now, too.

Young. Beautiful. Talented. She was a purebred Hollywood princess. At twenty, Waverly Sinner appeared to have it all. The California beauty had looks that could stop traffic. Her bank account was big enough to buy just about anything a girl could want, which made him curious why she still lived at home. In a city where wealthy teenagers snapped up multimillion dollar mansions like they were candy bars in the grocery store checkout line, Waverly was closeted away in her parents' pool house.

There were plenty of red carpet glam shots and magazine pictorials that promised tell-alls that amounted to next to nothing. *Favorite food: sushi. Favorite band: The Killers. How she got those abs for her role in Bleed Out? A personal trainer, a chef, and an assistant that slapped donuts out of her hand.* Many of her answers showed a tongue-in-cheek humor that seemed to go over the interviewers' heads. There were a handful of the requisite party girl club pictures but not enough to make him worry.

Xavier clicked on the YouTube results while the background check printed. One nice thing about guarding the rich and famous was the diamond mine of data available to him at his fingertips. The first video that caught his eye was almost sixteen years old. It was a clip from an entertainment news show and featured a young and striking Sylvia Sinner outside a trendy L.A. boutique, her entourage lugging a dozen shopping bags. Sylvia wore a form-fitting tank dress in siren red and stilettos with straps that wrapped halfway up her shins.

She was blowing kisses to the crowd of photographers and fans that had congregated at the store's entrance. Just behind her, in a matching dress, her silvery blond hair pulled back into a high ponytail, was five-year-old Waverly. The little girl was missing her front tooth and had plugged her fingers in her ears.

Her little diva sunglasses were a tiny replica of the ones Sylvia wore. An exact copy of her mother with the exception that Sylvia devoured the attention, reveled in it, while Waverly looked terrified.

"Come on, darling. Show the nice men how pretty you are," Sylvia coaxed. She lifted her daughter into her arms like a prize-winning pumpkin at the state fair. "Smile for the cameras, Waverly."

But the little girl's face was set in fearful lines. When Waverly buried her face in her mother's neck, Sylvia gave one last wave to the crowd. "I think someone is ready for her beauty sleep," she trilled. She set Waverly down, and Xavier wondered if it was because she didn't want a child ruining her exit or if she just couldn't bear the weight of the little girl with her bird-like arms.

Sylvia signaled her entourage. The photographers swarmed closer, and Xavier watched as Sylvia strutted off toward her next fabulous destination while her entourage—a team of beasts of burdens—hurried to follow.

In the chaos, Waverly was separated from them. He watched in disgust as the paparazzi swarmed like sharks scenting fresh blood. Flashes exploded in her face and loud men and women shouted questions at her.

"Are you going to be a movie star like your mommy?"

"Who's a better actor? Your mommy or your daddy?"

A photographer bumped her and Waverly took a tumble, landing hard on her knees on the sidewalk. Her mini movie star sunglasses were crushed underfoot. Xavier saw twin tears slide down her sweet, round cheeks and wanted to shoot every single one of the fuckers.

Finally, a hero appeared. A Middle Eastern guy wearing a ball cap and an apron elbowed his way through the crowd. He snatched Waverly up and pressed her face to his shoulder. Her little hands gripped his shoulders.

"Vultures!" he shouted. "She's just a little girl, not a carcass to feed on."

Xavier felt an echo of the man's rage inside him. A swift rush of adrenaline coursed through his veins as the spray tanned entertainment hosts with bleached teeth made jokes about Waverly's first paparazzi experience.

Poor kid never had a chance, Xavier thought as he took a deep pull of his beer.

Waverly had been summoned to the big house. *Lecture time again*, she sighed to herself, her bare feet padding over the sun warmed marble of the patio. She shoved her hands into the pockets of her hoodie and braced herself for passive aggressive manipulations or a diva-worthy meltdown. It all depended on her mother's unpredictable mood.

She could envision the stack of scripts at her mother's elbow, the look of motherly concern. Everything her mother did was playing a part. The woman had never had an authentic reaction to anything in her life.

Waverly let herself in through the TV room off the kitchen and ignored the giant bouquet of fussy white peonies. It was the twin of the one shoved in a corner of her living space. It was her father's showy apology for banging someone who wasn't his wife on his daughter's couch.

"I'm sorry Waverly. I'm under so much pressure these days. I don't know what I was thinking. Please don't discuss this with your mother," his card had said.

She had discussed it with her mother. Once, long ago.

Sylvia had shared neither Waverly's surprise nor devastation. Her mother was already used to it by the time Waverly caught on to the family dynamics. The next morning, her mother had cheerfully shown off a spectacular, new tennis bracelet and all returned to normal.

From that point on, Waverly had made it a point to keep her nose out of her parents' business. And she wished that they would return the favor. She hadn't mentioned her father's latest indiscretion to her mother, but her father had taken to covering all his bases. Every time an apology was owed to one of them, they both got one. Waverly had a drawer full of "I'm sorry" jewelry she'd never worn.

She turned her back on the peonies and what they represented and made her way into the kitchen. It was a space designed for magazine spreads with its wall of windows overlooking the gardens and thick timber beams that created a cathedral-like ceiling. The gleam of stainless steel and granite echoed everywhere.

Louie, her mother's personal chef, was running his knife through a small mound of radishes. His chevron mustache perched above lips that were set in a near constant frown.

"Good morning, Louie," Waverly greeted him with a peck on one of his perpetually ruddy cheeks.

"Bonjour, my dear," he said, his knife never ceasing its murderous precision.

Waverly helped herself to a glass of fresh lemon cucumber

water. "So what's the mood like in there?" She nodded her head in the direction of the morning room.

Louie's coal black eyebrows raised speculatively. "It's... interesting," he said finally. He put the knife down and wiped his hands on the checkered towel he always kept slung over his shoulder. "You're not going in there like that are you?" he asked, eyeing up her yoga shorts and hoodie.

"That's funny because there for a second I thought you were a chef, not my personal stylist," Waverly teased. If there was one thing Louie loved more than his precious cast iron skillets, it was fashion.

"I'm both to you until you finally develop some taste of your own. I can't understand why a girl who looks the way you do goes stomping around in sweaty gym clothes."

"A. I don't stomp," Waverly corrected. "And B. I just had a yoga session. I'm supposed to be sweaty."

It was an old argument between them, and a moot one at that, since Waverly and her assistant, Kate, deferred all decisions on her public outfits to Louie.

"You can help us go through the options for that thing this weekend if it will make you feel better," she promised him.

His frown deepened, but she knew from the pink flush on his ears that he was pleased. "That 'thing' this weekend is the Women in Hollywood awards, and you're presenting. Don't you ever look at your calendar?"

"Why would I do that when I have you, Louie?"

He shot her a dark look that had absolutely no effect on her. "I will do my best to choose something that doesn't make you look like a homeless Pilates instructor," he told her.

Waverly stuck her tongue out at him, and Louie tossed a handful of spinach at her.

"There you are!" A tiny woman dressed in head-to-toe gray bustled into the kitchen. Her dark hair with its spider web of silvery strands was pulled back in a severe bun. Marisol Cote topped out at five-foot-two, nearly a full head shorter than Waverly, but the woman carried herself with the aplomb of a four-star general. She'd been in Waverly's life from birth. Originally the nanny, Marisol had been promoted to house manager when Waverly hit her teens. Now she ran the family home—and the family—with a loving, if iron, fist.

"Morning, Mari," Waverly said, giving the woman an exaggerated kiss on her smooth cheek. Marisol was ageless, and she credited her unlined complexion to her Dominican blood and her deadpan expression. Her serene expression was even evident in her wedding pictures to the French Canadian she'd fallen for at nineteen. *No smiling, no frowning, no wrinkles* was her motto.

"Don't pucker, girl. It will give you wrinkles."

Waverly laughed. "Louie has not been a fount of information this morning, Mari. What's the big pow-wow about?"

"They tell me nothing," Marisol said evasively. She eyed Waverly's outfit. "This is what you are wearing?"

"Why does everyone suddenly care about what I wear around the house?"

Louie and Marisol exchanged a knowing look.

"What? If I'm going to be emotionally manipulated for failing to live up to the family legacy, I can at least be comfortable, can't I?"

Marisol took her by the shoulders and shoved her toward the door. "Go talk to your parents and remember that they do this out of love."

Crap. That wasn't a good sign.

Waverly let Marisol shove her out of the kitchen. She used the walk across the hallway to steel herself for whatever assault her mother had planned. She was an adult, Waverly reminded herself, and her desire to call her own shots was finally starting to override her need to not rock the boat.

She let herself into the morning room with a deep breath, the gold handles of the door cool to her touch. She was halfway into the room when she came to a halt, her bare feet buried in the snowy depth of the area rug.

The welcoming committee was bigger than she expected.

Her father was texting from a cream-colored wingback chair near the fireplace. Her mother was on the divan pouring tea no one wanted into delicate china. Phil, the agent that the two Sinner women shared, sat next to her mother. His thinning hair was trimmed short and inadvertently showcased the near-constant sweat that beaded his ever lengthening forehead. His customary wire-rimmed spectacles rode low on his nose.

But it wasn't the usual cast of characters that caught Waverly's eye. It was the man leaning against the mantel across from her. The man whose presence was definitely responsible for Louie and Marisol's preoccupation with her gym clothes.

He was tall, at least an inch or two taller than her father and more athletically built. His thick hair blurred the line between brown and blonde and was worn short enough to make Waverly think military. Eyes the color of amber studied her coolly. There was no hint of a smile on his firm lips. Broad shoulders wore the black Brioni suit with a careless confidence. His arms were crossed over his chest, his stance casual, but there was nothing casual about the way his gaze locked on her. *A hunter and his prey,* the thought came unbidden, spiking her pulse into a tattoo rhythm.

He wore a tailored suit, polished shoes, but there was a roughness around those edges. A sharpness in the eyes and the determined set of his well-defined jaw. In the way he held himself, Waverly sensed a restrained power like a beast waiting to be unleashed.

She knew danger when she saw it, and this stranger was lethal.

He wasn't an actor, some leading man sent to tempt her. She was sure of that. This was no golden boy, making bank from his pretty face. It wasn't pretty. It was breathtaking. Things that beautiful were always trouble, and she wanted no part of it, of him.

He smiled then, a lift of the lips, as if he read her mind. She swore she could feel the echo and pulse of his heartbeat from across the room. It matched her own.

"Oh, Waverly! There you are," her mother chirped, setting down the teapot with a clink.

"Here I am," Waverly agreed vaguely, trying to drag her attention away from the stranger with probing eyes.

"Come. Sit," her mother ordered.

Waverly made a valiant effort to stop staring back at the man and took a seat on the pearl pink silk sofa across from her mother and Phil. She refused to relax. There was an ambush coming, and she wanted to be ready for it.

"Xavier," her mother turned to the man by the fireplace. "Come join us," her invitation much warmer than necessary.

Waverly watched him as he pushed away from the marble surround and strolled toward her. She was at war with herself, wanting him closer and, at the same time, wishing he'd stay on the other side of the room.

Waverly wasn't aware of standing, but when Xavier stopped in front of her, she was on her feet.

"Waverly, this is Xavier Saint," her mother began.

Of course that was his name.

The man extended his hand, the same subtle curve of amusement on his sinful lips. A dare. After a brief hesitation, she accepted his offered hand. Their palms met, and she felt a crackle of electricity. Definitely a warning to stay away, she decided. She gripped his hand and shook it firmly pretending that it was Phil's cold spaghetti handshake instead of the confident, hard contact against her skin.

Xavier had yet to say anything, and Waverly was inclined to extend the silence between them. Rather than a barrier, it felt like a bubble with just the two of them inside.

"Xavier is your new security." Sylvia's airy announcement popped the bubble like a dart.

"Excuse me?" Waverly felt her insides ice over. She started to tug her hand free and glared up at him when he merely tightened his grip. In her bare feet, Saint still had several inches on her, and his gaze warmed considerably. He made her feel vulnerable, exposed. She didn't like it. Waverly set her jaw and dug her thumbnail into the flesh between his thumb and index finger.

She bared her teeth in a fierce smile as he tightened his grip crushing her fingers. "So nice to meet you, Mr. Saint," she said sweetly, drawing on her acting skills to dare him to contend.

"The pleasure is mine, Ms. Sinner." His voice was as rough as his edges and sent a delicious, unwanted chill down her spine.

"I told you they'd get along," Sylvia trilled to no one in particular.

Saint let go of her hand and Waverly felt the rush of blood returning to her digits. She didn't retreat to the empty chair at the end of the Lalique coffee table but reclaimed her spot on the sofa. Xavier laid claim to the seat next to her, unbuttoning his jacket as he sat gracefully.

Their shoulders brushed, and Waverly immediately shifted to get some distance. "I'm afraid there's been a misunderstanding, Mr. Saint," she began, interlacing her fingers on her knee. It was hard to look imperious in yoga shorts, but she'd make it work.

"Now, Waverly," Sylvia said, trying to head off Waverly's dissent. "Let's discuss logistics."

Sylvia loved logistics. Every moment of her mother's life was planned out in excruciating detail with the sole goal of maintaining her brand... and satiating her need for attention. When parts began to go to younger actresses, Sylvia effortlessly changed gears to focus on building Waverly's brand and career. She looked at her daughter as an extension of her own success.

"Darling, put that away so we can discuss this," Sylvia said to her husband.

Robert dropped his phone on a side table and pasted on an enthusiastic expression. *Nothing like a family of actors,* Waverly bit back a sigh.

"Yes. Let's discuss," Waverly said agreeably. "I don't need security. No offense, Mr. Saint," she offered.

"None taken, Ms. Sinner," he said coolly.

"Oh, come now. Let's not be so formal," Sylvia said, clasping her hands together.

"Fine," Waverly agreed. "No offense, *X*."

"None taken, Waverly."

She didn't like the way he said her name, as if it was a private joke.

"I don't need security," she stated again. She hated repeating herself because it meant that no one was listening to her, as usual.

"Now, Waverly," Phil spoke up for the first time, his round cheeks flushed. "After last week, it's clear that some measures must be taken to ensure your safety."

"Yes," Sylvia agreed, nodding her head vehemently until

her blonde curls trembled. "You certainly weren't taking any safety precautions when you flew out of here for some silly reason, and you were careless. What were the photographers supposed to do? Be understanding that you had a bad day and leave you alone?" She laughed at her own joke.

Waverly drummed her fingers on the linen arm of the sofa. "I didn't leave for 'some silly reason,'" she said, looking pointedly at her father, who suddenly became fascinated by the tips of his loafers.

"Waverly, you haven't been yourself lately. Not only were you careless last week with those photographers, you've been ignoring social functions, you haven't settled on a new project yet, you're refusing to do any press on the accident. Why, Zoey Grace had the cover of *Indulgence* last month. You go to the same gym, yet she manages to hit the gossip sites twice as often as you do."

Waverly realized that they didn't want security for her safety. They wanted security to keep her in line. "I wasn't being careless," she said, zeroing in on that offense. "I'm *never* careless. The photographer was the one who got out of line, not me. Why do you want to punish me when it was a grown man acting like a criminal?"

Sylvia sighed dramatically, a diamond laden hand floated to her heart. "Do you see what I have to deal with, Xavier? You try reasoning with her."

Xavier shifted his gaze from Sylvia the Martyr to Waverly the Enraged. She glared at him. If he couldn't read that his presence was unwelcome, he was an idiot.

"Waverly," Xavier began. Again, her name from his mouth was like a rough caress. "Security isn't meant to be a punishment. Regardless of whose behavior was out of line last week, you could have been killed. With your level of visibility, you face greater risk than the average twenty-year-old."

"Exactly," her mother interjected. "Darling, I know this is hard to understand. You're very young, and your father and I have done everything we can to protect you ourselves."

Waverly saw it, that quick tightening of Xavier's jaw, but it was gone just as quickly. She wondered what it meant. She wanted to make a smart remark, to get in a dig that would make her mother feel something real before she disappeared again into the scripted soap opera in her head. But she couldn't, so she bit her tongue and counted down from ten.

Her father crossed his legs restlessly. Conflict and confrontation were anathema to Robert Sinner. He preferred subtle, passive-aggressive tactics to get what he wanted. "Look, darling. You are an important, special person and unfortunately that puts you at a greater risk for unwanted attention."

"We tried security before," Waverly reminded them. Though, a sidelong glance at Xavier reminded her that the two goons Phil had hired were nothing like the man next to her. She'd spent the summer she turned sixteen slipping their coverage. After a few half-hearted attempts to catch up with her, they'd struck a bargain. Waverly would leave the house with Hoss and Lenny, and they'd all go their separate ways until it was time to return home. It worked for a month until the tabloids busted them by shooting Waverly at a tennis lesson while her bodyguards were caught "guarding the bodies" at a strip club.

"This time will be different," Sylvia predicted cheerily. "Xavier is the best at what he does, and you're not going to test him."

It was like waving a forbidden electronic device in front of a toddler. She shot Xavier a look. Those unreadable eyes met hers again and hardened. A challenge? Another dare?

"I'm not sixteen anymore. I can handle myself. I don't need a babysitter."

Her parents exchanged a glance, and her father cleared his throat. He plowed on with the script she assumed her mother had provided. "Waverly, you're misunderstanding this. We aren't doing this to control you. We're doing this to protect you. You are the most precious thing in the world to us, and you must be kept safe."

Waverly opened her mouth to argue, but her mother interjected.

"If you feel the need to fight us on this, we may have to review the terms of your trust," Sylvia said, taking a proper sip of tea.

Waverly could feel her heartbeat throbbing in her head. Her parents had tucked away every one of the paychecks she'd earned before she turned eighteen into a trust. A trust that would finally be hers in four months on her twenty-first birthday. She'd been careful with the money she'd earned on her own and, combined with the trust, it would mean freedom and independence. And her future plans depended on having that money in her control.

Of course her mother would threaten her with that. And of course she would surrender.

She listened to the nineteenth-century mantel clock as it ticked off the seconds. Waverly could kiss the next four months of her life good-bye since she would be stalked by the devil himself.

"Fine. Your fragile special snowflake will be under lock and key from now on," she said, rising abruptly. "Now if you'll excuse me, I have a fitting for a ball and chain."

3

He gave her a thirty-second head start before excusing himself from the back-patting fest in the parlor. Robert felt that it had gone better than expected while Sylvia was predicting to Phil that Waverly would be attached to a new movie by the week's end. They were all either blissfully ignorant to Waverly's rage or just didn't give a rat's ass. Either way, he was all too aware of what a pissed off starlet was capable of.

If she were anything like the other girls he'd guarded, she'd strike back with a drug binge or a sex tape.

But something told him Waverly was different. He'd seen pictures and videos, but nothing had prepared him for when she walked into the room. Flawless golden skin, mile-long legs that demanded attention in short Lycra shorts. She wore her corn silk hair piled on her head in some kind of sloppy knot, providing an unobstructed view of the graceful curve of her neck and her movie star face. She wore no makeup that he could see to enhance her high cheekbones over delicate hollows. Full, unpainted lips had parted when she spotted him watching her. Her gray-green eyes were wide and heavily fringed with lashes. And in those eyes, he could see storms brew as her parents broke the news to her.

She wasn't what he'd expected. And that was a problem. He'd thought he'd be meeting Sylvia's mini me. But she was different, and that was trouble. His physical reaction to her took him by surprise. He'd spent years honing his control, reining in his reactions. And all she had to do was walk into a room and get pissed off for his blood to migrate south.

The attraction wouldn't be an issue, he assured himself. He wouldn't let it. He'd get used to looking at her, and that punch-in-the-gut reaction would dull. And once he got to know her, the interest would be gone. He knew the spoiled princess type. There wasn't anything a girl could do on the outside to make up for being a vapid vacuum on the inside. He'd find the ugly or the annoying in Waverly and be back on an even keel before dinner, he decided.

He caught up to her by the pool, the crystal waters sending off blinding sparkles under the mid-morning sun.

"Waverly."

He was pleased when she stopped, automatically obeying the command. It was a test, as everything else would be over the next few days. He needed to know her so he could predict her. This job wasn't just about protecting starlets from outside threats. It was more often about protecting them from themselves.

She must have realized that she'd subconsciously obeyed because she straightened her slim shoulders under her hoodie and marched toward the pool house.

"Stop." He put enough authority into the command that it should have scared the girl. The time and energy it took to win a battle of the wills with stubborn and spoiled was a waste and Xavier had crafted a workaround. *First step: Make sure she knew he was in charge.*

Waverly turned around to face him and marched back to him, temper flaring. "You bellowed?"

If he didn't have to ensure her safety, he might have actually liked her. Her barely contained temper was entertaining. He decided to push her a little bit further. *Establish authority early.*

"For an actress, you don't hide your feelings well," he commented.

"For a bodyguard, you have a lot of opinions about my acting ability. I guess I'll just go cry myself to sleep over your review."

"You're not mad at me," Xavier said mildly. "You're pissed because you feel like the family puppet."

"Dancing monkey, actually," Waverly corrected.

"Potato, po-tah-to," he quipped. "The bottom line is you can cut the spoiled brat act with me and deal with the fact that I'm not leaving."

"Calling me a spoiled brat is you trying to cement our relationship? Clever."

He rewarded her with a smile to show her she wasn't getting to him. "You're going to have to get used to me, Angel."

"Angel?" Her well-shaped eyebrows arched.

"Your code name."

"Well, isn't that sweet?" she said, her tone dripping with sarcasm.

"I like to go for irony with my code names. Besides, if I used Bride of Satan it wouldn't be much of a code, now would it?"

Waverly's jaw dropped at the insult, but she recovered quickly. "What's the sentence for manslaughter in California?" she asked innocently.

Yeah, under other circumstances, he'd definitely like her.

"Three to eleven. But I wouldn't if I were you."

"Why's that?" she asked him.

"You'd be thirty and irrelevant before you got out."

It was meant as an insult, a dig at the Holy Grail of Hollywood, but the spark of yearning he saw in her eyes surprised him.

"Okay, you want to talk? Let's talk. Put your cell phone on the table." She nodded at the polished driftwood table next to him.

"Why?"

"I want to make sure you're not recording this conversation."

Protocol dictated a firm 'no' to diva demands, especially in the beginning when establishing authority. But if it helped to build trust, what could it hurt? He reached into his jacket and fished out his phone.

"Does that happen often?" he asked, placing the phone on the table. "Do people record you when you think you're safe?" He put a hint of sympathy into his tone to disarm her.

Waverly stepped past him to the pool's edge. Arms crossed, she stared out over the vista of hills and homes. *A lonely princess surveying her kingdom*, he thought.

"It happens sometimes." There was a quiver in her voice.

He moved next to her, and they stood shoulder to shoulder. To an outsider, they'd look like a united front. He let her brood, contemplate the unfairness of her lucky life. There were two security cameras that he could see from here. They'd need more and an upgrade to the overall system. He'd have his hands full, but they would all come around, and Waverly would stay safe.

"It must go with the territory," he answered her.

"So does this," Waverly sniffled.

He should have seen it coming, but damn if she didn't catch him off guard. In a move slicker than a ninja's, Waverly danced in front of him, hooking her arm around his neck. He thought for a split second that she was going to kiss him. And that thought, that anticipation, was enough to slow his reflexes.

She pulled and spun, yanking him off balance. There was no time to save himself, the crystal blue water was rushing up to meet him. But he managed to wrap an arm around her waist and drag her down with him. The heated pool water closed over his head and he heard her laugh. She was grinning at him, her hair floating around her like a golden halo.

She looked like a mermaid. A mermaid who needed to be taught a lesson.

He reached for her, contemplating the satisfaction of drowning her, but she flashed away, her long, slim legs pumping.

By the time he clawed his way to the pool's edge, she was pulling herself out of the water at the far end.

"How's that for acting, X?" She blew him a kiss and sauntered off in the direction of the pool house, water streaming from her clothes.

Waverly cued up a playlist on her phone and paired it to the speaker in the bathroom. She turned on the water in the shower and shucked off her dripping clothes. She tossed them in the claw foot tub to deal with later. The bathroom was miniscule in comparison to any of the eight in the big house, but Sylvia had managed to outfit it with all the luxurious necessities.

When Waverly turned eighteen and asked for access to her trust to buy a house, her mother had insisted she had a better idea. That idea involved a two hundred thousand dollar renovation of the already very nice pool house. Now, Waverly enjoyed a modicum of privacy surrounded by pops of saturated color that reminded her of a candy store and furniture that looked like a sorority pledge class had designed it.

Waverly ducked her head under the stream of water envisioning a soggy Xavier Saint sloshing his way home. She grinned. She may be trapped for the next four months with a babysitter, but at least she'd won a minor yet satisfying victory over him. He'd think twice before trying to play head games with her again.

She was a student of humanity, and for an actor, observation was essential. She excelled at reading people and their intentions. So she knew when Xavier was purposely pushing her buttons. It hadn't been flirting as some playground bullies still did. It had been more deliberate. Trying to get a rise out of her to show her he was in control.

Well, he hadn't looked in control when he was floundering around in his suit under water, Waverly congratulated herself.

She probably shouldn't have done it. There was something about him, something more than stereotypical bodyguard. The way he kept his back to the wall in the morning room, how his gaze constantly scanned for threats—there was training there that hadn't come from some private security firm. What she couldn't tell was if he was underestimating her like so many others had or if he was testing her.

She nailed the high note with Taylor Swift and twisted off the faucets with a flourish. After a quick towel dry, she wrapped herself in a short cotton robe and ran a comb through her wet hair. She needed to call Kate, she decided. Between the two of them, they could devise a plan to get rid of Xavier Saint.

Still humming, she strolled into the kitchen.

"Got an extra towel?"

She shrieked and rapped her elbow sharply off of the refrigerator handle. The knife she grabbed sang when she yanked it out of the wooden block on the counter.

Xavier was sitting on her couch his shirt and pants were inexplicably dry. A handgun was stripped down on the coffee table in front of him. His suit jacket hung on a peg just inside the front door dripping a steady patter of pool water onto the tile floor.

"How the hell did you get in here? Why aren't you wet? Why is there a gun on my table? Are you a freaking magician?"

He looked up at her over the slide of his gun. His eyes were as deadly as the weapon in his hands. "That's something you're going to have to get used to about me, Angel. I'm always prepared."

"My parents gave you a key." She closed her eyes. They were serious about this security business.

"This morning, before you threw your hissy fit in the parlor." Oh, he was pissed.

"Morning room," she corrected him automatically.

He continued as if he hadn't heard her. "And I had a change of clothes and a cleaning kit in the car." He kept his tone mild, but the way he slammed the magazine back into the gun told her he was good and steamed at her. She'd pushed him pretty far, but not far enough to make him snap. *Interesting.*

"Were you a Boy Scout?" she wondered out loud.

"Army intelligence," he replied.

Well, that explained the training...and the haircut. She rubbed her aching elbow and opened the refrigerator. Inside she found the daily pitcher of disgusting green juice that Louie made fresh for her to gag on. She poured herself a small glass and then shot a look into the living room before pulling down a second glass and filling it.

"Sorry about your gun. I didn't realize you were wearing one," she said, setting the second glass down in front of him.

He gave a harsh half-laugh. "Thanks for not destroying my phone."

Sarcasm? Perhaps there was something human in him after all.

"What's that?" he asked, eyeing the shamrock green liquid.

"Green juice. Or as I like to call it, garbage juice. Louie makes us drink pitchers of it when we're home. If I have to deal with you on a daily basis, the least you can do is help me with my share."

"You threw me in the pool."

"Nothing wrong with your short-term memory," Waverly quipped.

Xavier racked the slide and double-checked the safety before stowing the gun in a shoulder harness.

"Have a seat, Waverly," he said. His tone was calm, mild even. But the look in those eyes was hard, dangerous. Warning bells went off in her head.

She sat on the overstuffed armchair, avoiding the cushion next to him. Interlacing her fingers, she crossed her legs. The picture perfect listener.

"This may seem like a game to you," Xavier began, his tone was that of a professor instructing a deficient student. "But the real world isn't just parties and pretty dresses."

For a complete stranger, he had an uncanny knack for putting her back up.

"I am well aware of that—"

"I don't think you are," he cut her off, his tone clipped. "You seem to be operating under the misconception that you aren't an easy target. Those photographers could have gotten you killed, but you were too pissed off that Daddy wouldn't give you the keys to the Jag or whatever the argument was to take even the basic safety precautions. That all stops now."

Red began to creep into the edge of Waverly's vision. He was baiting her. He wanted her to throw a temper tantrum so he could prove that he was right, that she was just a spoiled little rich girl. *God, why did everyone have to push her for a reaction?* One of these days, she was going to get sick and tired of being pushed around, and she was going to give them all a reaction they'd never forget.

"My life is not a game," she said icily. "It's already as close to a prison as I'm willing to get. Having you lurking over my shoulder every time I step outside my door is not an option. I can't live like that."

"You don't have a choice."

And that was it. The problem. She didn't have a choice.

She leaned forward. "I'm twenty years old. That's legally an adult by anyone's standards. I sign contracts. I vote. I pay taxes. I should be making my own decisions."

"An adult doesn't throw a hissy fit and stomp her feet when things don't go her way," Xavier pointed out. "An adult doesn't knowingly take unnecessary risks just because she's having a bad day."

"Let's get this straight," she said quietly, picking up her glass of juice and sipping. "Your opinion of me—low as it is—means nothing. I don't need or want your approval on how I choose to live."

It was his turn to lean forward. Anger and something else smoldered in his gaze. "While we're getting things straight, I'm not some ass-kissing lackey who's going to bring you lattes. I'm here to do a job, and that's to protect you. So you can play the spoiled little rich girl card all you want, but there are two truths that you need to accept."

He held up a finger. "One, there are people who, for whatever reason, wouldn't mind seeing you hurt. Two—" he held up a second finger. "You have people in your life who, for whatever reason, want to keep you around. I am here to make sure that's what happens. And if you have a problem with that, I don't give a shit."

"And yet you'd take a bullet for me. Now, who's the one taking unnecessary risks?" she shot back.

Xavier picked up his glass. "You can throw your temper tantrums and play your little princess games all you want. But I'm sticking, and I will win." He knocked back the juice and downed it.

Waverly had to give him points for not flinching. Louie's recipe ran heavy on the celery and kale.

She could handle his assumptions about her. No one saw the person under the Hollywood polish. And who was she to disappoint him? If he wanted a spoiled rich bitch to shadow, she'd give him one.

4

"Are you listening to me, Kate?" Marisol admonished Waverly's assistant and friend.

"Nope," the blonde in the ball cap said, leaning over the sink to get a better view through the windows. Two inches shy of Waverly's five-foot-eight, Kate moved like a roller derby diva. Everything about her was energetic, edging toward frenetic. She chewed gum as if her life depended on it and preferred speed in all things. She wore her hair, a shade or two darker than Waverly's silvery blonde, in a perpetual ponytail.

Waverly beaned her friend in the head with a muffin. "Come on, Kate. He's not *that* hot."

Despite their age and cultural differences, Kate and Marisol managed to shoot Waverly twin looks of disbelief.

Waverly joined Kate at the wide window over the sink. Xavier was perched on the edge of the roof that covered the main house's expansive patio. Below him, a man on a ladder was installing a new security camera. Xavier's jacket was off, and his sleeves were rolled up. Waverly could understand how Kate and Marisol found him attractive. Physically, he was the perfect male specimen.

His face alone was worthy of being captured in marble. That perfect Roman nose, cheekbones so sculpted they would have guaranteed a modeling career. And those eyes. The color of melted caramel, they missed nothing.

They watched him prowl the edge of the roof. *Probably scouting more ways to invade her privacy*, Waverly thought. He stood, hands on hips, with his tie fluttering in the breeze.

"I mean, come on," Kate said. "That's just hot. I don't know how you can concentrate with that piece of gorgeous breathing down your neck."

"Easy. Just look past his god-like exterior and get to know him. He's got the personality of a Turkish prison guard."

"I'd go to prison for that," Kate mused.

Waverly crossed her arms. "He's condescending, rude, and entirely too opinionated. Now, can we please get back to our meeting?"

"He called her the Bride of Satan," Marisol piped up. "And that was before she threw him in the pool." She tried to look disapproving, but Waverly wasn't fooled.

They returned to the table where, with one last look of longing, Kate launched into Waverly's calendar. Details and schedules were her fetish. She rattled off a series of appearance requests and invites for the week while Waverly drummed her pen on the table.

"So, no to all, correct?" Kate asked.

But still Waverly drummed. If Xavier wanted to guard a Tinsel Town princess, then maybe she should give him a show. One that would have him packing his bags.

"Say yes," Waverly decided, dropping her pen.

"To which one?" Kate frowned.

"All of them."

"Wave, there's a dozen events here. Some that overlap," Kate argued.

"And?"

"And you don't do that. You don't go to these things unless your mother holds a gun to your head."

"Saint is putting in overtime to get to know me and my routine. Why not give him a routine that makes him regret taking the job?"

Marisol made a disapproving tut-tut. "Your parents hired him to keep you safe."

"My parents hired him to keep me in line," Waverly corrected. She got up to pace. "Kate, how do you think my mother will react when she hears about my new schedule?"

"She'll shit a brick of ecstasy," Kate predicted. "She lives to parade you around like a show pony. You're lucky that kid beauty contest TV show didn't exist when you were growing up."

"So if she sees me playing ball..."

"Then what does she need Mr. Hot Bod Sexy Face for?" Kate finished.

"Exactly! Ladies, we could be Saint-free in a week." Waverly twirled around the kitchen.

"I don't like when you two scheme," Marisol shook her head sternly. "Why can't you just let this Saint do his job?"

Waverly stopped twirling. "Mari, you know me. I can't live like this. I'm so close to finally doing what's right for me. I can't spend the next four months under lock and key so my mother can turn me into a puppet. She'll have me committed to projects two years out."

"But why can you not say that to Mr. Saint? Explain to him that you're leaving the business."

"Because Mr. Saint believes that I'm a spoiled little rich girl with an attitude problem. And I'd hate to disappoint him."

"Ay!" Marisol burst into a litany of blistering Spanish.

"I'm not stubborn as a two-headed mule," Waverly said

primly, topping off Marisol's coffee. The woman grabbed her coffee cup and rose stiffly.

"I want no part in this!" She muttered her way to the door complaining about mule-headed girls and blind men. Waverly watched her go. As much as Marisol pretended to bluster, she knew the adoration went both ways. Waverly was certain if she ever called Marisol from the scene of a murder she'd committed, her Mari would show up with a nice Persian rug and a roll of duct tape.

Marisol, still muttering, wrenched open the front door with a Latin flourish of temper. Xavier was on the doorstep poised to knock.

"Señora Cote." He stepped back as the woman bustled past.

Marisol made a show of crossing herself. "God be with you," she said, shaking her head fiercely.

If Xavier was bemused by the woman's exit, he didn't show it. The consummate professional, his face remained impassive as he took the chair next to Waverly at the table. Yesterday obviously hadn't dampened his determination to ruin her life. He stared her down, and Waverly met his gaze with disdain.

"I'm Kate," Kate announced, breaking their silent battle of wills.

"Xavier," he said, offering his hand across the table.

Kate grinned, shaking with enthusiasm, and Waverly kicked her under the table.

"I'm Waverly's personal assistant and whipping post," Kate said, sticking her tongue out at Waverly.

"Waverly's personal security and personal floatation device," Xavier answered with a ghost of a smile.

Waverly rolled her eyes. Kate had been Waverly's right hand for three years after they met on a movie set where Kate was working as a haggard, underpaid production lackey. She'd called an associate producer with a God complex and wandering hands a "weasel-faced asshole" and been unceremoniously fired.

Waverly hired her on the spot.

"We were just going over Wave's schedule for this week," Kate said, ignoring Waverly's disapproval. "I can cc you when I email her the finalized calendar."

"That would be great, thanks. What can you tell me about your email server?" Xavier asked, eyeing the carafe of coffee.

Waverly slid it and an empty mug to him. He poured and sipped while Kate gave him the details about the IT company she worked with for the website and email.

"We're going to want to keep any communications about Angel's schedule or plans or whereabouts on a secure server," he said, rolling down his sleeves.

"Angel?" Kate snorted.

"Don't start," Waverly grumbled.

She felt the weight of Xavier's attention on her. "I'd like to have our cyber team take a look. I don't have to tell you that email servers get hacked every day." He looked at her pointedly.

"Are you waiting for me to confess to having a treasure trove of naked pictures?" Waverly cocked her head. She poured a glass of the ever-present green juice and slapped it down on the table in front of him.

"This is serious business," he reminded her.

"And this is the price of doing business, X."

Those tawny eyes flickered. He raised the glass in a mock salute and drained it. "It's not as horrific as you make it out to be," he told her.

Waverly downed the last half of her juice and resisted the urge to shudder.

"God, how do you drink that crap?" Kate gagged. "It's like someone stomped on soggy lawn clippings."

"That's the wheatgrass," Waverly told her, washing down the juice with a belt of coffee. "X here helps with my daily quota and then I don't have to lie to Louie and dump it down the sink. So, meeting adjourned?" she asked hopefully.

"Actually, I think we should hear an update from X Factor here," Kate suggested.

At Waverly's stare of death, Kate shrugged. "What? He's here doing stuff. I think we should know what that stuff is."

"It's smart to be interested in security," Xavier said, giving her a nod of approval. Waverly thought she heard Kate purr.

"Ugh, fine," Waverly said. "Let's hear all about the prison you're building for me."

Undeterred, Xavier briefed them on the new security system that he was installing. Lights, sensors, cameras, off-site back-ups. The whole she-bang. He pulled out his phone and opened an app. When he tilted the screen, Waverly could see a rendering of the house and grounds.

"We added cameras here, here, and here," he said, pointing. "The perimeter sensors will go in at the weak points around the wall. I'm also changing the locks here and in the main house. You'll be able to lock and unlock doors with an app I'll put on your phone. Any alarms will be monitored by my internal team, and alerts will be sent directly to your phone."

"This all sounds like we're preparing for an attack," Waverly frowned. "What's next? Bulletproof gowns and secret bunkers?"

"Next is you and I spending some time reviewing your usual haunts, where you feel safe, what situations could be dangerous, and what steps we can take to keep you safe without locking you in a closet."

“She has a really nice closet,” Kate interjected.

“A nice prison is still a prison,” Waverly reminded her.

Xavier shook his head. “These are just standard safety measures. Being prepared for the unknown makes it easier to react effectively when there’s a known threat.”

“Speaking of known threats—” Kate began.

“We don’t need to get into that again,” Waverly sighed, grabbing for the folder that Kate was trying to shove at Xavier.

Xavier wrestled the folder from Waverly and slapped her hand away. “What’s this?”

“I run Wave’s social media accounts, and these are a handful of—shall we say ‘fans?’—that give me the creeps,” Kate explained. Her quick fingers paged through the printouts. “This bi-yatch here started an ‘I Hate Waverly Sinner’ group on Facebook. Her profile pic is a chick in a Confederate flag bikini flipping the bird.”

“Classy,” Xavier commented, skimming some of the more salacious posts.

“I’m pretty sure she’s just a troll. I friended her with one of my fake accounts to keep an eye on her. She basically spouts off on everything from puppy videos to baby pics. She may not be a ‘credible’ threat, but I don’t like it when she starts sharing nuggets like this.

Kate tapped a finger on a post on one of the papers. Xavier’s eyebrows raised and he let out a low whistle.

“Well, now you have to tell me,” Waverly sighed. As a rule, she ignored all comments directed at her whether positive or negative. She’d learned at a young age that those who wanted to see her fail were a lot louder than those who appreciated her work.

Kate cleared her throat and read in a breathy southern twang designed to downplay the vitriol. “Waverly Sinner should be hung from a burning cross for her views on mixing the races. I've got the gasoline. Who's with me?"

Waverly puckered her lips thoughtfully. "How many misspellings?"

"Three. Plus a misuse of a comma."

"Where's she from?" Waverly could feel Xavier trying to gauge her reaction.

"Whistle Swamp, Alabama, which does not exist. Neither does her alma mater, the School of Hard Knocks."

Waverly shrugged. "Well, she doesn't sound like much of an actual threat. More like everyone's racist aunt who gets drunk and talks politics at Thanksgiving."

"All the same, if you can do some digging, I'd rest easier," Kate told Xavier.

"Consider it done. Who's next on the list?"

"We've got this charmer here. Mikey D., which I'm positive stands for 'douche.' Mikey is a tad bit conservative, and he feels there's a special place in Hell reserved for Wave here since she did that movie where she was a teen mom who gave up her baby."

"Apparently he wasn't impressed with the Critic's Choice Award," Waverly quipped.

"The esteemed Mikey posts on her Facebook and Twitter accounts a few times a month and spews Bible verses and threats all over the place. I block him every time, but he just creates new accounts."

"'I hope you get raped and murdered while your parents watch. Even God won't save you,'" Xavier read out loud.

He looked at Waverly, who pursed her lips. "On that note, I think I'm going to pack my gym clothes and figure out what to wear to dinner," she said, rising and collecting the juice glasses and coffee mugs.

"What time do we leave?" Xavier asked. He wasn't even giving her a choice to go without him.

She took a breath, let it out. "Five for the gym. Dinner's at seven-thirty. Kate'll send you the details." She dumped the dishes in the dishwasher.

"Sorry, Wave," Kate grimaced. "Here's the happies to read while you raid your own wardrobe." She handed over a sheet of paper.

"Thanks," Waverly said, and wandered into the bedroom, shutting the door behind her.

Xavier watched her go and moments later heard the muffled chorus of "Uptown Funk" from behind the closed bedroom door.

Kate looked guilty. "I hate doing that to her. No human being should feel like a target like that and definitely not on a daily basis."

"She needs to be aware of potential threats," Xavier argued.

"I know, and so does she. There've been a couple incidents in the past, nothing serious, but enough to make her cautious. The whole car accident thing was a fluke. Something must have really pissed her off to make her take off like that."

She shook her head and flopped back down at the table. "It's these assholes who are allowed to spew poison all over her. It's like a whole different kind of abuse. Just because she stands in front of cameras for a living, people think they have a right to pick her apart like vultures and road kill."

Xavier didn't much care for it either. Even if Waverly was a pain in his ass, she didn't deserve to have that kind of hate directed at her. If someone were to say those things to one of his sisters, he'd be digging a shallow grave in the woods. But getting pissed off didn't help him do his job any better.

"What are the happies?" he asked Kate, changing the subject.

"Every time we have to talk about the psychotic dipshits of the world, I print out fifty happy posts or reviews. It takes the sting out of idiots who don't think before they post."

Xavier's lips quirked. "That's very nice of you," he commended.

Kate glanced toward Waverly's closed bedroom door. "I've got one more baddie in here, and it's the one I'd really like you to look into."

She shuffled papers to the top of the stack. "This Unabomber lookalike is Les Ganim. He sends Wave shit online all the time. Disjointed love letters about how they're destined to be together, and why won't she just acknowledge that they're in love?

She tapped the picture of a gaunt man with hollow eyes. "She gets marriage proposals and stranger booty calls all the time, but I started paying attention to this dude when he mailed his mother's wedding dress to the house."

"To this house?" Xavier asked, studying the man's face. He had a wiry build and hair that stuck out in tufts of curls. His broad, flat nose didn't fit the rest of his thin face.

"Yep," Kate nodded. "That was a few months back. I alerted Sylvia and Rob, but neither of them was too concerned. Honestly, stuff like this happens to every star. But it made me nervous, so I looked into him and found a couple of stalking and trespassing charges, which *really* made me nervous. So I'm pretty happy to dump the worrying onto you."

Xavier got a buzz off of the picture. His gut told him there was trouble here. "I'll look into him and see what I can find," he told her. "I don't like the feel of this guy either."

Kate looked relieved. "Good, because the last message he sent said he's moving to L.A. so they can start their lives together." She looked toward the bedroom door again and lowered her voice. "Listen, not to be disloyal or anything because I love Wave like a sister, but she's planning on shaking you loose. While I can understand why she wouldn't want to be smothered—even by someone as gorgeous as you—I don't like the idea of her running around unprotected with our pal Les lurking in the shadows."

Xavier packed the papers back into the folder. "You're a good friend, Kate. And I don't shake loose."

"Well, as a good friend, I'd be remiss if I didn't tell you that Wave isn't your typical Hollywood heiress. She's human. I like her. Don't be a dick to her."

Xavier made a noncommittal hum. "I'll do my best. And maybe you could convince her to go a little easier on me?"

Kate smirked. "I'll do my best."

5

Kate clearly hadn't had time to have her go-easy talk with Waverly. The girl had done nothing but argue with him since they left the house. First, she didn't like the route he took to lose the three photographers on the way to the gym. Then she wasn't happy when he announced he was staying for her private barre class. Next time, she informed him, he would be required to participate if he tagged along.

Xavier sat by the door and watched her stretch and contort her body for forty-five minutes until it was slick with sweat. The way she moved, flowing like water over rocks, gave him a healthy kick of appreciation for her very female form. Waverly Sinner earned her stunning body the hard way. After barre came thirty minutes of power flow yoga that had sweat dripping off her chin every time she swooped into up dog.

Loose and sweaty, she met a trainer in the weight room for another thirty minutes of lifting. As a man, watching her thruster form was as impressive as it was entertaining. As security, there was nothing entertaining about his client working out in a room occupied by half a dozen guys who looked like they could be drafted onto any defensive line in the NFL. None of them minded checking out the scenery.

One particular meathead had to be stared down before he went back to his bicep curls. Then, there was the trainer. A shorter, broader version of a Ken doll, who was a little too attentive in his spotting. He was going to have to talk to Waverly about reassessing where she did her weight training, Xavier decided.

Waverly usually avoided showering at the gym. At this particular gym, the member fees were high enough to dissuade most from taking and selling pictures of other members, but one could never be certain. However, with the tight schedule, it was necessary today. She left Xavier outside the women's locker room and pushed through the frosted glass door.

She paid a hefty monthly fee, which gave her access to the well-equipped locker room decorated in stainless steel and purple finishes complete with attractive mood lighting. It may have housed multi-jetted showers and a state-of-the-art steam room, but no amount of money could rid the space of the smell of sweaty feet.

She spotted actress Zoey Grace, her mother's version of her competition, lacing up gold, limited edition high-tops on one of the benches. Zoey was a painfully thin typical Hollywood girl—too much partying, not enough food—and Waverly had to resist the urge to shove a protein bar in the girl's bag. She settled for waving a greeting instead.

She grabbed her bag and took it into the shower's dressing

room with her. Waverly remembered the first time a studio suggested she drop some weight for a role. She'd very politely told them that, if they wanted someone smaller for the part, they could go hire someone and walked away from contract negotiations. She'd ignored their calls and apology gifts for a week before directing Phil to accept the hefty salary increase they offered.

Hollywood, she thought, stepping under the jets of water, *could either destroy a girl or make her stronger*. And by the time her career was done, she would be invincible.

She showered and changed in record time, pulling her still damp hair back into a sleek braid. She kept it casual with a simple V-neck t-shirt and distressed jeans that cuffed stylishly above caramel leather sandals.

It was just a dinner meeting with Phil. One that she'd put off for a few weeks now.

She slicked a taupey rose over her eyelids and applied a quick coat of mascara to her lashes. She knew exactly what Phil—coached by her mother—was going to say.

You need to pick a new project before the world forgets about you.

Well, she already had a new project in mind, but it wasn't one her agent or mother would approve of. And now was not a good time to show her hand. Not with Sylvia already toying with changing the terms of her trust. No, tonight she'd play along with Phil.

Playing along was what she did. But soon, in just a handful of months, she'd be able to play by her own rules, set her own goals, live her own life. She shoved everything into her gym bag and hustled through the locker room door.

She was so busy fishing her sunglasses out of her bag that she didn't see the wall of muscle until she'd walked smack into it. Strong hands gripped her shoulders. "Your attentiveness astounds me." Sarcasm designed specifically to piss her off resounded in Xavier's tone, but it came a distant second to the sudden rush of awareness that flooded her system.

His chest was as broad as it was solid. The heat pumped off of him through the crisp checked button down he wore under his jacket into her palms splayed across his chest. In her flat sandals, she had to tilt her head back to look him in his eyes. "Jesus, I wasn't expecting you to be lurking outside the locker room like a creep," she retorted. Her gym bag slid off her shoulder and smacked him in the shin. He shifted, pushing her against the wall as someone moved past them.

He was too close, and she didn't like it. It made her jumpy and anxious. She felt trapped. His grip on her radiated heat as did his honey-colored gaze and frowning mouth.

"When you want to yell, you get this little line right here," Waverly said, tracing the mark between his eyebrows.

"I don't want to yell," he argued.

"Your forehead wrinkles suggest otherwise." She brushed his forehead again. His grip on her arms tightened, and she felt an unwelcome rush of excitement.

"Behave yourself," Xavier ordered, his voice tight and rough.

It thrilled her to know that she'd pushed him off center. She liked having that ability, that power. She grinned up at him, "Come on, X. Let's go to dinner. You're probably just hangry. It means you get angry when you're hungry."

"I know what it means, and I'm not hangry," he grumbled, giving her a helpful shove toward the door. "I'm trying to keep you from walking into the arms of a serial killer and offering to drive to the kill site. It's exhausting."

Waverly laughed. "See? Hangry," she told him, savoring her victory.

"Just shut up and get in the car."

PHIL CHOSE a hot sushi place guaranteed for some pictures on the gossip sites. It was easier to get inside than usual with Xavier there. He guided her through the crowd at the door with one hand on the small of her back. Waverly kept her sunglasses on and her face Victoria Beckham-neutral for the photographers, but on the inside, her pulse was jumping.

She hated crowds, and adding to the anxiety was the heavy awareness of Xavier's warm, firm hand on her. She didn't want to be attracted to him, but her body seemed to have other ideas. He sent her heart rate skittering every time they touched, yet she felt oddly safe with him there frowning away the crowd. Inside, the restaurant was crowded, its red walls glowing, its chocolate brown booths and tables full. She nodded at a few executives she knew and posed for two selfies, one with a fan and one with a socialite who looked vaguely familiar, before they finally made it to the table.

Phil was already there. He'd reserved a table in the back room that was sectioned off but not quite private thanks to a handful of clever screens and a transparent wall of live bamboo. He made a show of greeting her with a hug and offered Xavier a hearty handshake. What was left of his silvery mane was combed back into a fluffy cloud. He wore a navy pinstripe suit and flashed a Rolex Yacht-Master on his wrist. When Xavier made a move to leave them, Waverly insisted he stay. She'd only been half kidding about the hangry. The man hadn't eaten all day that she'd seen, and, attractive pain in the ass or not, he deserved dinner.

The evening went exactly as Waverly had predicted. Phil

tried to play it as a friendly catch-up, but she knew better. Her guard was always up when it came to Phil.

"I'm glad to see you two are getting along," Phil said, taking an enthusiastic slurp of his miso soup.

"Oh, yeah," Waverly agreed with just a hint of sarcasm. "Just like synchronized swimmers."

She felt the pressure of a loafer sole squashing her foot under the table and hid her laugh with a cough. She thunked Xavier solidly on the shoulder as if they were old drinking buddies. "Yep, I can count on this guy to keep me safe from physical harm."

He gave a final, painful squish before moving his foot. She caught him in the shin with her bare heel and had the satisfaction of hearing a soft grunt.

Oblivious, Phil plowed on. "I'm going to take that as you forgiving me for my involvement in your little ambush about bringing Xavier on board. There's nothing that we all value more than your safety."

Oh, goodie. They'd moved on to the ass-kissing portion of the meal. She had no idea why Phil felt like it was necessary. He'd been her mother's agent since before Waverly was born. She'd known the man her entire life, yet he still couldn't be real with her.

She kept her pleasant mask in place and let Phil zig and zag his way to his point over edamame and sashimi. While Phil tried to pry information out of her, she watched Xavier eat. Even when dabbling with the wasabi, he never stopped scanning the room. He looked relaxed, engaged, but looks were usually deceiving in this town.

He seemed not to notice the appreciative gazes directed his way by the restaurant's female—and some of the male—clientele, but Waverly was certain he noticed and filed it all away along with the rest of his observations.

"So, my dear," Phil began, patting his thin mouth with a cloth napkin. "Have you given any thought to your next project?" He leaned in, his suit bunching at the arms, looking like a confidante.

Waverly finished her bite of tuna and casually reached for another piece. "I have," she told him, keeping her tone light. She punched up the energy to sound excited. "There are a couple of scripts that caught my attention."

Phil, sensing the prize he sought, cocked his head to the side. All ears. "Which titles?"

Waverly drew it out by taking a leisurely sip of water. "Originally I was considering Will Wakefield's remake."

"Really?" Phil's enthusiasm oozed through his pores. "That would be an excellent choice for you."

"I thought so, too," she agreed. "But the shooting would overlap with the European leg of the press tour for *The Dedication.* And with the buzz we're getting from advance viewings, I'm not willing to sacrifice that commitment."

"Hmm," Phil nodded. "I think that's a wise decision."

Waverly shot a glance at Xavier, noted that he was watching her closely. She turned back to Phil and tried to ignore the weight of his gaze on her. "I read through the one your office sent over last week, and I'm just not feeling it. I don't think it's going to get off the ground."

"Sound instincts," Phil commended.

She could have sworn she heard Xavier mutter "kiss ass" under his breath, but it was hard to tell with the background noise.

"I've got two more possibles that I'm looking at," she continued.

"If you have any questions that need answered, you know I'm just a phone call away. I'm happy to talk to the studios for you—perhaps get some preliminary numbers?"

"Thank you, Phil. I'll let you know."

Appeased that she was actually still planning to work for a living, Phil led the conversation down the path of industry gossip. Who had just been let go from what project, what the critics were whispering about so and so's new movie. Waverly listened with half an ear and wondered how much time she'd bought herself.

Finally, Phil had had his fill of both sushi and quality time and called it a night.

Xavier had the valet bring his SUV around while she watched the crowd outside from the host stand. Night had fallen, and thanks to a fresh-out-of-rehab soap star's arrival twenty minutes earlier, the crowd of photographers and fans had grown.

"Ready to go?" Xavier asked, studying her face.

Waverly pasted on a smile and dragged her sunglasses out of her bag. "Sure. Let's go."

As soon as she stepped outside the crowd pressed in. People were shouting her name, and the flashes were blindingly bright. She tried to concentrate on Xavier's hand on her back, but someone grabbed her arm hard and she stumbled. The noise turned to a dull throb in her head, and she felt the panic closing in.

Then Xavier was shoving her under his arm, holding her tight against him while blazing a path to the SUV with his free hand. Restaurant security took up her other side and held the crowd at bay.

She caught the gleam of teeth, the flash of a camera, her name on strangers' lips in a tornado of stimulus. Xavier yanked open the SUV door and all but deposited her on the seat.

"Angel."

She looked up at him, his face inches from hers. He was calm, completely calm. There was no danger, and it made her relax instantly.

"You gotta let go, Waverly," he said softly.

Glancing down, she saw that she had a death grip on his jacket.

"Sorry." The word came out a hoarse whisper. She forced her fingers to unwind themselves, and then he was shutting the door, separating her from the chaos outside. In the seconds it took him to walk around to the driver's side, she tried to get her breathing under control. She didn't need Xavier to know how freaked she'd been.

Still, she felt steadier when he slid into the driver's seat and eased away from the curb. She even managed a wave through the glass as they pulled away.

"You okay?" he asked, his tone mild.

"Yeah. I just ate too much. I feel like I'm going to burst."

"You were lying your ass off to Phil in there, and now you're lying to me," Xavier said, accelerating smoothly down La Cienega. There was no recrimination in his tone. He was simply stating facts.

Waverly watched as the designer furniture store her mother had used to redecorate the pool house slid past her window. She was tired. Bone tired. The constant battle of what she wanted versus what others wanted for her was an ebb and flow of disappointment and hope. Every time she lied about what she wanted, another spark of hope died. She worried that by denying it, she was slowly killing her dreams.

"What makes you say that?" she sighed, feigning disinterest.

"You hold your breath right before you tell a lie and when you're really trying to sell it you get this smile that never makes it to your eyes. Plus, you blink twice as often as you usually do."

Crap. He was even more observant than she'd given him credit for. He was entirely too tuned in to her, and that was dangerous.

"You've got walls," he continued conversationally. "I get that. How could you not given your situation? But we're on the same team here, and I need to know you."

She felt a surge of anger and welcomed it over the exhaustion. "Technically, X, you're on my parents' team. They hired you. They sign your paycheck. That has nothing to do with me."

"I'm protecting *you*," he pointed out. "And in order to do that to the best of my abilities, I need to know you."

"Why?" She held back the tears that suddenly clogged her throat. "What does it matter?"

Xavier slowed the SUV and pulled over under a streetlight. He put the vehicle in park and shifted in his seat to face her. "I'm not the bad guy here, Waverly."

Her name on his lips gave her a little, unwelcome thrill. How could she have a crush on a man she didn't like? She needed therapy... or a vacation.

She leaned in across the console. "I don't trust you, X, any more than I trust Phil, my mother's parakeet."

He moved in until he was barely inches from her face and took off her sunglasses, tossing them on the console. "You will. If you tell me why you were scared leaving the restaurant, I can make it better for you. We can avoid situations that—"

Her laugh was short, sharp. "X, there is no 'avoiding situations.' I am required to make appearances and behave in certain ways. It's like the saying 'with great power comes great responsibility.' Except in my case there's very little power. There's only responsibility. I owe people things. I owe my parents for providing this life for me. I owe my fans for supporting me movie after movie. I owe my staff a living because they have given their time and loyalty to help me build this world. And that means that I go places I don't want to go, sometimes talk to people I don't want to talk to, and occasionally make movies I don't want to make."

"Penance."

"Maintenance," she corrected him.

"You trust Mari and Louie. You trust Kate. You're going to have to trust me." His mouth was so close now, and Waverly couldn't stop staring at his firm lips. Her world had narrowed to just his face. There was a line of stubble on his jaw and it made him look even more irresistible.

"That's different. They're family."

"You don't trust your parents."

"Biology doesn't buy loyalty these days." She said it before she thought better then sighed. She'd said too much. Given him too much of a window into her. It was safer to keep Xavier at a distance.

He took her chin in his hand, held it steady so she had to look him in the eye. "Whether or not you trust me, I'll still be here."

Others had promised the same. Empty promises and Waverly didn't put stock in those words anymore. She could count on herself, and that's what she did. It was the price to pay for admission into this world, and she was willing to pay it.

"I'm not taking applications for a BFF. You work for my parents, and I tolerate you. That's the extent of our relationship."

He held her chin for a second longer, stared deep into her. Those amber eyes were searching for something, and she worried that he could see down into her very soul. Whatever it was he was looking for, she made sure he didn't find it in her gaze. She kept her eyes cool, and when he released her, she pulled back quickly. "Take me home, X."

"You got it, boss." *He was amused*, she thought, as if he was dealing with a kid's temper tantrum. But he hadn't seen anything yet. She'd shake him loose and wouldn't even miss that face, those strong shoulders, that broad chest...

They drove home in silence. And Waverly was grateful for the break. She felt oddly guilty about brushing him off and didn't know why. He wanted "in." And there was no way in hell she was letting that happen. He would just run right back to her parents with his report.

Neighborhood security had swept out any lingering photographers, she noted when they pulled through the tall, ornate gates at the foot of the driveway.

The Tahoe's headlights illuminated the cobblestone drive as they came up the hill to the house. The beams caught Sylvia in an ivory nightgown standing in the middle of the driveway, broken glass at her bare feet.

"Shit," Waverly said, under her breath, yanking her seat-belt off.

Xavier put the Tahoe in park and made a move to get out.

She grabbed his arm, her fingers digging in with urgency. "Please don't," Waverly said.

"I can help."

"I know, X. I know you can. But if she wakes up and remembers this tomorrow, she'll be humiliated." *Please don't do this to us*, she begged with her eyes.

Xavier studied her face and then looked through the glass at Sylvia.

"Go check her first. Make sure she's not hurt. If she's okay, I'll go."

Waverly exhaled her relief. "Thank you. Really."

She leaned over the console reaching into the backseat to grab her bags.

"Leave them. I'll take them to the pool house," he told her.

"You don't have to do that. I can take care of—"

"Angel, I've got them. Go help your mother."

Still, she paused. "Listen, please don't—"

"I won't say anything to anyone," Xavier promised, shaking his head. She believed him.

Surprising them both, Waverly brought her hand to his chest. She leaned in and brushed her lips against his cheek long enough to take a fortifying breath, drawing in his scent, his warmth, his strength. And then she was sliding out the door.

"Hi, Mama," Waverly said softly, picking her way around the glass to get to Sylvia.

"I can't find your father," Sylvia said dreamily, swaying in the moonlight in her own cloud of vodka.

Waverly tucked an arm around her mother's waist and guided her away from the shards of glass. Sylvia felt so fragile and thin. It was such a shock to her that Waverly wondered when she had last hugged her mother.

"Dad's not here, remember? He left today to shoot in Vancouver for a few weeks. He'll be home for a few days on Wednesday."

Sylvia stumbled and recovered, clinging to Waverly's free arm. "He is? I must have forgotten." She frowned, limping her way toward the house.

Waverly glanced over her shoulder at Xavier in the Tahoe. She nodded to him to let him know everything was fine.

Everything was far from fine, but it was normal.

It took her an hour to get her mother settled. She brought her some warm broth and water, trying to flush out some of the alcohol from her system. While her mother sipped, she tidied up the bedroom. Sylvia's suite was nothing shy of spectacular with its Austrian crystal chandelier hanging from the vaulted ceiling over the bed. As in her sitting room, everything here was shades of white from the tufted ottoman to the wingback chairs flanking the white marble fireplace that, to Waverly's knowledge, had never been used.

The rug that covered an acre of floor was thick and plush. The bathroom was fit for a goddess and trimmed in rose quartz and stocked with luxurious towels and the best beauty secrets money could buy. And the dressing room, well it was larger than the attached sitting room. Once Sylvia's pride and joy, Mari now ruthlessly managed the room and its contents. Waverly ducked her head into the dressing room and did a fast check for liquor bottles. She found one in the accessory island in the center of the room and another tucked into the calfskin boot on display.

She carted them out and emptied them in the bathroom sink. It did no good. She wasn't even sure why she bothered other than the fact that it would force Sylvia to order more, temporarily inconveniencing her problem.

When Sylvia finished her broth, Waverly curled up on the bed with her and turned on *Relentless Love*, the movie that Sylvia met Robert while filming. As precarious and damaged as her parents' relationship was, Sylvia always took comfort from the movie.

"Oh, how young I was," Sylvia sighed, her eyelids heavy under the weight of exhaustion and make-up. "And just look how handsome your father was," she sighed, pointing to the screen.

Waverly, aware of her role, hugged a silk pillow to her chest as she leaned against her mother's satin-wrapped headboard. "Very handsome," she agreed.

"Darling," her mother slurred, "we only have a small

window to solidify your career. To really make your mark. This business isn't kind to women who venture beyond forty." Her mother had drummed it into her skull since she was five.

It's all downhill after forty. Personally, Waverly was looking forward to a little downhill.

It was true—parts for her mother were fewer and farther between, but Waverly was aware of the role that alcohol played in that.

She distracted her mother, filling her in on her schedule for the week, noting the pleasure it gave Sylvia. "Oh! I'm so glad you're presenting at *Indulgence's* Style Awards," Sylvia sat a little higher against her pillows. "Isn't it exciting? Standing up there in front of all those people who wish they were you?"

"Sure, Mom." It was, sort of. But to Waverly, it didn't feel like a rush. It felt like a responsibility.

"You've got such a good following right now, and we need to make it stronger," her mother yawned. "We need to give them more. You need to pick your next movie. Maybe start seeing someone? Is there anyone you're interested in?"

Career and love advice from Sylvia Sinner. Because to her mother, who she dated, who she married, was just as much a part of her career as the roles she chose. Sylvia had been setting up Waverly with eligible and appropriate bachelors since she was fourteen. Every once in a while, Waverly had pulled off the impossible and quietly enjoyed a relationship that had nothing to do with her mother, sometimes an actor and sometimes a regular, normal guy. None of them stuck. There was the actor with the charming, crooked grin who used her connections to a producer to score a part. Then there was the musician who'd neglected to call for the duration of his world tour and then penned a song about her body as an apology that went unaccepted.

A relationship, fake or an actual attempt, was not something she was willing to throw into the mix right now. She needed to be unencumbered and ready to move.

"There's no one who makes me look at them like that," she said, gesturing at the screen where Sylvia was giving Robert one hell of a come hither look. And ignoring the vision of Xavier that immediately popped into her head.

"Don't put it off, Waverly," her mother said, her eyes closing.

"Don't put what off, Mom?"

"Life. Look at everything we have, everything your father and I built. We're counting on you to carry this on. Don't make all of this be for nothing. You have real earning potential, more than I did at your age. Don't waste that." The words slurred and slowed before fading away.

Waverly listened to her mother's steady breathing for a few moments and, satisfied that Sylvia was asleep, turned off the movie and gathered the dishes. She carried the bowl and mug to the kitchen, washed them in the sink, and armed the alarm before tip-toeing out the front door.

She had a broom and a dustpan in the pool house. She would clean up the glass in the drive before calling it a night, she decided, her shoulders slumped. One more task and then she could rest.

But the glass was gone. Not a sliver of it twinkled under the floodlights. *Xavier the fixer,* she shook her head. She was too tired to think about her warring feelings there. She let herself into the pool house, automatically arming the alarm, before venturing into her kitchen. Her purse and gym bag rested on the counter next to a plate with half of a peanut butter and jelly sandwich. A note was scrawled on the napkin.

Snack then sleep. See you in the morning, Angel.

X.

He could have just gone home, yet he'd stayed to make sure she got her mother safely inside and then cleaned up the mess. He'd delivered her bags and made her a snack. All after keeping her safe and calm in the midst of a trigger.

Hell, he was getting harder and harder to hate.

6

She was going to kick Xavier's ass.

"You're not wearing that," he announced again, his tone suggesting there was no room for argument.

But Waverly was in the mood for a fight. She whirled around in the mirror set up in her bedroom, her hands on her hips, to glare at him. "Exactly what is your problem with this dress?" she demanded.

It was Thursday in the week from absolute hell. She'd booked every spare minute in an effort to shake him loose, but he was only digging in harder. Through two red carpets, four lunches, five sessions at the gym, three cocktail parties, nine interviews, and even a damn baby shower for an actress she'd worked with once when they were tweens, he stuck.

The man was stubborn enough to make it look easy. She'd missed meals dashing from one event to the next, missed sleep, dragging her ass in the door at three in the morning from a cocktail party that turned late night pool party. The circles under her eyes were going to add an extra twenty minutes to her make-up for the event this afternoon. Yet Xavier showed no signs of cracking.

She hated him a little for it. Sure, he'd had the good manners not to mention the scene with her mother. But he'd spent every moment of the ensuing week annoying her with his mere presence. He'd gotten more vocal, too. He'd insisted on sitting in with her meeting with Kate and Mari again and dropped the bomb that Les Ganim had indeed left his job in El Plano and hadn't been seen in ten days.

Then he complained every time she left the house. She wasn't about to lock herself in a prison just because Wedding Dress Guy may or may not have come to L.A. She'd dealt with things like this her entire life. It was par for the course in her opinion and a legitimate threat in his. Just like everything else, they'd butted heads over. And then there was the picture that surfaced on the gossip sites after dinner at Nobu. She was tucked under Xavier's arm, her fingers clinging to him as he guided her into the SUV. The headlines had been about her escaping a raucous crowd, but what she saw when she looked at the pictures was a raw and intimate portrait of need.

Waverly whirled back to the mirror, turning this way and that admiring the way the elegant, sheer fabric clung to her like a spider web.

"I don't see what you could possibly have against this dress."

She skimmed her hands over the gauzy layers. Backless and cut impossibly low in the front, it wasn't a dress she'd normally have chosen. She'd have to tape herself in just to make sure she could avoid the weekly nip slip countdown. No, she wouldn't have agreed to wear it, but Xavier's dissent pushed her over the edge. She was prepared to prance out in public dressed like a girl with daddy issues.

"It's a security risk," Xavier snapped.

"How? I can't hide a handgun, much less a bomb under

this," Waverly smirked, hands on hips. He wet his lips, and she felt a thrill run up her spine.

Xavier Saint was attracted to her.

"I'm going to end up shooting someone tonight if you wear that dress."

Kate snickered from her sprawled out position on the bed. "Saint, you gotta get out more. There's going to be women wearing a lot less than Waverly here."

The vein in Xavier's forehead throbbed. "Kate, would you mind giving us a minute?" he asked pleasantly, rubbing two fingers to the line between his eyes.

"I'd be happy to," Kate said. "I need a snack anyway."

Waverly watched her friend saunter through the bedroom door and, tossing a knowing smile over her shoulder, shut the door behind her.

"You didn't have to throw her out," Waverly snapped.

Xavier rose and loomed behind her, glaring at her in the mirror. Waverly spun around to face him. He put his hands on her shoulders and looked ready to throttle her. "If you wear this dress, I'm not leaving your side this afternoon."

She slapped a hand to his chest. "How is that any different from any other day?"

"I mean it Waverly. You're asking for a lot of attention that you don't need."

"I'm not asking for anything. I look good in this dress."

"You look fucking beautiful in the dress, but you'd look that way in a dress that I can't see through. I am begging you, Angel, for the love of God, do not wear this dress tonight. I need to be on alert for threats, not watching to make sure your spectacular tits don't fall out of your dress."

Waverly opened her mouth. Shut it. Then opened it again.

"Shit. Sorry." Xavier backed away and rubbed a hand over his face.

The break in his perfectly professional façade shocked her, fascinated her. She was glad she wasn't the only one cracking from the pressure of constant togetherness.

"Hand me the red one?" she asked, taking pity on him and pointing at the next dress on the rack.

Without looking at her, Xavier grabbed it and handed it over. He looked like he wanted to apologize again. But Waverly didn't give him the chance. She ducked behind the screen and shimmied out of the gossamer thin gown and into the red.

It too was a stunner. The slim, strapless column flowed down her curves highlighting all the right places with its film siren red. A long slit hit high on the thigh and allowed for a bit of room to move. The hem pooled in the slightest fishtail train. The length would be perfect for those to-die-for crystal Gladiator sandals she had tucked in the back of her closet. Hair half up and curled, gold cuff bracelets, she'd look Greek goddess-like and not have to worry about her "spectacular tits" falling out of anything, Waverly decided.

"Better?" she asked, arching an eyebrow in the mirror.

He stared at her reflection, raking her with a look from head to toe, and nodded his assent, the tic in his jaw told her there was a lot he wasn't saying.

"Problem solved," she said.

"Thank you," he muttered the words through gritted teeth like it pained him to say them.

She brought her hands to her breasts and hefted them under the dress. "Still spectacular though, right?" she joked.

"Christ," was the only part of his retort that she caught as he stalked out of her bedroom.

She laughed, loud and long, and then went to find her accessories.

Xavier did another scan of the room, noting again the exits, the blind spots, the faces. Waverly had been a hit on stage presenting tonight and was reaping the benefits by being dragged around the after party, weaving in and out of the columns in the museum's rotunda.

He stood with his back to a wall where he could survey the room yet still get to her if he needed to. Xavier didn't like letting Waverly wander far without him, but situations like this required give and take. Security threats were rather low at an event like this. Just getting into the ceremony had been a circus of reporters, photographers, museum staff, and event and venue security. He'd worked with the security team in advance to make sure they were briefed on Ganim just in case the man actually showed his face. The possibility of him showing up here to get a look at Waverly was low, but Xavier always covered his bases.

The awards ceremony and late lunch had taken place downstairs in the museum's theater and the celebration continued two floors up under twenty-foot ceilings and the glass atrium that lit the entire building via the four-story rotunda. Low techno music pulsed from speakers tucked behind exotic plantings and statues. It was a very Garden of Eden vibe the party organizers had gone for.

Everything glittered from the diamonds on necks and wrists to the high-tech lighting displays around the bars and photo stations.

Waverly didn't glitter. She glowed.

She looks incredible, he thought, watching her with a woman who spoke animatedly with both hands glittering under jewels. They shared a laugh and Waverly brought a hand to her chest.

Thank God she hadn't worn the other dress. His eyes would have been glued to her. It was hard enough to stop looking at her in this one.

He circled around the edge of the crowd and came up by the column at Waverly's back. It was time to check in before drifting away again and watching from the sidelines.

"I've got a project in mind for you, Waverly," the woman was saying. She was tall and slim, her hair was a natural mass of ebony curls. She wore thick purple-rimmed glasses and her smile was more genuine than ninety percent of the other attendees.

"I'm not really in the market for any projects right now, Malia," Waverly confessed.

Malia cocked her head to the side. "I'm intrigued. Spill it, kid."

Waverly glanced around to make sure they wouldn't be overheard, and Xavier resisted the urge to move closer.

"I'm thinking about getting out of the industry."

Malia's brown eyes widened. "Waverly, you have a talent. Normally I would applaud anyone who wanted to leave this vapid hellhole, but you're the reason people like me make movies."

"I want to go to college."

"You didn't even go to high school," Malia reminded her.

"That's exactly my point. I want to go somewhere that my parents can't control or can't grease the way, and I want to decide what's right for my life. I want the choice," Waverly said in a rush. Xavier could feel the passion in her tone.

Malia contemplated. "What would you study?"

Waverly shrugged. "I'm not a hundred percent sure, but I think psychology would be at the top."

"Hmm. Would you be giving up acting completely?"

"I honestly don't know. Acting is the only thing I know in

my life, but I don't see studios being eager to work around a full-time student schedule," Waverly answered.

"I think if it's something you feel strongly about, you should absolutely do it. But this project I've got, it starts filming in June. We'd be done by the first or second week of August, tops. And the lead, honestly, I signed on for it with you in mind."

"Really?"

"There's no pressure, but if you can have both, why not?"

"Send me the script, and I'll take a look."

The women wandered off toward the bar, and Xavier slipped back into the crowd.

College? That was interesting. He imagined Sylvia wouldn't be excited to hear about that prospect. Not that she'd hear it from him. He didn't get involved with family squabbles unless one of them threatened a client's physical well-being. He'd stay out of this one and file the information away.

Waverly and Malia had parted ways, and a new woman sidled up next to his charge. The brunette stood just a little too close and was waving her martini around like she was an enthusiastic drum major.

Her body language told him drunk. Her facial expression told him bitch.

Xavier worked his way through the crowd, keeping his eyes on Waverly. The woman she was talking to had her back to him, but he had a clean line of site on Waverly's face. She had her blinding, fake smile firmly in place.

"I *know* the only reason you got that role is because you were fucking Sidney," the woman announced in a loud hiss. She leaned in, but rather than looking threatened, Waverly looked bored.

"Is that so?" Waverly asked.

"That part and that award should have been mine."

"Geneva," Waverly sighed. "Don't you think this industry is tough enough without trying to pit against each other as enemies?"

"Don't pretend to go all 'girl power' on me. You are the enemy. You *stole* that part from me!" Geneva gestured with her glass and sloshed vodka onto the museum's marble floor.

Xavier circled around and came up behind Waverly. He put his hand on the small of her back, but said nothing. She was tense and vibrating under his palm, but her voice was as smooth as honey. "Let's get this straight, Geneva. I didn't steal that part from you. I auditioned and landed it. I beat you fair and square. You're a decent actress. You could be better if you'd lay off the booze and the coke, which by the way is still visible under your nose."

Xavier felt an odd burst of pride as Waverly defended herself. Classy and indomitable.

"You're a fucking whore!" Geneva snarled and reached out with her talon-like claws. Her pretty face rearranged into an ugly mask of hatred. Xavier didn't wait to see whether she was planning to slap, shove, or rake her nails over Waverly. He simply grabbed her by the bony wrist and squeezed.

"Let's get one more thing straight," he said in a friendly tone. "If you touch her, I will take you down and restrain you in front of all these nice people. Then, I'm going to press charges and, you can spend the next six months of your life pretending to be sorry for what a miserable asshole you are and trying to clean up your image with endless hours of community service. And in the end, no one is going to buy it because, as previously stated, you're a miserable asshole."

Geneva's glossed up purple lips gaped open on a gasp. She bared her teeth and sneered, "You can't talk to me that way!"

Her voice was a screech and curious people in gowns and suits were starting to look.

"Geneva! There you are," a woman in a navy pantsuit with a short brown bob bustled over. She grabbed Geneva's other arm. "If you'll excuse us," she said, flashing a desperate smile at Waverly. "Geneva's car is ready to take her home."

"I don't need to go home. She needs to go home," Geneva said, jutting her chin in Waverly's direction.

Xavier waited until the suit had a firm grip on Geneva's arm before letting go of her wrist. "Lovely meeting you," he called after them as Geneva was hauled off.

"Did you just swoop in here and White Knight me?" Waverly said, raising her glass to her lips.

"No, I *intervened* when I detected a potential security threat," he corrected her. They watched Geneva get dragged into the elevator by her handler.

"Who was that?"

"The screaming maniac throwing accusations or the overworked woman who corralled her?"

"Both."

"Geneva St. Regis, totally not her real name. She's an actress who is still very upset about a part that I beat her out for when I was fifteen."

"You were fifteen, and she accused you of sleeping with someone to get a part?"

"Par for the course, trust me. The woman who swooped in and saved us all some embarrassment is Geneva's long-suffering agent. Probably hoping to get one last movie out of her before dumping her in rehab."

"Speaking of rehab. What's in the glass?" He frowned at her drink.

"Relax, Saint," she rolled her eyes. "It's club soda. I don't drink."

"Ever?" he asked.

"Ever. You seem surprised. It's not even legal for me to drink yet."

"I've been at bar mitzvahs in this town that served booze to kids," Xavier told her.

"Money can buy your way around a lot of laws," Waverly reminded him. "But in my case, my mother drinks, so I don't drink."

"Simple as that?"

"Some things are that simple, X." She smiled up at him, and he felt a funny twist in his gut. She was using her real smile on him, and it worked better than any weapon of destruction.

"There's my favorite Sinner."

Xavier didn't like the flirty British tone or the look of the man who'd bent Waverly back in a dip deep enough she was in danger of falling out of her dress.

He wore the light gray suit sans tie and with the carelessness of someone who'd been born with his own tailor. His shirt, a pale blue check, was unbuttoned, giving him a rakish look. His frame was lean, and his grin was toothy. Subtly highlighted hair glinted gold under the lights. His Rolex was real, his tan was fake, and his resume was full of more than a dozen blockbuster films.

Waverly laughed as Dante Wrede, Hollywood's most eligible leading man, righted her.

"My mother would be crushed if she heard you say that."

"Then it will be our little secret," he said, with a devilish wink before turning his attention to Xavier. Xavier returned the man's once-over.

"Dante Wrede," he said, extending a hand.

Xavier took it, gripped. "Xavier Saint."

"Ah, Mr. Saint. I've heard good things about Invictus Security," Dante said, returning the crushing grip.

A well-informed most eligible leading man.

"Glad to hear it," Xavier said stoically.

"I believe you did some work for Roy Krasinski over at Metro Studios," Dante said, finally relinquishing the handshake.

He had. It was a short-term assignment involving extortion and a kidnapping threat. It took Xavier little more than a week to identify the extortionist, Krasinski's entitled stepson who wanted a bigger allowance. The matter had been solved privately and without police.

"Yes, we worked together briefly. How do you and Waverly know each other?"

Another toothy grin. "Everyone knows everyone in this town. But I had the good fortune to shoot a film with the lovely Ms. Sinner and fall madly in love with her while on location in Africa."

Waverly laughed again. A real laugh. "You're ridiculous, Dante."

"It would have been a torrid love affair if she'd only given me the time of day," he sighed dramatically. "Oh, well, I'll just keep wearing you down until you agree to marry me."

"And become the third Mrs. Wrede? Be still my heart," Waverly said, fanning herself.

"Your casual handling of my feelings guts me. Now if you'll excuse me, I'm going to go lick my wounds at the bar and see if that lovely little redhead can heal my broken heart."

He dropped a loud kiss on Waverly's cheek and zeroed in on the woman in the short gold dress like a shark scenting fresh blood.

"Why the face?" Waverly teased Xavier as he watched Dante leave.

Xavier frowned. "I don't like him."

"He's harmless," Waverly laughed.

"Even golden retrievers have teeth."

"If I didn't know better," Waverly said innocently. "I'd say you sounded jealous."

"Jealous?" Xavier scoffed.

He wasn't jealous. He just didn't like that a man could put his hands all over her, and she'd smile up at him like he casually announced a cure for childhood cancer. That wasn't jealous. That was... concern.

"I'd rather spend time with Geneva. She's more straightforward about being an asshole," Xavier muttered.

Waverly elbowed him in the gut. "You *are* jealous!" She was gleeful now.

"I'm your security. Security doesn't like it when people manhandle the women they're guarding."

"It was a hug."

"And a kiss," he reminded her.

She grinned, the full on wattage again. "I like seeing this human side of you."

"I'm not jealous, and I'm not human," he argued.

When she said nothing, he felt compelled to solidify his argument. "You're not my type. You're too young. You're..." he trailed off. He couldn't think of another valid argument why he wouldn't be jealous.

"A spoiled Hollywood princess?" Waverly supplied.

He winced when she threw his own words back at him. "Maybe that was a little harsh."

She gave an unladylike snort. "Xavier 'Calls Them As He Sees Them' Saint. A. Of course, I'm not your type. You go for the girls who laugh at girls like me. B. I'm twenty. You make it sound like you're seventy-eight."

"I'm seven years older than you."

"And you think that'll stop you from admiring all this?" she teased, gesturing down at her dress.

"Shut up, Waverly."

"Whatever you say, X," she patted his arm. "You're not my type either. Of course that doesn't mean I don't think you look incredible in that suit."

He grunted.

"I'm going to go get another non-alcoholic beverage. Can I get you one?"

"No," he grumbled. But he did watch her walk away.

What the hell was he doing? He was a professional. He didn't get personally involved with his clients. Yet here he was pissed off because he wasn't her type. He bet money that Dante Wrede was her type. The shiny golden boy oozing with charm and money.

"Mr. Saint?"

Embarrassed that he'd been caught staring at Waverly's retreating ass, Xavier turned. It was one of the guards from downstairs.

"Jim," Xavier greeted him with a nod. Jim looked like a very tall, very strong Stevie Wonder, but he spoke like a librarian in the stacks.

"We may have a sighting of that sub you briefed us on," Jim said quietly.

Xavier felt a boost of adrenaline. "Is he still here?"

Jim nodded. "I came straight up. If you have time, you can confirm," Jim said, gesturing toward the stairwell door behind them.

Xavier glanced at the door and back at Waverly who was engaged in another conversation, this time with the host of the ceremony and the man's husband.

"I can keep an eye while you head down," Jim offered.

"Let me introduce you first," Xavier decided. Jim followed him across the room to Waverly. She took one look at Xavier's face and smoothly excused herself.

"What's wrong?" she asked him.

"Nothing's wrong," Xavier assured her. "Waverly, this is Jim. He's going to be hanging out up here with you for a few minutes, okay?"

"Hi, Jim," Waverly said, distractedly offering her hand. "Where are you going?"

"Security downstairs may have spotted Ganim in the crowd."

Waverly's eyes widened. "Here? Wedding Dress Guy is here?"

"We don't know for sure. I'm going down to see if I can spot him. I need you to stay here with Jim. Okay?"

Waverly looked like she was going to argue with him.

"I mean it, Angel. Stay here. I'll be right back." He knew he had her when her bottom lip poked out just a bit. It was another one of her tells.

"Be careful," she warned him.

Xavier nodded and turned back to Jim.

"Just ask for Ricardo down there. He'll hook you up."

"Thanks, Jim. Keep an eye on her," he said, jerking his thumb at Waverly. "She's sneaky."

Waverly rolled her eyes and Xavier winked at her.

Downstairs he found a makeshift security hub commandeering the section just left of the entrance. Ricardo was as short as Jim was tall, and he moved in quick, jerky movements.

"Yeah, yeah, yeah," he nodded vigorously at Xavier. "Saint. Jimbo said he'd send you down. We got a possible suspect a few rows back behind the barricade. Black ball cap and a Texans t-shirt."

He tapped the screen of a security monitor showing a live feed of the crowd on the right hand side of the red carpet. "Can't tell on this piece a' crap. But Jim spotted him when he was doing a sweep outside."

"Mind if I take a look out there?" Xavier asked, fully intending to do so regardless of the answer.

"Have at it," Ricardo nodded. "Grab a walkie so you can let us know if you need backup."

Xavier snagged a radio out of the charger, slipped on his sunglasses, and ambled out the door. He'd make it look like a routine sweep. He walked down the inside of the barricade behind the mini makeshift stages where entertainment reporters had recorded interviews with new arrivals. The crowd started up against the front of the wing of the museum, still several rows deep despite the fact that it had been hours since anyone had arrived. He took his time scanning each face, running it against the pictures of Ganim he'd memorized.

He was almost done with the sweep when the black ball cap caught his eye. He was further back from the barricades now and not very tall so it was harder to spot him. He was looking down at his hands, probably at a phone.

Come on, buddy, look up. Let me see your face.

He could only stare into the crowd so long before someone caught on that there was an issue, and he didn't want Ganim to get nervous and run. If he could get to the man, he could detain him, ask him some questions, and alert the cops if there was any trouble. But he knew full well that no action would be taken until Ganim made some kind of move. There was nothing illegal about mailing a wedding dress.

"Come here often?" The question came slyly from a woman in overalls clutching an "I HEART DANTE" sign.

Xavier pretended not to hear her, and the man in the hat finally turned. He got a hit on the profile. Ninety percent sure it was him.

"Come on. Come on," Xavier muttered. "Show me."

His radio squawked. "Any familiar faces out there, Saint?" Ricardo's voice crackled.

"Got a possible," Xavier answered back. Only one way to find out, he decided. "Hey, Ganim!" he shouted over the din of the crowd. Ball Cap lifted his head and looked Xavier in the eyes. Those dark, empty eyes widened. Xavier could see the thoughts swirling for a full second before the man spun around and took off at a dead run.

Xavier knew that jumping the barricade and fighting his way through the crowd was futile. Instead, he sprinted down the remainder of the red carpet into the street and fought his way through the line of limos and cars parked on the street. By the time he ran behind the crowd, Ganim was gone, lost in the bustle of Wilshire.

"Fuck," he muttered under his breath.

"Missed him?" Ricardo skidded to a stop next to him, not even breathing heavily.

"Yeah," Xavier straightened. "It was definitely him, though. Good eyes on your team's part."

Ricardo shrugged jerkily. "Most action we get at these things are cat fights and coked up D-listers tryin' to get in. Maybe once in a while a bum takes a piss on some signage. Was nice to have something to do," he said. "Expectin' trouble from him?"

"Always a possibility," Xavier said mildly as Ricardo led the way around to a side door, keyed in the entry code. Xavier's phone signaled in his jacket.

"Kate," he said by way of a greeting.

"Hey, X Factor. I just got a Facebook message from Les Creeper. He's there. He sent a pic of the museum and said he's waiting outside for Waverly. I think it's for real."

He could hear the edginess in her voice.

"He was here, but ran before I could talk to him," Xavier told her.

"So Wave's safe?"

"She's hanging out with the equivalent of a big, black brick wall that isn't going to let anyone near her."

Kate blew out a breath in his ear. "That makes me feel better. What should I do with the message?"

"Don't respond. Just send me a screenshot of it. I'll add it to the file. I can take it to the cops, make sure they're aware of the situation. But—"

"But they still won't be able to make a move until he does something creeper-ier."

"Exactly. Send me the screenshot. I'm going to go find Angel."

"Thanks for sticking, Saint."

"Yeah." He hung up and shoved the phone back in his pocket.

He gave the carpet and crowd the once over again. Both sides of the red carpet were lined with TV cameras and production crews. On the far side, there was one camera facing the right direction, he noted. It would have been directly across from Ganim. He crossed the carpet and stopped near a production assistant who was kneeling down packing up equipment.

"Excuse me," he said.

"What?" She slammed the top on a stainless steel case and looked up at him. Irritation shifted to surprise. "I mean, uh, how can I help you?" She shoved a hand through her frizzy dishwater hair, yanking out the tie that held her ponytail in place. She lost her balance and fell backward, rapping her elbow sharply on the case.

Xavier held out a hand and hauled her to her feet while she cursed.

"Shit. Ouch. Damn it," she muttered, scrubbing her hands over her plaid shirt and jeans.

She wore tortoise shell glasses and had a slight gap between her two front teeth. The blush that was working its way over her face could have ignited a forest fire.

Xavier boosted the charm. "Sorry for startling you, but I need your help."

She was nodding, her mouth slightly open.

"I'm sorry," Xavier said, flashing her a smile. "I'm getting ahead of myself. I'm Xavier. Xavier Saint." He offered her his hand.

When she just continued to nod at him he took her hand and shook it.

The contact seemed to bring her back from her reverie. "Saint. Uh-huh. Right."

"I'm here on a security job, and we just had a little incident over there a few minutes ago," he gestured at the crowd behind them. "I was hoping you could get me a copy of the footage you shot today."

Her eyes blinked behind her glasses. "Footage. Uh-huh."

"What's your name?" Xavier asked.

She visibly shook herself. "Amy. I'm Amy," she told him.

"Amy," Xavier smiled down at her. "Would you be willing to do that? I don't want you to get in any trouble."

"Trouble? No," she shook her head violently from side to side. "No trouble. Do you need all the footage? We shot a lot and it's mostly skinny women talking about dress designers."

"I'm looking for any crowd shots you'd have. And it's gotta be kept pretty quiet. Client privacy, you know?"

She stopped shaking and started nodding. "Sure. I can do that. Yeah."

Xavier reached into his jacket and pulled out a business card. "You can reach me at any of these numbers. Let me know if you have any trouble with your bosses. I really appreciate it, Amy. Really."

When he walked into the building a few minutes later, he was already formulating a game plan. Ganim had made a move, and it was enough to convince Xavier the man was a credible threat. He'd get the footage, compile the report, and pay a visit to Micah's detective friend. Getting the ball rolling on that end now would make it easier to press charges if Ganim tried anything serious.

A flurry of activity near the security desk caught his attention.

Waverly.

"What the hell, X?" she pushed away from the chair that Jim was trying to make her sit in. "You disappear to check out a security threat and then tell me nothing? I have to hear from Kate who isn't even here that you chased some guy out of the crowd?"

Xavier grabbed her arm and started dragging her toward the stairwell. "I told you to stay upstairs." He shoved the door open, pushed her inside.

"And I did," she snapped. "Until I didn't hear from you. And then I see you're hanging out outside *flirting*."

He pushed her up on the first step of the stairwell so they were eye-to-eye. "When I tell you to do something, Angel, you do it."

He was working his way up to being good and pissed. Not only had he had and missed a shot at talking to Ganim, but he now had to reiterate for the millionth time that he was in charge. "I'm protecting you, *not* controlling you. The sooner you get that through your thick skull, the better for us both."

"I don't like being left in the dark."

"I was coming back upstairs when I got waylaid."

"Oh, is *that* what the kids are calling it these days?" Waverly shot back, her tone laced with sarcasm.

Xavier gripped the railings on both sides so he wouldn't give in to the desire to strangle her. "Now who's the jealous one?" he asked coolly. For a second, he thought she was going to slap him. He could read the impulse in the flash of anger in those beautiful gray-green eyes.

But she pulled it back inside, and her expression shifted imperceptibly until she looked bored. "It's none of my business what you do or who you do it with."

He showed his teeth. "Well, isn't it too bad that what you do and who you do it with is my business."

"We'll see about that, X."

Before he could argue, she was pushing her way past him.

"I'm ready to leave now." She arched an eyebrow at him. "That is, if you're done with your friend out there."

Xavier followed her out of the stairwell taking slow deep breaths. He'd never wanted to throttle someone so much in his entire life. And he wouldn't be able to get away with it here. Too many witnesses.

He texted the driver while Waverly sashayed off toward the security desk. He watched her shake Jim's hand and then take a few minutes to chat with the rest of the team, signing autographs and posing for pictures. There wasn't a hint of temper on her face, at least not until she shot a look at him that would have had a lesser man withering in his shoes.

But Xavier Saint was no lesser man, and he would put her in her place...even if it killed him.

7

It was a chilly, silent ride home. Waverly stayed glued to the limo door and refused to even glance in Xavier's direction. The man's expertise at pissing her off continued to reach new heights. And her overwhelming awareness of him sitting just inches away pissed her off.

Why couldn't she just ignore him? Tune him out? Pretend he didn't exist? And why did it bother her that he'd been turning on the charm with someone else. They didn't even like each other. Yet when she'd spotted him on the security monitor grinning down at the adorably disheveled tech, she'd felt a sharp flare of something she didn't like.

Waverly stewed in her thoughts even as Xavier obliviously texted next to her. Her phone rang in her Ferragamo clutch. Her mother, of course.

"Hi, Mom," Waverly answered, biting back a sigh.

"Darling! I'm coming to meet you at whatever fabulous after party you're headed to. Just text me the address," Sylvia chirped in her ear. That manic level of happiness was often reached by her third martini. That's when everything became a party to Sylvia.

"I'm actually headed home. I have a huge headache." She glanced at Xavier. It was the truth. It was a man-sized headache.

"But, Waverly!" her mother wailed. "I just put on a new dress, and I can't think of the last time you and I went to a party together."

It was two years ago, and Waverly had to drive her mother home in a borrowed car because Sylvia had gotten so drunk she couldn't stand up.

"I'm sorry, Mom," Waverly said. "We'll go out another time. Why don't you and Dad go out to dinner tonight instead? Make him buy you something shiny."

"Well..."

She could hear Sylvia weighing her options.

"I did see the most adorable little convertible the other day," her mother mused out loud.

Waverly knew she was off the hook this time. Although her father might kill her. But he would do what he always did, go along with Sylvia's demands affably until something shinier or younger or more adoring came along.

She declined her mother's invitation to join them, told her to have fun, and hung up. She wanted to close her eyes and lean against the leather of the seats. But that would be a tell, a sign of weakness. And she wasn't about to give Xavier yet another one.

Her stomach reminded her of its emptiness with a yawning growl. There was nothing in her fridge at home, and she didn't want to chance sneaking into her parents' kitchen for a snack in case they tried to wrangle her into dinner and car shopping.

Her only other option sat next to her.

Waverly closed her eyes and took an inaudible breath.

"Could you please ask the driver to take us through a drive-thru?" she asked in a frostily polite tone.

"No." Xavier said without looking up from his phone.

"No?" Waverly blinked.

"No."

"There's a taco place coming up on the next block," she informed him.

Xavier slid his phone back in his jacket and sighed. "We don't have time. I need to report to your parents before they leave and then run some errands."

Report to her parents? The man couldn't even tell her what happened with her own potential stalker. But he could go running to her parents'. If there had been any doubt before, Xavier's loyalties were now clear. Her parents' signed the checks, and he would do whatever they asked. Including holding her prisoner.

She'd had enough of the prisoner routine. And it had been a while since she'd escaped. Waverly fired off a text to Kate.

Up for a nice, quiet evening in?

The response came a few seconds later.

Sure, but are you sure that's the best idea with Creeper running around?

Waverly's thumbs flew over the screen.

I'm desperate. It's either this or you lock me up in a mental hospital.

She waited for a response. Waverly could practically feel Kate's indecision. Listen to Xavier and keep Waverly on a short leash, or let her friend blow off some steam?

Ugh. Fine. But you owe me and if Creeper murders you I'm going to be really pissed.

Waverly's lips turned up at the corner. Freedom was just a few miles away.

When the car came to a stop in her parents' driveway, Waverly hopped out without waiting for Xavier. She just had to play the part for a few more minutes and then she could finally relax.

Xavier got out on the other side of the car. "Waverly," he called to her.

She turned. "What?"

"You're not going anywhere for the rest of the night."

He made what should have been a question sound like a command.

They both turned when Kate's Explorer pulled into the drive and skirted the limo to park in front of the garage. Kate bounced out, pizza box in hand, and waved.

"Just a quiet night in," Waverly told Xavier.

"Then I'll see you tomorrow."

Waverly gave him a curt nod with a chilly glare. She waved to the driver and practically skipped toward the pool house.

She found Kate inside, spreading out pizza and paper and a rainbow of colored pencils on the table.

Waverly threw herself at her friend's feet. "Oh my God, you're the best! Now take off your clothes."

Ten minutes later, fortified by a slice of Kate's pizza and her friend's sweatshirt and baseball hat, Waverly bounced from foot to foot in the kitchen.

"Kate, he's never leaving!" she moaned as she willed Xavier's SUV to pull out of the driveway from the security feed on her phone.

"Maybe it's a sign you shouldn't go," Kate said, shading in a cartoon super hero's bulletproof corset.

"If I don't get away from everything Waverly Sinner-related for a few hours I can't be held responsible for my actions. Did I tell you what he said to me?" she spun around, sending her ponytail whipping over her shoulder.

"Mmm. The part where he acted all jealous over Dante or the part where he wouldn't let you have a burrito and told you your business is his business?"

Waverly rolled her eyes. "I can tell that you're absorbed in your art, so I'm not going to hold your inattention against you."

"Appreciate that," Kate said, taking a bite of pizza and selecting another pencil. "I still think you going out tonight is kind of dangerous. We know that that Ganim guy is here in town and looking for you."

"But he's not looking for *you*," Waverly pointed out. If she didn't get out, get away, she was going to suffocate. She could feel it creeping over her like a dark cloud.

Kate kicked back in her chair and gave Waverly the once over. "I think with sunglasses you'll pass on the security feed. Just go now while you still have daylight to enjoy. It makes me nervous when you ride at night anyway."

Waverly shoved some cash and her license into the back pocket of her jeans. "You're the best friend slash assistant slash artist a girl could have."

"Just please don't get caught...by Creeper or Saint. I'm not sure which one of them scares me more." Kate scrubbed a hand over her face. "If X Factor finds out I helped you escape your ivory tower, he'll turn that stern look on me, and I'll turn into a puddle of fear and lust."

"You, my friend, are into some weird stuff. But I respect that, and you're totally getting an amazing present for this."

"Yeah, yeah. Just don't get murdered," Kate called after her as Waverly danced through the door and locked it behind her.

Waverly slid on a pair of sunglasses that hid a good portion of her face and hurried to Kate's SUV. She slid behind the wheel and turned the key and was battered by the wailing guitars of an eighties rock ballad. *Fitting*, she grinned.

She put the Explorer in drive and started to ease around the circular drive.

Shit. Shit. Shit. Xavier chose that exact second to walk out the front door. *Be cool,* she told herself. *You're just Kate headed home.*

She raised a hand in a casual wave and held her breath when he returned it as he unlocked his SUV. She wasted no time navigating the curving drive and didn't breathe again until the gates closed behind her. Her eyes stayed glued to the rearview mirror, but by the time she hit the stop sign at the end of the street with no sign of Xavier speeding after her, she punched the volume on the stereo and rolled down her windows.

She was finally free.

XAVIER'S MOOD hadn't improved after his short briefing with the Sinners.

He'd explained the incident with Ganim and also gave them a toned-down version of Waverly's run-in with Geneva St. Regis. But Sylvia seemed more excited than concerned. It was a measure of her daughter's success, she had gleefully informed him. Stalkers and public feuds were good for a few gossip site mentions.

Robert, on the other hand, seemed ambivalent to the entire situation. Neither of them seemed to care to grasp the seriousness of the situation. Their daughter had a stalker who was fixated enough that he moved states to get closer to her. If that wasn't a loud and jarring warning bell, he didn't know what would be.

He saw Kate in sunglasses and her ball cap guiding her Explorer around the drive. She sent him a wave, which he returned. His hand was on his door handle when he felt the buzz. Something wasn't right. He watched the taillights on Kate's SUV as it pulled down the driveway. *But that wasn't Kate behind the wheel.*

He took off at a dead sprint around the side of the main house, skirting the pool, to the pool house. The front door was locked and he wasted precious seconds fishing in his pocket for the keys.

"What did you forg—oh fuck."

Kate stared at him wide-eyed from the kitchen table. She jumped up and pulled her chair in front of her as if facing a lion. It was then that Xavier realized his fury had carried him all the way into the room.

"Where is she?" he demanded.

Kate flinched. "I'll tell you but you have to promise not to murder her when you get there."

"Where the fuck is she, Kate?" His shins were touching the front of the chair she wielded.

He stared her down until she wilted like a daisy. "Shit. Fine. Okay. She's going to my house. It's no big deal. She does it all the time."

The glare he shot her was deadly and had her backpedaling against the kitchen counter. "Don't even think about warning her," he growled.

"Couldn't if I wanted to—which I don't because you're terrifying," she inserted quickly. "She left her phone here. She thought you'd track it." Kate pointed to the phone charging on the counter.

She thought right.

"When I get back I'm murdering you both," Xavier

promised and started for the door. His gaze fell on the empty pizza box. He shot another look at Kate.

"Don't judge me," she told him.

"Text me the address," he said heading for the door.

It was a fifteen-minute drive to Kate's, and it was more than enough time to have Xavier's temper spike to heights previously never explored. Waverly had known that Ganim was in town, knew he posed a threat. And yet here she was sneaking out of her house like a rebellious kid.

That's what she was, he reminded himself. A spoiled, selfish kid.

God knew what she did at Kate's house. Drank herself into a stupor? Had sex? Whatever stupid, rebellious thing rich, undisciplined kids did. Well, if her parents were incapable of laying down the law, he was happy to step in. Fucking thrilled.

He'd let her push him around all week, giving her time to get used to the idea of him. But that was a mistake. Waverly obviously needed a firmer hand.

His GPS directed him into a cul de sac of pasty townhouses with orange tile roofs and gravel landscape. Kate's was the third on the right, and her SUV was in the driveway sitting in front of the beige garage door. Xavier parked his Tahoe behind the Explorer, cutting off any possible escape and slammed the door with enough force to send the vehicle rocking.

He was debating the best access point that wouldn't alert the neighbors but still scare the shit out of Waverly when Lady Luck finally smiled on him and the garage door began a creaky ascent.

~

Waverly breathed in the scent of leather and gasoline. It was the smell of happiness and giddy freedom.

She revved the throttle and the BMW sport bike under her purred to life as the garage door opened behind her. She picked up her helmet and prepared to stash her hair up into it when she spotted something in the rearview mirror.

She knew those shoes, those nicely tailored pants, those strong arms and broad shoulders. And hell if she didn't know that scowl. She was toast.

"How—" She barely got the word out before he pounced.

Xavier stormed in, turned off the bike, and with one arm, plucked her off of the seat. He pinned her against the drywall with enough force that her teeth jarred together.

"What in the ever-living fuck is wrong with you?" he growled.

Waverly struggled against the crushing grip he had on her arms, but he merely lifted her off the ground and held her there so they were eye-to-eye. Fear shifted gears into anger. "Damn it! How the hell did you find me?"

It was the wrong thing to say. She watched his pupils contract to slits. Rage, hot and primal, pumped off of him in waves.

"Are you stupid?"

"What?" She slapped her hands to his chest and shoved with all her might. He didn't budge.

"Answer the fucking question, Waverly. Are you stupid? Or are you having some kind of psychotic break?"

"You're the one manhandling me like a freaking pro wrestler," she wheezed, aiming a kick at his shin. "That seems like both to me."

The kick glanced off of him and resulted in him pinning her to the wall with his body. His hips crushed against hers and she immediately stilled. His hands dug into her upper arms and she could feel the silk of his tie pressed against the skin above the low v of her t-shirt.

The line between his eyes was crater deep and there was a vein in his forehead. Their mouths couldn't get closer without touching, and there was nowhere to go. She felt his breath, hot and ragged, on her face. And then she felt him go raging hard against her.

"God damn it." His voice was jagged. "I can't decide if I want to kiss you or choke you."

When her jaw dropped, her lower lip scraped his and that was all it took.

His mouth crushed down on hers, claiming, demanding. Teeth scraped, and lips bruised in a violent clash. He gave her no room to breathe, but oxygen was suddenly the last thing she needed. Their tongues met and tangled in an aggressive battle.

She had never been kissed like this before, possessed like this before.

Her breasts were smashed against his rock-hard chest as the edges of their bodies fused. His erection, as powerful and as impressive as the rest of him, flexed into her and she hooked a leg over one of his slim hips desperate to get closer still. He groaned at the friction and fisted a hand in her hair to change the angle of the kiss.

God, yes, her mind chanted. This is what had been missing. This tangle and mess of emotions and need. He forced her to take and take and take.

Xavier fed on her mouth, stealing her breath, robbing her of the will to think. She whimpered against his hard lips, craving more, but the sound tore him out of the fray.

"Damn it, Waverly," he gasped for air, resting his forehead on hers. "What the hell have you done to me?"

He released her, and she slid bonelessly to the floor, her

heart pounding like a drum line. She dragged in a breath and then another one, wondering what had just happened inside her. Xavier bent at the waist, looking like a man destroyed.

Their gazes met and held, and he returned to her and carefully pulled her to her feet. He rubbed a thumb over her swollen lip and swore.

"Angel—" he began.

Waverly slapped his hand away and dug her hands into the lapels of his jacket. "If the words 'I'm sorry' come out of your mouth, I will *never* forgive you. Don't try to ruin what was the most incredible kiss of my entire life."

"It never should have happened. I shouldn't have let it," Xavier said, his hands reaching for her and then fisting at his side instead. He looked panicked and angry.

"Xavier, just breathe," Waverly told him. She spotted a camp chair under a shelf of plastic totes against the back wall of the garage and pushed him into it. He dropped his head in his hands, and the vulnerability Waverly saw tugged at her still hammering heart.

"Wait here," she said.

He lifted his head. "If you make me chase you again, I'm stuffing you in my gym bag and carrying you home."

"There's the Saint I love to annoy." She patted his knee. "I'm getting us some water. The kitchen's right there. I'll leave the door open," she promised. He let her go and she took a moment to calm herself down in Kate's tan on cream on beige kitchen.

Waverly grabbed two bottles of water from the fridge and pressed one to the overheated skin of her neck. The kiss had melted her from the inside out and she was having trouble recovering. She felt raw, terrified, energized.

She returned to the garage where Xavier was in the same position. She'd finally pushed him over the edge, and now she didn't want to be free of him. The irony brought a soft smile to her ravaged lips. She handed over a bottle. His fingers lingered on hers for a moment until she met his eyes. In them, she saw concern and questions.

"Did I hurt you?" he asked.

She shook her head and felt her cheeks flush. "More like stunned. Did I hurt you?"

He shoved a hand through his short hair. "You wrecked me." The words were almost a whisper.

"X," she began, but Waverly didn't know where to go from there.

"One second you're a pain in my ass, and the next you're hydrating me."

"I'm co-dependent. Daughter of an alcoholic," she shrugged. "I'm responsible for causing and healing all pain and discomfort."

He shook his head at her. "Just go over there so I don't grab you again," he pointed at the bike. He couldn't be feeling too bad if he was back to giving her orders already. Waverly hit the button on the door opener and the garage door creaked down to give them some privacy. She draped a leg over the leather seat of the bike and sat.

"I'm breaking rules left and right," Xavier said half to himself. "I'll call Micah. I'll have someone else assigned to you," he said flatly, reaching for his phone.

"You're overreacting."

"And you're underreacting. Angel, I grabbed you. I lost control, and I took advantage of you."

"Okay, now you're being dramatic," Waverly rolled her eyes. She leaned her elbows on the bike's tank.

"I don't recall you asking me to haul you up against a wall and..."

"Kiss the ever-living crap out of me?" she supplied.

"I can't get physical with you in any way, violent or otherwise. I'm protecting you. That line can't be crossed. It puts both of us at risk."

"Rules are important to you," she stated.

"Obviously there's something about you that makes me forget how important those rules are. I'm out of control."

"I pushed you. Hard. All week I was pushing," she confessed.

"I know you were, but I'm supposed to be better than that."

"Above annoyance and physical attraction are we, Saint?" She was teasing him now.

"This is serious shit, Waverly. I mauled you. We can't work together anymore."

"Why not?"

"Because you're making me lose my mind. I'm exhausted. I chase after you all day and half the night and then I go home and think about touching you... or strangling you." His fingers brushed over the line between his eyes. "You might break me."

Shit. If she had been hot for the demanding and angry Xavier, the wounded one was going after her heart like a master thief in a gallery. He was being candid, and now it was her turn.

"X, do you know why I was trying to shake you loose?"

Xavier shot her a look that said "duh" through the hands he held over his face. "Because your life is a prison, and there's no freedom being you," he said as if by rote.

"It's a prison on another level, too. I can't be with you every day and be worried about what kind of information you're feeding my parents or how you're manipulating me to get what you need. I can't have that kind of relationship close to me."

"You think that because your parents hired me, I'm an extension of them. I'm on their side, which pits me against you. They bought a service, Waverly, not a loyalty." Xavier rubbed his temples as if he was trying to ward off a migraine.

"You're so by-the-book I didn't know that it was possible you could be on my side."

"I want to keep you safe, Waverly. Not in a prison. And I never had any intention of tattling on you to your parents. You're an adult. Maybe it's time you start acting like one."

"It's not that easy. There are consequences that I'm still exposed to even as a legal adult. But that's beside the point. If this is going to be a professional, working relationship, we have to be a team, not two people playing each other."

He looked up at the ceiling of the garage as if praying for patience. "Christ, Waverly, isn't that what I said from the beginning?"

She smiled softly. "Yeah. But now I'm not trying to shake you loose."

"You mean since I had a complete mental breakdown and tried to throw you through Kate's drywall before kissing the shit out of you?"

"Since you behaved like a human and not some snooty security robot."

From the look on his face, Waverly felt certain no one had ever called Xavier Saint snooty before.

"This can't happen again." His tone was earnest. "It can't, Angel. One of us won't survive it, and it would probably be me."

"Relax, X. A torrid affair with you is not something that fits into my plans either." That was an understatement. The last thing she needed was some orgasmic crush. Sex was like all other areas of her life. It needed to be on her terms. If that kiss was a sneak peek, her "terms" would end up on the floor on top of her underwear. She'd get hurt when it ended. Badly hurt. "Let's just chalk it up to exhaustion and rage-fueled passion. You were kissing me, but you really wanted to strangle me."

"You make me so irate and so... hard. Sometimes at the same time."

Waverly laughed. "This new human Xavier Saint is really honest."

"I think a dam broke," he said wryly. "Are you seriously okay? I wasn't exactly gentle."

"I'm better than okay. In some weird way, I think I needed that."

He nodded in agreement. "Let's just make sure neither of us needs it again in the future."

"Deal. Out of our systems." If something like that could ever just disappear. "But while we're making deals, I want to know what's going on with my security quandaries. I don't want to have to get information from Kate or wait until you're done briefing my parents—who probably weren't too concerned. My safety is my business."

Xavier sat straighter and took in a breath. "That's fair. In my defense, I didn't mean to leave you in the dark like that. I got distracted, first by Kate calling to tell me Ganim messaged you from the museum and then by—"

"A cute production assistant?"

"A *source* at the network who had been shooting crowd shots from the right angle all afternoon. I wanted the footage of Ganim in the crowd."

Waverly winced. "And I accused you of flirting instead of doing your job."

"I was flirting, but it was in the line of duty."

"I was a tiny bit jealous," she confessed.

"I was jealous of Wrede."

"If it's any consolation, you're a much better kisser."

"I'd bet that I'm better at a lot of things," Xavier muttered.

"A lot of things that are off the table," Waverly reminded him. "Oh, God. This is going to be awkward. First I didn't want you around, and now I'm going to be thinking about how good it felt when you—"

"Don't even think about finishing that sentence," Xavier threatened. "We need to make one more deal."

"What are the terms?" Waverly asked.

"You can't run from me again. It turns me into a predator."

Waverly caught her breath and held it. "That feels like a commitment."

His grin was wicked this time. "It is. I need you to trust me, Waverly."

He was asking for the nearly impossible. "We'll play it by ear." It was as far as she was willing to go.

"Fair enough." He rose and crossed the short span of concrete to her. "If the negotiations are over..." Xavier held out his hand.

They shook solemnly and Waverly tried not to remember what it had felt like minutes before to have those big, hard hands on her.

"Now, let's talk about why you're sitting on a motorcycle in Kate's garage when I told you to stay home."

Waverly heaved a sigh. "You're just going to get mad again." Although that might lead to another kiss, so it wasn't entirely a lose-lose.

"Try me," he said.

"Don't you ever just want to be someone else? Even just for an hour?"

He crossed his arms, considered her. "Everyone does."

"Well, I spend my entire *life* being someone else. Whoever my agent, the studio, the director, the journalist, my parents need me to be. Sometimes I want to be just me."

"Who are you?"

She shrugged her shoulders in a quick lift and drop. "I don't know, but I'd like to find out."

"And you're going to find out on a one-hundred and seventy-five-horse street bike?"

"Very good, X. You know your bikes."

"How long have you been riding?"

"Four years. I learned for a movie before the insurance put the kibosh on me doing the stunts. But it was too late. I already loved it." She patted the gunmetal gray tank. "This was my secret birthday present to myself when I turned eighteen."

"Are you any good?"

She grinned. "Hell yeah, I'm good. Do you ride?"

"I've done my fair share."

"I've got another one, if you're interested," she nodded toward the bike-shaped tarp in the corner.

8

Xavier wasn't exactly clear on how Waverly had talked him into it, but he found himself astride her sweet Victory Hammer cruising toward the coast with the balmy summer breeze ruffling his suit jacket.

He'd at least had the presence of mind to secure two promises from her. She'd buy them dinner *and* stay under the speed limit. They'd ridden through neighborhoods, past gated homes with emerald green lawns and crews of gardeners, through streets neatly lined with identical townhouses in beiges and stucco. When they hit the PCH, the Pacific waters glittering below them.

Once he was confident in her competence on the bike, he let Waverly have the lead. She obviously had a destination in mind, and he was content to watch her back.

With her thick curtain of hair tucked up under her helmet and molded dark backpack, she could have been just another anonymous rider on the road. Except for that long, lean body with curves more impressive than the highway under sexy biker jeans and a tight leather jacket.

He'd had his hands on those curves. And Xavier wasn't sure how he was ever going to forget it. Or stop wanting more.

They crested a hill, and he watched as Waverly let the bike move with the road, flying downhill. Her laugh through the headset in his helmet went straight to his groin. He accelerated smoothly and pulled alongside her, ready to let her see his displeasure for breaking the rules. But the smile, the unadulterated joy on her face, had him grinning back at her through his visor.

"Try to keep it under eighty, Sinner," he told her.

She whooped in his ear, and together, they flew through the descent. He knew what she was after, what she'd found in that moment. Freedom. And it was heady.

They slowed with the next ascent, and Xavier spotted a road sign promising food at the next exit. "I think I found dinner," he said into his headset.

Waverly glanced at the sign and laughed. "Perfect."

They found the Taco Bell tucked away on a side street in a tiny beach town and parked side-by-side in a parking space. Waverly tugged off her helmet and shook out her hair. Xavier cut the throttle and pried off his own helmet.

"That was *awesome*," Waverly said, twirling in a tight circle between the bikes.

"You can ride," Xavier admitted, running a hand up the back of his head. She was tantalizing when she was happy. She'd scrubbed off her event makeup and with nothing more than lip gloss and flushed cheeks, she was perfection. The walls were down and she was just a happy, beautiful, California girl.

She shot him that grin that had his cock stirring restlessly.

"You're not so bad yourself," she winked.

"Well, I didn't have professional stunt training, but I get by."

She grabbed his hand and tugged him off the bike. "Come on, X. I'll buy you dinner."

"You take your dates to the nicest places," he commented, letting her pull him into the restaurant.

They went blissfully unidentified at the counter and took their bag of tacos and nachos to go.

Back on the bikes, he let her lead the way to their final destination. She navigated through the little town and just beyond where the traffic was nearly non-existent. There, squeezed between cliff and sea, was a quiet ribbon of sandy beach.

They parked against the dunes, and Waverly shucked off her helmet and jacket. Her boots and socks came next. "Strip," she ordered, giving him the once-over.

"This isn't a nude beach is it?"

"No, but I'm sure they'd make an exception in your case."

"Funny." He shoved his tie in the saddlebag.

"You can lose the jacket, too," Waverly suggested.

He opened his jacket to reveal his shoulder holster.

"Right. I forgot," she said. She picked up her backpack and tossed it to him. "Here, pretend you're a mere mortal for a few minutes."

Warily he scanned the parking lot. There was one other vehicle, a hatchback with stickers proclaiming the driver's love for rescue dogs and Valley Sun Preschool. He sighed. *How many other rules would he break tonight?* he wondered as he slipped out of his jacket, draping it over the bike and releasing his holster.

He checked the chamber and safety before slipping the gun and holster into the backpack's molded compartment. When he moved to unbutton his shirt, he didn't miss the way Waverly's eyes flickered over him. Maybe he wasn't the only one struggling with the idea of "out of the system."

He stripped down to his undershirt and stepped out of his oxfords. He slung the backpack over one shoulder. "Happy?" he asked her.

"Ecstatic."

They trudged over the dunes, his free arm draped loosely over her shoulder. They could have passed for a typical couple enjoying a romantic evening picnic. The only other beach occupants were a family of three and their two dogs, some kind of retriever mix and a bulldog that seemed more content on the blanket than chasing the surf with his friend.

"They don't look overly threatening," Waverly teased.

"Neither does Les Ganim," he reminded her.

They chose a spot in the sand above the tide where Waverly could watch the waves roll in while the sun sank lower in the sky. Xavier angled himself so he could keep the family and Waverly in his line of site. The backpack stayed open and within arm's reach.

Waverly unloaded the food and bottles of water into a haphazard pile. She tossed him one of the tacos and unwrapped one herself. "What's your take on him? On a scale of one to 'I'm Going to Murder Waverly,' where does this guy fall?"

She took a healthy bite of taco as if they were discussing the weather or baseball.

"I think he's a concern. One you should think about before you try sneaking out again," he said as sternly as he could while eating a taco.

"I gotta ask," she said through a mouthful of chicken and cheese. "How did you know it was me? My own mother has seen me leave as Kate before and had no clue."

Xavier felt his eye twitch. "Christ, Waverly, how often do you do shit like this?"

"Uh-uh. My question first."

He thought back. "Your jaw lines are a little different and I noticed yours was still, which meant you weren't chewing gum. Then there's the wrist tattoo," he said, wrapping his fingers around her right wrist and flipping it palm up. "Kate has a sun tattooed here." He ran his fingers over her where her pulse flickered just a little faster.

He released her hand, took another bite.

"Damn," Waverly sighed. "I underestimated you."

"Yeah. Right back at you. I didn't expect someone who just had an encounter with their stalker to decide it would be a great night to ditch her security and run amok."

She pretended not to hear him. "I'm going to have to wear a cuff bracelet and shove a fistful of Big League in there next time."

On the words "next time," Xavier flopped back into the sand and stared up at the sky. "Please, for the love of all that's holy, be joking right now."

Her beautiful face hovered over his. She was smiling and the sky was going to gold behind her. "Relax, X. Maybe you can come with me next time instead of scaring the hell out of me."

"Angel, I still don't think we should be working together." He sat up and wiped his palms on his pant legs.

She arched an eyebrow. "Why not?"

He shot her a hard look.

"Ohhhh," she drew it out sarcastically. "Because we kissed. You're afraid you won't be able to control yourself around my hotness."

He gave her a shove and she landed on her hip in the sand. "You're such a smart ass. First off, that was *not* just a kiss. And I'm less concerned with my desire to kiss you again than my desire to throttle you."

She snorted and wiggled her ass into the sand to sit cross-legged. Behind her, the toddler wandered over to the bulldog and sat on him.

"Don't you get tired of always being on alert?" she asked him, licking sauce from her thumb.

"You get used to it," he said, finally glancing in the direction of the ocean. "For the most part."

"Is there anywhere you can just relax?" Waverly wondered.

He crumpled up an empty taco wrapper and shoved it in the plastic bag. He shrugged. "My parents' house, I guess."

"Do they still live where you grew up?"

He nodded.

"My parents' house isn't very relaxing."

"No it isn't," he said, thinking back to his conversation with the Sinners. "You looked pretty happy on the bike, though."

"That was freedom," she explained with a wry half smile. "I'm not sure what happy looks like." The surf rolled in on a rumble. It threw a tangy mist heavenward. Seagulls swooped and cackled near the trashcan on the way to the parking lot. The sky was fading to washed out water colors, and Waverly turned her face toward the glow of the sinking sun.

His golden girl, he thought. *No, not his,* he corrected himself. *The world's.*

He was building a business. For the first time, he called the shots in his life, not some commander behind a fancy desk with a luncheon or a golf game to get to. He had things to do, a reputation to build, money to make. He wasn't ready to add someone into that mix. Especially if that someone was Waverly Sinner.

Xavier's phone burst into Katy Perry's *California Gurls*.

"Fuck." He frantically dug through his pants pockets.

"That's an interesting ring tone you've got there, Xavier," Waverly said, opening the nachos.

"It's my sister," he said, fumbling with the phone. "She

thought it would be hilarious." And now he was going to have to kill her.

"She was right," Waverly snickered.

When his thumb hovered over Ignore, she slapped at his hand. "It might be important," she warned him.

He swore under his breath and answered the call.

"Chelsea."

The irritation he'd let seep into his tone had no effect on his sister. "Oh, my God," Chelsea hissed in his ear. "Xavier, Mom is driving me insane. She won't listen to me." Her voice echoed on the line.

"Why do you sound like you're in a canyon? And why are you whispering?"

"I'm in the bathroom at Mom and Dad's."

He felt his eye twitch again. "Why are you calling me from their bathroom?" he sighed.

"Mom's got one of those pop-ups on her laptop telling her she has a virus and to call this number for tech support."

"Christ. Just tell her it's a scam."

Xavier yanked the phone away from his ear so his sister's indignant screech didn't puncture his eardrum. "I take it you already tried that."

"She won't listen to me. She wants to hear it from the prodigal."

"Mom doesn't need to hear it from me. Try reminding her of your college education in computer crap that they paid for."

"I'm putting her on."

"No! Don't put her on the—Hi, Mom." He rubbed the spot between his eyebrows and felt a headache begin to brew.

He glanced over at Waverly who was eating and watching him like she was enjoying a matinee at the movie theater. She looked thoroughly entertained.

His mother held a PhD in history and taught at a local

college but was somehow technically deficient when it came to personal computers.

"Xavier!" she sounded thrilled to hear his voice, and he instantly felt guilty for not thinking to call recently. "What are you doing calling your sister?"

Well, at least he'd get the points.

"I, uh, have an issue with my email, and I wanted to ask a computer expert," he fibbed. "What's going on with you and Dad?"

His mother launched into a description of their garden, the neighborhood's new playground, before finally circling back to her laptop. Xavier inserted "uh-huhs" where appropriate and snagged a nacho from Waverly.

"I don't know, Mom. I think you should listen to Chels. You know she's a genius when it comes to this stuff. That's why I go to her with all my IT stuff." Waverly nudged him with her foot, and he captured it, warming it in his hand. She purred when he pressed his thumb into the arch.

"Well, okay. I just don't want the FBI thinking I'm downloading porn or trying to buy missiles or something if it's a virus."

"Mom!"

"Just kidding, sweetheart. What are you doing tonight?"

"Right now?" he asked. He shot Waverly a sideways glance and squeezed her foot. "I'm enjoying a beach picnic."

"With a beautiful woman I hope." He could hear the smile in her voice.

"As a matter of fact, she is, and before you ask, no I'm not sending you a picture."

"Well, don't let me interrupt. Call us this weekend, and we can talk about your visit home, which is...?"

"Soon. I promise," Xavier said, smiling.

They hung up, and Xavier tucked his phone back into his pants pocket.

"You lied to your mother, X! I'm shocked," Waverly teased.

"You think you're the only one who does that? My motives are pure."

"It's nice to know that you're a little bit human," she smiled softly.

His hand tightened on her foot, thumb in the in-sole. "A little too human sometimes," he said quietly.

"Well, I admire the way you handled the problem while turning all future responsibility back on your sister."

"It takes a great mastermind to recognize one," he said dryly.

Waverly smirked and stared out at the sea. "They sound blissfully normal, you know? My family dynamics are closer to a hostile takeover," she said wryly.

"They care about you," Xavier told her.

She arched an eyebrow.

"In their own way," he amended.

Still, she stared at him, looking like she was trying to work something out. Finally, she spoke. "What do you think of them? Of me?" she wondered out loud.

He shook his head. "Waverly, my opinion isn't important. What matters is my ability to protect you."

"Fine. Forget opinions. You're an observant man. What are your impressions?"

He shot her a look.

"Oh, come on, indulge me."

"You might not care for my impressions," he warned her.

"I've had people critiquing my work, my face, my wardrobe, and my body since I was six. I think I can take it."

Xavier released her foot and took his time unwrapping the taco. "Your parents—your mother specifically—hired me to protect you when what they really want is to keep you in line. Performing in whatever capacity she, or they, see fit. They pull your strings, and you're starting to pull back. It terrifies your mother. You're supposed to be Sylvia 2.0, her best chance at remaining relevant."

He paused to assess her reaction, but Waverly's flawless face was impassive. Accepting her indifference for permission to continue, he moved on.

"Your mother's a functioning alcoholic, but the functioning part is beginning to slip. Your father checked out of your life and his own a long time ago."

He saw her wince and wrinkle her nose.

"That brings us to you. You're beautiful, even by Hollywood's standards. Talented. You were born into this bubble. But instead of spoiled, I'd say smothered. Everyone pulls your strings. Everyone wants a piece of you. You learned how to get what you want the same way. You don't trust easily because you've been burned too many times, been left unprotected by the very people who should have been guarding you."

A vision of her at five years old with the paparazzi closing in on her surfaced in his mind.

"You're about to get your hands on some legal and financial resources available to you, but you aren't sure who you are without the strings. Or what you want. Besides college."

He saw the sidelong glance she shot him.

"I hear things," he said, answering her unasked question. "You're smart, very smart. You're observant to the point that you read people like a ninety-nine-cent book. Yet none of them have ever tried to scratch your perfect princess surface. You take your work seriously but have trouble committing to the trappings of being famous. And tonight is the only time I've seen you genuinely enjoy yourself."

"Oh, is that all?" she asked, letting grains of sand slip through her fingers.

"One last thing. There's something so appealing about you, like having the front row seat for fireworks or getting there seconds before the bud blooms."

He saw goose bumps rising on her arms. She blew out a long, slow breath. "I've never been assessed and boxed up so concisely before."

"Hazards of asking your highly trained security detail for their observations."

"I think I'm starting to like you, Xavier."

"Back at you." Only what he felt was a lot darker than like.

9

Xavier had barely settled into the chair behind his desk before all six-feet five-inches of his partner ambled through his doorway.

"I see you found your way back," Micah said, folding himself into one of Xavier's visitor chairs.

"Didn't even need the GPS," Xavier quipped.

"Sure is homey in here." Micah's gaze rolled over the blank, beige walls, the mahogany desk and matching credenza, all void of personal effects.

Micah's office, by contrast, had been decked out by his wife, Suzette, during her interior design phase. Handsome backlit bookcases showcased family photos and tasteful yet masculine accessories. The walls were painted a warm khaki and served as a backdrop to framed diplomas, awards, and more photographs. Micah had five potted plants in his office and a small aquarium that was usually fishless.

"I'll get to it," Xavier said. "Eventually."

"You've been using that line for two years. You're out of the service, in case you haven't noticed," Micah ribbed. "You don't have to keep living like you might have to bug out in thirty seconds."

It was true, Xavier thought. He'd spent most of his adult life avoiding roots and any other entanglements that would pull at him. But now he was digging roots with Invictus and digging them deep. What had started as a two-man operation was now a team of forty that included experts in the fields of personal protection, investigation, and information security. Each employee had been handpicked, scrutinized, and tested before being brought into the fold. Whenever he walked through the frosted glass doors of Invictus, he felt a quick burst of pride at what they'd already accomplished.

He kicked back in his chair and eyed his friend. "Maybe after I'm done chasing starlets, I'll fix it up. I'm thinking about stealing one of your houseplants."

"That's quite the commitment for someone who sees the inside of this place once a week," Micah mocked. It was a running joke between them that Micah never left the office, and Xavier couldn't find it. "The Sinners giving you any trouble?"

Xavier raised an eyebrow at his friend and kept it light. "If by trouble you mean an obscene disregard for personal safety, then yes. A metric shit ton of trouble."

Micah's grin crinkled his eyes. "You could have had a nice, quiet desk job and left the fieldwork to better swimmers."

"I knew I'd regret telling you that," Xavier muttered. Micah had laughed until tears came out of his eyes after hearing Xavier's version of his swim with Waverly. And when Xavier's secretary, Roz, came in to check on them, Micah had repeated the story. Roz had helpfully composed an intra-office memo to relay the experience to the rest of the team.

It was still in the lead for their monthly internal Worst Client Experience competition.

"A few more years, and I'll be ready to give up the field," he promised. Maybe sooner rather than later. If last night was any indication, his control was slipping.

Restless, he rose and crossed to the coffee maker.

"You want one?" He held up a mug to Micah.

"Nah." Micah shook his head. "Wife's got me on green tea again."

"Lucky you." Xavier programmed a cup for himself.

"Speaking of, when are you going to get yourself one?"

"A wife?" Another old conversation between two friends. Family man Micah couldn't comprehend a life that wasn't crowded with commitments and responsibilities of the family sort. *And just why the hell did an image of Waverly laughing up at him present itself as if it were an answer to Micah's question?*

Xavier swiped a hand over the back of his head and felt the buzz of nerves. He'd crossed a line last night. One that was a fireable offense for anyone else on his team. And what worried him more was the fact that he was afraid it would and wouldn't be the last time.

"I'll get around to one of those too someday," he said vaguely. He stared out at the bustle of L.A. three floors below.

Guilt divided between the original offense and now keeping a secret from his partner ate at him. He made it until the stream of coffee sputtered dry.

"I fucked up last night," he said, ignoring the coffee and pacing in front of the windows.

Micah gave him a look and then got up to close the door. "How many bodies do we need to get rid of?"

"I'm serious, Micah. I crossed a line in a big way."

His partner sat back down and crossed ankle over knee. He looked entirely too relaxed for Xavier's liking.

"I kissed her." The confession snapped out of him like a whip. And saying it out loud made it real.

"Uh-huh." Micah said and cocked his head waiting for more.

"I was pissed off. She actually got away from me last night —and you tell anyone this story, and there will be a body that needs disposing—but I tracked her down, scared the hell out of her, and then just..." There weren't words for what he'd done next. Attacked? Mauled? Seduced? Marked?

"You're wearing a hole in our industrial grade carpet over a kiss?" Now Micah was amused.

"It wasn't just a kiss it was...it was...You remember the feeling right after a bullet bites into the wall behind you or you feel the breeze of it over your head?"

Micah nodded. No one forgot that rusty bite of fear chased by the elation of cheating death.

"That's what it was. This rush." He clenched his hands into fists in front of him as if to hold on to the feeling. "She had to get me water afterward."

Micah put his head in his hands and his shoulders started to shake silently.

"Jesus, are you crying or laughing at me?" Xavier demanded.

Micah looked up and it looked like he was doing both. He hooted, and a tear escaped the outer corner of his eye.

"It's not funny."

"Brother, from where I'm sitting it's fucking hilarious," Micah said, gasping for breath. "First, I'm expecting you to tell me that you got sick of the Hollywood princess act and held a pillow over her face, and I'm wondering how I'm gonna get you out of the country before the cops show up. Then you tell me you kissed her, and I'm waiting for you to say it was in the middle of some god damn red carpet spectacle, and you proceeded to do the funky monkey in front of TV cameras." He wiped another tear away on a gasp.

"The funky monkey? Christ, Micah, how do you even have kids?"

"I'm sorry," Micah made a sound like air escaping an inflatable kiddie pool. "Okay. I'm sorry. I've just never seen you rattled before. Never thought it would be over a girl. I'm prepared to take your problem seriously now." He wiped his palms on his pant legs. "Let's start over. What's at issue here?"

His friend's shoulders were still shaking from silent laughter, but Xavier had to get it out. "I crossed a line. Rule number one: Don't get personal."

"Uh-huh." Micah nodded his dark head. "And why does that rule exist?"

"So bodyguards don't go sticking their dicks in every client." Xavier's frustration was mounting. *Micah was supposed to be as appalled as he was,* he told himself.

"Exactly. We don't want the lesser ethically minded security officers taking advantage of their position of power and responsibility. Now, given the fact that you've got your head shoved so far up your ass with guilt, I'm gonna save you some time and tell you that that's not you."

When Xavier started to argue, Micah held up a hand. "Shut it. You started this confessional, now you get to find absolution." He got up and snagged Xavier's untouched coffee and took a sip. He leaned against the credenza. "The second reason for the rule is because real feelings can get all tangled up in an agent's instincts. If you're too worried about Princess Buffy saying she's chilly or you're off in the corner having a quickie, you might miss the armed assassins busting through the windows."

Xavier stared at Micah for a long moment. "What is it like to live inside your head?"

"Hey, we're making fun of you now. Not me."

"My apologies," Xavier said dryly and programmed another cup of coffee.

"Here's the thing. You're not the kind to take advantage of a woman. Ever. I know it, and deep down you know it. If things got out of control last night, I have no doubt that Angel helped shove you along down your path of sin. And if anyone can have tangled up feelings about someone and still maintain the level of awareness needed to do this job, it's you."

"Micah, I messed up. You should be sidelining me until I can get my head on straight."

"Is that what you want?"

"Hell no. I don't want anyone else guarding her."

"Then the solution is simple, man. Don't let it happen again."

"That's it?" Xavier asked.

"You're not a power-hungry, pussy-hungry asshole, Saint. Just tap into that insane control of yours and don't let it happen again."

Xavier slid down in the visitor chair Micah had vacated. "I've never fucked up like this before."

"Maybe it wasn't a fuck up. Maybe it was fate."

"For the love of God—"

"Relax, kid. I'm messing with you. Nobody died, and from your latest report it sounds like she could use some up close and personal support."

"I can roll your body up in this carpet and have Roz drag you down to the dumpster," Xavier threatened. But he felt lighter. The weight was off his chest with Micah's absolution. Maybe it wasn't the end of the world.

And if it never happened again, he could just forget about it and move on.

Micah must have considered the case closed because he

moved on to more entertaining subjects. “So, she snuck out on you last night, huh?”

“Dressed up like her damn assistant and left in her SUV.” Xavier let his head tip back against the seat back. “She freaking waved to me on her way down the driveway.”

Micah cackled and took another sip of the forbidden coffee. “How do you know she’s staying put today while you’re here?”

“She wouldn’t dare pull a stunt like that again.” But to be on the safe side, he pulled out his phone and rattled off a text to Waverly.

Proof of location?

He hit send and her response was immediate.

Gee, X, so glad we got these trust issues worked out.

Her message included a picture of Louie waving a knife in her direction from across the island, a stack of scripts in the foreground. Xavier smiled with what he told himself was relief.

Good girl.

“Glad we’ve solved all your problems, Boy Scout,” Micah said. “Now listen, I’ve got some money riding in the office pool that Angel is going to leave you tied naked to a flagpole by the end of the month. Help me out, okay?”

“This is why I don’t come into the office.”

THE ANGEL BRIEFING was a lesson in efficiency. Invictus Security didn't sit back and wait for a threat to require neutralizing. They went on the offensive. Xavier and Micah sat at the glossy, round conference table while four team members from research—affectionately known around the office as stalkers—walked through the details of Les Travis Ganim's life.

Ganim was thirty-seven years old, and until ten days ago, had spent the last fifteen years working as a systems analyst for a health insurance conglomerate in El Plano, Texas. His father had gone out for cigarettes when he was seven and never returned. His mother, a fundamentalist Christian, had raised him alone, leaning heavily on a church that she tithed ten percent of her income to. He'd been homeschooled, judging from the lack of public school records. He had a Facebook profile that counted twenty-two friends. On the surface, he was a lonely computer tech from a broken home.

The deep background check painted a darker picture. His criminal history showed a disturbing pattern of escalation. Three years ago, Ganim had been charged with two counts of criminal trespass and harassment in connection with a woman in his hometown, a diner waitress. The terrified waitress had moved out of town immediately after filing the complaint and refused to pursue charges. He'd also skated a year later on criminal stalking and attempted abduction charges involving a dancer who had her own rap sheet full of possession and DUI charges.

The charges were dropped when the dancer disappeared, sending the investigating officer an email claiming she'd made up the whole thing and was moving back to Oklahoma to take care of her mother.

Speaking of mothers, Ganim's had died of breast cancer five months ago. The day of Mrs. Ganim's funeral was the day the wedding dress had arrived at Waverly's house.

Ganim had been the sole heir to his mother's modest fortune, which included a small IRA, $15,000 in savings, and the two-bedroom cottage that he'd grown up in. On his tablet, Xavier flipped through the street view images of the property from a private investigator they'd hired. The PI's write-up of her interviews with Ganim's supervisor and cube mate were also covered.

Every social media interaction had been combed through and examined by his team. And a three-generation family tree had been established.

"I want to talk to the waitress and the dancer," Xavier told Cayman, the hyper-fashionable thirty-four-year-old head of research.

"On it," Cayman promised, stretching his arms and revealing cufflinks shaped like magnifying glasses.

Xavier turned to members of the advance team. "What do we have on Ganim since he came to town?"

These results were scant at best. He'd checked in on social media at a pizza shop in Brentwood and a convenience store in Los Feliz. But those were the only traceable activities. There were also no pops on his credit report to suggest he was renting a place in town.

"He's probably paying cash for a motel. See if you can get me the plates and description of the car he was driving when he went to the convenience store. We don't know if he has the one registered to him in Texas or if he's using a different one." Xavier said. "Hopefully their security feed wasn't wiped yet." The advance team tapped notes into their tablets.

He made a mental note to check with Waverly on her whereabouts both days to see how close Ganim had gotten to her. The Brentwood pizza shop was only a block away from her gym.

Song, a woman they'd tempted away from the CIA when

she graduated from NYU with a dual major in cyber security and computer engineering, swiveled her chair toward him. "I had a hit on a sealed juvie record, but I couldn't get around it in any legal way."

The way she emphasized "legal" made it sound like she was hoping to be given the go-ahead to use any means necessary. Song's hacking skills were terrifyingly brilliant and came in handy.

"Let's keep this by the book for now," Xavier said, hiding a smile.

"I'll see if I can get a buddy down in the Texas court system to help us out on that," Micah offered. Micah's "buddies" were a revolving list of people in various law enforcement organizations who owed him favors that never seemed to expire.

Xavier helped himself to a bottle of water from the tray in the center of the table.

Roz, in her ice blue Chanel suit, passed him a flash drive and two printouts. She tapped them with her burgundy nails. "Copies of the report and findings that you can take to the police. I included a summary with the pertinent points and the applicable laws Ganim is in violation of in case the detective isn't particularly interested in reading." She had a voice that always reminded Xavier of a glass of brandy.

He'd fallen in love with Roz from their first meeting when she'd swept into the interview. She'd ditched her calf-length cashmere coat on an empty seat, announced she was tired of retirement, and demanded he give her the job. She'd spent thirty-five years with the FBI doing admin work, the last fifteen as office manager of a field office. She'd taught Xavier and Micah more about efficiently running the business side of operations than anyone else. He'd hired her on the spot and never regretted it.

"Thank you, Roz, everyone," Xavier nodded at his team.

"This is a good start. Let's keep it pushing and get this guy contained."

Micah pushed back from the table. "We'll meet tomorrow with Advance to talk about the logistics for Angel's premiere next week and start laying the groundwork for the international side of the publicity tour."

He glanced at his watch and dismissed them. He had to get to a meeting with a Detective Hansen, another of Micah's buddies, to open the lines of communication about a stalking complaint. It was the first day in a week he hadn't spent with Waverly. He missed her. And that annoyed him.

He pulled out his phone, started a text, and then changed his mind. There was no professional reason why he should be checking in with Waverly right now. Unless she changed her mind about going out? Or she needed him for something and didn't want to ask?

He pulled his phone back out of his suit jacket and dialed her number. She picked up on the first ring before he could convince himself to hang up.

"Hi," she said a little breathlessly.

"Hi." *Smooth, real smooth, idiot.* He cleared his throat. "Just checking in to make sure you're still where you're supposed to be."

"I'm being held captive by Mari and Louie who want to start planning my tour wardrobe," she said in a stage whisper.

"Don't you have him running over here guns blazing," Mari grumbled in the background. "Being held captive, bah!"

"Mari says hi," Waverly said. He could hear the smile in her voice.

"Tell, Mari, I said hi back," Xavier told her. "Is there anything you need? I have some meetings, but I could swing by later today…" *God, what was wrong with him?*

"Actually, that would be great. Kate still isn't convinced

you're not ready to string her up by the toenails for helping me last night. So it would be nice to clear the air there. Unless you really do want to string her up, in which case she just got a pedi and you probably shouldn't mess it up."

"I promise no maiming. And I can give you an update on where we are with Ganim."

"Sounds good."

So did her voice.

"Okay, I'll text when I'm on my way. Oh, and I have to discuss changes to your security detail with you, too."

"You're not quitting!" She sounded worried, and he liked it. She wanted him around.

"I'm not quitting. But I want you to have a dedicated driver for the time being. Only if you're comfortable with him or her, though."

"If you're comfortable with them, I'm comfortable with them." She covered the phone and murmured something to someone in the background and then came back on the line. "See, X, isn't it nice when we play nice together?"

WAVERLY HUNG UP THE phone and dropped it on the bed. She bit her lip and then immediately thought of the last person who had bit that lip. To be fair, she had thought of little but Xavier since last night. The fight, the kiss, the whole evening played on a loop in her brain. She'd enjoyed herself. Hell, she'd enjoyed him. And never in all of her twenty years had she ever been kissed like that before.

She wondered if she ever would again.

"Uh-oh. I know that look," Marisol tsk-tsked, emerging from Waverly's closet with an armful of clothes.

"What look?"

"That look!" She pointed a finger at Waverly's face. "The look of love. I looked at my Henri like that and BAM!" She clapped her hands together. "We were married in a month."

"I do not have the 'look of love,'" Waverly argued. If anything it had been the look of lust, which was entirely different though no less dangerous.

Louie looked up from the rolling rack of dresses he was organizing by color and harrumphed.

"You look like that when you talk to this Saint on the phone. I wonder what you look like when you kiss him?"

"How did you—Mari!"

Marisol waved a slim hand. "You just told me. See? Not just actors can be sneaky. I have learned a thing or two from you Sinners."

Waverly felt her face flood with heat. She brought her hands to her cheeks. "Mari, you can't say anything to anyone. It was a heat of the moment kind of thing and nothing else happened… but you just can't breathe a word of this. You either, Louie."

Marisol looked indignant. "When have I ever betrayed a trust, ah? You forget who you talk to."

Louie winked at her. Waverly flopped backwards on the bed and pulled a pillow over her face. "I'm sorry, Mari."

Marisol perched next to her like a dainty Latin bird and pulled the pillow away. "So? What was it like?"

10

Xavier pulled up to the Sinner estate's gates and prepared to push the opener when his attention was caught by what looked like a wrestling match in progress on the side of the road. He keyed in an alert on the security system app on his phone and jumped out of the SUV.

It looked like two photographers in a half-assed street fight.

"Give it to me!" the rotund one in the headlock screeched.

The second photographer, the taller of the two who weighed half of what the other did, was winning. He clutched a manila envelope high overhead while fighting off the flails of the first man. His camera bag clanked around his legs as he spun around.

"It's an invasion of privacy," the tall one yelled.

"Duh! That's what we do, you fucking moron!" The first photographer was starting to gasp for air.

"Gentlemen." Xavier had his jacket open, weapon in easy reach.

The taller man froze. He was a lanky six-foot with shaggy light brown hair. He released the other photographer from the headlock and straightened his Avengers t-shirt. "Are you Xavier Saint?" he asked.

Xavier raised an eyebrow. "Who's asking?"

"I'm Arnie. Some guy just left this here for you." Arnie held out the envelope. The other photographer took one last wild lunge at it and came up short when Xavier snatched it out of his reach, which wasn't surprising because one of his arms was in a sling and none of the rest of him looked like it was moving well.

The outside of the envelope did indeed have his name scrawled across it.

"Arnie, you look familiar," Xavier told him.

"Douchebag Joe and I hang around here a lot," Arnie said, shooting a look at Joe who was leaning against the side of a Toyota and wheezing. "Hey, don't dent the fender," Arnie warned him.

"Fuck you, Arnhole."

"Ah, the Douchebag Joe who tried to get my client killed," Xavier said, his tone ice cold.

"Yeah? Well fuck you, too. She almost ran me over. I was just minding my own business," Joe sputtered. "I should fucking sue. Then I'll live in this house, and Arnhole here can wait around to take my picture."

"Yeah, because that would happen," Arnie rolled his eyes.

"Tell me about the man who dropped this off," Xavier said, waving the envelope.

"He wasn't famous," Joe snapped. "So I don't give a shit about him. I don't get paid to—"

"When I want you to talk, I'll tell you," Xavier said. He let his jacket gap just enough that Douchebag got a good look at his holster. He turned his attention back to Arnie. "The guy who dropped this off."

Arnie shoved his hands into the pockets of his jeans and

hunched his shoulders. "Uh. He was about Douchebag's height but way less fat."

"Fuck you."

"I'd guess around one sixty, maybe one seventy. His hair was like a blah brown. He had sunglasses on. But there was nothing special about him. Just kind of ordinary."

"What was he wearing?"

"Khakis and a t-shirt," Arnie shrugged.

"What kind of car did he drive?"

Arnie shook his head. "No car. He walked up to the gates, which is weird. This isn't exactly a foot traffic kind of neighborhood, no sidewalks or anything."

Xavier pulled up a picture of Ganim on his phone. "This the guy?"

Arnie squinted at the screen. "Yeah, I think that's him. Hard to tell because of the sunglasses, but I'm pretty sure."

"How long ago did he leave?" Xavier wanted to know.

"About five minutes before you pulled up. He was real squirrely. Didn't talk, just stared at the house and then us for a while and then walked away. Douchebag wanted to open the envelope when the guy left it at the gate."

Xavier eyed up Joe again. The man had bandages and gauze wrapped around his good arm and a nice scrape along his jaw. He walked like a ninety-year-old after a marathon. Apparently he was still healing from his near death experience with Waverly on the highway.

Another Tahoe rolled up behind Xavier's, and two Invictus staff members got out. "Is there a problem, Mr. Saint?" one of them asked.

"Do me a favor, run a patrol through the neighborhood. Our person of interest was here. He's got a five-minute head start heading south on foot."

The men took off and Xavier handed Arnie a business card. "You see this guy again, you call me."

"Is he dangerous?" Arnie asked, frowning.

"What's in the envelope, man? You could at least show us, let us take a few snaps," Joe whined.

"How do you stand hanging out with this guy all day?" Xavier asked Arnie.

"Hey, I'm standin' right here!"

Arnie shrugged his skinny shoulders again. "Tuning him out really helps me work on my Zen."

Xavier left the bickering photographers and pulled up the driveway. He called into the office and talked to the monitoring department. They had the gate footage, which corroborated Arnie's story. Ganim had walked up to the gates coming from the south, deposited the envelope, and stared at the house as if waiting for someone to magically appear. He'd walked off but not without staring directly into the camera mounted over the intercom.

Xavier decided that he'd review the system footage himself. He parked behind Kate's Explorer and stared at the envelope on the seat beside him. Whatever was inside wasn't going to be good. But it wasn't going to open itself.

Carefully, he worked the seal open. A dozen photographs spilled into his lap. All of Waverly. All recent, he noted, his mind working calmly, methodically even as his body registered the threat with a surge of adrenaline. Waverly leaving her gym alone. Waverly and Kate entering a designer's studio. Waverly through a window, half-naked being pinned into a gown. Waverly and Xavier entering Nobu. The two of them on the carpet at the awards show yesterday. And another one of Waverly last night in Kate's Explorer at a stop sign. He'd been so close, and Xavier hadn't known.

He shoved his way out of the SUV and tried to calm his

need to run. He wanted to see her, to touch her, and make sure she was okay. The pool house felt like it was a million miles away, and he was in a half-jog by the time he burst through the front door.

Startled, Waverly looked up from a pot on the stove and then smiled brightly. She was wearing leggings and a tank top with her hair piled up on top of her head. Her feet were bare. "I thought you were going to text me when you were on your way?"

She was safe and here and smiling. She was okay.

His momentum carried him into the kitchen and then he was reaching for her. He pulled her into his arms and his mouth found hers in a fierce, possessive kiss. He wanted to brand her, to claim her so no one else could touch her.

He spun her away from the stove, bumping them against the island. His tongue invaded her mouth with a swift thrust. She moaned into him, and he clamped his hands possessively on her hips.

"Holy shit! I mean—"

Xavier spun around, pinning Waverly against the island with his back.

Kate stood in the doorway of Waverly's bedroom gaping like a guppy and peering through her fingers.

"Uh, X?" Waverly's voice was breathless from behind him. He moved off of her, turned to face her. She looked as though she'd just been ravaged, her gray-green eyes were wide, her lips swollen. It made him want to kiss her again, but he backed off.

"Should I, uh, leave?" Kate asked, still in the doorway.

Xavier shoved his hands into his pockets. Less than twenty-four hours prior, he'd vowed never to touch her again, a promise he'd also made to his partner this morning. And here he was devouring her in her own kitchen.

"We need to talk," he told Waverly.

She nodded wordlessly, her mouth still open as if the kiss had stolen her senses.

"I can just go home," Kate suggested again.

"We're all staying," Xavier said flatly.

For the first time, the state of the kitchen registered. The counter tops were littered with ingredients and utensils and something that smelled like heaven was simmering on the stove. "What's going on here?"

Waverly recovered her speech capabilities. "I'm making us all dinner."

He ruined their cozy little evening with work. He sat Waverly and Kate down at the table and walked them through the day's events starting with the Ganim investigation. He'd systematically worked his way through Detective Hansen and was explaining what happened at the gates when his team returned. He met them in the driveway where they reported what he'd expected. Their canvas had turned up no signs of Ganim.

Xavier sent them on their way with orders to knock on a few doors—or security gates—to see if anyone would be willing to share their security footage.

When he returned to the pool house, he carefully spread the photos out on the coffee table for Waverly and Kate to examine.

"That creepy motherfucker," Kate said, voicing Xavier's sentiments.

Waverly remained silent as she stared at the proof of the invasion of her privacy. She picked up the photo of her dress fitting. "This is my premiere dress," she said quietly. Waverly flipped it over.

Tell her to wear red for me.

It was scrawled across the back of the picture in the same handwriting that was on the envelope.

Xavier swore quietly and searched the rest of the photos for more notes, but they were all blank.

"Can we take these to the police?" Waverly asked.

Xavier nodded. "We can."

"But it's still not actionable, is it?"

"No," Xavier agreed. "But it helps establish a pattern."

"Would it help if I personally went to the police and filed a complaint?" she asked, still staring at the pictures.

Xavier hated to see the vulnerable look on her face and packed the photos back into the envelope. "It still isn't enough for Hansen to move on Ganim, but I think us going in will help remind him of how serious this is."

"Okay. We'll go tomorrow," Waverly said with a curt nod. "I'm going to stir the asopao de pollo." She started to rise.

"Waverly?" Xavier's tone was serious.

She looked at him, and he saw that those green eyes had lost their light.

"Are you a good cook or should I call for pizza?"

A ghost of a smile played across her lips. "I guess you'll have to stick around and find out for yourself."

"It's kind of like to-die-for jambalaya but Dominican," Kate explained, scenting the air like a bloodhound. "It's Mari's recipe, and Wave's been making it since she was a kid."

"So, no on the pizza then?" Xavier joked.

Kate waited until Waverly was busy at the stove.

"Couple of questions here. What does this mean for her premiere? She can't not go. It's seriously like the biggest film she's ever done. Do you guys have any idea where he might be? Are the cops even looking for him? Do you think we should add a few more bodies to the detail?"

He waited until she paused for a breath. "Anything else going on in that hyperactive brain of yours?"

"Uh, yeah. Are we not going to talk about that kiss? Was that the first one? Was it the last one? Oh my God, are you guys going to get married and make babies so beautiful that mere mortals can't look directly at them? Can I start calling you Xaverly?"

"Shut up, Kate," Waverly and Xavier said in unison.

THEY ALL HAD dinner together and pretended it was nothing out of the ordinary, even though Xavier kept leaving the table to take the half dozen calls that came in from the office. And every time he excused himself, Waverly found herself being grilled by Kate. In fits and starts, she told her friend most of the details.

"So you vowed never to do it again, and then he just storms in here and lays one on you?" Kate wanted to know. Waverly had no answer for her. Getting it out of her system was feeling less and less likely. *God. When he touched her everything inside her unlocked and came alive.* But she had other things on her plate that needed to be considered. Les Ganim was able to walk right up to her front door to personally deliver evidence that he'd been following her, closely.

Yet the creeping fear that she knew she should feel hadn't made itself known. He wouldn't get to her. Xavier wouldn't let him and she knew that. When he'd burst in through the door, the look of relief and worry and need on his face told her he cared. And not because he was paid to. And not because she was a Sinner. He cared about her, and he would protect her.

Xavier returned, a grim look on his face. Waverly picked up his plate and popped it in the microwave. He'd been working on the same helping for forty-five minutes, and it was beyond cold.

He told them his team had finally hit pay dirt with a neighbor's home security system and got footage of Ganim getting into a car. They got a solid description of the car and a partial plate.

"It's a place to start," he said grimly.

"Then why do you look like you just knocked down someone's grandma?" Waverly asked.

"It's not enough. We need to find this guy, and we need to get the cops to move on him. Until we get him, you're going to be in a virtual prison because I can't just let you walk out that door."

Waverly rubbed her hands over her face. The microwave dinged and she brought his plate back to him.

"Please don't fight me on this," Xavier said quietly. "You either, Kate. From now on, security takes you to and from here. And it would be better if you could stay here for a few days, at least until the premiere."

"I guess we can have Padma come here," Waverly said, thinking of her dress designer who was going to freak when Waverly told her she couldn't wear that dress now. She thought of the picture and shuddered.

"We could probably pull in a trainer from the gym, or we could go old-school and dig out those Jillian Michaels DVDs your mom has squirreled away. Oh, and I can reschedule your meeting with the publicist." Kate suggested.

"Ugh, Media Barbie. I forgot about her," Waverly groaned. Her mother's publicist Gwendolyn—never, ever Gwen—was fanatical about media relations and press junkets and press statements. "Just move the meeting here. Otherwise my mother will sic her on me when I'm not prepared, and she'll lecture me on eyebrow grooming again."

Kate snorted and dumped her plate in the sink. "So listen, X-Man. Since I'll be Wave's new roommate, do you have any hot security guys who want to follow me home so I can pack some stuff?"

"I don't know where they fall on the hot scale, but yes, I've got one waiting outside for you. Take the Tahoe," Xavier told her, handing over the keys.

"Woo! Air-conditioned seats for my ass. I'll be back in an hour unless the guard is really hot." Kate winked and pranced out.

Xavier finally got to finish his meal and leaned back in his chair. He looked tired and angry. Waverly cleared the table.

"Hey. In my family, you cook you don't clean," Xavier insisted. He joined her in the kitchen, opening the dishwasher and loading in the plates. "It was really good, by the way."

Waverly gave him a tired smile. "Thanks. I'll tell Mari you approve."

He rummaged under the sink for the detergent and started the washer. "Is it shitty of me to say that I'm surprised to see you cooking and cleaning up?"

"Yes, yes it is," Waverly laughed. She led the way into the living room where they both sank down on the couch. She pulled her feet under her and hugged a pillow to her chest. "I don't like having a lot of extra people around in my personal space."

"You're the toilet scrubbing kind of Hollywood princess?"

Waverly snorted. "I wouldn't go that far. A very discreet housekeeping service comes in once a week when I'm at the gym, which I'm sure you already knew."

"It's good to know that you're not too human," he teased.

They fell silent for a moment.

"I need you to not worry, Angel. I'm going to take care of this. I'm going to take care of you." Xavier's voice was firm.

"I know you will, Xavier."

"Then why do you look so worried?" Xavier's hand rested on the cushion between them. It felt like an invitation to touch him. She scooted her foot toward him, and he took it in his hand.

"Why was the envelope addressed to you?" she asked. It had bothered her since she saw it. "He's supposed to be fixated on me, but now he's sending you fan mail."

Xavier took his time answering, rubbing lazy circles on the bottom of her foot with his thumb. "I'm no psychologist, but I'd say that he sees me as an obstacle and wants me to know that he has every intention of getting around me."

Waverly had suspected as much. "That worries me," she admitted.

"Don't. I'd much rather he tried to come after me. I'm not an easy obstacle to get around."

"I've noticed," she said dryly.

"I've got a guard on the grounds now twenty-four seven. He'll monitor the systems on-site and be able to respond to any visitors or deliveries. Ganim won't get near you here," Xavier promised. "I'll talk to your parents tomorrow about all this so they know what's going on. Unless you want them to know tonight."

She shook her head, a headache threatening. "Tomorrow's soon enough for everyone to find out. Actually, do you mind if I talk to the publicist before you talk to my parents? I need to know if news like this can damage the premiere or if it'll somehow boost it."

"That's pretty sick," Xavier sighed.

"Welcome to my world."

"Is there a reason you want me to wait on telling your parents?"

Yes. "I just want to make sure I've got all my bases covered," she answered.

"Okay," he ran a hand over the back of his head. "Do we need to talk about that kiss?"

"You mean us breaking our pact less than twenty-four hours after we made it? Nothing's changed has it? You're still code-bound, and I'm still… not looking for any complications."

Xavier nodded his head. "We'll consider the subject closed."

They stared at the blank TV screen for a few moments, each lost in their own thoughts.

"I met your pals at the end of the driveway," Xavier said finally.

"The photographers?"

"Arnie seems pretty nice. I think he's in the wrong line of work. But that Douchebag Joe? He was made for this."

Kate returned with a bag full of necessities the night before, and they'd crashed on the couch and streamed half a season of *Arrested Development*. Xavier had set up shop at the kitchen table reviewing security footage, coordinating with on- and off-site Invictus staff, and occasionally smirking at the entertainment on the screen.

When Kate had crawled off to the guest room close to midnight, Xavier closed the lid on the laptop.

"Long day?" Waverly asked from her perch on the couch.

"I've had longer." He interlaced his fingers behind his head. "You should get to bed."

Waverly wet her lips. "Are you leaving?" She didn't want

him to go. Even with a guard outside, she still felt safer with him here.

Xavier was silent for a long moment. "I'd prefer to stay here—on the couch. Just for tonight, until we have a better handle on things tomorrow. But I'll go if you want me to."

"Stay."

He looked relieved, and she wondered if he was as reluctant to leave as she was to let him. Xavier nodded. "I'll grab my bag which, by the way, now contains an entire micro wardrobe thanks to my swim here with you."

"So you don't need to borrow any pajamas?" she grinned, not the least bit apologetic.

"Got it covered."

"You're such a Boy Scout," Waverly teased.

She lingered in the living room until he returned with a duffle bag. "I feel bad about relegating you to the couch. Why don't you take my room, and I can—"

Xavier shook his head and pointed at the front door. "Anyone comes through that door, I want them to have to get through me to get to you."

Since when did she find over-the-top protectiveness hot? Waverly wondered.

"I'll get you some bedding." She padded barefoot into her room and returned with a pillow and two neatly folded cashmere blankets. "There's towels in the bathroom and leftovers in the fridge. Help yourself to anything."

He nodded and watched her fuss over the bedding.

"Is there anything else—"

"Go to bed, Waverly."

Even with the couch between them, the tension was palpable. He'd ditched his jacket earlier in the evening and rolled up his sleeves. With the holster and gun and the ready-for-action look in those whiskey eyes, Xavier looked dangerous and made her feel safe.

She looked her fill for a moment, taking in the pure perfection of his face, the graceful strength of his body. Her guardian. He'd keep her safe. *But who would protect her heart from him*, she worried.

With a palpable sense of reluctance, Waverly drifted toward her bedroom. She glanced over her shoulder. One last look. "Good night, X."

"Good night, Angel," his voice was a rasp of warring want and restraint.

11

She woke the next morning groggy and disoriented. Just the thought of Xavier sprawled shirtless on her couch—which she knew he was because she'd peeked in the middle of the night—had kept her up most of the night.

Renaissance masters would have spent lifetimes trying to capture his perfection in marble. He slept with one arm behind his head, the other splayed across his muscled stomach, his fingertips tucked just beneath the untied waistband of his cotton pants. He was hard in his sleep—the rigid length of him visible through fabric had her breath catching in her throat. The moonlight played over his broad chest, the subtle hollows of his cheeks. A day's worth of stubble made him look more bad boy than Boy Scout.

Waverly felt her body react with a hot fist of lust. He was so close, so touchable. *What would he do if she traced her fingers over those planes and valleys, lower and lower...*

She'd gone back to bed, tossing and turning, thoughts and fantasies swirling in her head. Frustrated and exhausted, she'd finally fallen asleep and dreamed of her guardian ranging himself over her, taking what he wanted.

He'd made coffee. The scent of it dragged her out of bed and into the kitchen before seven. And, because she blamed him for her restless night, she glared at him when she accepted the mug he held up for her.

He hadn't even bothered to put on a t-shirt yet, and his spectacular form was on display. She hated him, just a little bit, for being so beautiful. He was staring at her, no, *glaring* at her.

"Don't piss me off already, Saint," she said, sighing into the coffee.

"Then put some fucking clothes on," he snapped.

She looked down. Her nipples were trying to fight their way out of the white cami she'd slept in. In her exhausted funk, she hadn't bothered to pull on shorts over her pineapple print underwear that cut high on the thigh and butt. *Oops.*

Judging by the morning wood that was straining against his pajama pants, Xavier Junior liked what he saw.

"What about you, Mr. Coffee-making Adonis. Put a damn shirt on before Kate wakes up and I have to pry her off of you with a crowbar."

"I don't have time for games, Waverly. You're not getting laid, so get your ass in there and put on something that holds those things in," he waved a hand at her chest.

"Excuse me? You think I'm trying to get laid because I walked into my own fucking kitchen for a God damn cup of coffee?"

"You do not wander around here dressed like that," he argued.

"This is what I slept in!"

"Well, you're not asleep now so cover the fuck up!" He stepped in on her, looking good and pissed. She held her ground with a stubborn jut of her chin, and they glared at each other for several tense seconds.

Waverly wilted first. Exhausted and angry, she sprawled over the countertop of the island and put her forehead on the cool granite.

"Why are we fighting?" she groaned.

"Jesus, don't they make underwear with more material?"

"Oh my God, stop looking if it bothers you."

"Angel, my team is going to be in and out of here constantly. You can't prance around in shit like that or I'm going to have to fire every single one of them."

"Ugh. Fine. But at least get that thing under control," she said, pointing at his throbbing cock. "And put on a damn shirt."

She stormed into her room and pulled on a two-piece bathing suit and cover-up. She'd hit a few laps in the pool before sneaking into the gym in the big house. She needed to burn off some of this frustration before Gwendolyn got here. If she didn't, she was guaranteed to say or do something her mother would make her regret.

"I'm going for a swim," she said brusquely, heading for the front door.

"Waverly." Xavier closed the refrigerator. He'd pulled on a t-shirt, though it was fitted enough to leave little of his spectacular physique to the imagination.

"What?"

"I'm sorry for yelling at you." He made it sound like it pained him to apologize. "I didn't sleep well last night, and I took it out on you."

"I didn't get a lot of sleep either," she admitted.

He gave her a long look. "Maybe it was for the same reason."

A blush heated her cheeks. She had a feeling he wasn't talking about Ganim. Had he seen her in the doorway?

"I'm sure we both had a lot of things on our mind," she said diplomatically.

He gave her a half-smile. "How about I make breakfast while you swim? Consider it part of the apology."

"I like my bacon extra crispy," she said, keeping it cool.

She didn't bother easing into the water. The pool was heated to prevent the mundane suffering of cold pool water on a sensitive belly. Waverly shed her cover up on a lounger and dove into the crystal blue waters. She surfaced and cleanly carved through the water with a freestyle stroke.

Her very first movie at the tender age of six had been a reimagined, modern day *Swiss Family Robinson*. The swimming lessons had stuck and now she could outswim just about anyone who dared challenge her.

She let her mind empty of thoughts of Xavier and Ganim, the premiere, and where she wanted to be at summer's end. Emptied until the only things left were the count of her strokes, the steady pull of her breath. Here in the water was peace and presence. Here everything was fine and safe. Waverly powered through a dozen laps and then slowed to a more leisurely pace for the last few. When she finally surfaced at the end, bare feet greeted her.

Xavier set her coffee mug down on the stone edge of the pool. "Breakfast is ready."

"Thanks," she said breathlessly.

He held out a hand to her, and she took it, letting him haul her out of the water with ease.

She grabbed a towel from one of the stations that ringed the pool. "Kate up yet?"

"Yes, and whining that she's going to waste away before you—and I quote—'get your ass out of the pool.'"

Waverly sighed. "Let's get this day started."

"Are we good?" Xavier picked up her mug and handed it to her.

"Yeah, we're good."

GWENDOLYN RIDDINGTON-MACKS WAS A COOL, cunning, ball-busting power publicist. Her client list included the crème de la crème of Hollywood's A-list. She had single-handedly rebranded dying franchises, launched unknown talents to spectacular heights, and kept the wraps on all her clients' secrets. Her fees were astronomical. Her honey blonde hair was always styled into a chic chignon. Her pencil skirts always ended three inches above her knees and her heels were never under four.

Waverly couldn't begin to guess Gwendolyn's age. The woman had the enviable twin fortunes of good genes and a very skilled plastic surgeon for a third husband.

"Waverly," Gwendolyn offered a cool, firm handshake when she was escorted into the parlor in the main house. There was no smile or pleasantries. Her clients didn't pay her to be warm and fuzzy. "I understand you have some business to discuss before we talk about your tour."

"I do. Would you like some water or tea?" Even with Gwendolyn, Waverly found herself unable to dispense with those pleasantries. She led the way to the round pedestal Hepplewhite by the windows that Mari had set with meeting goodies, including crystal glasses of cucumber water and an artful display of MarieBelle chocolates.

Gwendolyn sank gracefully onto the silk covered, armless chair. She ignored the spread before her and brought up a photo on her phone. "Is this, by chance, what you wanted to talk about?" She turned the screen to face Waverly.

Her stomach clenched. "I'm going to kill her," Waverly whispered. This time her mother had gone too far.

There on the gossip site was a blurry picture of Xavier and Waverly by the pool. From Xavier's attire and their close stance, the story the picture told was clear. And for those too lazy to draw their own conclusions, the caption spelled it out. "Waverly Sinner has upgraded to twenty-four seven security. Her new bodyguard enjoyed a cozy breakfast with his charge after spending the night. We wonder how secure her bedroom was last night?"

"We've talked about this before," Gwendolyn continued. "You can't let her keep feeding them. Especially not without passing the stories through me first. She's getting sloppy, and I'm not going to be happy about cleaning up another one of her messes."

"Short of taking her phone away from her and locking her in Betty Ford, do you have any suggestions?"

Gwendolyn drummed her white nails on the mahogany. "Let me handle Sylvia this time. She needs to have the shit scared out of her again."

"I'd appreciate that. I'm not sleeping with my security, by the way," Waverly told her.

"It doesn't really matter whether you are or aren't," Gwendolyn responded in her trademark tone of disinterest. "It's the perception we need to weigh."

Waverly bit back a retort and smiled politely instead. "Of course. The issue at hand is I have a stalker situation that's begun to escalate. Xavier and my assistant spent the night last night after an incident here at the house. My concern is the premiere and what impact additional safety measures and media attention about the case will have."

"Mmm," she said noncommittally. "How serious a threat are we talking?" Gwendolyn asked, typing notes into her tablet. Waverly had the impression that literally everything had happened to Gwendolyn's clients, and she already had a protocol ready to put into effect. Nothing fazed the woman.

"I'm filing an official complaint with the police today."

Gwendolyn nodded and continued to type. "All right. I'd like to speak to your head of security before I leave. I'll have a statement drafted by noon, and we can at least refute the banging the bodyguard rumor. Is there anything else, or can we move on to the premiere?"

Gwendolyn's concern for her welfare was underwhelming.

"By all means," Waverly said, helping herself to a glass of water and envisioned herself throwing it in Media Barbie's face.

"Now, I'm sure I don't need to remind you that *The Dedication* is the biggest film you've done to date and has the largest potential to influence your future career. If you handle the publicity for the film in the right way, and it does what's expected at the box office, you could be naming your price for your next project and the next."

Waverly let her prattle on about branding, staying on message, appearing friendlier in interviews. Gwendolyn had already drafted talking points about the movie, her co-star, the director, and run them by the studio for approval. She'd even included a few "amusing" stories that Waverly should feel free to share during interviews.

There was, of course, the list of things not to discuss, such as the fact that Waverly had made twenty percent less than her male co-star even while garnering more screen time.

By this point in the meeting, Waverly was digging her fingernails into her leg to give herself something to focus on besides Gwendolyn's droning offense.

"I'd like to touch on this bodyguard issue briefly again as it ties into the premiere and tour," Gwendolyn said. "This movie is a love story, and audiences need to believe that it could come true."

"Liam is married," Waverly reminded her.

Gwendolyn waved his marital status away. "You two wrapped filming before they were married so I don't see any issue in hinting at a past relationship and making sure the audience can still sense a chemistry."

"We didn't have a past relationship." Annoyance was charging into pissed off territory.

"What they want to see is that you two have a connection. The film will sell better and you will sell better if you give everyone what they want. And they're going to want you and Liam, not you and some nameless security guard."

"Xavier isn't a security guard," Waverly snapped. "He owns Invictus Security."

For the first time, Gwendolyn looked interested in the conversation. "Well, well. Maybe Sylvia didn't get everything wrong this time." She arched an exquisite eyebrow.

"I think we're done here," Waverly said. She'd been bumped over her tolerance level about ten minutes ago.

"Nice seeing you again," Gwendolyn said without looking up from the screen of her tablet. "Don't forget to send in your security."

Waverly paced off her mad in the kitchen while Louie dodged her.

"Why don't you sit and pout," Louie grumbled, smacking his stainless mallet against a sliver of pork with more force than necessary.

"I'm *not* pouting," Waverly shot back.

"Well, I can't help you if you won't tell me what's wrong."

What was wrong? Oh, just the usual. Her stalker was on the loose, but he wasn't dangerous enough to warrant police intervention. Her mother had once again sold her out to the tabloids showing an outrageous apathy toward her reputation in favor of garnering attention. And then there was that hot, liquid pooling she felt between her legs every single time she looked at the untouchable Xavier Saint.

An unfamiliar laugh, warm and bright, echoed off the marble floor of the hallway.

Waverly and Louie shared a glance.

"Is that Ice Queen laughing?" Louie looked as incredulous as Waverly felt.

"That's not possible," Waverly shook her head.

They raced to the door and pushed it open at the same time. Louie's jaw hit the floor when he saw Gwendolyn facing Xavier with a dazzling smile on her face. "Well, I must say it was a pleasure, Mr. Saint."

"Please. Call me Xavier." He turned, sensing them in the hallway, and his gaze told Waverly he was anything but happy.

Oblivious to the tension between them, Gwendolyn gave her trilling laugh again and patted Xavier on the chest. "Oh, I can work with this, Waverly," she said, her smile still at full wattage. "I'll be in touch. Off to speak with your mother."

"Good luck," Waverly whispered after her. She wasn't sure which of them would need it more.

"I need to speak with you," Xavier said, all charm vanishing from his face.

Waverly and Louie backed into the kitchen, and Xavier advanced on them.

Louie, the coward, abandoned her and busied himself on the safe side of the island when Xavier shoved the swinging door open. It bounced off the wall. Waverly backed into a barstool as his hand clamped over her wrist.

"Let's take a walk."

"But… I'm helping Louie."

"No you're not," Louie the Traitor announced, his relief evident when Xavier hauled her out the door.

"What the hell, X?" Waverly asked, trying to yank her arm loose. But he wasn't giving up. He pulled her around the side of the house toward the garden with its cobbled walkways and pristinely trimmed hedges.

"Your mother sells information about you to the tabloids, and I have to find this out from your publicist?" He finally released her, and she took a step back, turning to get a bit of distance between them.

"I'm sorry about the picture, X. Gwendolyn will fix it. She always does."

"Always does, as in this isn't the first time."

"I promise, I won't let this damage your reputation or that of Invictus either."

"Actually, according to our friend Gwendolyn a juicy little scandal like this would bump up the exposure of Invictus and have female clients flooding in."

"Everybody wins," Waverly said weakly.

"You know that's not what I'm after, and I'm also not after you apologizing for your mother's behavior. You have nothing to apologize for."

"Then why are you yelling at me?"

"I'm not yelling," he yelled. "I'm being upset on your behalf in a loud manner."

"Oh good. Glad we cleared that up."

He turned her around to face him, this time gently. "I have to ask you something, okay? And I need you to be honest."

"If I can, I will be." She could tell he wasn't particularly pleased by that answer, but he pressed on.

"The topless pictures of you from the tabloid…"

Waverly took a slow deep breath and let it out. She could lie to him, but he'd know. It seemed like he already knew. "She took them."

His hands tightened reflexively on her arms, and he muttered out a string of curses.

"She's sick, X." Her shoulders slumped. Somehow, her mother's indiscretions made Waverly feel like both a victim and a failure.

"No shit. What kind of a mother sells out her own daughter like that?"

"She'd been drinking for a week straight. Her 'baby' was turning eighteen, and that meant she was old enough to be the mother of an adult. Aging in this industry can be traumatic, especially for women. The drinking makes her do things that she wouldn't normally do."

"That's no fucking excuse," he said, and then he was pulling her in and holding her. "I knew from the angle that someone had to take them from inside the house. I just assumed it was some asshole guest."

She could hear his heart beating steadily against her ear. Its staccato beat told her he was still angry, but it wasn't with her for once. He was angry on her behalf.

"I had a photo shoot coming up and didn't want tan lines. I thought I had the place to myself. The pictures came out on my eighteenth birthday, but I knew from the landscaping and other details that they were taken earlier than that. So I stormed into my lawyer's office that afternoon, just a few hours before my party.

"He reached out to the publisher immediately, saying we had proof that these were taken when I was underage. And five minutes later the guy was on the phone, dropping the bomb. My mother sent them the pictures. There was a part that I was up for, but it was more adult than my other work.

She thought it would help the studio with their decision." She gave a bitter laugh and rested her cheek against his chest. "I had to leave my lawyer's office and go to the party that she and my father threw for me."

Xavier's hand stroked her hair, the back of her neck. It felt so good and so safe to be in his arms.

"I had to call Gwendolyn in to help clean it up. The tabloid could have gone public with it all, but between Gwendolyn and my attorney, they backed down fast. The settlement with the tabloid was that they wouldn't reveal their source if I didn't pursue charges and a lawsuit. None of the parties involved would ever speak of it again. And it worked. I got the part. Everybody won. Gwendolyn told my father what had happened, and the next day, we checked my mother into rehab."

"I'm so sorry, Angel," he said, his lips moving against her hair.

"I should be apologizing to you," she said, pulling back to look up at him. "She's not just screwing with my reputation now, she's dragging you into it."

"Don't worry about me."

"You made Gwendolyn smile. And laugh," Waverly said.

"This face is a curse sometimes," he said, raising the back of his hand to his forehead.

The martyr act got a laugh out of her. "Poor Xavier Saint. Too pretty for life."

"What is it they say about honey and flies?"

"Aha! So you were after something," Waverly said, crossing her arms. They began to walk slowly around the corkscrew path that led inward to the statue garden.

"She was very adamant about you doing all of the pre-premiere press, which meant you'd be running all over L.A. for the next week."

"Gwendolyn wasn't overly concerned about Ganim," Waverly said. "I think she's seen it all before, and if I get kidnapped and murdered, it would make the movie a blockbuster with all the press attention."

"Sometimes I feel like I'm working for Satan and the Nazis in this town," Xavier sighed.

Waverly laughed again. "Now who's being dramatic?"

"Anyway, Gwendolyn and I were able to hash out a deal that we both find acceptable for your media appearances. You'll be doing all the radio shows from here and the shoot for the Behind the Scenes blog will be moved from the hotel to the main house."

"My mother will approve. She loves having shoots here."

"Then instead of a dozen interviews scattered all over town, you and Liam will do a screening and press junket at the Four Seasons for a day. She's having a press agent make the arrangements now."

"That was a very productive twenty minutes," Waverly said.

"I have to coordinate with Kate, but I think we're going to be able to keep your outside exposure limited before the premiere."

"Is that security speak for keeping me under lock and key?"

"I thought it was a much nicer way of putting it, though now that I know we have a direct threat living on the property, I'm considering locking you away in a remote cabin with no running water or Wi-Fi."

"Haven't I suffered enough?"

"I'm going to have to talk to her, Waverly." She knew it would have to be done. If Gwendolyn couldn't convince her mother that not all attention was good attention, Xavier could at least scare her into behaving for a while.

“I feel like I should be the one having the conversation with her,” she admitted. “She’s my responsibility. Not yours or Gwendolyn’s.”

Xavier shot her a look. “She’s your mother. She’s her own responsibility, maybe your father’s, and definitely Gwendolyn’s. That’s what the woman is paid to do.”

“But—”

“No buts. You are not responsible for her behavior, her drinking, or her choices. Stop trying to be.”

“Maybe we could lock her away in that cabin with no water or Wi-Fi,” Waverly said wistfully.

12

The days before the premiere flew by in a blur. Waverly's complaint with the police went, predictably, nowhere. And thanks to Gwendolyn's master puppeteering, every major media outlet had picked up the story of her stalker scare. Not only was she getting sympathy points, the rumors about Xavier had dried up. Although, with the exposure, he'd now become a favorite with the paparazzi thanks to an insatiable female demographic, and his face was splashed across as many gossip sites as Waverly's.

With Waverly ensconced at home and Xavier heading the Ganim investigation—and no longer sleeping on her couch—they barely saw each other except for short, daily catch-up sessions. Each was preparing for the premiere in their own way. Waverly and Kate worked with the dress designer, trainers, the studio's publicity team, and spa staff leading up to the big day.

Xavier, meanwhile, had gone on the offensive. He'd called a meeting with Sylvia and Robert where he dropped the bomb that Sylvia's tips to the tabloids and paparazzi had been how Ganim was able to track Waverly's movements in L.A. It had led to an ugly scene between the couple. Xavier felt like a marriage counselor as he extracted a promise from each of them that it would never happen again.

Ganim had remained quiet and just out of reach.

One of Invictus' research staff had hit a hot tip doing cold calls to motels. A man matching Ganim's description had stayed there for four days, paying cash, but had checked out that very morning. The front desk clerk, whose only on-the-job excitement to-date had been the night the ice machine broke, had been only too happy to provide the alias and license plate number that Ganim had registered under. She even invited Invictus to search the room since the cleaners wouldn't get to it for another hour.

What they'd found had warranted an actual visit from Detective Hansen. While most of the room had been wiped clean, an eagle-eyed tech had discovered traces of black powder on the rickety particleboard desk.

Black powder meant either ammunition or explosives. Neither was good. Hansen made no promises, but said he'd have some uniforms "look into it."

Xavier had grimly increased the coverage to include Sylvia, Robert, and Kate. Everyone now had a driver and a guard.

He worked daily with event security for the premiere and coordinated with the LAPD officers who would be on duty at the event. He made sure every member of the team had memorized Les Ganim's face and finally secured permission to have Invictus staff positioned in plainclothes throughout the crowd, on the carpet, and inside the theatre.

Two days before the premiere, Xavier had put the team to the test at the press junket. Invictus invaded the W Los Angeles hotel with exterior, lobby, and floor coverage, ensuring that no one could get to Waverly without first getting through Invictus.

He'd been impressed by Waverly before, but today he was captivated. She sat on a low leather couch in the presidential suite next to her co-star Liam MacGill, answering the same questions over and over again with sincerity. The interviews were scheduled in strict fifteen-minute increments, and reporters and bloggers cycled through the chairs across from the actors like clockwork. All the while, Xavier stood by, positioning himself between Waverly and whoever came through the door.

Between interviews, stylists freshened Waverly's hair and make-up and Gwendolyn reviewed talking points with her. Phil spent most of the day on his phone answering emails and sneaking snacks off the food table.

"This whole BFF thing you guys are going for is falling a little flat," Gwendolyn announced after a blogger left the room texting madly on her phone. "If you're hell-bent on that angle, try punching up the pranks angle next time, bigger smiles, bigger eye rolls."

Waverly made fake look so real that he was almost unnerved by it. She slipped behind her carefully crafted public façade so easily that Xavier felt like he was staring at a different woman. She could make people believe whatever it was she wanted them to. On camera, Waverly couldn't live without her Bulgari sunglasses and her Seven jeans and her Crème de la Mer. Interview Waverly loved her protein smoothies and ate a strict fourteen hundred calorie diet. Public Waverly was not a tacos on the beach or motorcycle road trip kind of girl.

Waverly caught Xavier watching her and winked at him over her Perrier. He joined her at the long glass table the hotel's catering staff had laden with every kind of celebrity food favorite imaginable.

"Who are you?" he asked her as she loaded up a plate with crudité and avocado hummus.

"It's all about perception, X." She wriggled her eyebrows at him. "Here." She pressed a plate into his hands. "Eat."

"I don't need to eat."

"It's three in the afternoon, and we didn't have lunch. I don't need you getting lightheaded and faint when some bad guy breaks down the door."

Xavier reluctantly tossed a burger slider on his plate. "Happy?"

"Eat it like a good boy."

He took a bite, and his eyes rolled back in his head. "Oh, my God. What is this?"

"Kobe beef," Waverly grinned. "So what do you think?"

"I think I just put actual heaven in my mouth."

"No, I mean about the junket. Do you think it's going well?"

"Why are you asking me?"

"You're a trained observer. Gwendolyn seems to think we're doing a shit job selling the film and ourselves, and if I asked Phil, he would just tell me I'm brilliant and pat me on the head."

"Point taken. What do you want to know?"

"What do you think is coming across to the press?"

He took another bite of slider and thought before speaking. "What people find interesting about stories is the relationships. So whether it's between you and Liam in real life or as characters, that's what they want to hear about. So your interactions with a co-star or a director or the author of the book, even your own stalker. It's the relationships that matter to people."

Waverly looked pensive. "Still waters certainly run deep. Thanks, X." Then she snagged the rest of the slider off his plate and ate it.

At least the real Waverly was still in there somewhere, Xavier noted. He was glad she and Liam had foregone the "ex-lovers" angle. Even if the relationship was fake, Xavier would have still wanted to beat the hell out of the guy, and Liam seemed like a decent man. Not like that Dante Wrede.

Kate signaled to Xavier, and he crossed the suite to her.

"Got another message from our pal," she whispered.

He took her phone and glanced at the screen.

I look forward to seeing you at the premiere. It'll be our night.

KATE WAS READYING for battle with her arsenal of boob tape, safety pins, floss, markers, and a cosmetic bag full of beauty tools spread out over the European down comforter in one of the main house's upstairs guest rooms.

"I feel woefully unprepared for a stalker attack," she muttered, shoving beauty supplies into her sleek tote.

"Hey! Don't jinx us," Waverly complained from her perch on a tufted ottoman in front of the mirror.

"Hold still," Marisol commanded, the pins between her lips moving as she spoke.

"Sorry, Mari," Waverly said and tried to stop fidgeting.

"I feel like I should at least be packing pepper spray or a Taser or something," Kate frowned. "Unless I can like stab him with this." She picked up an eyelash curler.

"This is why we have security: so we don't have to be the ones doing the stabbing," Waverly reminded her.

"Yeah, but, aren't you mad? I mean, don't you kind of want to have the pleasure of kicking this guy in the balls yourself?"

Waverly's stomach took a sick slide at the thought of being that close to Ganim. She was mad, yes, but fear was right up there on the list of things she was feeling leading up to the premiere. She already felt woefully unprepared to deal with the mental side of the evening—the crowd, the photographers, the interviews. And adding worries about Ganim to the mix could have her curled in the fetal position if she let herself think too much. But Kate the warrior wouldn't understand. She'd punch trouble in the balls without a second's hesitation.

"I don't care who kicks him where," she confessed. "I just want him gone from my life." She thought about the envelope that had arrived today from Stanford. The one from Admissions. The one she'd been too terrified to open. It was the news she'd been waiting for, and now she was too freaked out to find out whether or not she got in.

As long as the envelope was still sealed, her dreams could be both alive and dead. She couldn't imagine getting a yes and then trudging around campus with a security detail and a stalker. Normal would never be within her reach if Les Ganim stayed free.

"Don't get her all riled up," Mari said sternly to Kate. "This is a big night and Waverly does not need to be worried about anything. Worry gives you wrinkles."

Waverly met Kate's gaze in the mirror, and they rolled their eyes at each other.

"I saw that," Mari announced without ever lifting her gaze from the seam of Waverly's top.

"Spooky," Kate hissed. She flopped on the bed.

"Don't wrinkle your dress," Waverly warned her. "You look amazing in it, by the way."

Kate stood and obliged with a slow twirl around Waverly's footstool. The navy sheath dress nipped in at the waist giving

Kate a hint of curves she'd never quite sprouted on her own. She'd pulled her hair back in a serviceable ponytail and added a bit of curl to class it up. She wore two pairs of diamond studs in her earlobes.

"Think Simon will like it?" Kate asked. Simon Shipley was the host of an entertainment news show. He'd been flirting with Kate for the past year whenever their paths crossed on red carpets.

"You'll have him drooling after you like a dental patient," Waverly predicted.

Kate looked satisfied. "Speaking of drool, how do you think X-Man's going to feel about this little number?" she asked, eyeing up Waverly's dress. They'd scrapped the red gown Ganim had photographed her in and worked feverishly with the designer to come up with a new concept for the event. The dress was a two-piece in sinful black. The top was a fitted satin crop with cap sleeves, while the skirt fell away into airy layers of tulle. The pieces were separated by two inches of bare torso. She looked glamorous and edgy in it. And with hair and make-up she'd be fierce, at least on the outside.

"I showed him the dress on a hanger and he approved it," Waverly told Kate. "I think he was relieved to see so much material."

"But you are no clothes hanger," Marisol reminded her, tucking another pin into place.

"That's why I'm staying up here until the last possible second so there won't be time to change," she smirked.

"There," Marisol said, smoothing down the seam. "Now it is perfect. Just don't breathe too much."

"Thanks, Mari. Your talents know no bounds," Waverly told the woman.

Marisol paused while gathering up her sewing tools. "Be

careful tonight, okay? Don't ruin my hard work, and do what Mr. Saint tells you."

Waverly patted her on the arm. "Don't worry about me, Mari. I'll be good."

Marisol pointed a finger at Kate. "I'm counting on you to keep her out of trouble."

"Yes, Mari," Kate promised.

Waverly's phone signaled. "That's Mom. Hair and makeup are ready for me."

"Take off the dress and I'll finish the stitches. It will be ready in half an hour," Mari ordered.

Kate excused herself to load her supplies in the car and flip-flopped her way downstairs. Waverly handed over the dress and changed into a short satin robe. She headed across the hallway to the skinny room her mother had dubbed the glam room.

One long wall was dominated by a twelve-foot slab of marble counter divided into three vanities with professional lighting and outlets galore. Sylvia was perched in the first chair while Chase, her long-time make-up artist, finished her eyeliner.

"There you are, darling," Sylvia greeted Waverly with a pucker of her freshly painted lips. "Am I gorgeous, yet?"

"You're always gorgeous, Mom," Waverly said indulgently and winked at Jenni, the hairstylist who was a pixie-sized version of Halle Berry.

Sylvia Sinner lived for premieres, and the only thing as good as one of her own was her daughter's. She would plan her look for weeks out, and on the big day, not a drop of alcohol passed her lips. It wasn't that she wanted to be sober. It was because she didn't want to carry an extra ounce of water weight in front of the cameras.

Yes, there was nothing that made Sylvia happier than a red

carpet with her husband and daughter by her side. "We are other people's dream come true," she often said.

Sometimes Waverly wondered how her mother could see their lives as anything but a nightmare. But today, Sylvia glowed.

Chase had performed his special kind of magic to hide the circles under her eyes and fill out her sunken cheeks with subtle contouring. The bronzer and blush brought a dewy freshness to Sylvia's face. It made Waverly think of days when Sylvia had been naturally vibrant and full of life. But alcohol had slowly robbed her of that, and now she could only enjoy a temporary facsimile of that effervescence through the miracle of paints and lotions.

"Ready for me, Jenni?" Waverly asked.

Jenni spun her chair around and patted it. "I know your dress changed. Are we still going for a wild, jungle chic?" the stylist asked, plucking gently at Waverly's tresses.

"You changed your dress?" Sylvia swiveled so suddenly that Chase almost lined her forehead.

"Mmm-hmm," Waverly said mildly.

"But I planned my entire look around the red!" What she meant was that she had planned her gown to outshine Waverly's original pick. Sylvia may have been bursting with pride over her daughter's accomplishments, but that didn't mean she wanted to be overshadowed on the red carpet.

Waverly tried to rally herself to comfort her mother. The tension she always felt before big events was already blooming in her belly. But she couldn't have her mother melting down now.

"You're wearing the gold Marchesa, aren't you?" she asked while Jenni deftly stabbed pins into her hair.

"Well, I *was*," Sylvia wailed. "This is so inconsiderate of you, Waverly. You know how much work and planning went into this outfit. And now it's all ruined." Chase began a frantic search for tissues and Q-tips to minimize the damage if Sylvia turned on the waterworks.

Waverly decided to save him the effort and dug her phone out of the pocket of her robe. "Nothing is ruined. This is the dress I'm wearing." She pulled up a picture from one of her fittings. "I think the gold is going to look even better against this, don't you?"

Sylvia snatched the phone out of her hands and held it out at arm's length, turning her head this way and that. "Well, I suppose I can make do with this," she sighed. "Yes, I think the gold will still work. But next time, you must talk to me before you decide to do something drastic."

Waverly made eye contact with Jenni in the mirror. The stylist winked as she wrapped a section of hair around the barrel of a curling iron. Waverly wondered what Jenni and Chase heard behind the chairs of other mother-daughter duos in Hollywood. Was it the same story everywhere? The same war between pride and envy? Of family responsibility and a desire to be one's own?

With the crisis averted, Sylvia leaned back and let Chase set her makeup with a few deft sprays. "I told Kate to make sure Hollywood News gets a shot of all three of us together," Sylvia said. "Oh! And Gwendolyn wanted me to remind you to make sure you mention how much you adored working with Liam. She felt you went a little light on the message at the junket."

"Mm-hmm," Waverly said, noncommittally.

Sylvia sighed dramatically. "I wish Liam wouldn't have run off and gotten married. An affair between the two of you would have been just too perfect."

Waverly let her mother chatter on and tried to relax. She had a routine that she religiously adhered to leading up to big events to help keep the panic at bay. At best, the energy at these events was exhausting. And if she wasn't properly prepared, it could be a trigger. The press of the crowd, the atmosphere of excitement. Then there were the journalists and bloggers and TV hosts, all wanting the sound bite that people would talk about for days. Everyone wanted something from her.

To be the focus of so much energy was enough to spike anyone's anxiety levels. But to Waverly it was a special kind of torture. She'd never been able to bask in the attention as her mother did. She felt guilty at times, living the life that so many others dreamed of yet not finding the happiness and fulfillment that were supposed to be there.

The panic attacks were practically non-existent these days. Thanks to the therapy she'd secretly completed, she had the tools she needed to cope. And she would have Kate and Xavier with her. She'd be steadier with them next to her.

She stole a glance at her mother who puckered prettily so Chase could check her lip stain. Sylvia never felt a moment's nerves on the carpet. She was born for it and would never understand how the place she felt the most at home was a secret torture for her own daughter.

Jenni combed her fingers through Waverly's tresses, and she closed her eyes and blocked everything else out to focus on her breath.

Her mother left to dress after a final reassurance that the Marchesa was still stunning and perfect, and Waverly, now with miles of wild waves, moved to Chase's chair. She thought of it as armor. Her hair and makeup were always several steps in the opposite direction of what she would personally choose. It was her way of creating a distance, a persona. The persona could come under attack, and Waverly would still escape unscathed.

Chase finished up, and when Waverly opened her eyes, she didn't even recognize herself in the mirror. In her place was a woman with flawless skin, a mysterious pout, and enough smoke around the eyes to dazzle on camera. Her hair was ripe with a riot of waves with tiny braids tucked here and there for texture and drama. It was the perfect homage to her character in the movie who often wore her hair wild.

"You guys are miracle workers," Waverly sighed. She gave Chase and then Jenni a quick hug.

She left them to pack up and returned to the guest room across the hall where her finished dress hung over the cheval mirror. Waverly preferred to dress alone and use the time to settle her nerves and mentally prepare. She pulled on the skirt and smoothed the tulle over her hips. The satin top laced up the back in a kind of corset to highlight her silhouette. She loosened the ties and slipped the top over her head. She'd get someone downstairs to lace her up properly, Waverly decided.

Overall the look was dramatic and intense without losing the sense of youth. It would certainly cause a stir on the red carpet. She made a mental note to send Padma flowers after tonight to thank her for her emergency dress services.

A knock at the door pulled her attention from the mirror.

"Come in," she called.

The door swung inward and her breath caught in her throat when Xavier walked in. Even in a tuxedo, his raw, masculine energy made itself known. Where others would have looked elegant in the satin-lapeled Brioni, Xavier looked dangerous. There was power in the way he prowled into the room, authority in the way he looked at her.

He paused and took in the view and Waverly felt her temperature rise from the weight of his gaze. "That dress didn't look like that on the hanger," he said finally.

"Hmm, no it didn't," Waverly said innocently. "Can you lace me up?" she asked, turning her back to him.

He joined her at the mirror and she felt his long fingers brush the skin at her back as they plucked at the satin strings of the corset.

He pulled and she felt the tension around her breasts increase. "Tighter," she said.

He met her eyes in the mirror and she felt the strong tug at her back.

The tension she felt now shifted to pool between her legs. Each time his fingers brushed her bare skin, tender goose bumps erupted.

"Better?"

"I can still breathe, but it looks pretty good." She put her hands on her hips and nodded at her reflection. "Is it time to go?"

"We have a few minutes. I have something for you." Xavier pulled a small box out of his jacket pocket.

Waverly turned around to face him. "You got me a present?"

"Invictus got you a present," Xavier corrected her, opening the box. It was a delicate anklet in platinum with a small round heart charm encrusted with tiny diamonds dangling from the thin chain.

"Xavier—"

"Before you embarrass us both and think this is some kind of romantic gesture, I'd be remiss if I didn't tell you it's a GPS tracker."

Waverly felt twin pangs of relief and something almost like disappointment. "You want to put a tracking device on me?"

Xavier ignored her and knelt down in front of her. He tugged her right foot up onto his thigh. She had to steady herself by putting her hands on his shoulders. "You can't complain about it. It's shiny and pretty," he said, clasping it around her ankle.

"Your male clients must love wearing these," Waverly joked, and her voice wavered. Every time Xavier touched her, her body reacted with an intensity that unsettled her.

"They usually get phony wedding rings or a high-tech belt buckle."

"It's beautiful," she said, admiring the charm.

"I was going to have the designer make it a ball and chain, but I thought you might like this better," Xavier straightened. "You don't have to wear it all the time, but I'd like you to whenever we're away from the house."

He didn't realize how telling his words were. He'd known she wouldn't like yet another reminder of her prison sentence, so he'd tried to make it something pretty and sweet to take the sting out of it. Waverly bit back a sigh. If she had to spend too much longer with Xavier, her heart would be taking a hit. A hard one.

"Are you ready?" Xavier offered his hand.

Waverly took a deep breath. Would she ever really be ready?

13

Xavier felt the tension in the back of the limo like it was a smothering blanket. Waverly was sitting, back lance straight, on the lush leather seat next to him. Her hands were clasped in a white-knuckle grip as she stared out the window taking long, slow breaths.

On the bench seat with her heels stowed next to her purse, Kate texted maniacally.

"Your mom and dad are meeting us in the holding area. They'll do the first half of the carpet with you and then peel off so you can alternate interviews," Kate said, glancing up from her phone at Waverly.

When Waverly didn't respond, Kate caught Xavier's eye and then made a pointed look at her phone and back at him. Her thumbs flew over the screen, and Xavier felt his phone vibrate in his jacket.

He fished it out.

She gets nervous at these things. She'll be okay. Just stick close.

As if he would let her out of his sight for a second tonight.

Will do.

Her response was rapid fire back.

You look tense too. Do I need to freak out?

Xavier gave her an exaggerated eye roll.

Everything is under control and no one is going to freak out.

He wasn't tense. He was focused. He knew Ganim would show his face tonight, but what Xavier wasn't sure of was the man's intentions. Would he just watch from the shadows like before, or would he make a move tonight? Either way, Xavier was not leaving Waverly's side for a moment. He would stand between her and any threat.

He glanced at her again, noticed that the thumb and forefinger of her left hand were moving rhythmically back and forth over the surface of something shiny. A lucky coin, perhaps?

He fitted the earpiece that would connect him with the rest of his team in place and fired off an ETA text to the Invictus staff already on-site.

His phone vibrated again with a text message from one of his men.

NSS.

It was Invictus speak for "no sign of subject." Xavier had the utmost faith in his team and their preparation. He knew exactly where the crowd would be, where the exits were located, and what to expect once they were inside the theatre. He'd arranged for a second car and driver to be waiting at a side entrance as Plan B. Event security was on the lookout for Ganim and the seven other problem suspects on the "unfriendly" list.

They were ready for Ganim, and perhaps tonight they would get lucky.

Now that the cops were interested in the case, Ganim would be taken into custody if he was detained by Xavier's team or event security. He hoped it would be that easy, but his gut told him otherwise.

The man may be crazy, but he wasn't stupid. Every movement he made in L.A. had been carefully cloaked except when trying to get Waverly's attention.

The noise outside the car grew louder as the limo edged past crowds lining the sidewalk. They were still two blocks away from the theater, and the crowd outside couldn't know who was in the limo, but it didn't matter. Their enthusiasm overrode everything else.

Both sides of the street on the theatre's block were lined with waist-high metal fencing that served as a barricade. Cops walked the block directing traffic and keeping spectators on the sidewalks.

The theatre appeared on their left, and as the limo rolled to a stop, the crowd outside grew raucous. Waverly was still rubbing the coin between her fingers and staring as if unseeing out the window.

"Geez, they don't even know you're in here yet," Kate grumbled. "They'd probably go nuts no matter who got out of the car. 'Ohmigod! It's Mr. Potato Head. Let's get his autograph and maybe rip off his nose for a souvenir!'"

Kate's snarky humor dragged Waverly from her fog, and Xavier watched her eyes refocus on the interior of the limo as if she was seeing it for the first time.

"You ready to go be adored by hoards?" Kate asked her.

Waverly shot her a bright smile that wasn't fooling anyone. "Let's do it. Oh, and I'm thinking pizza or fried chicken for late night."

"If you're a good girl, I'll get you both," Kate promised. "So recap. As soon as that door opens, you've got four minutes with the crowd to give our buddy Saint here a heart attack. Then we drag you away from your adoring fans, across the street to the holding area. We'll meet up with your parents, run the first half of the gauntlet, and then dump the 'rents and trade them for Liam and his wife."

Waverly gave a nod. "I'm ready. Just point me in the direction of my loving admirers."

She looked steadier than she had. Her color was up, and there was light in her eyes. But Xavier wasn't sure if it was excitement or fear. Or both.

Xavier exited first, nodding at the guard who opened the door. They made room for Waverly on the street, and when she stepped out, the crowd behind the barrier went wild.

People were screaming her name. Flashes from cameras and cell phones lit up the evening like lightning. Xavier didn't like how charged the crowd was already, and it only heightened when they realized she was coming their way.

Their little entourage picked up another guard and two cops. Xavier kept his left hand on the small of Waverly's back and walked her right up to the crowd. He had a surreal moment where he felt like he was dangling a tasty morsel in front of a starving dog and expecting to pull back with all his fingers intact.

The noise was so deafening, Waverly could do nothing but smile at those she greeted, their comments, questions, and requests lost under the din.

"Waverly!"

Her name was shouted from all directions. She began with a pair of giddy teenage girls, signing the publicity headshot that the one with braces handed over. She obliged them with a selfie that brought tears of hysteria to the teens and then moved down the line. People shoved pictures and magazines at her to sign. Cell phones recorded her every move. From the third row a middle-aged giant with the collar popped on his lime green polo clutched a fistful of pictures.

Hulking over the crowd, he shoved them in front of her,

and as soon as Waverly signed one, he shuffled it to the bottom of the stack and followed her down the line, leaning in again with a fresh picture.

Xavier let him do it twice until the man elbowed a woman holding her young daughter in the face. He took the marker and tossed it over his shoulder. "No more," he told him and moved Waverly down the line. When the man protested, one of the cops stepped in and gave him the option to calm down or leave.

Kate hovered at Waverly's elbow acting as photographer for fans and ready with a metallic marker if it was needed. Waverly scrawled her signature on just about anything that was shoved in front of her. Until some smartass in a backward trucker hat held out a grainy copy of one of the topless shots.

Kate snatched it out of the guy's hand. "Real funny, asshole."

Trucker Hat didn't think it was so funny now that his picture had been confiscated. He charged the barrier, reaching toward Kate. Xavier grabbed his arm and held it in a crushing grip.

"Stay behind the barrier, sir," the cop behind him shouted and the crowd turned their cell phones to capture the scuffle. Trucker Hat backed down quickly, but the crowd was even more amped. A woman with a mousy brown perm and a kitten sweatshirt vied for Waverly's attention by grabbing her arm and holding it in a death grip. Xavier couldn't hear what she was saying. Judging from the woman's animated expression, it could have been praise for a movie or some kind of political rant. Or maybe she was just rattling off the list of names of her cats.

Either way, Xavier had had enough.

"Enough," Xavier said, shaking his head at Kate. "Let's get her out of here before someone rips her hair out as a souvenir." He separated Waverly from her rabid fan who was still yelling something. The rest of the entourage closed ranks around them and Xavier guided them back across the street to boos from the crowd.

"Well, that was fun," Kate said, hustling to keep up. "Did you see X Factor put the kibosh on eBay Eddie?"

Waverly gave him a weak grin and winked.

They reached the relative safety of the other side of the street and the opening of the large tent that served as a holding area for the red carpet walkers. Xavier thanked the cops and guard for their help and was surprised when Waverly took the time to do the same. She shook each of their hands, asked their names, and thanked them. Waverly also scrawled a quick autograph and delivered it with a wink to Officer Kinnekut who claimed his wife was a huge fan. But Xavier judged by the star-struck expression on the man's face the autograph would never make it home to the missus.

Kate discreetly tapped her wrist signaling that it was time to move on. Xavier stepped in and whisked Waverly into the tent. Inside, it was a different kind of excitement.

Here, celebrities and their guests were corralled and released in a controlled trickle down the red carpet to ensure a steady flow of traffic for the photographers and reporters. Before their release into the wild of the carpet, stylists fluffed and dabbed, assistants snapped "candid" shots of their clients for Instagram and Twitter, and agents shooed their charges away from the complimentary pizza that had the potential to ruin a ten thousand dollar designer gown.

The excitement ratcheted up another notch when the inhabitants of the tent realized that Waverly was with them. She was immediately surrounded by well-wishers both sincere and fake.

Xavier stayed close and spotted Big Mike Mahoney a few

paces away, maintaining a discreet distance from the soap actor he protected. The actor, as Xavier discovered in yesterday's event security briefing, had a little trouble with a fan who was convinced his character was real and that she was pregnant with his love child.

Big Mike gave Xavier a nod, and Xavier threw him a mock salute. They'd run into each other at similar events in the past. It was impossible to miss the man when he towered head and shoulders over the rest of the crowd.

He took a moment to report to his team and let them know that Waverly was on schedule and in the holding tent. Everyone checked in with all clears in their respective areas, and Xavier began to wonder if Ganim wasn't ready to make his move tonight.

Gwendolyn weaved her way through the crowd to Waverly's side and air kissed her on both cheeks. "You look incredible. Any incidents I need to be aware of?" she asked.

"You missed Saint here almost lay out a lady in a cat shirt," Kate said helpfully.

"I thought she might have rabies," Xavier quipped, and Waverly laughed.

Gwendolyn ran her gaze over Xavier and gave him a feline smile. "Well, I'm sure I'll enjoy the video of that later. I'm going to collect your parents. Phil's babysitting them right now. See you on the carpet." With one last look at Xavier, she disappeared back into the fray.

Waverly excused herself from a conversation and leaned in. "You did well," she said, patting him on the arm. "The crowd signings are the worst part of things for security. They can be really unpredictable."

"Then why do it?" he asked. God knew his heart rate would be a little more under control without worrying the entire crowd was going to jump the barrier and tear Waverly into tiny souvenirs of flesh.

Kate guffawed. "If Wave skipped the crowd, her mom would do something even more camera worthy like forcing a nip slip on camera or something."

Xavier didn't think she was joking.

"Any sightings of… him?" Waverly asked in a whisper.

Xavier shook his head. "All clear."

He let her go back to her friends and fans with a reassuring nod. "It's all good, Angel."

The accolades came in left and right—well wishes for the movie, compliments on the dress—and while the delivery was slightly different, Xavier got the same vibe as outside. Everyone wanted a piece of her.

"Your parents are here," Kate said, looking up from her phone. "I'm going to meet them." She teetered off on her heels.

She returned a few moments later with Sylvia, Robert, and Phil in tow. The crowd around Waverly parted for the family reunion. "Darling! You're absolute perfection," Sylvia crowed as she leaned in for another round of air kisses. Xavier caught a whiff of her floral perfume.

Cameras snapped left and right, capturing the moment. Robert stepped in and gave Waverly a kiss on the top of the head. "You look wonderful, sweetheart." They made a picture, the three of them. Robert, debonair with a deep tan and his impeccable tux. Sylvia in the glittering gold gown that clung to her tiny figure. And Waverly, the picture of youth and vitality, glowing like the star she was in the middle of it all.

She made him catch his breath.

Robert put an arm around each of them. "My two beautiful girls," he crooned, and the crowd took it as an invitation to snap away. Everyone had a cell phone in hand to record the beautiful family.

"I heard there was an incident with the crowd." Sylvia's eyes glittered. "I hope someone got it on video."

"Waverly's fine, by the way," Xavier announced coolly.

"Of course she is. Why wouldn't she be?" Sylvia giggled as if he'd made a joke. "Darling! How wonderful to see you!" And just like that, their little circle opened up to include the crowd. All three Sinners were pulled in different directions. Xavier stuck with Waverly as she kiss-kissed and smiled and selfied her way through the tent. She made it look easy, natural. Waverly paused and introduced him when appropriate, giving Invictus a little bump each time. He was careful to maintain the line between security and guest, knowing that every impression was a reflection on Invictus.

She knew nearly everyone, had a grasp of names and faces, and remembered little tidbits of information about each person. She would have made a great diplomat, he thought.

Richard, an executive from Breitling Studios was a secret violin maestro. Tilda with her short red hair had starred in a popular nineties TV comedy and was slated to guest star in the reboot that fall with her niece.

He watched Kate expertly juggle the Sinners and their industry following, constantly maintaining forward progress toward the front of the tent.

Finally, their little group was on deck for release onto the carpet. The Sinners each checked their reflections in the hand mirror that Kate produced from the depths of her bag. They smoothed hairs, blotted, puckered. And, with the final prep behind them, were presented to the carpet.

The pit of photographers was every bit the hell Xavier had predicted it to be. Hairy guys in t-shirts and ball caps clamored for the Sinners to look this way and that. "Now just mother daughter." "Now just Waverly." Snap. Snap. Snap.

It was like watching a solar system of stars explode at the same time.

Xavier waited just off camera with Kate while Waverly turned this way and that, smiled here and then there. One of the photographers made a move to lean over the barrier hidden behind printed movie graphics for *The Dedication*. "Remember me, cupcake?"

Xavier rolled his eyes behind his sunglasses. Douchebag Joe had decided to make an appearance. Despite being physically hindered by the sling, his personality was still in full noxious power.

"Hey! Remember me, Waverly? You too good to look at your old pal?" Joe leaned precariously over the barrier.

Xavier took a step closer. "Just give me a reason," he muttered under his breath.

Waverly continued to smile and pose as if Douchebag Joe didn't exist in her universe.

Which didn't go over well with the photographer. "Hey! Fuck you anyway! I'm sending your stupid ass my medical bills, ya fuckin' bitch."

Xavier stepped up just as two event security guys appeared.

"We're going to have to ask you to leave," said the one built like a brick shit house.

"That's bullshit," Douchebag Joe screeched. "This is freedom of the press!"

He leaned all the way over the barricade trying to shoot around Xavier and the other two guards. "Do not cross the barricade, sir."

"She's just being a cu—"

He was cut off when the skinny shadow of Arnie kicked

Joe's knee out from under him. Joe went down like a ton of bricks taking the barrier with him. He was hauled away, shouting threats of lawsuits before he could even regain his feet.

Waverly, who had seemed oblivious to the exchange, suddenly left her mark and crossed the carpet to Xavier. She stopped in front of Arnie.

"I remember you. Arnie, right?"

He nodded his shaggy head.

"Thanks for the help, Arnie," Waverly said.

He held up the camera hesitantly. She gave him a nod and then blew him a kiss. Behind the camera, Arnie turned the color of an heirloom tomato as he grinned and snapped away.

The talent manager, a haggard looking man in a rumpled suit whose glasses kept steaming up from the sweat pouring forth from his forehead, finally signaled to Kate that it was time to clear the carpet. Kate and Xavier led the way to the first TV host. Each camera crew commandeered a tiny radius of the carpet with a camera, a host, a floor manager, a producer, and talent manager. It was pure chaos off camera, but Xavier could tell it was all par for the course with Waverly.

She breezed through two interviews with charm and grace, and on the third, Liam "surprised" her. They provided a united front on camera, just two friends proud of a project. Together they laughed off rumors of a romantic relationship, and Waverly scored points when one particular host kept pressing on that front. Waverly tugged Liam's wife up on the elevated scrap of stage and told a behind-the-scenes anecdote about the happy couple.

They had just moved as a unit to Simon Shipley's perch on the carpet. The pleasantries had just begun when Xavier's team came to life in his ear.

"Suspect spotted. West side in the crowd."

"Keep eyes on him," Xavier ordered quietly. He gave a nod to the undercover on his right. Darius was one of Xavier's contract employees who did surveillance work when needed. He breezed in at just under five-feet nine-inches but was built like a body builder. Darius sidled off the carpet onto the walkway that was cordoned off behind the movie posters and took off toward the call.

Kate caught Xavier's eye and he gave her a curt nod.

"He's on the move. Heading toward the theatre," came the voice in Xavier's ear. The tone was calm, blasé even. But Xavier knew every member of his team was primed and ready to go.

Something wasn't right, Xavier's mind scrambled for possibilities. There was no way Ganim could just stroll down the carpet and grab Waverly. He wouldn't make it past the pit without being detained.

The sound of the explosion had him diving for Waverly. He snatched her off the stage and had her down on the ground under him in less than a second, yanking Kate and Liam's wife down with them. "Get down," he yelled. But his command was lost in the second explosion, this one much closer.

14

Panic filled the carpet as people screamed and ran. The TV cameras panned the chaos as the crowd across the street broke through the barricades to escape the acrid smoke, snarling traffic.

"He's on the carpet!" someone shouted in Xavier's earpiece followed by a fit of coughing. Celebrities, fans, and executives ran and shoved their way down the carpet in a bid to get to the safety of the theatre.

Xavier caught a foot in the back as someone tried to jump over them. He needed to get them up and out or they'd be trampled. Liam crawled down from the stage and grabbed his wife and Kate. Xavier hauled Waverly to her feet and pulled his gun, his gaze scanning the crowd for Ganim's face. "Get them out of here! There might be more bombs," he yelled to Liam.

"I'm not leaving Wave," Kate shouted, trying to come back for Waverly.

"I've got her. Get out, get safe," Xavier assured her. Liam had to drag Kate away, but he got both women through the shrubs behind the camera to the sidewalk.

Simon still stood on his stage, microphone in hand gaping at the scene as hundreds of people tore down the red carpet. His cameraman panned the scene, chewing gum with a mechanical rhythm.

Thick black smoke began to descend on the carpet, intensifying the panic. He could barely see a foot in front of his face. There were people everywhere frantically running for safety. Waverly clutched Xavier's arm and screamed.

Xavier's heart stopped, but his body moved on instinct. He turned, pulling her hard against him and found Ganim just feet away staring at them, a sick smile on his face. The crowd parted around him as if he was a rock in the river and for a second they just stared at each other. His teeth were worn down in a straight line, his cheeks were hollow, and his complexion sallow and pale as if he hadn't seen the sun in years. His brown hair looked like it was rarely washed or combed, and the eerie light in his almost black eyes spoke volumes of obsession and craving.

Xavier made a move forward, but Waverly trembled behind him and dug her fingers into his jacket. Every instinct shouted at him to neutralize the threat, but he couldn't leave Waverly. A woman in a glittering gown sobbed her way past them, blood leaking from a wound on her forehead. Taking a shot was impossible with the pandemonium around them—too many bystanders.

He forced the shivering Waverly behind his back. "Suspect engaged on carpet," he called to his team.

Ganim brought his left hand up and wiggled his fingers in an obscene wave. "Come and get me, asshole," Xavier called. "I dare you."

He spotted Darius closing in from the right, but Ganim must have known his luck was up. Another cloud of smoke drifted between them, and by the time it cleared, Ganim was gone.

"Suspect on the run," Xavier shouted.

He felt Waverly's fingers slip from his jacket. She was being carried away by the crowd that was still surging toward the building. The terror on her face froze in his mind, and he fought his way to her.

"Come on, Angel. Come on, baby," he chanted, pulling her off the carpet and under the scaffolding that bore movie graphics with her face. They made it to the alley before Waverly's legs gave out, and Xavier scooped her up at a dead run. He thanked the gods of planning when he noted the Invictus SUV was still waiting by the side exit.

"Christ, Saint. What the fuck happened?" the driver demanded. Jada was barely five feet tall and built like a fireplug. She was the best damn driver on his staff and Xavier would have kissed her if they had a second to spare.

"Drive!" he shouted, tossing Waverly onto the backseat and sliding in next to her. He kept his gun drawn. Jada had her piece ready, too.

They flew down the alley in the Tahoe at highway speed. Traffic on the street was a tangled mess of chaos, but Jada forced her way through and across into another alley. By the third block, traffic had thinned, and she gunned the V8 heading west.

Xavier knew he didn't have to tell her to run a surveillance detection route. Her gaze scanned from the road to each of the mirrors in a methodical rotation.

"Angel is secure," he told his team. "Darius, you're in charge. Get those people out of that building in case it's rigged."

Xavier finally allowed himself to look at Waverly. The terror on her face had nearly stopped him cold on the carpet, a reaction that could have been deadly. He couldn't let that happen again. Now, she was bent at the waist, her hands over her face.

"Waverly," he said softly. "It's okay, baby. You're safe."

He ran a hand down her back and felt her spine tense like wire. She was trembling.

"Hey, Angel." He leaned down and brought his lips to her ear. "It's all okay."

"P-people got hurt," she stammered through chattering teeth.

"We don't know what happened yet," Xavier told her, stroking her back.

"P-people got hurt because of me. M-my movie. My stalker."

"Hey," his voice was less calming now. "Don't be an idiot. The only person to blame here is Ganim, and he will pay."

She was rocking herself, curled in a ball, and it finally clicked for Xavier. *Panic attack.* He'd battled a handful of them after his second tour of duty in Afghanistan. Given her history as a kid of crowds and chaos, he should have guessed earlier.

He hauled her up and into his lap, tucking her head under his chin. He wrapped his arms around her. "I've got you, Angel. I'm not going to let anything happen to you."

"We're clear," Jada said, cool and composed from the driver seat as if they were out for a quiet Sunday ride. They meandered north while she waited for a destination.

He gave her an address, a place he could be sure was safe and quiet.

"Hang in there, Angel. We're going home."

~

It was the first time in his life that Xavier had ever carried a woman across his threshold. He shoved the front door open with his foot and dropped the key ring that dangled from his finger under Waverly's legs on the table inside the door.

Judging from the shivers that wracked her body, he knew she wouldn't be interested in a tour of his apartment now, so he bypassed the living room and carried her down the hallway to the master.

When he tried to set her down on the bed, one or both of them refused to let go.

Xavier swore under his breath and toed off his shoes. Using his hand that held her legs, he yanked the covers back and sat down against the pillows and headboard, cradling her against him.

He shrugged out of his jacket and pulled the earpiece out. Waverly curled up against his chest, a scared girl in miles of tulle, and he felt her tears leak through his shirt. Xavier tugged the covers up around her and just held on for dear life.

She must have fallen asleep, Waverly realized, as she slowly clawed her way through the darkness to consciousness. And it all came flooding back to her. The explosions, the panic, the press of the frightened crowd. Ganim.

She jerked awake, and strong arms soothed and held her. She was surrounded by Xavier, his warmth, his scent, his touch, and just like that, the fear began to slip away. In its place came a bone-deep embarrassment. He'd seen her in the throes of a panic attack, and who knows how many others had witnessed it, too. Her dark secret was out, and she'd just handed Xavier a weapon to use against her should he ever need one.

"X?" she whispered. The room was dark, and she couldn't tell where they were other than someone's bed.

She felt his lips move against her hair. "Shh, Angel. You're safe."

She sat up again. "Kate? My parents? Liam?"

"Everyone is okay."

"The… bombs?"

"Homemade flash bangs," he said quietly. "Lots of smoke and noise, but no shrapnel. Only minor injuries."

"Oh, thank God," she breathed. "Was it Ganim?"

Xavier pulled her back down against his chest, and she listened to the steady rhythm of his heartbeat.

"Don't think about it right now," he told her.

She resisted the urge to ask more questions for a minute and then two, lulled by his closeness. "Where are we?" she finally asked.

"My place."

"I dropped my quarter," she said mournfully.

"Your good luck charm?" Xavier asked.

He felt her nod against his shoulder. "I lost it on the carpet when the first explosion went off."

"How long have you had it?"

"Since I was five." And Xavier knew then where it had come from. The news stand vendor. The man who had pulled Waverly out of the paparazzi frenzy. He'd given her a shiny quarter to play with to calm her down, and she'd kept it all these years. His heart broke a little more for the five-year-old girl who needed a talisman to protect her.

"I'll be your lucky charm from now on," he told her gruffly.

It got a snicker out of her. "You're not going to fit in my purse."

"I'll get you a bigger purse," he promised. He stroked a hand down her back and when she realized his palm was in contact with bare flesh the entire length of her spine, she yelped. "Xavier, where is my top?"

He cleared his throat and shifted, and it was then that she realized he was hard as stone beneath her. "I tried to untie the corset so you could breathe better, and the whole damn thing came apart."

Waverly tugged the sheet up around her chin.

She could feel him laugh softly. "Relax, Angel. It's pitch black in here. I can't see a damn thing."

"Darkness doesn't mean you can't *feel* things," she said, and to illustrate her point she wiggled higher up his chest, brushing against his erection with her side.

"Behave yourself," he said gruffly. "It's a natural reaction to having a half-naked woman curled up on top of you for an hour."

"An hour? Oh my God, X, everyone must be worried sick!" Waverly tried to pull away and, in the ensuing struggle, lost the sheet. She found herself face down against his chest, her bare breasts pressed against his stomach, and the throb of his hard-on nestled against her abdomen. Xavier's sharp intake of breath told her he felt the friction, too.

She stilled immediately.

"Everyone who needs to knows that you're with me. Kate is the only one who knows that you're here, and she'll be here in an hour with food and clothes and whatever other necessities she deemed appropriate."

"Are you sure everyone's okay?" Waverly asked tentatively, certain he must be hiding some horrible disaster from her.

His phone vibrated on the comforter next to them, but he ignored it.

"Positive. Though we're going to have to give Gwendolyn something to give the media soon. So far, no one's made the connection between Ganim and the explosions, but there are reports that you're missing. On the bright side, the cops are now in a manhunt for Ganim."

Waverly dropped her forehead to his chest. "I can't believe this is happening."

"We'll get him, Angel." His palms skimmed up from the small of her back to her shoulders and down again. It felt so good that she sighed and then felt his thick shaft pulse against her.

"I should probably get up and find some clothes," she breathed. His hands skimmed up and down again, this time his thumbs brushed the lush sides of her breasts. And she finally felt something besides icy fear. Her blood rolled into a low simmer, breath caught in her throat.

Using her knees as leverage, she climbed his chest until the nipple of her right breast brushed against the light layer of chest hair that peeked out from open buttons. She gave a little gasp at the delicious contact. Her lips parted, and she laid them on his neck, just over where his pulse labored in staccato.

"Waverly." Her name was a low warning.

But she was alive, and she wanted to feel like it. She worked the next button in his shirt free and the next until she could feel his chest and chiseled abdomen bare under her palms. She moved her lips from his neck to his jaw, nipping and nibbling. Her nipples dragged over his skin and puckered, igniting a flame.

Xavier swore quietly. His body hummed beneath hers, and when her lips melted over his, she felt the quick lunge at his own wall of control before he pulled himself back.

"Why is your heart beating so fast?" she whispered over his firm, hard lips.

He groaned. "Adrenaline," he whispered back, tasting her with a quick thrust of his tongue.

"Is that why mine is pounding?" She took his palm and laid it over her breast. He squeezed it reflexively, and when she moaned into his mouth, his control snapped like a leash. This time when he lunged, nothing stopped him. He had her on her back splayed across the bed before she could catch her breath.

"You drive me insane," Xavier growled, ravaging her mouth as he roamed her body with his callused hands. When he cupped her breasts with those rough, warm palms, Waverly's hips pistoned off the mattress.

She raced her hands over him, desperate to strip him bare, to have no more layers between them. She shoved his shirt off his shoulders, touching every inch of his muscled torso. He levered up and off of her to help. When her fingers dipped into the waistband of his pants, he dropped his forehead to hers panting.

"We need to slow down, Angel."

But she didn't want slow. She wanted the speed and thrill, like she was on the back of a bike. She undid his belt with trembling fingers and impatiently waited while he took care of the pants. He kicked them off, and she shoved a hand inside the band of his briefs. Finally, she closed her fingers around his shaft. Thick and long, it grew impossibly bigger in her hand as she stroked him once from root to tip. And then again and again.

He gritted out unintelligible words of praise and dug through the layers of her skirt. She knew the exact second that Xavier gave up on finding the clever hidden zipper. The sound of fabric shredding brought a smile to her lips, which turned into a gasp when he lowered to lap at one of her lonely nipples.

She moaned loud and long, and he closed his lips over the nub, drawing it in with long, deep pulls. Every nerve in her body came to life and caught fire. He licked and sucked until the worshipped point strained with need. And when she thought she could take it no longer, he shifted and took the other into his mouth while his fingers massaged and tugged her abandoned breast.

This was what it felt like to be revered, Waverly thought. It wasn't the need from the crowd or the calls on the red carpet. It was Xavier's desire to possess her body.

She arched up against him, begging him with her words and her body. She pleaded for something she knew she might never be ready for.

Impatiently, he skimmed a hand over her stomach until it came to the lacy La Perla barrier that separated him from her. Rather than remove the briefs, he yanked, shredding the air-thin lace and baring her to him.

His fingers skimmed, whisper soft, against her aching center where the slickness betrayed her need. With a deft move, Xavier parted her folds and stroked the sensitive flesh between them. In the darkness, she could just make out his form above her. And when he brought his fingers to his mouth to taste her, something in Waverly broke. She reached between their bodies and gripped him hard in her hand. Moisture that beaded on the broad crown of his cock slicked her hand and dotted her stomach.

His breath came in short, desperate pants.

God, he was made to light a fire inside her. She stroked him with a grip that was so tight it was almost painful. The throbbing between her legs intensified. She felt so empty, the need for Xavier had hollowed her out.

His thumb brushed over her most sensitive spot, the tiny bundle of nerves that ruled her world in the moment, and when she spasmed from the contact, he thrust a long finger deep inside. Waverly cried out in pleasure so intense she thought she might come right then and there.

"God, you're so ready for me, Angel. So ready to take my cock."

His words pushed her beyond reason. Her hips rocked up to meet the thrust of his finger. Then it was two fingers, working her in a slow, rocking rhythm. Xavier lowered his mouth to her breast and thumbed over that sensitive slit once more, catapulting Waverly over the edge. His mouth and fingers moved in a hypnotic rhythm to carry her through the shockwaves of her release.

She heard him whisper in the dark as her blood sang and her body quivered.

"You're so perfect," he said, releasing her nipple to nuzzle her breast.

"Please, Xavier. I need you inside me," she begged, still not nearly finished with the pleasure he was offering.

He shifted over her, his cock probing restlessly between her legs.

"Birth control?" The question came out on a rasp.

"On it. Condom?"

"Drawer...I think. Don't fucking move," Xavier ordered, pulling away from her.

She liked that he wasn't one hundred percent sure if he had condoms on hand. And the crash of the drawer hitting the floor and the swearing told her he was as desperate for her as she was for him. She only prayed that he wouldn't stop and overthink it. It was need, a desperate, hungry need that they both wanted to satisfy.

But he was back on her in a flash, a condom wrapper crinkling in his hand.

She helped him roll it on, slide it over that heavy column of flesh. And the second it was in place, he was shoving her back down to the mattress and ranging himself over her. "Hang on to me, Waverly. Tight."

And then he was groaning in agonized pleasure as he eased into her.

God, he was big. Just past her limits big, and Waverly struggled to accommodate him. She pulled her knees up and the last aching inch slid into her on a cry.

"So fucking tight." His breath came in short gasps, and they were both coated in a sheen of sweat. Waverly was stretched to capacity. He'd taken her up to and beyond her limits, and she was pinned to the bed with the most excruciating fullness she'd ever experienced.

"Am I hurting you, Angel?" Xavier panted.

Waverly shook her head. She could feel his breath on her face.

"I can't see you, baby. Are you saying yes or no?"

"You're not hurting me," she promised.

"Thank fucking God. I don't think I can stop now." To prove it, he pulled out slowly, slowly, slowly and then sank back in on a groan. This time her body accepted all of him, and Waverly sobbed into his shoulder.

She dug her nails into his back and used her hips to urge him on. Faster. A little harder. A little meaner.

Xavier obliged, and she knew when he'd passed the point of control. His lust for her obliterated his need to take care, to protect. He fisted one hand in her hair to hold her in place and slammed inside her. She felt her breasts tremble against his chest with every powerful thrust.

"You. Are. So. Perfect." Every word was emphasized by another plunge into her core, and on every drive, he hit the end of her.

"Xavier!" His name exploded from her. Waverly was too far beyond caring about anything but finding her release. She'd never been dominated like this before, never felt this helpless. She'd given up her own control to him, trusting him to take her where she needed to go. To make her feel something besides terror and guilt. He filled up all the emptiness in her, quieted the fear until there was nothing left but his driving need for climax.

"Come when I tell you," he growled, and Waverly gripped him with her thighs as he rocked into her. "My beautiful, Angel."

Her cry was a sob that caught in her throat. She was overcome with the desire to see where Xavier could take her. She'd never given anyone else free reign over her body before, and Xavier Saint was showing her just what was possible.

He whispered dark promises as he laid her bare with pleasure. "I feel you rippling around my cock, Waverly. It's driving me insane."

"Please, Xavier. Please, please, please," Waverly chanted the words. She could do nothing but hold on as he battered into her, the spike of pleasure so sharp and so high it terrified her.

"Come!" He gritted out the command, and Waverly was shocked when her body did exactly what he told it to do. She erupted around him, and as he hit bottom and held there, his entire body tensed. The groan—guttural, animal—was sinful pleasure to her ears. His orgasm controlled hers, and she shuddered around him as he thrust wildly, emptying himself inside her, using her hungry squeezes to stroke out every drop of release from him.

"Waverly. Waverly. Waverly," he chanted her name like a mantra.

15

They were still tangled around each other, still stroking and petting when a distant knock cut through their haze.

"Fuck," Xavier sat up. "Kate's here."

"Shit. Shit. Shit," Waverly hissed and jumped up. She blindly felt for wall and hit the nightstand instead. "Ouch!"

Xavier flipped the light switch and flooded the room.

They stared at each other, and Waverly clapped a hand over her mouth to stifle the laughter that threatened to erupt.

"What?" he hissed.

Waverly snickered. "You look debauched!" she said, taking in his messy hair, his shoulders riddled with scratches. "If you answer the door like that Kate is going to pass out, and when she wakes up she's going to know exactly what we did."

Xavier frantically grabbed for a pair of sweatpants and yanked them on. "Better?"

She looked pointedly at his half-mast cock that was proudly fighting its way out of its cotton prison.

"Fuck." He pulled on a t-shirt. "I'm not going to get unhard with you standing there naked."

"Where would you like me to go?" Waverly asked accommodatingly. "You shredded the only clothes I had."

He grabbed for her and shoved her and her ruined dress into the master bathroom. He threw a clean t-shirt after her. "Go take a shower, and don't come out until you look like you didn't have sex," he ordered.

But when she took a step toward the shower, he was pulling her back in and kissing her hard. "Talk later," he promised, and then he was hurrying out the door.

Grinning, Waverly shut the bathroom door behind her and took stock of Xavier's bathroom. It reflected the man who owned it. Subtle polish in the granite and the tile, the glassed-in shower. But it was Spartan in its order. Nothing was out of place. She couldn't tell which side of the double vanity he used because both were spotless. A single toothbrush occupied a stainless steel holder halfway between the sinks. It, and a bottle of hand soap, were the only items on the sparkling white countertop.

The only female presence was the one she spotted in the mirror. Her hair was a wild riot that had clearly had a man's hands tangled in it. Her cheeks were flushed and rosy. Her lips were swollen from frenzied kisses. And her eyes? Well, they held the knowing light of what it was like to be worshipped. That's how she felt, as if Xavier had witnessed her at her very worst and only saw the good, the bright, the beautiful.

Faintly, she heard voices coming from the other room. *Kate*. She'd need to get her head on straight before she faced Kate or anyone else for that matter. She ducked into the shower and turned on the faucets, setting the water on the edge of scorching. There was so much to consider. So many things had happened tonight, and she didn't know what a damn one of them meant for her future. But that was for later. For now, she would bask in the steam of the water and the certainty that her body had been used as nature intended, perhaps for the first time ever.

Xavier did his best to control her exposure to the news until Waverly snatched the remote out of his hand and replaced it with a fried chicken breast. "I know you don't want me going all to pieces, X, but this is the best way for me to deal with it," she told him, not taking her eyes from his giant flat screen.

It wasn't just that the coverage of the explosions was riveting. It was that it had pierced the fragile bubble that their lovemaking had created. She was ripped back to a reality full of questions. The drone of the TV provided a barrier that bought her time while her mind frantically shuffled through what ifs and outcomes.

Kate snorted with indignation from her slouch on the floor where she was working her way through a plate of pizza, chicken, and mashed potatoes. "These idiots are doing everything they can to turn this into another New York or Paris," she said, stabbing her plastic fork at the TV.

"Supposition sells, not facts," Waverly sighed, pushing coleslaw around her plate. The relief that no one had suffered serious injuries was tempered by the guilt she felt at bringing this on the event. Her world, along with a sidewalk trashcan and a planter, had blown up. The events of the night were going to have long-reaching effects and not just for her.

A frantic Kate had busted into Xavier's bathroom to see for herself that Waverly was okay. Her friend had been so upset she hadn't mentioned the shredded designer gown and sex-tangled sheets. But Waverly knew it was only a matter of time before Kate's brain processed everything and then the questions would start.

Over a smorgasbord of comfort foods Kate had shared her version of events. Liam had dragged her off the carpet with his wife in tow, and the three of them had dashed down the sidewalk under the scaffolding. They raced four blocks down the street until they found a sports bar where Kate called Ubers for them. She'd gone straight to the Sinners' estate, and Waverly's parents, Gwendolyn, and their security showed up minutes later. Kate dialed frantically until she finally got a text from Xavier that they were safe.

Gwendolyn, in true Media Barbie fashion, had crafted two press releases, one reporting that Waverly was safe and sound, praying for the rest of the attendees and crowd, and another announcing her disappearance. Thankfully, Waverly was present and accounted for and could sign off on the safe and sound release.

Xavier had listened to Kate's version of events, asking careful questions to get a clearer picture. Waverly could see him sorting and adding information to the report running in his head.

Meanwhile, the TV played the video footage from Simon's live coverage of the carpet on a loop. There was the glittery before of smiling faces and beautiful gowns and then there was the after of terror and tears. It took an hour before one of the entertainment news anchors had finally speculated that perhaps the explosions were somehow linked to Waverly Sinner's stalker and the story took off from there. Twenty minutes later the police released photos of Ganim labeled only as "a person of interest."

The news program ran the steady stream of pictures and video clips that came pouring in from those who witnessed the chaotic scene. On the third replay of Xavier tackling Waverly to the ground, Xavier took the remote back.

"Enough," he said when she began to protest.

They shared a moment thick with tension, and she saw it then, the heated gaze, the tightness in his jaw. Xavier was angry. At what she could only guess. Ganim. Her. Himself. The fact that there was a maniac on the loose, and he was holed up in his apartment babysitting her. Waverly wanted to reach out, to touch him. Thank him. But the moment had passed, and his phone was signaling another incoming call.

He took it into the kitchen, and Waverly flopped back against the couch cushion. He'd certainly been there for her tonight. Not only had he saved her life, but he'd also dragged her out of a panic attack. It shamed her to know that he'd seen her at her worst. At her most vulnerable. Xavier hadn't used it against her, hadn't even mentioned it. He hadn't judged her. *Yet.*

Everything had changed tonight. The premiere that was supposed to set her career for the next five years hadn't even happened. The stalker who terrified her had gotten closer than she ever expected. And Xavier. Well, Xavier had happened. She'd given up all her need for control and let him rule her body.

Just thinking about it made her breasts feel heavier, her core hotter. They had succumbed to the growing attraction, and it was going to complicate things whether it was the first or last time.

Xavier had been in touch with his team, with Micah, with the cops, but he still hadn't left her side. She wondered how much of that was duty and how much of it was his heart. The way he held her in the car, the soothing words he'd whispered to her when he cradled her in his own bed. That wasn't an obligation of the job. Xavier Saint had feelings for her.

But having feelings for someone doesn't mean you don't eventually screw them over, she reminded herself. She had far too much personal experience to dismiss that as a possibility.

"So was it really Ganim?" Kate asked, dragging Waverly back to the present.

She nodded, suppressing a shudder at the image of Ganim smiling at her just feet away. That odd, gleeful wave as if to say, "Look how close I can get to you."

"Yeah, it was him. He just stood there, smiling. But he didn't try to come any closer." Waverly frowned. There'd been something odd about the way he came so close and then just stopped. He could have grabbed her in the chaos and tried to drag her off. Wasn't that his end goal? But instead he'd just stood and stared. *Why?*

"Did you get any messages from him on Waverly's social media?" Xavier asked, coming back to the living room and his abandoned plate of food.

"To be honest I didn't think to look. Let me log in," she said digging through the food containers in search of her phone.

"Why don't you use my desktop in the guest room?" Xavier suggested. "It's secure, and you can stow your things in there too since you'll be staying the night."

It wasn't an offer. It was an order. "Thanks for the invite, X Factor," Kate smirked, and then winked at Waverly. She picked up her purple duffle and bounced off down the hallway.

Alone with Waverly, Xavier muttered something about coffee and abandoned her on the couch. Avoidance, she recognized. Well, she was the only one allowed to play that game. He didn't get that luxury. She corralled Xavier in the kitchen, a galley layout outfitted with dark cabinets, sleek appliances, and quartz countertops. He stared out the window while his coffee maker burbled to life.

"Are you mad that you're stuck here with me when you want to be out hunting for Ganim?" she asked.

He turned to face her, leaning against the curved edge of

the counter, arms crossed. He looked sexier than anyone had a right to in sweatpants and a t-shirt.

"Waverly, there is nothing that could tear me away from you right now." He rubbed a hand over the back of his neck, and she could see the tension vibrating off of him. "There is no one else I would trust here with you. It needs to be me."

She took a deep breath and plunged. "Am I just a job?" The words tumbled out of her mouth. She didn't want an answer, not really. Because she already knew, just as she knew it wouldn't change anything.

"You were never just a job." Those brown eyes warmed as they stared into her.

"But?"

"But I have a job to do."

"And?"

He gave her a sexy half smile. "Angel, nothing has changed."

"That's funny," Waverly said with a sad smile. "I feel like everything changed tonight."

After a confirmation that there were no messages from Ganim and then an emergency feel-good viewing of *Dirty Dancing*, Xavier sent both women off to bed, insisting that Waverly take the master. He'd sleep on the couch. It wasn't just chivalry. He wanted to put himself between her and anyone foolish enough to try to get through the door. And, a dark part of him admitted that he wanted her sprawled across his bed, cuddled under his covers and dreaming about him.

Xavier lay on his back, staring up at the dull white ceiling. He fought the pull in his body that wanted him to slide under the covers of his bed and pull Waverly against him. Hold her, stroke her, brand her.

She was digging trenches in his brain, and he worried that this is what it felt like to be obsessed. Was this how Ganim felt? Waverly was *never* out of his mind. It wasn't just keeping her safe, it was the way she looked over her shoulder and smiled at him. How quickly her mind worked when she schemed. The way she took care of her mother, even with all the resentment she felt.

His conversations with her played on a loop in his head every night. He liked talking to her, liked watching her shift from private Waverly to public and back again. He liked knowing that she let him see the real her as she had tonight. She'd been completely vulnerable to him, and he knew how terrifying that was for her. He wouldn't let Waverly down and be yet another disappointment in her life. He cared too much.

When he wasn't near her, he wanted to be. He sought her out with no other reason than to be close to her. He touched her as often as he thought he could get away with without raising eyebrows. Yet none of it was enough until tonight, and now that he'd touched her, tasted her, he knew he'd never be free of her again.

He'd never experienced sex like this before. Never lost and then found himself in a woman. Waverly Sinner had hooks in him and not just because she needed protecting. She was his dream girl and that's what she would stay until... Until when? He couldn't see past the immediate danger. They'd catch Ganim. And then what? Would Waverly seek out her college dreams? Or would she succumb to family pressure and stay the course? Would she still need him?

God, he was living a fantasy, he cringed. *There was no future for them.*

There was a price to pay for the line he'd crossed tonight.

He'd slept with a client. He'd broken the trust, not just between himself and Waverly but with Waverly's parents. Just because they didn't know didn't mean his actions hadn't been wrong. He didn't take his word lightly, yet he'd still broken it just to have her for one night.

He'd broken his own rule, crossed a line that couldn't be uncrossed. And now he had to pay the price. He'd stay close to Waverly, he'd protect her with his life, but he couldn't touch her again. The center of his world slept in his own bed, but he couldn't fill her again and make her sigh out his name in wonder and pleasure. The only thing he could do now was to make sure it never happened again. It wouldn't make up for the mistake, but it would stop a downward spiral that was inevitable if he let himself touch her again.

Xavier didn't know how he was going to handle it. How could he turn these feelings off? He couldn't go five minutes without thinking about her before tonight. It was going to be a thousand times worse now that he'd experienced heaven.

But these weren't the questions to be asking tonight, he reminded himself. There were more pressing matters at hand.

Someone wanted to take her away from him. And even if she couldn't ever really be his, he vowed to keep her safe. He needed her safe, and compromising his instincts with the physical demands of his body wasn't going to save her.

Xavier closed his eyes and willed himself to walk through the events at the premiere. He was missing something. There was something about the way Ganim stood—close, but not close enough. Waving and smiling. There was something there. And he would find it.

MORNING CAME TOO SOON for the residents of Xavier's condo.

Waverly had dragged herself out from under the covers where she'd slept a surprisingly deep, dreamless sleep. Wrapped in Xavier's scent and the memories of their lovemaking, she'd drifted off secure and comfortable. But morning brought its own challenges.

She found Xavier and Kate already up and arguing. Xavier from the kitchen where he was putting on the coffee and Kate from his living room where she poured over social media and news reports on her tablet.

"I can't tell if this is a PR nightmare or a God send," Kate muttered, frowning fiercely at her screen.

"I don't give a flying fuck what it is. We aren't parading her around like a duck decoy to bump up ticket sales," Xavier snarled from the kitchen where cabinets slammed closed.

"I'm not saying use her as bait. I'm saying we can't keep her on lock down here in town. The international leg of the publicity tour starts in eight days. What do we do with her until then?"

"Does 'her' get a say in any of this?" Waverly grumbled.

"Of course, her do," Kate shot back.

"No, her don't," Xavier shot back from the kitchen.

Waverly pulled the sides of her long cardigan together over her shorts and tank top and padded into the kitchen. He was still in the sweats and t-shirt from last night and still sexier than she wanted him to be.

Wordlessly, Xavier handed her a mug of coffee. His gaze traveled from her head to her toes resting very briefly on areas that he'd so recently become familiar with.

She gestured for another mug and took it back to the living room to Kate.

A quick review of trending headlines revealed that the world wanted proof that Waverly was okay and that *The Dedication's* opening night had sold out in theaters across the country. In the light of day, it was confirmed that there had been no serious injuries after the attack, which loosened the guilty fear Waverly had held tight in her chest. In an early morning press conference a block from the theatre, police discussed the improvised explosive devices used in the attack and speculated that the perpetrator used them as a diversion rather than a means of harm.

It didn't make sense to Waverly. Why would Ganim go to that much trouble to get close enough to her without attempting an abduction or some kind of physical harm? Was it because Xavier had been so close? Had his mere presence scared Ganim off?

Xavier entered the living room, his own mug in hand, and leaned over the back of the couch. "We're all going to the office, so everyone needs to shower and pack in case we can't come back here tonight."

Waverly met his gaze. "Expecting trouble?"

"Expecting a logistical nightmare," he clarified. "We're pulling in everyone including your parents, Gwendolyn, Phil, and Detective Hansen's team. And did I mention the FBI is now involved?"

Her parents. *Crap.* It hadn't even occurred to her to call them last night. Had they been worried? Or was her mother thrilled at the prospect of so much publicity? She'd find out soon enough.

Kate took her leave to hit the shower first, and Waverly watched more news coverage. The studio would have been in touch with Phil and Gwendolyn by now. Decisions being made for her left and right. Someday she would call her own shots. She thought of the letter from Stanford, tucked away in her bedroom in the pool house. Maybe sooner rather than later.

Xavier's house phone rang, and he frowned at the readout on the caller ID.

He took the call in the dining area, his voice low. He was already reaching for his cell phone before he disconnected the call. He spoke quietly, his free hand on his hip, his head bowed.

"What is it?" Waverly asked when he hung up.

"There's a delivery for you at the front desk." His tone was chillingly calm.

Waverly sat ramrod straight. "Who knows that I'm here?"

"The three of us and two of my team."

"My mother..."

"She doesn't know where you are. I told her I was taking you to a hotel."

Waverly felt a sad roll of relief.

"What's the delivery?"

"I had one of my team watching the parking lot overnight. She's checking out the package at the front desk." He prowled now, back and forth by the front door, pausing to pull a handgun out from a false bottom in a side table drawer. He tucked it into the waistband of his pants, and together, they waited in silence.

A knock sounded on the front door. One hard rap followed by two short, sharp ones. Xavier checked the peephole and opened the door.

A woman in her mid-thirties wearing nondescript jogging clothes entered. She looked like any busy mom out for some early morning exercise before work, but Waverly saw the canniness in her eyes. Field training of some kind, she speculated.

"They were flowers," the woman started without preamble. "White roses. I left them at the desk in case they'd been tampered with. But I brought this up."

She handed over a generic card. Xavier read it and the line between his eyes deepened.

His gaze returned to her and after a moment's debate, he handed the card to Waverly.

Don't worry, my love. I just wanted to be closer to you last night. We'll be together soon enough.

She shook her head. It wasn't possible. Ganim had found her here. No one knew where she was.

Xavier and his investigator quietly discussed the situation while Waverly's head spun.

Hunted. It's what he wanted her to feel. Trapped. And it was working. Anywhere she went, she would be putting people in danger.

She wanted to disappear, to run. Alone. At least no one else would be exposed to the threats she faced.

But she felt Xavier watching her, felt the weight of his gaze so unbearably intimate as if he knew what she was thinking. He stood between her and the door. Between her and freedom. Between her and danger.

16

He dragged them out of his apartment ten minutes later. A complaining Kate with wet hair and an unshowered Waverly in the clothes she'd slept in piled into the backseat of Xavier's Tahoe. They'd packed quickly and ran a complex surveillance detection route that took them into Glendale and Eagle Rock before heading downtown to Invictus Security offices where traffic was only mildly oppressive at this early hour.

It was housed in one of the glossy high rises that reflected the early morning sun in blinding brilliance. He parked in a reserved spot and was met by a three-man security team that escorted them up to the building's third floor, home of Invictus Security.

"Thought you'd have the penthouse, X-Man," Kate said with disappointment.

"Never house your office higher than the ladders of fire trucks can reach," Xavier lectured her.

The smoked glass doors to the suite opened with a swipe of a badge, and they were ushered inside. They hustled past a long front desk guarded by two staff members who looked more like sentinels than secretaries.

Xavier led them left past rows of cubicles and a handful of offices, all occupied by busy-looking staffers. A woman with a razor sharp bob and exotic eyes rattled away on the phone in what Waverly thought she recognized as Korean. Her office-mate was reviewing traffic camera footage on a monitor the size of a jumbotron.

She saw a sleek, modern kitchen tucked away in the back and a wall of glassed-in conference rooms. Employees in sharp suits held animated discussions with men and women dressed in anything but office attire. Undercovers, she assumed.

The entire operation reflected efficiency and a single-minded intensity, a devotion to the task at hand. She'd known Invictus was at the top of the private security game, but what Waverly hadn't realized was just how top.

Xavier pushed open an office door and ushered Waverly and Kate inside. He spoke quietly to the rest of the entourage and closed the door.

"We're meeting with Hansen and one of the FBI suits in half an hour. Waverly, there's a bathroom with a shower through there." He gestured to a door on the far wall. "My admin, Roz, will be in shortly. She'll get you anything you need." He stopped, considered Kate's mess of wet hair. "I'll see if she can dig up a hairdryer for you so you don't scare the cops off."

Kate stuck her tongue out at him, and Xavier gave her a harried half grin. "I'm going to brief the team. Neither one of you is to leave this room until I come back for you, got it?" The finger he pointed landed squarely on Waverly. "I mean it."

He stared at her for a beat longer and then nudged her

under the chin. "Hey. Chin up, Angel. We'll get this figured out. It's nothing for you to be worried about."

She wasn't sure if the "this" he was referring to was Ganim or what was happening between them.

Xavier left them, closing the door behind him and Kate busied herself setting up her laptop and planners. She pulled out a digital camera from her bag, explaining Waverly's fans would be clamoring for a proof of life shot sooner or later.

Waverly's good night's sleep now forgotten, she felt the exhaustion of despair weigh in on her shoulders. She headed toward the bathroom, hoping a shower and fresh clothes would somehow make it all better.

She returned to the office with clean skin and clothes. She couldn't stomach the thought of donning the pencil skirt and heels Kate had packed for her and instead went with a comfortable pair of black athletic pants with cargo pockets and a long cashmere cardigan over a white tank. She'd used a light hand with her makeup to chase away the paleness caused by worry over her immediate future.

She didn't know where she'd be laying her head tonight, but Waverly was sure it wouldn't be in her own bed. Or Xavier's.

The meetings were an eye-opening experience for Waverly. Xavier introduced her to his partner, Micah Ross, in the hallway outside the conference room.

"Ms. Sinner, it's a pleasure to meet you," Micah beamed, shaking her hand with the enthusiasm of a sports fan meeting his hero.

"Really?" Waverly asked in surprise.

"Do you by chance have a flagpole at your house?"

"Okay, no more talking," Xavier said, shoving Micah into the conference room ahead of them. "Remind me not to explain that to you later," he told Waverly with a grimace.

Detective Hansen and his team had been busy in the last twelve hours. While uniforms and forensics examined every speck of dust on and around the theatre, the detective had techs methodically work their way through surveillance footage in a four-block radius of the blasts. They'd hit pay dirt when they spotted a figure acting inconsistently with the rest of the traffic on the sidewalks on the grainy camera footage of a convenience store.

They'd caught up with him half a block later on an ATM camera and then again after he turned down a side street and got into a ten-year-old sedan matching the one identified by Xavier's team. With a full plate number and some traffic camera luck, they'd been able to track the suspect to a motel in Hawthorne.

Their luck had run out there. By the time they'd sifted through the footage and tracked the car, Ganim was gone. He'd left the car behind in the motel parking lot and the room had once again been wiped clean. They were back to square one.

The FBI agent, who had been on the case a grand total of six hours, was a grumpy looking man close to Xavier's age. Agent Malachi Travers was exactly what Waverly pictured for the quintessential FBI agent. He was overworked, underpaid, and had been with the bureau long enough that the idealistic bloom had worn off of him. He was dressed in the on-the-job law enforcement uniform of a wrinkled button down with rolled up sleeves that he'd already spent too many hours in.

Without preamble, he announced that the FBI had unsealed Ganim's juvie file. It wasn't good news.

"We've got an animal cruelty charge when he was sixteen,"

Travers began, tossing out papers to all those assembled around the table except for Waverly. "Ganim killed the family dog of a neighbor girl who'd turned him down—not very gently—when he awkwardly asked her out."

Waverly saw Xavier's jaw tighten at the news, and she suppressed a shudder. Violence against animals was a common indicator of a serious mental disturbance. Not that building and using explosives was a ringing endorsement as a human being, but it showed a pattern. Waverly realized they weren't just investigating, they were building a case—one that they could prosecute whether she was alive or not.

Hansen, shifted his bony frame in the chair across from Waverly. "Ms. Sinner, I assure you, it's only a matter of time before we find this guy."

Travers agreed that she could rest easy with the resources of the LAPD and FBI behind her. He'd struck at some of LA's most elite citizens last night, and the city wouldn't stand for it. They'd have him in custody in thirty-six hours, Hansen predicted.

As the meeting wrapped up, Xavier and Micah extracted promises from Hansen and Travers to share information as they worked the investigation from both ends.

Yet Waverly felt no safer than she had the night before. Ganim had a plan, of that she was sure. And she felt like every step was bringing him closer and closer to her. There was a possibility that no one could stop him.

The next meeting didn't make her feel any safer. They exited one conference room of law enforcement and entered another full of executives. And it was there that Waverly experienced one of those moments of knife-edge clarity, an almost out of body experience, as a dozen people who earned huge fees for their particular areas of expertise argued about what was best for her.

Exactly when she had become a commodity, she wasn't sure. Waverly had a suspicion it had been at conception. Her mother's pregnancy, she'd learned years later, had served to quiet the infidelity rumors that had begun to surface. But with such undeniable biological proof of her parents' love, the rumors had withered and died.

Now, she sat at a long glass conference table, Xavier on her left arguing a point on safety with Gwendolyn while her parents, Kate, Phil, and a handful of studio execs chimed in with their opinions. Micah and a few of the Invictus team filled out the empty seats.

Everyone had a say but Waverly. And as she took in the scene with an eerie sense of calm, she felt the reality she'd built begin to swallow her whole. Somehow, she'd allowed herself to become this valuable, delicate thing. An asset of great worth yet easily damaged in capricious hands.

And so an army of agents, executives, and security experts rallied to protect her from harm while keeping her on display in her gilded cage.

She took a lull in the debate of her future and excused herself from the room. She needed a break so she didn't break, not in front of all of them. Waverly quietly let herself into Xavier's office and closed the door behind her. She didn't bother turning on the light, just stood in the dimly lit office and wondered how she'd gotten to this point.

The door opened and closed behind her, and she could sense Xavier's presence. He didn't order her back to the conference room. He didn't say anything at all as he pulled her into his arms. She let herself sink into him. Breathing him in, Waverly let the heat that pumped off of his body start to thaw the ice collecting in her veins.

His heart beat slowly, steadily, under her ear, soothing her. There was no danger right here or right now. Just the unknown of the future she needed to face and the reality of the present that she'd allowed to exist.

She felt his lips brush the top of her head before moving to her forehead. Somehow he knew. He sensed that she was just hanging on by her fingernails, ready to rail at the ridiculousness that had become her life. The intimacy of last night had bled into the light of day, and she once again felt bared to Xavier.

But she couldn't lean on him. She couldn't depend on Xavier to protect her from everything, couldn't trust him not to betray her. She needed to start standing on her own two feet and stop expecting everyone else to take up the fight. She would get through this with the help of her army, and once Ganim was behind bars, she would take her life back. And maybe then she would figure out if she and Xavier fit together.

Decision made, Waverly felt fortified. She smoothed the lapels of his jacket under her palms and straightened his tie. And then she'd stepped out of his arms and walked back to the conference room, a new layer of calm protecting her.

She walked into a heated debate.

Sylvia was on her feet shooting a withering screen goddess glare at one of the studio suits. "I understand your point, David," she said, color rising to her cheeks. "But this is my daughter we're discussing. And we're not compromising her safety so you can sell more movie tickets. Parading her around the talk show circuit to discuss her psychotic stalker is just going to bait him into making another move. And I'm *sure* that's not what you want."

It was a glimpse of the mother she'd known and loved. She was still in there somewhere. Waverly offered Sylvia a small smile and received a regal nod in return.

Gwendolyn smoothly assumed control. "I agree with Sylvia here. If anything, we could put more focus on the international tour by keeping Waverly under wraps until the London premiere. The press will be clamoring for a personal statement. I think this—" she paused and glanced in Sylvia's direction, "unfortunate situation could provide a great deal of publicity for the film."

"So what do we do with her for eight days?" one of the suits wanted to know.

SHE WOKE as the jet began its slow descent. Stretching, Waverly craned her neck to catch a glimpse outside the window. Idle Lake, Colorado, spread beneath her, a tiny lake town basking in the late afternoon sun.

There were no high rises, no snarls of traffic, not even an international airport. They were putting down on a skinny municipal strip used mainly by the local flying club.

"You grew up here?" she asked Xavier as she peered out the window.

They were the first words spoken since take off. And in the silence, Waverly had done a lot of thinking.

A plan had been crafted at the offices of Invictus. Xavier had ushered everyone out of the room except for Waverly, Kate, Micah, and Robert and Sylvia. Robert had offered up a last-minute family vacation on the Mediterranean. It would put her closer to her London premiere, and he just happened to know a friend with a yacht. *God, Waverly hoped his friend was a man.*

With one phone call, it was arranged, and Monday, the Sinners would convene on a cozy one-hundred and sixty-foot luxury yacht for six days before Waverly kicked off her six-city international publicity tour for *The Dedication*.

Until then, Waverly needed to get out of L.A., away from

Ganim. She hadn't known where until they got to the airport. Two days in Xavier's hometown at his parents' house. Even Kate, who'd returned to the Sinner estate under guard and packed for Waverly, had no idea where she was.

No one but Xavier and the pilot.

What made Waverly nervous wasn't being out of touch with everyone. If she was being honest, the idea of being incommunicado for two days was incredibly appealing. What did get her pulse jumping and the butterflies fluttering was meeting Xavier's parents. It wasn't like she was meeting a boyfriend's parents for the first time. But it certainly felt like it. She wanted them to like her just as she wanted to see him at home in an environment he was comfortable in.

He leaned forward to look through his seat's small window, and his fingers drummed a beat on his knee. Maybe she wasn't the only one who was nervous?

"This is it," he said finally, a ghost of a smile playing on his lips. She doubted he knew it was there. Though he'd gotten even less sleep than she had in the past twenty-four hours, there was an energy, a lightness about him that she'd never seen before. Right now, he was just a man recognizing home. And she was going to get an up close look at Xavier Saint's personal life.

Waverly knew virtually nothing about Xavier's family. His parents were married, his mother was a professor, and he had two younger sisters. But she'd walked into more enigmatic situations before. After years of being interviewed, Waverly had learned how to get information out of people. She'd get to know them and, through them, Xavier.

They still hadn't talked about what had happened the night before. Her skin heated at just the thought of their love-making. She wasn't sure either of them was ready to face the consequences of last night, and the longer they went without acknowledging it, the longer they could pretend that everything was normal.

As normal as their lives could be, she thought wryly.

She leaned back in her seat and slipped on a pair of oversized sunglasses as the jet touched down on the skinny ribbon of a landing strip.

On one side of the strip, a thick copse of scrubby pine trees spiked toward the blue sky. On the other, the rolling green of mountains dominated the horizon, still white capped even in June.

The plane came to a neat stop, and Idle Lake's population had just increased by two, Waverly thought.

The attendants cleared their exit, and Xavier led the way down the plane's stairs to the tarmac. The Colorado sun warmed her cool skin, and the change of scenery so different from Bel Air distracted her from the nerves collecting in her belly.

A shrill whistle cut through the air, and Waverly spotted a man approaching the plane. He wore neatly pressed charcoal chinos and a button down, sleeves rolled up in deference to the weather. Even from this distance, she could see the family resemblance: the way he moved, that ambling stride of purpose and the grin, though she'd only seen it rarely on his son.

Xavier met him on the asphalt and wrapped the man in a bear hug, slapping him on the back. She couldn't hear their exchange, but their laughter carried.

Had she and her mother ever been that happy to see each other? Had they ever exchanged such an easy and bright greeting?

Both men turned as she approached, and Xavier held out his hand to her. She took it without thinking and let him pull her into his family fold. "Waverly, I'd like you to meet my father, Emmett. Dad, this is Waverly, your house guest for the weekend."

Waverly smiled and offered her hand to the man. "Thank you for letting me invade your home, Mr. Saint."

"Please, call me Emmett," he said, engulfing her hand in his. "And I should be thanking you for putting my son on a plane to see us."

She waited for the inevitable awkwardness that usually arrived hand in hand with an introduction, that flicker of recognition and the ensuing judgments that followed. But there was nothing but easy friendliness in Emmett's eyes.

Xavier certainly came by his looks honestly, Waverly decided. Emmett's hair was a shade or two darker and flecked with silver. It took to curl on top, and Waverly wondered if Xavier's would do the same if it were longer.

Emmett's eyes were a gray blue and crinkled at the sides when he smiled. And that smile, just slightly off-center, reminded her so much of his son.

Their bags were loaded into a tidy late model crossover, and Emmett slid behind the wheel. Waverly grinned when Xavier made a move to slide into the backseat next to her. "I think I'll be fine back here by myself, X."

"Old habits," he said with a wink and took the passenger seat. Emmett navigated through the cozy mountain town calling out landmarks of interest to Waverly. The high school where Xavier had captained the cross-country team. The community pool where Xavier had lifeguarded for two summers and where he'd saved little Alex Lewis. And did Xavier know that Alex was a sophomore in high school now and just passed his lifeguarding exam?

When Emmett pointed out the park where Xavier had gotten caught necking with a girlfriend in high school, his son drew the line.

"Dad."

"Uh-oh, Emmett. He's using the 'you're-in-trouble' voice on you," Waverly teased from the backseat.

"I see you're familiar with my son's bossy tone. He gets it from his mother." Emmett winked at her in the rearview mirror.

The Saint men bantered back and forth through the downtown, where Emmett had someone to wave to on every block. Idle Lake had all the feel of a frontier gold mining town with its cluster of painted wooden storefronts and boardwalk-style sidewalks. Down cross streets, Waverly caught glimpses of the glittering lake water that beckoned residents on a lazy summer afternoon.

The storefronts ended, and miles of sidewalk began. Houses styled after log cabins dotted the streets on spacious lots. Every home had a view of the mountains that loomed over the town, and every neighborhood was prettier than the next, and then they were turning onto a paved driveway.

She wasn't sure where she'd pictured broody, perfect Xavier growing up, but it wasn't here in the stucco and stone home with its copper and cedar shake accents. It wasn't grandiose like the neighborhoods Waverly had grown up in. But it had charm from its traditional architecture blending perfectly into the wooded lot. An emerald green lawn rolled out from the front porch to the sidewalk and street.

No need for security gates and walls here.

The house said family, tradition, foundation.

They would know their neighbors here, Waverly thought. *Kids would play together moving from backyard to backyard while parents enjoyed a drink and the sunset from the deck.*

Emmett eased up to the detached two-car garage in the same stucco and stone as the house. "We're home," he announced, shutting off the engine.

Waverly saw the curve of Xavier's smile as he peered through the windshield at the house. Xavier Saint was home.

They piled out of the car and followed Emmett toward a side entrance facing the garage when a giant gray furball shoved its way through the screen door.

"Hamilton!" The delight in Xavier's voice tickled something deep in Waverly's chest.

The dog lumbered its great bulk down the three short steps to the walkway and romped into Xavier's waiting arms. When he dropped to his knees to give the dog's fur an appropriate ruffle, Hamilton jumped his meaty paws to Xavier's shoulder and licked the sunglasses off his face.

Xavier laughed.

Waverly shook her head. "I've spent nearly every waking hour with this man in the past few weeks, and I've never seen him this happy."

"A boy and his dog," Emmett laughed. "No love story can top it."

They watched the love fest unfold as Xavier and Hamilton tumbled over in the grass.

"Come on," Emmett said. "We'll let them get reacquainted, and I'll introduce you to Xavier's mother. She can tell you several embarrassing stories about him before he notices we're gone."

Waverly laughed and trailed Emmett up the steps and through the screen door. They entered a large kitchen crowded with cabinets, a butcher block island on wheels, a huge oak table with mismatched chairs that seemed to be doubling as a desk, and floor-to-ceiling bookcases.

Pots bubbled and steamed on the gas range. Bowls and other cooking accessories littered the worn wooden counters. Jars of spices and the remains of a rainbow of ingredients clustered around the range and sink.

In the midst of it all, a tall, narrow-framed woman swore a blue streak at whatever was cooking in the oven.

Emmett had to cup his hands and shout to get her attention.

"Carol!"

The woman jumped and yanked the ear buds out of her ears. Even from across the kitchen, Waverly could hear a soaring aria.

"Jesus H. Christ, Em! You scared the shit out of me." Carol shoved a hand through the sweep of sandy blonde hair going silver. Her brown eyes, Xavier's brown eyes, held none of the reproof of her tone. Her gaze traveled over Emmett and landed on Waverly.

"Oh." Her eyes widened, and in them, Waverly saw recognition and realization. "Oh!"

"Hi," Waverly waved awkwardly.

Carol wore an apron decorated with cardinals and sprigs of holly over holey, low-slung jeans, and a University of Colorado t-shirt. And a murderous expression on her face.

"I'm going to kill him," she announced, slamming down a spoon and advancing on Waverly. "Emmett, where is our son?"

"Out rolling around on the lawn with the dog." Emmett didn't look at all perturbed by his wife's anger.

Carol came to an abrupt stop in front of Waverly, who resisted the urge to take a step back.

"'I'm bringing a guest,' he says. 'She's a client,' he says. But do the words 'Waverly Sinner the actress' cross his tight lips?" Carol ranted.

"I'm guessing they did not?" Waverly ventured.

Carol rolled her eyes heavenward and surprised Waverly with a hard hug. "Welcome to our home that I would have redecorated from basement to attic if I had known you were our guest. You're welcome to stay even after I kill my son."

Waverly gave a relieved laugh. "Thank you, Dr. Saint. I appreciate your hospitality. You have a lovely home."

"Call me Carol."

"See? Bossy tone," Emmett said, elbowing Waverly. "Dear, uh, how do we know Waverly?"

Carol rolled her eyes again. "You'll have to forgive my uneducated husband, Waverly. He hasn't been to the movies since the late nineties."

"Ah, yes. I believe it was *Titanic*," Emmett said thoughtfully. He brightened. "Are you in movies?"

Waverly nodded in amusement. It was refreshing to meet someone who didn't know, nor particularly care, that she was an actor. "A few."

"I'll educate you later on Waverly's body of work, but first, before my soon-to-be deceased son comes in, please tell me that you're dating Xavier and not 'just a client' as he made sure to mention eight times on the phone."

"Stop pumping Waverly, Mom," Xavier said from behind her. The screen door thumped closed. His suit had sprouted a thick coating of grass and dog hair, and his tie had been dislodged. The grin on his face told Waverly that he was confident he could coax his mother out of her anger.

Hamilton, a similar grin on his furry face, abandoned Xavier's side and shoved his nose into Waverly's crotch in greeting. She ruffled his ears and guided his nose to less personal areas. He bounded away from her under the table and returned, nudging a worn hamburger toy into her hand. The cloth was hard, suggesting many hours of dog slobber exposure.

Waverly took the burger and tossed it toward the refrigerator and Hamilton lunged after it.

"Well, I know how Waverly will be spending her weekend

now," Emmett sighed, as Hamilton romped back with the burger.

Carol gave the dog an absent-minded pat as he barreled past her to get to Waverly.

"I am not happy with you," she said, jabbing an unpolished finger in Xavier's direction.

He caught her wrist easily and reeled her in for a hug. "If I told you who I was bringing, you would have had the house torn apart and refitted for royalty, which Waverly wouldn't have wanted." He winked over his mother's head at her. "Is that pot roast I smell?"

"Yes," Carol said extricating herself from her son's hug. "And you can watch the rest of us eat it." She wasn't quick to forgive, and Waverly could respect that.

A horn sounded three short bursts from the driveway, and Hamilton, burger in mouth, skidded for the door.

"The girls are back," Carol said. She gave Xavier a sharp tap on the cheek. "You thought my reaction would be bad? I can only imagine what Chelsea and Maddy will do."

"That's why I told them already," Xavier grinned that heart-breaker smile.

At Carol's gasp of indignation, he laughed. "Mom, I didn't tell you because I didn't want you to go psychotic on the hospitality. I told them so they wouldn't completely humiliate the rest of us by asking what co-star is the best kisser or squealing like a twelve-year-old."

Just such a sound tore through the kitchen, and the screen door slammed shut behind the two women who had entered. Hamilton plowed under the table, bumping chairs out of his way.

Xavier swore and put himself between Waverly and the new arrivals.

"I told you she was coming!" he protested.

Both girls strained to see around his broad shoulders. Once again, the family resemblance was unmistakable. They had their mother's nose and cheekbones, their father's coloring, and Xavier's mouth. The one Waverly judged to be slightly older wore slim gray pants and a navy silk blouse. The younger one rocked denim cutoffs and a faded Idle Lake High t-shirt that had seen more than a hundred washings.

"Yeah, but now we're actually seeing her," the younger of the two said, bouncing on her toes. Her ponytail sprang over her shoulder. "Oh my God. Waverly Sinner is in my kitchen!"

"You make one move toward that cell phone, and I will put you in the oven with the pot roast," Xavier threatened.

His sisters were obviously immune to Xavier's threats. Ponytail rolled her eyes in an exact replica of their mother. "Relax, big brother."

"No pictures," Navy Silk said gruffly in a spot-on imitation of her big brother.

"No Tweeting," Ponytail added in the same.

"No Facebook, no SnapChat, don't tell Mom..." they continued to tick off Xavier's commands one by one, and Waverly snickered.

"I'm disowning you all," Carol said and stormed back to the stove. "Waverly and Em and I will enjoy this delicious dinner, and the rest of you can scrounge for scraps with Hamilton."

At the word "scraps" the dog thrust his head between two dining chairs and barreled over to Carol. "I was making a point, buddy, not offering a meal," Carol told him. The dog slunk back to Waverly and gave her a devastated look.

"Come on, Zav," one of the sister's begged. "You can't keep her from us the whole weekend.

"Fine," Xavier relented. But before they could rush her, he grabbed both in a headlock and spun around to face Waverly.

"Waverly, these mutants are my sisters, Chelsea and Madeline, who have promised to behave themselves or they'll be banned from the house this weekend. Mutants, this is Waverly. Don't bother her."

He released them and looked as though he immediately regretted his decision when they rushed her for hugs. "Oh, for Christ's sake!"

"Shut up, Zav," Madeline squealed. "We're hugging famous!"

17

They settled her into Chelsea's old room, a bright upstairs bedroom with a Jack and Jill bath and a view of the lake that butted up against the property's backyard. The walls were a mossy green, the furniture decidedly feminine, and the bed soft. Carol had offered her the master, but Waverly had politely and firmly declined. Twice.

Waverly stashed her suitcase in a corner near the closet and took a few minutes to freshen up in the bathroom to erase the travel weariness. As she changed into a long, flowy skirt and simple black tank for dinner, she could hear the sounds of family rise up from the first floor. Raised voices, excited chatter, and quick bursts of laughter.

Xavier's room was next door to her own, and when she saw the door open, she paused. He had changed, too, she noted. He lay on top of the handmade quilt on his double bed in casual khaki shorts and a t-shirt. His feet were bare, hands tucked under his head as he stared up at the lazily circling ceiling fan.

Hamilton was flopped over on his back next to Xavier on the bed, his tongue lolling happily out the side of his mouth.

"I've never seen you this relaxed," Waverly said from the doorway.

He didn't spring to attention as she'd have expected. Instead, Xavier rolled his head to the side and beckoned her in. He patted the mattress, and she sat to face him as he propped himself up on an elbow. Hamilton grumbled at the intrusion.

"Sorry about my family," Xavier said, his tone low.

"Relax, X. If anyone needs to apologize for their family, it's me. I like yours. They're...real."

"Real crazy."

Waverly smiled. "They're nice. Normal."

"Give it until this time tomorrow, and you'll be begging me to call the jet," he teased.

"It's nice seeing you so happy," she said, changing the subject.

"I'm taking five before I connect with Micah and Hansen and the rest of the team. And I need your help."

Waverly couldn't remember the last time anyone had asked her for help. "Name it."

"You're going to regret offering," he said, with a devilish grin.

"What do you need?"

"We've got about half an hour before dinner. I need you to keep my family distracted so I can get caught up. Mom will microwave my phone if she thinks I'm running the business instead of spending quality time with the family."

"On it," Waverly said, springing up from the mattress. "Close your door and run the water in the shower. I'll see you in thirty."

"Devious mind." He reached out and caught her hand before she could escape. "We're going to have to talk about last night soon, Angel," he warned her.

Talking would only ruin it, she thought. "Let's focus on tonight for now," she said, giving his hand a squeeze and escaping through the bedroom door.

VERY LITTLE HAD CHANGED in the Saint household since Xavier had left for the military. Maybe there were more knickknacks on the endless bookshelves, definitely more books, and the furniture in the family room had been replaced, but the bones of the house and the dynamic of family were the same.

The four upstairs bedrooms still housed the same furniture they had for the better part of two decades. Downstairs, his mother's study was a crowded, chaotic mess of books and papers whose piles never got smaller. His parents' master suite add-on was on the other side of the study, accessed through the family room. They'd built it for sanity when Xavier and his sisters were all in the throes of their teenage years.

The dining room across the foyer was still crowned with the flea market-find chandelier that only worked sometimes. The table was set for dinner, he noted as he headed to the back of the house for the kitchen. There would be no casual family dinners around the kitchen table or the coffee table in the family room while Waverly Sinner was a guest.

He hoped he hadn't made a mistake bringing her home.

The news Micah had given him had added a new, disturbing layer to the darkness that surrounded Ganim, and Xavier prayed his instincts were right about coming to Idle Lake. The man was devious and mobile, but he didn't have the deep pockets to be chartering planes to follow Waverly from state to state or country to country.

He didn't need to put anyone else that he cared about in

the line of fire where Ganim was concerned, especially not his own family.

He did care. About Waverly. If he hadn't, last night wouldn't have happened. He'd never been a one-night stand kind of man. Not the son of Carol Saint.

The flashes of Waverly under him in the dark had him pausing in the hallway to will away the erection that threatened to embarrass him. He'd been out of his mind to give in to those desires. And now craving her again, especially knowing what waited for him with that lithe, responsive body of hers, would keep him out of his mind unless he could find a way to shut it down.

She needed his protection, not his devotion. He would toe the line until Ganim was behind bars or wiped off the planet. And then... And then what? Could there ever possibly be a relationship between them? He with his growing business, she with her thriving career—would there ever be a middle ground to start a life together?

It was a question for another day. Now, he needed to keep his head clear and thwart a new kind of threat: his mother and her uncanny suspicions that his relationship with Waverly wasn't one-hundred percent professional. If she had the slightest hint of how much he really cared for Waverly, she'd be like Hamilton with his hamburger. Relentless.

Erection under control, he followed the laughter back to the kitchen.

"I knew it," Chelsea said triumphantly. "Dante Wrede just *looks* like he'd be an incredible kisser."

"He's certainly one of the better ones," Waverly agreed.

Madeline swooned against the counter. "What about Liam MacGill? He's just too pretty to look at."

Emmett looked on from the island with interest while

Carol danced around the crowd in the kitchen putting the finishing touches on their meal.

Xavier did not like where this conversation was going. On set or not, Waverly kissing any other man did not sit well with him.

"Guys, I told you to make Waverly feel welcome, not interrogated." He stuffed his hands in his pockets to keep himself from putting them on Waverly's shoulders like he wanted to do. "Why don't you tell her a little bit about yourselves so she doesn't think you're completely insane?"

His mother shot him a knowing look with the arch of an eyebrow.

"Already done," Madeline announced, giving the floor to Waverly with a dramatic wave of her upturned hand.

Waverly cleared her throat and began her recitation. "Chelsea is the middle child, and, as such, is often overlooked in favor of the prodigal son who can do no wrong."

"Until he starts lying to his mother about weekend houseguests," Carol reminded them. "Chels, you and Mad can battle it out for favorite tonight."

Chelsea whooped in approval.

"Chelsea is twenty-five and works for a large information technology company as a network security administrator. She lives in Boulder and is dating—"

"You can skip that part," Chelsea said, jumping in with a pointed look at Xavier.

"Who are you dating?" Xavier demanded.

"Madeline, or Mad, is twenty-one and finishing up a degree in environmental design at University of Colorado Boulder. She plays volleyball and plans to hike the Pacific Crest Trail from Oregon to Washington after graduation."

"You want to do what?" Xavier asked, incensed. His baby

sister hiking alone through the wilderness was giving him heartburn.

"I need less testosterone in this room," Carol said. "You two with the penises, get out."

Emmett pulled two beers out of the fridge and jerked his head toward the deck. Xavier followed him.

"Dinner in ten," Carol called after them.

Xavier accepted the beer his father handed over and they stood shoulder-to-shoulder facing the lake and trees. He marveled at his ability to relax here. Waverly was in the kitchen unsupervised—because his mother and sisters were no kind of supervision—and he was enjoying a cold beer with his father and not wearing a gun.

He wondered if it was his instincts that told him everyone was safe here or an ignorance based on the false sense of security home bred. Whatever it was, he knew with a mystic certainty that Ganim would never touch this place or anyone in it.

"So how much trouble is she in?" Emmett asked finally.

Xavier wondered when the excitement of celebrity would give way to making the connection to current events. "A good bit." *A good bit more than even he had realized.*

"I Googled her," his father said, looking out through the trees toward the lake. "A lot of results in the last twenty-four hours. A lot of results that mention you. Your mother is going to go ballistic when she sees the footage from last night."

Xavier grimaced. "I'm surprised the girls haven't shown it to her yet."

"I don't know if they've seen it. Chels picked Mad up on campus from a camping trip on her way in, and Chels was in the office until early morning today, thwarting some cyber-attack on their server."

"I don't know why she won't come work for me," Xavier sighed.

His father laughed. "Don't you? Does Chels seem like the type to enjoy being the boss's sister?"

"I'd treat her fairly," Xavier protested.

"You'd protect her. It's what you do. Why do you think they haven't told you about any of their boyfriends in the last year?"

"I thought they weren't dating!" Visions of boyfriends not vetted by him taunted Xavier.

Emmett clapped him on the shoulder. "Son, sometimes our women don't want to be protected. They want to be supported when they go out and kick ass on their own."

Xavier sighed. "You're a wise man, Dad."

Emmett raised his beer. "Your mother is responsible for that."

Dinner was a loud, casual affair. Pot roast, mashed potatoes, carrots and peas, and homemade apple pie for dessert were doled out around the table as everyone talked and argued over each other. The easy affection Xavier and his sisters shared made Waverly wonder what it would have been like to grow up with siblings.

And then there were the stories. Waverly was treated to volumes of Saint history, the more embarrassing the better. There was the time Emmett was late for work—he ran a civil engineering firm—and forgot to put the garage door up before driving through it. One Easter Eve, Carol had hidden three-dozen hardboiled eggs in the yard after hosting a particularly thirsty wine club. Only twenty-two eggs had been found, the rest rotted in the yard for the better part of the spring, making the entire neighborhood smell of sulfur on breezy days.

And there were stories about Xavier. Waverly's personal favorite was when Xavier overheard Chelsea's new boyfriend bragging about his less than respectful weekend "plans" in the locker room. It had taken the gym teacher and football coach to unwedge him from the locker Xavier had stuffed him into.

Family came easily to them. Affection, love, and a fierce acceptance of each member in its fold.

It hit her like an arrow to the heart. This is what she'd wanted growing up. This is what she'd want for a family of her own someday.

After dinner came clean up, in which everyone except Carol participated. Carol took her glass of wine and sat at the island directing. Once the dishwasher was loaded and running and every surface was spotless, one of the girls produced a Blu-ray of *Dark Waters*, Waverly's thriller with Dante Wrede.

"No. Absolutely not," Xavier said, drawing the line.

"Come on! Please!" Madeline begged. "This is one of my all-time favorite movies, and Waverly is here! It'll be like having backstage access."

"A lot of actors don't like to watch themselves on screen," Xavier argued.

"Do you mind watching yourself?" Madeline asked, her big brown eyes pleaded with Waverly.

"I've done it before," Waverly said diplomatically. It was impossible for her to enjoy watching a movie she'd been in. There was no way to suspend disbelief after you spent two months on set dealing with thousands and thousands of takes, hours of make-up, shoots that ran right up to dawn, and the inevitable personality conflicts whether it be with a co-star, crew, or studio rep.

"See!" Madeline crowed in triumph. "Waverly, will you watch this with us, pleeease?" Chelsea poked her head over Madeline's shoulder and they both stuck their bottom lips out.

"Oh, for God's sake. Haven't you outgrown that yet?" Xavier grumbled.

"Why would we?" Madeline wanted to know. "It still works."

"Don't fall for their shit, Waverly," Xavier warned.

"What's this movie about?" Emmett wanted to know. Madeline handed it over without breaking her pouty face. Her father pulled out a pair of reading glasses and perused the back of the case.

"Don't be such a Grumpy Gus, Zav," Chelsea mocked.

Xavier playfully shoved her in the shoulder. In seconds it was a free for all with Xavier's sisters jumping him in a coordinated attack. Chelsea went for the shoulders, and Madeline swept his legs. Xavier put up a good fight but ended up going down and shoving the rolling island a good foot in the opposite direction.

Emmett stepped out of the way of the fray still reading. Carol looked on over the rim of her wine glass. "Children, please," she said half-heartedly.

They rolled, a tangle of arms and legs, into Waverly, and she went down on top of the pile. Xavier finally clawed his way off the bottom and pinned all three of them beneath him by laying across them.

"Say 'Xavier is the greatest,'" he ordered. "Ouch! Stop biting, Mad."

"Girls, what is Waverly going to think about our family?" Emmett sighed.

"That we're awesome?" Chelsea wheezed. "Oh my God, get your fat ass off of me, Zav!"

"Say it."

He added tickling fingers where he could reach and had all three of them shrieking the words.

"Xavier Saint, get off your sisters and your client," Carol ordered. "Do you see why I never go anywhere public with you idiots?"

"Ah, Mom, you love us, and you know it," Chelsea said, pulling Madeline to her feet.

"Movie time?" Madeline danced from foot to foot.

Xavier slid his hands under Waverly's arms and pulled her to her feet, checking her for damage. "Let's watch a movie," Waverly sighed.

They'd crowded into the family room, pausing for popcorn breaks and what felt like a hundred questions, but Waverly enjoyed it. She'd curled into the corner of the sofa, Xavier next to her and told the Saints everything they wanted to know about the making of the movie. The stunt double that showed up drunk so Waverly performed the jump off the building before the producers figured it out and freaked. The way the director, a charmingly brusque man who knew what he wanted and couldn't understand why actors just couldn't deliver it without having their hands held, told her they couldn't break for lunch until she stopped screwing up a scene. "Just do it better!" Waverly mimicked his bellow and had the Saints rolling with laughter.

And she took pleasure from the fact that Xavier had to cover his eyes during the big kiss scene. While his sisters cooed at the impossible romance of it all, he'd leaned in and whispered in her ear. "I really hate that guy."

The rest of the family was much more vocal about their approval, and Waverly felt oddly proud. She'd spent so much time over the past few years thinking what she did for a living was silly, it was nice to be reminded that people really did care about her work.

That night, she lay between crisp sheets while crickets sang outside her open window and wondered if the Saints knew how lucky they were. She fell asleep thinking about Xavier: his heat, his heart, wondering if she would ever find what he already had.

18

The next morning, Waverly woke with the sunrise as it peeked through the room's bay window. She lay and listened to the comfortable silence of the house. With the exception of Xavier, the rest of the family were late sleepers, and she realized that for the first time in what felt like an eternity she could be alone and not just by shutting herself in a room.

She tip-toed out of bed and pulled on gym shorts and a t-shirt. She plucked the still unopened Stanford letter from her bag and stuffed it in the waistband of her shorts. Quiet as a mouse, she eased open the bedroom door and tip-toed into the hallway. The silence of the house enveloped her like an old friend.

She paused outside Xavier's door and, hearing nothing, padded downstairs. She started a pot of coffee and snagged a crackle glazed mug of cobalt blue from the glass doored cabinet.

Through the sink window and beyond the trees, the lake waters sparkled and shimmered, beckoning. She took her coffee and her letter and let herself out the back door. The grass gave way to a forest floor, and she followed a meandering path worn by two decades of family sojourns to and from the lakefront.

A stack of kayaks rested upside down, ready for a day of fun. The lake waters lapped quietly at the rocky shore. A dock jutted out over the water, and two dull red Adirondack chairs faced the waters. She carried her coffee down the dock, feeling the worn wood beneath her bare feet. How many times had Xavier sprinted down this dock to jump off the end? How many fish had been caught here? How many bonfires were lit in the ring on the pebbled shore?

This place would endure with its foundation of memories and stories to be built on for generations to come. The sun, pink and gold, peeked over the far shore's trees. A new beginning for a new day. It was as good a place as any for Waverly to find out if she too had earned a new beginning.

She settled onto one of the chairs and took a deep breath.

The letter felt heavy with importance in her hands. She'd wanted things before. Parts, mostly. Movies that she just knew were meant to be hers. But this was different. She'd been born into that world. This was a choice she could make for herself. A path to a future that *she* chose.

She tore open the envelope, shook out the papers inside, and, holding her breath, read the first line. She was out of her chair on a triumphant cry. Stanford University was willing to take a chance on the movie-set schooled Waverly Sinner.

The letter fisted in her hand, she twirled, arms stretched overhead.

"Someone had too much coffee."

The dry comment came from behind her. Xavier, dressed only in a pair of gym shorts and holding a mug of the coffee she'd made, watched her from the opposite end of the dock.

Embarrassed, Waverly shoved the letter behind her back.

Xavier ambled down to her. The only escape, which she always took to noting when Xavier was near, was the black as midnight lake water.

"I didn't run away," she said, automatically on the defensive. "I just came outside to be alone for a whole thirty seconds of my life, so don't even start with me."

Xavier sipped his coffee and said nothing. Stubble covered his jaw, and his perfect pecs drew her eyes despite her best efforts. Xavier Saint was an Adonis by anyone's standards, and it wasn't fair, trying to focus when he stood there looking like every woman's fantasy.

"You got in, I take it?" he asked finally.

"How the hell did you—?"

"Angel. There is nothing that happens to you that I don't know about. I knew you were looking at college. I saw that letter from Stanford that you've been carrying around with you. Add the fact that I'm not an idiot, and there you go."

He took another sip. He was cocky, confident, and she wondered why she found that so attractive. *She was just dazzled by his bare torso, that was it*, she decided.

"Don't let me ruin your celebration. I believe you were squealing and prancing around?"

"There was no prancing," Waverly insisted. "It was a very dignified celebration."

"One worthy of a Stanford student," Xavier teased.

Her lips curved and a smile bloomed. "Oh, what the hell?" She threw her arms around his neck and landed a loud, smacking kiss on his cheek. "I'm going to Stanford!" she announced to the birds, the lake, and the morning sun.

Xavier held his coffee at arm's length so it didn't slosh on them and laughed. "Congratulations, Angel. What are you going to study?"

Waverly pulled back and frowned. "I have no idea."

"You'll figure it out," he predicted. "Come on. Let's go back and make breakfast and wake everyone up. They hate getting up early."

As they walked back together, Xavier slung his arm over her shoulder and brushed his lips against the top of her head.

XAVIER FOUND himself not saying a lot of things.

He wanted Waverly there, in his family's home at their table laughing over eggs and bacon and pancakes. He wanted her making plans with his sisters for a lazy afternoon on the lake and sharing secret Hollywood recipes with his mother.

He didn't want this to be her last visit. But there was no one to confess to. This was the mess he'd created and the one he was tasked with cleaning up. But cleaning it up was getting less and less appealing.

He was getting by on less and less sleep these days given her proximity. He checked on her a few times a night. Just sticking his head in her room, making sure she was safe, comfortable. But every time it was harder than the last to close that door and go back to his own empty bed. A part of him hoped that she'd be awake, that she'd say his name and hold out her hand to him. How could he say no to that?

He wanted things he couldn't have.

She was a client. She was only twenty. They came from different worlds, and their personal aspirations were not relationship material. He had a business to build. And Waverly? Waverly needed time to find herself, finally, without the interference of family or a lover.

So he stayed silent, as he had when she'd talked about Stanford.

Xavier hadn't wanted to bring up security concerns of

what college life would mean for her plans. Just as he hadn't wanted to tell her what he'd learned about Ganim yesterday, not while she was enjoying herself like this with the people he loved the most in the world. He didn't want her to associate his family home with learning that the man obsessed with her was already a murderer.

If Les Ganim were still out there in the world by the end of summer, there was no way Waverly was going to college.

19

After a casual lake weekend with The Saints, Xavier felt a bout of culture shock coming on when he boarded the yacht Robert had borrowed for their last-minute cruise.

The azure waters of the Aegean Sea shimmered beneath the white hull, all one hundred and sixty feet of her. Waverly accepted the hand of a steward, who introduced himself as Leonidas, and climbed off the tender onto the lower deck of the yacht. Xavier followed. The deck, a glossy teak, climbed twin staircases and continued around both the starboard and port sides of the boat on the main level.

There was yet another level above that. Each with a wraparound deck and dark reflective windows promising no paparazzi lens could penetrate the privacy of the interior.

"Think this would fit on the lake at home?" Xavier quipped, peering up behind his aviators.

"Just a nice, quiet family vacation," Waverly sighed.

"Your parents don't do anything small."

While a second steward unloaded their bags from the tender, Leonidas led them up the port stairs to the main deck.

They walked aft almost the entire length of the yacht, passing a covered outdoor deck scattered with loungers. A large sofa in marine-grade white fabric faced a large teak table and chairs that sat just outside a wall of retractable glass doors. They entered what Xavier assumed was the main salon. A grand space for grand people was the only way he could describe it. Two seating areas were organized on opposite sides of the room. For casual conversations, there was a gigantic sectional sofa, again in white, and an uncomfortable-looking divan. Glass-doored bookcases that would make a librarian weep housed important tomes as well as trashy paperbacks and stacks of fresh, glossy magazines.

On the opposite side of the space was a bar with backlit shelves filled with every high-end liquor known to man. Here dark leather club chairs and a low, white sofa were clustered around an ornate coffee table. The rugs, antique Persian, offered a soft wash of color in navy and gold.

Beyond the living space was the salon's dining area with service for twelve with tufted leather scroll back chairs around a glossy walnut table that mimicked the inlay of the room's ceiling. Wide windows ran the length of the salon. Unshaded, they invited the Greek sun inside.

"Holy crap," Waverly whispered.

"Be cool, Sinner. You're used to this kind of insanity, remember?" Xavier teased.

Leonidas led the way down an interior stairway. "Ms. Sinner, you are in here," he said in his thick accent. He opened a stateroom door for her. "Mr. Saint, you are across the hall here. Mr. and Mrs. Sinner are awaiting you aft on the upper deck."

Waverly thanked him and ducked through her door.

Xavier ignored his room and followed Waverly into hers. It was spacious for boat living. The queen-sized bed buried under ivory linens had a curved, padded headboard that reached the ceiling. A long window offered a sea level view over the built-in dresser. The floor was some kind of zebra-wood. An attached bath was accessed through a door next to the bed. Two built-in wardrobes and another dresser framed a flat screen TV on the wall opposite the bed and a silk upholstered couch took up most of the space on the interior wall.

"Didn't security already sweep the yacht, X?" Waverly reminded him.

Twice actually. The *Sea Goddess* had been swept for stowaways, listening devices, and explosives. Each crew member had been vetted and required to sign a non-disclosure agreement. In addition to the usual staff, the crew now included two contract security personnel from an established Athens firm who would shadow Robert and Sylvia when they left the boat.

It had been impossible to keep the news of the Sinner family vacation from the media, but keeping the yacht moored offshore cut down on any unwanted paparazzi attention.

"Just doing my job, Angel."

"I thought you were trying to figure out the best way to sneak in here at night," she said, batting her lashes at him.

He frowned at her, but she'd spent too much time with his sisters and shrugged it off with a laugh.

"At least tell me this," she amended. "Do you think about… us? About what we did?"

"Only every second of every day," Xavier admitted. He knew what it felt like to have his hands on those breasts, to have her breathless and wrapped around him. To hear his name on her lips as she came.

She let out a breath. "Thank God. I thought I was the only one."

He closed the distance between them and brushed her hair over her shoulder. A gentle, intimate gesture that had the tops of his fingers skimming her neck. "Almost makes me wish the timing were different."

"Yeah, me too. Almost."

He grinned. "Get changed, and we'll go upstairs... or whatever you call it on a floating palace."

Xavier's room was nearly identical to Waverly's, but his adjoining bathroom—head, he corrected—didn't have the cauldron-like soaking tub. He changed out of his travel-worn suit and pulled on a pair of golf shorts in a dark gray and a light blue button down with short sleeves. He debated and then tucked his gun into a waistband holster. He'd keep it on him for now, at least until they were underway.

Waverly was waiting in the hallway, and he gave her outfit an approving nod that had her rolling her eyes. He was thankful that her cover-up was an ankle length dress that hid her bikini from him. The last thing he needed was to be distracted by her spectacular body in front of her parents.

They found Sylvia and Robert lounging on an open deck, frothy pink beverages in hand. Sylvia was curled on the sunken horseshoe-shaped couch against plush white cushions. Huge Dolce and Gabbana sunglasses hid most of her face. She wore a short white kimono over a high cut white one-piece bathing suit. Her blonde hair was pinned up and covered by a black and white scarf. She was the epitome of classic Hollywood style.

Robert wore an unbuttoned white linen shirt and walking shorts in navy. He was reading a newspaper and smoking a cigar on a lounger with an unobstructed coastal view.

Beyond him, Santorini rose from the water, a dazzling array of white washed buildings that sat like sugar cubes chiseled into cliff. Two blue domes the exact shade of the sea below topped two tiny churches.

"You guys sure can pick a spot," Waverly said by way of a greeting.

"There you are!" Sylvia gained her feet and tottered over on ridiculous heeled sandals. "Can you believe this is our first family vacation in four years?" Sylvia air kissed Waverly's cheeks and then gave Xavier the same greeting.

Robert folded his newspaper and wandered over, martini glass in hand.

"Hello, sweetheart," he greeted Waverly with an awkward hug and then offered his hand to Xavier. "Who's ready for a drink? Talia makes a delicious grapefruit martini."

Xavier declined Robert's offer as did Waverly, but they did accept tall glasses of ice water that Leonidas appeared with.

"Empty, Leo!" Sylvia wiggled her glass in Leonidas' face, and Xavier saw Waverly wince. She snatched the glass out of her mother's hand and turned a much warmer smile on for the steward's benefit.

"I'm sorry, Leonidas. It looks like my mother is in vacation mode already."

"It is no problem," he said with a white-toothed grin. "I will be happy to bring a refill."

"Maybe a water, as well," Waverly suggested.

"My pleasure."

"Xavier," Robert said, clapping a hand on his shoulder. "Why don't we take a tour of the sun deck?" He pointed up yet another set of stairs that led to the very top of the yacht.

"Of course." Xavier knew a man-to-man talk when he saw one and wondered what this one was regarding. He was entirely unprepared for the wave of guilt that crashed over him. He'd slept with the man's daughter, a man who was paying him to protect her, and in that moment, he felt lower than Douchebag Joe. He'd betrayed the trust of a client, crossed a line, and there was no way to fix it. Even ensuring that it never happened again wasn't good enough.

He just hoped to God whatever Robert wanted to talk about wasn't how Xavier had made love to his daughter and refused to find her another security team.

Mid-crisis of conscience, Xavier turned back to Waverly and Sylvia. "Behave ladies," he said in mock sternness.

Sylvia giggled, but Waverly looked a little sick, and he wondered if she was thinking the same thing he was.

"We'll do our best. Come on, Mom. Let's see what kind of snacks we can find," Waverly said, steering her mother toward the doors.

Xavier followed Robert up the stairs and onto an open deck with a small pool, a hot tub, and yet another lounging area. The area surrounding the hot tub was a series of pads, turning the entire space into one large bed. Huge colorful pillows were stowed in a cabinet built into the deck.

Robert took a seat on a white lounger while Xavier positioned himself at the rail facing the stairway.

"I understand the investigation is proceeding," Robert remarked, his expression unreadable.

Xavier had checked in with Micah when they'd landed in Santorini at the ungodly hour of three a.m. in L.A.

"It's proceeding, but we're not seeing the results that we need yet."

Robert nodded and stared into his glass. "When we hired you, I was mostly doing it to keep my wife happy," Robert said.

He didn't seem to require an answer, so Xavier stayed silent.

"I didn't really grasp the physical danger Waverly was in until Friday night. When I heard those explosions and knew my daughter was still on the carpet, my heart stopped." He shook his head.

Again, Xavier stayed silent.

"I haven't done the best job protecting her," Robert admitted. "It's par for the course in this industry. There will always be someone who has unhealthy feelings toward you. And when you're used to something, it's not as scary as maybe it should be. But you identified a threat the rest of us would have ignored. Without you, Waverly could have been snatched off that carpet." The man's shoulders slumped. "I could be looking for my missing daughter right now instead of enjoying a few days on the Mediterranean with her. I owe you for that."

Xavier's guilt wouldn't allow for compliments. "It's all part of my job. I'm not going to rest until we find Ganim and neutralize him."

"You'll do what you need to do when the time comes," Robert said. Xavier knew what the man was saying, just as he knew how far he was willing to go to keep Waverly safe.

"I will."

Robert gave him a nod. "I'm counting on you. Waverly is lucky to have you."

DINNER WAS a candlelit affair on deck with the lights of Santorini twinkling off the port side. Tonight they would weigh anchor and start their leisurely tour of the islands. Waverly hoped she could survive it. Paradise just wasn't paradise when her parents were involved.

She thought about her good-bye with the Saints. It had been surprisingly emotional for her. In a way, she felt like she was leaving her own family rather than Xavier's. And she wasn't ready to let go. She told herself it was because they'd been so welcoming, so blissfully normal and kind. Carol had given her one last hug on the airport's tarmac. "I know I'll be seeing you again," she'd whispered in Waverly's ear. And Waverly fervently hoped that Carol was right.

She glanced over at her mother as Sylvia hefted her second martini. She forced herself not to worry about it. Her father was aboard. He could deal with a drunken Sylvia for once. She speared a delicate piece of roasted eggplant and glanced across the table at Xavier. Her mother had insisted he join them for dinner. She had also insisted that their first dinner aboard be formal attire.

So it was out of the sexy summer shorts and back into a sexy suit for Xavier. Waverly had donned a backless black halter dress with plenty of sparkle and not a lot of skirt. She knew her mother would approve, and Xavier would squirm. It was the perfect choice.

He'd barely taken his gaze off of her all evening. They'd had no chance to speak privately though. She was dying to know what her father had cornered him about. For just a split-second, Xavier's face had betrayed him, revealing the guilt he felt most likely over their "transgression".

She'd tried to see it his way. Xavier was a Boy Scout. Rules didn't just exist to be occasionally observed. They provided a code to live by. By slipping and sleeping with her—a client—he'd broken a rule and an important one.

But damn it, when something felt that life altering, she was having trouble seeing it as a negative. It had been something they both wanted, and, sure, it made being around her parents a little more awkward, but it wasn't as if Xavier had taken advantage of her or had a serious breach of ethics... as both her parents continued to have.

But Xavier held himself to a higher standard. And if she were being honest, it was one of the things she found most attractive about him. She'd never known anyone like him, so committed to integrity, so determined to do the right thing.

"How's your sea bass, Xavier?" Sylvia asked, preening as if she had steamed the fish herself.

"Delicious, Sylvia. Thank you again for the invitation."

Waverly met his gaze across the linen topped table. Yesterday they had dined on bacon from a paper towel, drinking coffee out of mismatched mugs. Tonight they dined with china and crystal on a five-star "red carpet-friendly" meal prepared by a private chef, and she knew without a doubt they both were wishing they were crowded around that kitchen table in Idle Lake.

Reading her mind, Xavier gave her a discreet smile.

"Darling, your father and I are going ashore on Ios tomorrow for a little shopping. Will you come?" Sylvia asked hopefully.

Waverly glanced at Xavier, who gave a subtle shake of his head. She figured there was no way he was letting her off this yacht without an army before they flew out for her London premiere.

"I think I'll stay behind. The jet lag is bound to catch up with me tomorrow," Waverly told her. Sylvia's face crumbled.

"But if you're shopping, maybe you could find something for me?" Waverly asked.

"Of course!" Her mother was cheerful again. She loved to buy gifts, the sillier the better, and was actually quite thoughtful about it. "What would you like?"

"Something that you see, and it makes you think of me," Waverly decided.

"Oh, what fun!" Sylvia clapped her hands together. She'd gotten a little sun today but not enough to change her ivory complexion to pink. Waverly watched as her father put one of his hands over his wife's and brought it to his lips.

The last time she'd witnessed any kind of physical affection between them was... most likely on the red carpet. Just for show. What had begun as a red-hot love affair had morphed into a never-ending volatile argument and then, in recent years, an icy indifference as they'd each floated along sharing the same space, the same town, the same job.

Maybe a family vacation would be the beginning of a newer, healthier relationship between the Sinners?

Waverly's short-term hope vanished when Sylvia handed over her empty martini glass to Talia, a tall, lithe woman with dark hair and eyes. Both her parents' vices in one package. A talented bartender for her mother and a beautiful young woman for her father. Waverly prayed her father wouldn't pursue anything there. He had a weakness, and she worried that Talia's exotic olive skin would be too much for him to resist while Sylvia drank herself to unconsciousness.

"Oh! Did I mention that the chef has fresh baklava for dessert tonight?" Sylvia asked the table brightly.

Waverly perked back up.

"None for you, sweetheart. That premiere dress has zero give in it," Sylvia said wagging a finger at Waverly.

"Thanks for always watching out for my dresses, Mom," Waverly grumbled.

"You'll thank me when you see the pictures and no one is speculating that you're pregnant."

Depressed after watching everyone else fork up delicious, air-thin layers of baklava, Waverly excused herself early for bed. Her mother was already slurring, and for once, she was determined to not be the caretaker.

She kicked off her sandals and flopped back onto the bed.

She'd change out of her dress in a few minutes. She just wanted to lay in the quiet now.

The tired was setting in. She felt it like a fog in the brain, a heaviness in her limbs. It was hard to believe that she'd run halfway around the world just to avoid a man. A dangerous one, of course, but still just one human being had the power to keep her locked in a cage.

At least it was a luxurious, floating cage.

There was a quiet knock on her door. One rap followed by two short knocks.

"Come in," she said without bothering to sit up.

The door opened, and she lolled her head to look at Xavier.

"Do all you Invictus people knock the same way?" she asked.

"What way?"

She rapped her knuckles on the teak nightstand.

He gave her a crooked smile. "It's just another little layer of security. That way you always know it's Invictus knocking."

"Smart," Waverly yawned.

He stayed in the doorway.

"What?"

"You look like a bored, high-priced call girl waiting for her client," he told her.

"That's the worst pickup line I've ever heard."

"How about this one?" Xavier pulled his hand from behind his back with a flourish. He held a gold-rimmed plate, and on it was an impressive slab of baklava and one fork.

"Oh, my God. I love you." Waverly sat upright, reaching both hands for him.

The color drained from his face.

"Jesus, X. I was talking to the baklava. Gimmie." She wiggled her fingers until he entered, delivering the plate. She forked up a flavorful bite and rolled her eyes heavenward. "Oh, my God this is orgasmic."

"As someone who has had a front row seat to a few of your orgasms, I object," Xavier protested.

"Xavier Saint with the jokes."

"It's the jet lag," he yawned and flopped down on the foot of her bed. "Please tell me you're going to bed and staying there for twelve hours. I might throw you overboard if you say you're getting up for a six a.m. Pilates class."

Waverly laughed between bites. "My ass will remain glued to this bed as long as I can get away with it."

"If you leave your cabin, come get me, okay?" He grabbed her bare foot, squeezed.

"We're on a yacht in the middle of the ocean with crew that you personally okayed, X," she said dryly.

"Humor me."

Waverly feigned a sigh. "As if I could say no to a devastatingly handsome man begging from the foot of my bed."

He pinched her in the calf. "You know I don't beg, Angel."

"And the winner with the innuendo," Waverly said archly. "What did my father want to talk to you about this afternoon?"

Xavier snagged her fork and helped himself to a bite of dessert. "He had some questions about the investigation."

"You feel guilty."

He looked at her through those thick, dark lashes. "I suppose we're not talking about the investigation now."

"We are not."

He sighed, reluctant to talk. "Yes, I feel guilty. I broke a rule, *the* rule. And so when your father thanks me for doing my job, all I can think about is how I wasn't doing my job when I was defiling you."

Waverly laughed. "Defiling? Xavier, we made love."

"Why don't you try yelling that a little louder? I think there's a hard-of-hearing grandmother in Santorini who didn't hear you."

She poked him in the very firm abs with her toes. "You didn't take advantage of me, and it was amazing. End of story."

"I worry that I won't be able to control myself again," he admitted.

"We're on a bed now, and we're behaving," she reminded him.

His eyes narrowed, considering. He dipped his mouth to the arch of her foot, and she felt his tongue dart out to tease the sensitive skin.

The purr caught in her throat, and she saw his eyes warm. *Testing himself*, she thought, *wanting to see how far he could push himself*.

But his test didn't take into account how his touch affected her. She didn't know if she could trust her own control if pushed too far.

She put her foot against his chest. "Go to bed, X."

"Sweet dreams, Angel."

20

True to her word, Waverly slept late the next morning. Xavier got a solid seven hours before he heard the tender leave taking Robert and Sylvia to shore. He dressed and opened the door to his cabin so Waverly wouldn't be able to sneak past him.

Instead of setting up at the narrow desk in his room, which would force his back to the door, Xavier propped himself up on the mountain of bed pillows and opened his laptop. He spent the next two hours sifting through Invictus reports and firing off emails to his team, the FBI investigator, and Hansen.

He pulled up the report Roz had put together for him.

Daisy Louchner had been a waitress at the Rail Car Diner, two blocks from Ganim's mother's El Plano house. At twenty-two, she was a bubbly blonde according to the Facebook pictures his team had dug up—one of her playing softball with the diner team, another at a local fundraiser wearing a hot pink shirt that rallied readers to Save the Ta-Tas. She shared an apartment with a high school friend and enjoyed baking and a good party. She had her stomach pumped onc for alcohol poisoning and a blip for underage drinking when she was nineteen.

She had no family to speak of. Her father had died when she was a kid and her mother when she was seventeen.

Daisy hadn't posted to Facebook, filed a tax return, or had a single credit card transaction since she left El Plano three years ago.

The roommate, now living in Dallas, had been thrilled to talk to someone who was finally taking Daisy's disappearance seriously. She'd told local police when Daisy didn't come home that September night that the creepy guy from the diner had something to do with it. But there had been no proof that she was even missing, let alone abducted. She was probably out partying, the cops had told the roommate. After days ticked into weeks, they assumed she had just left town on a wild hair. Besides, Ganim had been alibied by his mother on the night Daisy disappeared from El Plano.

Tiffani Plotts was a nineteen-year-old dancer at a shithole club called Castaway Dolls on the outskirts of El Plano. She had run away from her Oklahoma home when she was sixteen and ended up in El Plano after a zig-zagging path through Louisiana and Mississippi. She dyed her hair a goth black and wore enough make-up for an entire dance troupe of drag queens.

She dated, frequently older men, but nothing stuck, and ually when one relationship ended, she breezed on to the t man in the next town. She'd lived in a trailer court less a quarter mile from the club and walked to and from She was saving for a car that would get her out of this and she told anyone who would listen. Unlike Daisy, n't have any close friends. So when she didn't show one day, the only fuss had been which girl had to shift.

Ganim had visited the club regularly and had gotten creepy enough that Tiffani had finally refused to go on stage if he were there. After an altercation one night in the parking lot involving Ganim and the trunk of his car, Tiffani had filed a complaint. But it was her second complaint since landing in town a year ago, and with her record of a DUI and a handful of possessions, the local cops hadn't taken the investigation very seriously and a week later, the lead investigator received an email from Tiffani claiming she'd made the whole thing up and was moving back to Oklahoma to take care of her ailing mother.

Mrs. Plotts, too, had been happy to talk to Invictus regarding her daughter. When asked about her health, Mrs. Plotts informed them if it came out of Tiffani's mouth it was safe to assume it was a lie. Just like when, at fourteen, she chased off Mrs. Plotts' second husband by making noises about him assaulting her. It was consensual, that much Mrs. Plotts was sure about. As for her daughter's whereabouts, she didn't much care. As long as she wasn't calling and begging for money, Tiffani could live her life, and Mrs. Plotts would do the same.

Xavier made a note to do something very nice for his own parents at his earliest convenience.

As with Daisy, Tiffani had fallen off the face of the earth. No convictions, no taxes, nothing on Instagram. She'd simply vanished.

He tapped his fingers restlessly and then fired off an email to Micah asking him to get the El Plano investigator who handled Tiffani's complaint to let them have a look at her email. Maybe they could learn something by tracing it.

He had two missing girls that no one wanted to believe were missing and a third target, none of them seemed t have anything in common besides being young and pret which could have been all it took to catch lonely Ganim's eye.

Xavier brought up the photos from the motel room Ganim had abandoned the night of the explosions and clicked through them. Not many clothes, leading him to believe that L.A. wasn't a permanent destination.

The laptop left at the scene would hopefully yield some useful information. A detailed manifesto with a list of hiding spots, perhaps? It was never that easy, but at least it was a starting point. He wondered where on the priority list the case fell for the FBI. It couldn't hurt to reach out and offer some of Invictus' services if it got the investigation moving.

He cued up the video shot from an abandoned TV camera on the red carpet. It had captured the exchange between Xavier and Ganim. He watched it on mute, paying close attention to Ganim's movements. He'd stopped and slid his right hand into his pocket a moment before Waverly had seen him.

Xavier backed it up, played it again. Was it a weapon in his pocket? Was he reaching for a gun? Why hadn't he tried for her? Why had he given up when he was so close to what he wanted?

The FBI hadn't released Ganim's identity yet to the public, but they had gotten a warrant to search his mother's house. It was still furnished, and Ganim still had possessions there. They were speculating that he planned to return at some [illegible]int. But "at some point" wasn't good enough.

Ganim had been quiet since the premiere. No messages [illegible]es the flowers he sent the next day. Maybe things hadn't [illegible] plan that night on the carpet? Maybe he'd intended to [illegible]verly, and he was off somewhere licking his wounds. [illegible]ooked too smug, too satisfied, standing there just

[illegible]

[illegible], they needed a break, and they needed one fast.

Xavier felt reasonably safe with Waverly on the other side of the world. However, when her tour ended, she still had to go home. The longer they went without answers, the colder the trail got, and he wasn't going to let that happen.

Not with the other timeline hanging over his head. He'd bide his time before telling Waverly that Stanford might not be an option this year. He hated to crush her dreams. That's why he was dragging his feet. He was hoping for a miracle. That Ganim would slip up and get taken down at a Pinkberry, and Waverly could have everything she wanted.

"You look like you have the weight of the world on your shoulders."

And just like that, there she was in his doorway. She wore her hair up in a high ponytail and a very small, very flattering black string bikini. She looked refreshed, rested. Unfairly beautiful.

"Good morning," he said finally.

"Oh good, I thought you'd lost the power of speech," Waverly winked. "Want to come up and have breakfast with me? I'm thinking about a swim after."

He could think of nothing he wanted more in the moment.

"Sure," he said closing his laptop before she could try for a peek at his screen.

"Do me a favor before we go up?" she asked. She held up a bottle of sunscreen. "Can you get my back? I don't want to ask the crew to do it."

And he would have no problems tossing the lucky guy overboard. "Sure," he said again.

She tossed him the bottle and brushed past him. She hinged forward just a bit against the mattress, and he wen from half-mast to rock hard when he caught the rear view.

The bottoms, which had been tiny from the front, w

minuscule from behind. The rounded curve of her perfect ass cheeks demanded attention under the high cut bikini.

"Oh sweet Jesus," he muttered.

Waverly pulled her ponytail over her shoulder. "Problem there, Saint?"

Maybe if he closed his eyes, the white hot lust that had electrified his body would start to dissipate. He opened the bottle, squeezed, and with eyes closed rubbed his palms over her shoulders and down her back.

The lotion smelled exotic, like oils and spices from the Middle East. Trust the Sinners to not have a spray bottle of Coppertone lying around.

She gave a little sigh of appreciation that had his cock flexing. "Please don't make that noise again," he pleaded through clenched teeth.

His hands skimmed over her low back and around the curves of her hips.

He blew out a breath. Eyes closed wasn't helping. If anything, it was making it more sensual. He opened his eyes, saw that she was bent over, elbows on the mattress now. It was an unfortunately seductive position.

"Did you get…lower?" he asked.

"Hmm?" she murmured lazily.

"Your ass. Did you put sunscreen on your ass cheeks?"

"Jeez. Such violence when you talk about my ass. And no, t I can—"

He shut her up by shoving her all the way forward. er squirt of lotion, and he was coasting his hands e rounded cheeks. His thumbs brushed together her thighs and this time her sigh was a gasp. d his breath, willed himself to think about reports, and skimmed the tips of his fingers e ge of her bikini bottom. He didn't want her burning if it rode up, though God knew where it could ride up to.

"There," he said, backing up like she was a toddler with a piñata bat. "Please do not ask any member of the crew to ever do that. I won't survive it, and I'll make sure they don't either."

"Gee, Xavier. I thought you never begged." she teased.

His palm landed soundly on her right ass cheek with a satisfying smack. She yelped, and he grinned.

"Don't play games with me, Angel. I always win." He smirked, enjoying the view of his handprint on that lovely ass as he followed her upstairs.

THE CREW ARRANGED a breakfast of French toast, berries, and yogurt on the covered main deck. The espresso chased away the cobwebs of travel and jet lag, and Xavier soon got his second wind. He opened up his laptop at the table while Waverly moved out into the sun with a novel for now and a script to be reading when her parents returned.

She sprawled face down on a soft deck bed, and Xavier did his best to concentrate on the screen and not her ass. He took half an hour and cleaned up some personal business—investments, bills, birthdays—and when Waverly rolled over to sun her front, he switched back to Invictus business.

Her front was just as distracting as her back.

Leonidas had to ask him twice if he'd like another espresso before it registered. And judging by the sly smirk on Waverly's face, she'd heard the exchange and guessed the cause.

The advance team had sent over yet another final, final tour schedule for London. The studio had squeezed in a one-on-one with one of the biggest newspapers in the UK. He was still waiting on a floor plan for the hotel from their head of security. He reviewed the profile of the driver they'd be using while in London and approved.

He glanced up again, and it looked to him like Waverly's top had gotten even smaller.

Xavier gave up. It would still be hours before Micah or Roz or any of the team was ready to connect. He was on a yacht on the Aegean Sea with Waverly Sinner. Twenty years from now, would he look back and be glad he spent so much time on paperwork instead of enjoying some non-life-threatening time with Waverly? He could afford to take an hour or two and just relax.

He shut down his laptop and wandered over to Waverly.

"Ready for that swim?" he asked, nudging her bed with his foot.

She dropped the book and smiled. "Let's go."

He let her lead the way up the flight to the upper deck and around the port side to the stairs to the sun deck.

While he shed his shoes and his shirt, Waverly studied the small pool pensively. "I don't think we're both going to fit in there," she decided.

"You'll just have to make do," Xavier told her. He draped his shirt over a lounger and nearly had a heart attack when he saw her climbing the rail.

He plucked her off and spun her around. "What the hell are you doing?"

"There's a lot more room in the sea, X."

"If you want to swim in the sea, we can walk down four flights of stairs and you can jump in from the very nice swim platform on the stern."

"First of all, there's an elevator we could use instead of the stairs—"

"Of course there is."

"Secondly, the swimming isn't the point. It's the jumping."

Xavier peered over the side. In his young and dumb youth, he'd jumped off cliffs with a shorter fall than this.

"You're not jumping."

"Jump with me. Come on," she pleaded when he started to shake his head. "Don't you want to feel a little self-induced danger for once? I'm tired of feeling afraid. I want to jump off the side and years later still have this memory to pull out and enjoy. I'll text you wherever we are then when I think about it, 'Hey, X, remember the time we jumped off a yacht together?'"

He was already going to have to crush her life's dream about college. Maybe he could give her this. He admitted the idea of being a treasured memory to her stroked his ego. If he couldn't claim her, he could at least claim a memorable moment in her life.

"I can't believe I'm considering this."

"What will metaphorically push you over the edge?"

He grumbled. "Call the captain, find out how deep it is, and if we're likely to die on impact."

Waverly squealed and clapped her hands. She danced away to a white phone mounted on the wall.

He looked over the side again. Had the ocean gotten farther away? This was crazy. He was crazy. Crazy about her. She'd talked him into a motorcycle ride careening up the coast. Now, all she had to do was blink those sea witch eyes at him, and he was trussing them both up as shark bait.

Shit. He should have had her ask the captain about shark activity.

She skipped back over to him. "We're at sixty feet right here. Perfectly safe!"

"I highly doubt he used those words."

She ignored his sarcasm. "They're deploying one of those floating trampoline platforms off the stern so we can swim back to it and lay out."

"If we're not eaten by sharks first."

"Don't be such a baby, Xavier. Get your ass up there on the rail!"

They climbed over together and stood, knees quaking.

Waverly didn't look scared, she looked energized. *His little adrenaline junkie*, he thought. So many years without any control over her own life had made her hungry for choice, for action, maybe even for consequence.

She looked at him, eyes glittering with excitement. "Trust me, X?"

"I'm putting my life in your hands, Angel. Be gentle."

She took his hand. "On three then. One. Two. Three."

They fell for what felt like forever before dropping into the warm waiting waters. He still had a grip on Waverly's hand, and before he could start dragging their bodies to the surface flickering with sunlight, she appeared before him.

Her lips brushed his once, twice. And then she was pulling them up toward the light.

SYLVIA AND ROBERT returned to the *Sea Goddess* with shopping bags galore.

"Is there anything left on the island, Mom?" Waverly asked with a laugh as Leonidas called in reinforcements to help tote the bags into the cabin.

"Only what she couldn't carry," Robert teased.

"Let me change, and then it's present time," Sylvia announced, clapping her hands. Her filmy maxi dress fluttered around her legs in the breeze. She blew them all kisses and fluttered and fussed her way into the master cabin.

"Speaking of gifts," Robert said, he pulled a tiny canvas

bag out of his shirt pocket. "I saw this and thought of you." He handed it over to Waverly.

She opened the delicate little drawstring and a woven bracelet in turquoise and gold fell into her waiting palm. It wasn't an expensive trinket, not like the drawerful of apology glitter she had back home, but it was obviously handmade.

"A little girl was selling them by the dock. She and her grandmother sit down every Saturday afternoon and make them," Robert explained.

Charmed, Waverly slid it onto her wrist. "Thank you, Dad." She hesitated and then threw her arms around his neck for a hug. The awkwardness reminded her that there had been a lot of disappointments and disagreements between them and their last hug.

"I'm just really glad we're all here together," her father said haltingly, as ill at ease as Waverly.

She smiled at him. "Me, too."

"Who's ready for their present?" Sylvia asked, clapping her hands as she reappeared. She'd changed into a snake print kaftan and a pair of matching platform sandals. She held a large shopping bag emblazoned with Greek in one hand and a significantly smaller bag in the other. "One for each of you," she announced, shoving the big bag at Waverly and the little one at Xavier.

"I can't accept—" Xavier began.

"Don't bother, X. My mother doesn't take no for an answer," Waverly warned him.

"Open, open!" Sylvia chirped.

Within her bag, Waverly found an oversized, floppy sun hat in white linen. It screamed Hollywood. She laughed and placed it on her head. The brim was so wide it drooped to her shoulders. She put her sunglasses on and posed, hand on hip, looking off into the distance. "How do I look, dah-lings?"

Sylvia giggled. "Oh, please, can I take a picture?"

Waverly felt her spine stiffen and then relax. At least this picture had no ulterior motives, just Sylvia's daughter enjoying their family vacation. She could give her this one. "Sure, Mom."

Sylvia gleefully plucked her phone out of her bathing suit strap. "Over by the rail so we can see the island in the background," she ordered.

Waverly posed for six or seven shots before her mother was satisfied. "Now how do I find those filters Kate showed me?" Sylvia muttered to herself. She wandered off to the shade to edit the picture to perfection.

Waverly returned to Xavier who was still staring into his bag.

"Did you get a matching hat?" she teased.

Xavier shook his head. "Uh, nope." He pulled a piece of material out of the bag, held it by two fingers.

"Oh, my God. Mom!" Waverly screeched, snatching the red and blue Grigioperla swim trunks out of Xavier's hand. "That is so inappropriate!"

"What?" Sylvia asked innocently. "I didn't know if Xavier had brought a suit, and I wanted him to be able to enjoy the pool."

Waverly covered her mouth to hide her horrified laughter. "You're unbelievable."

"Darling, he's got just an amazing physique—you really do, Xavier," Sylvia beamed at him. "It would be a crime to put him in some voluminous, knee-length discount store trunks."

Xavier snatched the trunks back, held them over his hips, and Waverly got a good look at just exactly what would be barely covered by them.

"Too bad we already had our swim today," he whispered.

"At least they aren't thong."

Late that afternoon, Waverly went below to grab a nap before getting ready for dinner, and Xavier used the time to call Micah in L.A.

"How's the high life, brother?" Micah's voice came through the phone crystal clear.

"Oh, you know, just another day aboard a multi-million dollar yacht."

"Yeah, I bet all those islands start to look the same," Micah mocked.

"You get my emails?"

"All eleven of them," his friend snorted.

"What's new since then?" Xavier asked, squinting off the bow into the cerulean horizon.

"FBI's decided to take a look at our two missing persons, see if they can't scare up any information or bodies," Micah told him.

"Are the locals going to release that email from Plotts to us?"

"I'm talking to them and the feds. Feds have jurisdiction, but they're backlogged into next year with cyber shit."

"Well, keep offering. I don't want this guy to slide because some ten-year-old embezzling court case is hogging up staff capacity."

"Will do. The feds are also releasing Ganim's identity to the press today. The tips have started to slow down on the sketch alone. They were hoping he'd try to run back to El Plano if he thought they hadn't connected him to the case. But no such luck. So they're going to go public with what they have."

"Are they going to mention the missing girls?"

"Dunno. They aren't real open and into sharing if you know what I mean."

Xavier had expected it. "Well, keep pushing with Hansen. He's not going to want to get cut out of this either."

"How's our bombshell client these days?"

Xavier thought about the drop of his stomach as they'd jumped into the sea, her laughter when they surfaced together. "She's good. It's good to get her out of town, away from it all."

"There's going to be a lot of questions for her in London, especially if Ganim's name goes public."

Xavier leaned over the rail and sighed. "She'll handle it. She's tough."

"Uh-huh." Micah said a lot with very little. "Any other ethical slips I need to be aware of?"

He thought of Waverly under him, screaming his name as she came.

"Nothing you need to worry about," he said evenly. There was no point in confessing. His partner would just try to drag him off the job and replace him with someone else. Someone he couldn't trust to be as good as he was. He was the one who needed to be here with Waverly. He'd deal with the fallout later.

"Good," Micah said even though he didn't sound convinced. "Look, seriously Saint. If you've got anything you need to talk about..."

"I'm good. Everything is good. Or it will be once we find this bastard."

21

The day started off as all the others had, blissful and beautiful. Today, it was Mikonos off the starboard side of the *Sea Goddess.* Their anchorage in a sheltered bay brought them much closer to shore than they had been before. Waverly felt like she could almost see into the cliff top homes.

She took her breakfast, a goat cheese omelet with fresh squeezed orange juice, on the main deck with Xavier. He scrolled through news from home on a tablet next to her while she dug back into her novel. She had just lifted her dainty cup of espresso to her lips when they heard a shrill scream from the salon.

"Stay here," Xavier ordered her as he jumped up from his chair. As he ran toward the salon doors, Waverly saw him reach behind him for the gun that wasn't there. He hadn't been carrying since the first day onboard. A sign that he was relaxing a bit... and probably regretting it now.

She ignored his order. She knew one of her mother's screams when she heard them. It could be over an old enemy appearing in a guest role on a popular TV show or the glimpse of a spider.

By the time she entered the salon, her mother was sobbing on the couch. But the cause of her reaction was still evident. Talia, the stunning Greek girl, was close to tears herself. Guilt and fear made her dark eyes wide as a full moon eclipse. Her lipstick, a dusky rose, was currently painting Robert Sinner's mouth.

"Sylvia, for God's sake, calm down," Robert begged.

"How could you?" Sylvia glared at him, mascara streaking down her cheeks. The wounded wife. "You're on vacation with your wife and daughter, and I catch you with this Grecian whore!"

Xavier smoothly shifted into non-life-threatening crisis mode. He signaled for one of the other guards who had appeared to escort the now-sobbing Talia out of the room. Waverly felt bad for the girl. So many girls before her had fallen victim to Robert Sinner's smooth charm. It made them feel special, important. But sooner or later, it always ended the same. Robert never left the wife he promised them he didn't love, and the girl drifted away feeling used and less worthy than before.

When Robert made a move to lay a hand on Sylvia's shoulder, she flinched and shrieked.

"Stay away from me! I hate you!"

Robert shriveled back, and Waverly made her way to her mother's side. She put a protective arm around Sylvia's shaking shoulders and telegraphed to Xavier that he needed to get her father out of the room before there was bloodshed.

Xavier put a hand on Robert's chest and spoke quietly to him. Her father didn't take much convincing, and Xavier guided him out of the room opposite the way Talia had exited.

Sylvia's tears showed no signs of slowing. Waverly got up

and found a bottle of water in the small refrigerator behind the bar. She pressed it into her mother's hands. "Here, Mom. Drink. You'll make yourself sick if you can't calm down," Waverly said gently.

Sylvia blinked back tears as she looked down at the bottle in her hands, and then she hurled the bottle across the salon. "Who does he think I am?" she railed, getting to her feet. "I made him. Me marrying him was the best thing that ever happened to his career, and he thinks he can just sleep with anything with a pair of legs? Six days. I asked him for six days with us, and he can't even give us that."

"I'm sorry, Mom." Waverly felt her mother's rage as if it were a physical presence in the room. But she'd seen it before, and it had always passed. She always forgave, or if not forgave, then forgot.

"Everything I have done in this life is for us. I play this role so that we can have the life we deserve, the life everyone wants. But your father is content to throw it away. And for what? So he can fuck a girl his daughter's age to feel important, desirable."

Sylvia stormed over to the bar and wrestled a bottle of vodka free from the shelf.

"Mom, I don't think that's a good idea."

Sylvia turned on her. "How about after you spend your *entire* life trying to keep a family together and three careers on track, *then* you can tell me what's a good idea." She wrenched open the bottle, poured a shot, and then downed it.

"Why don't you leave him?" Waverly had never asked the question out loud before. Only a dozen times a week in her own head. God knows he'd given his wife plenty of reasons in their twenty-one years of marriage. "Why do you keep settling for this?"

"Settling?" Sylvia's face went white. "This is what everyone in the world dreams of having." She threw her arms out wide, keeping the bottle clutched tight in her fingers. "You wouldn't be basking on a yacht in the Mediterranean if it weren't for all the sacrifices I've made. You would be making B-list movies with your tits out. No one would care about us if your father and I had divorced over his first infidelity. But together, we're more. Together, we're stronger."

God, she was talking about their brand, not their family.

Sylvia poured herself another shot and downed it, oblivious to the tears that still fell. It was crushing to know that her mother still felt the pain this deeply. As celebrated an actor as Sylvia Sinner was, movies hadn't even begun to scratch her depth, Waverly realized.

"You could be happy if things were different. You're obviously not happy now," Waverly tried again.

"What does happiness add up to in the end? Loss. You marry someone you love and then you lose them. Where's your happiness then?" Sylvia demanded. "But if you build something, a legacy, no one can take that away from you. I did this for you, and you ask me why as if I should be ashamed of myself. Everything I've ever done has been to build this legacy for you. You'll never know what it's like to be no one, to not matter."

"Mom." Waverly didn't know what else to say.

The fury had blown out of Sylvia. Her shoulders stooped. She reached for a glass behind the bar and filled it with ice.

"Next time you feel like judging me," she said, pouring a stream of vodka over the ice, "you just remember that everything I've done in this life is for you."

Drink and bottle in hand, Sylvia quietly left the room, climbing the interior stairs to the master cabin. "Have a steward move Mr. Sinner's things from the cabin." Waverly heard Sylvia snap the words at someone. "I don't care what you do with them. Throw them and him overboard for all I care."

Thank God for non-disclosure agreements, Waverly thought.

She ventured outside to see how the other half of her gene pool was fairing and found her father slumped in a chair at the dining table, staring off at the horizon. Xavier was pretending to mind his own business on an overstuffed armchair near the door.

Waverly took the chair next to her father. "Why, Dad? Seriously. I just don't get it."

Robert sighed, the weight of the world on his chest. "It's one of those things I hope you never understand."

"Help me understand. It's getting harder and harder for me to forgive you. What compelled you to stick your tongue down our bartender's throat with your wife just feet away?" Waverly could hear the anger in her voice, knew it would shut him down. But her control was rusty. She just wanted to shake him.

"Waverly, this is between your mother and me." His tone was tired. He was already withdrawing from her, from himself. "Maybe you could tell her—"

"Why does it have to be me? Why can't you tell her what you want her to hear?"

"She's upset right now—" Robert began.

"*I'm* upset right now. She drinks all the time, Dad. You're never around because you're so busy trying to screw your way through the West Coast, which by the way, what do you think that does to your twenty-year-old daughter? How much longer do you think you two can go on like this? Someone is going to get hurt, and it's not going to just be me this time."

Robert put his head in his hands, and she knew he was done. There would be no more discussion, no more answers.

She let her words hang heavy in the salt air and the

sunshine. Let them absorb the exotic paradise that surrounded them and leave nothing but ugliness and emptiness. Maybe it was what they all deserved. Maybe this was all there was.

Just like her mother, the fight drained out of her. She would never understand, never be able to fix it. And with that crystal clear knowledge, that final acceptance weighing on her, she walked past Xavier into the salon and down the steps to her cabin.

XAVIER DIDN'T BOTHER KNOCKING. He just opened the door and closed it behind him. She was sitting on the bed propped up by pillows staring blankly. She looked shell shocked. No tears, he noted. Just the exhaustion of a fighter who had finally given up.

He debated sitting on the couch, then decided he'd feel better closer. So he sprawled across the foot of her bed again. Without acknowledging him, she scooted her feet closer to him, and he took them in his hands. They were cold. The rest of her probably was, too. And not just from the Arctic air conditioning.

"What can I do?" he asked.

Waverly just slowly shook her head. "Nothing. There's nothing you can do and nothing I can do to fix this," she said, head still shaking. "I have no control over them, no matter how much I want it, no matter how much better I could make them."

"It's not up to you, Angel."

"But I could help. I could have fixed it before it got to this."

Xavier scooted up the bed until he was sitting next to her. He threw an arm over her shoulders. "Angel, it's not your job to fix them. They're damaged, but they are responsible for their damage. And they're responsible for fixing it."

"Am I damaged?" Waverly asked.

"You've got a few dents and dings, but I don't think you're damaged."

"I need to get away from all of this, X," she said. "If I don't, it's going to suck me in, and I'll never get out."

"Angel, you make your own choices just like they do. You won't make their mistakes," he promised her.

"I guess Stanford couldn't come at a better time," she said with a sad smile.

Fuck. Now was not the time to ruin that for her. He couldn't do that to her.

"What is it?" she asked, her eyes widening.

"What's what?"

"I say Stanford, and you get rigor mortis."

"It's nothing," he said, trying to brush it off. "Do you need a drink or something?"

"Don't lie to me, Xavier. I seriously can't take it from you, too."

He wanted to. He wanted to promise her that everything was okay and she could finally go live the life she chose. But he couldn't. He didn't.

"Stanford may not be an option."

He winced when she shrugged off his arm. "What do you mean 'might not be an option'?"

"If we don't catch Ganim, you can't go." Sometimes blunt was best.

"I think I'm having an aneurysm or something because it sounded like you said I can't go."

"Angel. He may have killed two girls in Texas. They both had stalker issues with him, and both of them disappeared. I think it's permanent, and the FBI is looking into their cases. If he's a murderer and he's still on the loose, fixated on you, you can't go. You can't go spend your days on a college campus with 16,000 other people."

"So come with me then." He heard it, the fear in her voice that she was losing the one thing left she had to hold on to.

Xavier reached for her hand and held it tight. "Think about it, Angel. You'd have a predictable schedule and anyone who paid the least bit of attention would be able to find a way to get to you. Even if I could guarantee your safety in classes, what kind of experience would that be? Normal students would be afraid to talk to you. The only ones left would be the assholes who just want something from you. Is that how you envisioned it?"

She shook her head slowly, sadly. And his heart hurt for her.

"When will it be a definite 'no'?" she asked.

"It already is, Angel."

She had asked him to go. And he'd gone, even though she knew he wanted to stay. He hadn't meant to hurt her. Her parents probably hadn't either. But the hurt was there all the same.

This legacy had robbed her of any hope of normal.

Her one out, the thing that she really wanted for herself had just been taken away from her. And what was she left with? Yes, other people would kill for this life. Some would look at the costs as being a fair trade for the luxury and the fame and the money. But Waverly wanted normal, she wanted happy.

A hot tear worked its way free and slipped down her cheek. She gave herself a few moments to mourn the life she'd dreamed of, let the tears fall silently. She'd asked Xavier if she was damaged and he said no, but she wasn't so sure of that. How could she remain unscathed, and would she if she stayed?

She wiped her face with the backs of her hands and then went into the bathroom. She washed her face slowly, carefully, and patted it dry with the cloud-soft towel. She found her phone in the nightstand drawer. She'd kept it turned off since they boarded. Kate was on vacation with her parents and she was the only one who would have called the number anyway.

Waverly powered it on and dialed.

"'lo?" Kate's voice was thick with sleep.

"Oh, shit. I'm sorry, I forgot about the time difference," Waverly apologized and felt like an idiot.

"Wave?"

"Yeah, I'm sorry I just missed you and forgot. Go back to bed."

"No, s'cool. I was just dreaming about serial killers again anyway."

"You're so weird," Waverly said with affection.

"You have your 'I'm not crying, you're crying' voice on," Kate yawned.

"Yeah well, I'm on vacation with my parents so..."

"Seriously, Wave, what's wrong? I'm awake now, and if you don't talk to me, I'm going to post that pic of you pretending to pick your nose with the salad tongs on your Instagram account."

"Who said I was pretending?"

"Har har. Spill sister."

"I got into Stanford."

"Are you kidding me? That's amazing! Holy shit, when are you coming back? Oh my God, we have to go school shop..."

"And I see you just landed on the conclusion that I completely missed until Xavier told me five minutes ago."

"Oh my God. You can't go."

"Not until Ganim is caught."

Kate swore ripely in Waverly's ear. "Listen, don't give up on this, Wave. We'll come up with something even if we have to trap the asshole ourselves."

Waverly felt her lips curve. "I miss you. I wish you were aboard the floating loony bin with me."

"Things that good, huh?"

"Mom caught Dad licking the tonsils of the twenty-two-year-old bartender in the grand salon."

"Guess that means your mom is mixing her own drinks, ha. Sorry. Bad joke."

Waverly laughed anyway and then sighed. "Am I damaged? I mean, it's not possible to come from them and not be damaged, is it?"

"If you are, you're the least damaged damaged person I've ever met. And I've met a lot of damaged people."

"Awh, thanks, pal."

"Anytime. So I guess I'll see you in London in a couple of days," Kate said. "We can start scheming how to catch a creeper and get your ass to college."

"Sounds good. Go back to sleep."

Waverly stayed in her room until late afternoon when her stomach demanded sustenance. She'd yet to hear a peep through her door or see any bodies flung over the side through her window. She hoped it was a good sign.

She decided it was as good a time as any to go up on deck, maybe let the sun bake away some of her pain. She changed into a new bikini, grabbed her sunscreen, and headed out.

Even after her talk with Kate, dejection clung to her like a florid perfume. She could see no way out, and if she were confined to this life much longer, she might never find one. *Should she just embrace it as her mother had? Or was normal worth fighting for*? Waverly wanted to know.

She trudged up the stairs and finding no signs of life on the main or upper decks she climbed to the highest level. She found Xavier on the sun deck, dressed in shorts and an open button down shirt.

There was a beer on the table in front of him.

"Rough day?" She heard the bitterness in her own voice and shook her head. "Sorry. I don't mean to take anything out on you." She sat down on a sunny bed and tried to focus on the beauty of the view.

Xavier picked up his beer and joined her. He said nothing just sat next to her in silence.

It was quiet up on deck. The lap of the water against the hull was far below. A light breeze teased her hair and relieved the unrelenting heat. Mikonos rose before them out of the water like a statue.

"Not all men are like your father," Xavier said finally.

"Thank God for that."

"I mean, not all men think only with their dicks."

"Why are you telling me this, X?"

"I don't want you to think that what we did was because you're young and beautiful, and I was trying to prove something," he said rolling the bottle in his hands. "You are young and beautiful—I mean. Shit, I'm making a mess out of this."

"Maybe start over?" she suggested.

"You asked your dad to think about how his actions affect you. You're his daughter, and you see him running off with anyone with a rack and a mouth. Girls your age. Not all guys are like that. They don't just take something because it's pretty, and they think it reflects on them. And then throw it away after it's served their purpose. That's not why I... why we..."

"You're not like my father, Xavier. I know you're not."

"It would kill me to think that I used you and then threw you away."

"I know why we aren't revisiting what we did. I get it."

"You're not disposable, Angel. Don't ever let any man make you feel that way."

Waverly blinked back unexpected tears at the tenderness in his voice. "You know, X? I think you're going to be a really good dad someday."

"You've been talking to my mother," he said dryly.

"I wish. I really, really liked your family, Xavier. Be good to them."

He covered her hand with his. "I'm sorry, Waverly."

"About what?"

"About just about everything at this moment. I'm sorry that you had to grow up how you have. That you're missing out on yet another shot at normal. That we aren't revisiting what we visited—which was mind-blowing, by the way. I'm sorry that your family can't see how lucky they are to have you and that you can't see what an incredible woman you are because, if you really did see it, you'd never settle for anything less than what you want again."

Waverly let her breath out in a stream. When he talked that way, it stirred things inside her. He didn't just see an actor or a bank account or the daughter of a genetic lottery. Xavier saw *her*. But even that wasn't enough. They had a complicated working relationship if she were to call it what it was.

Embarrassed by his frankness, Xavier scrubbed a hand over his head. "You put any sunscreen on yet?"

She shook her head and handed over the bottle. He gestured toward the bed and Waverly lay facedown and squashed the urge to cry at the unfairness of it all. *Xavier Saint was just one more thing that she couldn't have.*

His hands smoothed lotion over her shoulders and down her back, skimming under the purple ties of her top. The way he touched her said so much more than words. Gentle and soothing now, his hands worked over her lower back in long, smooth strokes. Waverly rolled her head to the other side when his fingers nudged under the side ties of her bottoms.

Movement caught her eye on the stairwell.

"Mom!"

Waverly sat upright. Her mother peered through the railing holding her phone outstretched in one hand and a bottle in the other. Waverly jumped up, but Xavier was faster.

He pulled Sylvia carefully up the stairs and pushed her toward a chair.

"Say cheese," she ordered Xavier with a slur so thick is sounded like an accent. "Smile pretty for the camera."

"Stop it, Mom," Waverly ordered.

The bottle in Sylvia's hand was only half empty, meaning it was her second bottle of the day. She leaned hard in the chair as if her world had shifted on its axis.

Sylvia pulled the phone up to her face and hooted. "These ought to stir up some attention for your tour." She poked at the screen with a finger that had lost its polish.

Waverly snatched the phone out of her hand. "We've had this discussion before. You can't just take pictures of me!"

Sylvia snorted. "I made you, you ungrateful bitch. I'm still making you. You should be thanking me." She lurched to her feet and Xavier stepped between them.

"You don't need to protect me from my own mother," Waverly snapped. She stepped around him to face Sylvia. Her mother had on rare occasions called her names. It was nothing a thousand other people hadn't said about her.

"You're going to drink a gallon of water, eat some soup, and go to bed and sleep this off, Mom."

"Gimmie back my phone. I'm going to make you famous," she said, pointing unsteadily at Xavier. "You'll be grateful, won't you? Not like *her*. She thinks this life is a *burden*." She sneered in Waverly's direction. "Everybody wants to be famous."

"Not everyone, Mom. Leave Xavier out of this."

Sylvia reached for the phone and missed, scratching at Waverly's wrist instead. "Give it back to me," she said, angry now. "It's mine. I won't have you taking what's mine!"

"You want it so bad? You want to hurt me and ruin Xavier's reputation by spinning more lies about him? Then go get your fucking phone." Waverly whirled and tossed the phone over the rail.

Sylvia's scream of despair was an echo of the morning's. "How could you?" she shrieked. "I *hate* you!" The slap caught Waverly completely unprepared, and she took a step back. Her cheek stung and so did the knowledge that her mother had never struck her before.

Waverly grabbed Sylvia's wrist as Xavier gripped her shoulders. She was a wild woman now flailing and screaming. Waverly squeezed her wrist painfully. "Look at me. Look at me, now! Do you see what your legacy cost?"

Sylvia refused to look at her. The woman threw herself into Xavier's arms sobbing.

The anger and adrenaline were too much. There was black around the edges of her vision. A panic attack or something even worse was coming on, and there was only one escape.

"I'm done," she whispered the words.

Over Sylvia's wails, Xavier heard them. "Waverly." He said her name calmly as if he was talking her off a ledge.

But she was shaking her head at him. "I'm done," she said again.

"Get out of here," Sylvia screamed, thrashing against Xavier's chest. "You're ruining everything!"

Waverly did what she'd wanted to do for nearly a decade.

She escaped. Without a backward glance at her mother or Xavier, she hopped over the rail and dropped into the sapphire waters.

22

The sea closed over her head and as she sank down, down, down, a fleeting thought wondered how it would feel if she didn't fight her way back to the top. But the flickers of fading sunlight beckoned her back. This was her life, currently an empty shell but one that would be filled as she saw fit from now on.

She kicked her legs and swam for the surface. No more living to fix her parents. No more hiding behind walls of protection or artifice. No more following someone else's rules. She was taking back her life.

Her head broke the surface, and without a backward glance at where she'd come from, Waverly stroked her way toward shore. The sun was beginning to fade behind the island that loomed in front of her, and there was a chill in the water, but she'd never felt more alive. She was swimming for her life.

She heard a splash behind her. *Xavier*, she thought.

But this time, she wasn't going to let him win. She almost felt sorry for him, caught in the crossfire. But he was just another person in a very long line of people who needed her to do what he asked of her.

She wasn't going back, not without a fight. And that's exactly what Xavier would get if he caught her.

Adrenaline pumped through her, fueling her limbs with the power of desperation. She didn't turn to look for Xavier. She didn't need to. She could sense him like prey could sense the nearness of a predator. She just carved her way through the sea, swimming toward freedom.

Finally, her knees dragged against the sandy bottom of the shore and she dragged herself out.

Even though the beach that stretched before her was empty, the heat of the day still clung to the golden sand beneath her feet. Waverly spared a glance back at the water. Xavier was there, powering through the seawater and closing quickly. She had a choice—old life or new—and the decision had to be made here and now.

She took off down the sand at a run. It was a quiet crescent of beach with no umbrellas or chairs. There were no resorts, no crowds to get lost in. Just sand and rock and a softly falling dusk.

"Waverly!"

She didn't stop, didn't acknowledge that she'd heard anything. She just ran harder. *She couldn't out run him, but if she could find a place to peel off, to hide...*

She could hear him now, pounding after her. He was a predator and she the prey. Her breath was coming in jagged draws. There was a bend up ahead where the sand seemed to end. Was that light that glowed around it? Did it mean people and crowds? Could she make it?

Faster, her long legs ate up the wet sand as she sprinted for freedom, slipping and sliding as the sand deepened. She was the quarry. The point was just ahead. She threw a glance over her shoulder and regretted it. He was so close and closing, his face a mask of fury. He wouldn't stop, not until he had her. But she wasn't giving up. Waverly Sinner was never going down without a fight again.

She reached the point on a triumphant gasp, which immediately turned to desolation. In front of her was a sheer rock face, behind her two hundred pounds of angry Xavier. The light she'd seen came from the last sliver of sun as it dipped behind the cliffs above her.

She was no closer to freedom off the yacht. He was coming to reclaim her. Drag her back. She was trapped. Again.

She gave it her all, one last futile effort, pumping her legs across the thin slice of sand between cliff and ocean. But there was nowhere to go and no one to save her.

He caught her in a full out tackle, and they tumbled over the sand, a tangle of limbs. He rolled on top of her, pinning her down with his big hands shackling her wrists overhead. She didn't want to look at him, to admit her defeat. So she escaped the only way she had left and closed her eyes.

"Look at me." The order was hoarse and his breath was uneven.

Waverly's chest rose and fell against his as she tried to catch her breath. Her breasts were crushed against him, beaded wet from the ocean. When she refused to look at him, he used his free hand to circle her neck, his thumb and finger holding her jaw.

She let her eyelids flutter open and stared up at him through watery eyes.

"Don't ever run away from me again." The harsh words were accompanied by a squeeze around her neck. "Do you understand me?"

When she didn't answer fast enough, Xavier squeezed harder. "Answer me, Waverly," he growled.

"I won't," she whispered.

"You won't what?"

"I won't run away again," she gasped against the pressure of his grip.

"He's killed, Angel. I can't prove it yet, but I will. Two women are dead, and I'm not going to let you be next. So you will *never* do this again."

She hadn't been thinking of murder and danger. She'd only been thinking of the slow death her old life would lead to. The slow, sad death of the unfulfilled. And here was the jailer to return her to that life.

But there was something besides anger in him. A primal drive to claim. He was achingly hard against her. She could feel every inch of his erection as it pressed against the juncture of her thighs. Their flesh was separated by only two thin, wet layers of bathing suit.

He shifted just an inch, and the pressure of his shaft against her delicate lips had her instinctively moaning. She instinctively lifted her knees and gasped. He moved again, this time a slow glide against her bikini that parted those lips through the fabric as the broad head of his cock moved deeper between her thighs.

She couldn't tell if it was an exquisite reward or torture. Waverly only knew that she wanted more of it, more heat, more friction. She wanted to feel him inside her again, filling her once more.

"Xavier." She whispered his name on a plea, a prayer.

He clamped a hand over her mouth. His breath was still coming in short pulls, but she knew it wasn't from exertion now. No, this was something baser. The need to take and to brand. The need to drive himself into her waiting, wet flesh. She could see the pulse thunder at the base of his throat, the war behind his eyes.

She did the only thing she could and arched against him, pressing herself to his hard-on, flattening her breasts against his chest.

On a sound that was barely human, Xavier tore his gaze away from her face. Her bikini top hadn't been made for running, or wrestling for that matter, and her right breast had burst its way free. Her bare nipple brushed his chest, perking against the smattering of chest hair she'd found so fascinating.

Her breath came out on a shaky sigh. How could he fight it when he already knew what it felt like? Was his control really that powerful that he could deny himself what they both craved?

It wasn't. She read it in the way he looked at her. His desire for control and his need for her were wrapped up in one undeniable urge.

"Take me, Xavier."

The words broke him, shattering his restraint and freeing the caged beast.

Without releasing her hands, Xavier dove down and took that straining nipple into his mouth. The heat, the surprising suction of it had her gasping. His tongue laved the peak until her breast felt heavy with need, her nipple begged for more. When he closed his lips over it and began to suck, Waverly arched hard against him and was rewarded with a shallow thrust of his cock between her legs.

He brushed aside the useless cup covering her other breast and plumped the flesh with his palm. The sound that escaped him was somewhere between a purr and a groan. And when his mouth settled over that nipple, his hand returned to the first breast, tugging and squeezing at the tip. He suckled with an intensity that had Waverly seeing a black sky of stars behind her closed eyes. She felt his need as he devoured her breasts in a relentless assault.

Her own desire skyrocketed when she opened her eyes and watched him worship her nipple with his slavish mouth. Deep pulls on each peak were echoed between her legs. She fought against the grip he had on her wrists, wanting to touch him, to taste him. But he held her still and licked his way back and forth over her straining tips, the cool night air teasing the one that wasn't in his warm prison.

"X," she gasped. She was so close already, and all he'd done was touch her breasts. She was vaguely aware that a desire like this was dangerous. But she didn't care. She didn't want safe now. She wanted Xavier. She wanted this prison of lust. He slammed his hips against hers, thrusting again at the opening between her legs that wept for him. And through the layers of clothing, still wanting more, Waverly came. It was a hard, brutal release that ripped through her before she was ready. Her entire body tensed under Xavier's, forcing more of her breast into his mouth as she fought the tremors.

He groaned against her and dragged his hand down over her stomach to her hip. With one hard tug, he'd untied the string of her bikini bottom. Still pinning her, still feeding on her, he rose to his knees. He yanked away the material that hid her from him and with the same swift movement, freed his straining cock from the confines of his shorts.

He released her breast with a pop and levered himself over her. He fisted his erection with his free hand and Waverly gaped. He was even bigger than she remembered. He dipped the head through her spread center, brushing her still shuddering clit and lower to slide through the juices at her opening and back again.

The broad crown of him was slicked in moisture, and she saw a bead of it bleed from the slit. He stroked himself from root to tip, watching her. Waverly's breath was coming in gasps. She was so desperate to be filled she was afraid she'd black out from need.

No, she thought, taking a shaky breath. *She would remember this forever.*

He was stroking himself with barely restrained violence, staring at her. There was nothing left of the man that had teased her, the man who had tenderly held her and wiped away her tears. He'd been replaced with a primal warrior who had one goal, one desire. Taking her.

She was hypnotized by the way he stared at her. Anger, hot and primitive, poured off of him. *Was he punishing her or himself?* she wondered as still he made no move to enter her.

She was bared to him, her knees open wide, her bikini yanked open and cast to the side. Nothing separated them now. He changed the angle of his strokes so the head of his penis brushed over her primed lips, parting them.

The moan that broke free from her throat had him growling, a guttural rumble. With one deft thrust, he surged into her. "Waverly!"

She was stretched beyond capacity and didn't care because it was her name he shouted. Xavier flexed his hips, holding himself against her until she relaxed millimeter by millimeter and he slid all the way home in a glorious surge. Every inch of him was surrounded by her wet walls, clenching him tight. He held there, at the very bottom of her, and another orgasm rushed up inside her.

Waverly quaked around him, enjoying the slivers of pain laced through the thick cloud of pleasure as she clamped down on him with each tremor. This, this was what she had craved. To be claimed by Xavier. She was dizzy with it. Impossibly, she wanted more even as the release began to fade.

He withdrew slowly, inch by inch, leaving her empty and needy. His jaw ticked when he slammed back into her. The pleasure, a special kind of torture to him, too. This time, she didn't need a minute to adjust to him. She welcomed his full shaft. Again and again he drove into her. There was no finesse, no teasing, just a hard sprint for the finish. When he hit the end of her, Waverly saw the greed in his eyes. Oh, he liked what he was doing to her, liked that it hurt her just a little. He never broke away from her gaze as his pace quickened frantically.

She could read the message in his eyes loud and clear. *Mine. Mine. Mine.*

Sweat beaded between their bodies, her breasts rebounded, and her hips pumped with every thrust. Her arms sang from their restraint, but still he pounded into her, and she took it, she demanded it. She craved his surrender to his need. And when his eyes closed, when each thrust drew a soft grunt, she knew that he was finally giving her that surrender.

She gave herself over to him, to his need, and felt the first trickle of panic when the wave began to build. She wouldn't survive this one, she was sure of it. Xavier Saint would drown her in pleasure so deep, she would never resurface.

"Xavier!" The panic made her voice sound foreign to her own ears. The wave began to crest inside her. Higher and higher it carried her, threatening her with its promises.

"With me, Angel. With me," Xavier ground out the order. And then he was shouting her name as he pumped into her. She felt it. Hot spurts of semen exploded inside her, and the rawness of it shoved her over the edge. She was coming, a brutal detonation that echoed in every cell of her body. She tremored around him and forced more from him. Xavier jerked against her, in her. Grunting in surrender, awash in desire. He emptied himself inside her as she exploded around him. And as the wave of pleasure broke over them, there were no more barriers between them.

The quiet surf lapped at Waverly's toes, bringing attention to a sensation other than that of Xavier's body pinning her to the sand. Her world got marginally wider as she began to register the cooling sand beneath her back, the blanketing heat of Xavier covering her front. She could see stars now in the dusky navy sky as evening fell. The moon was nearly full and fat as it hovered above the horizon.

A catharsis. That's what had happened, she reasoned. All the anger and hurt and frustration they both felt had imploded in a nuclear reaction. Her body still hummed with aftershocks. She felt as though he'd hollowed her out, taking her turmoil and doubt and releasing it.

"Mmm." His lips moved against her neck and shoulder where his face was buried.

It took so much effort to form the words, but they needed to be said before anything was ruined. "If your next words are 'this can never happen again,' I will literally kill you right now," Waverly warned him.

"Mmm," he said again, but this time he stirred. He pressed his forearms into the sand on either side of her and shifted some of his weight off of her.

They stared into each other's eyes in the fresh twilight. The anger had dissipated, making way for a tenderness she'd never seen before. Xavier stroked a hand over her cheek.

"Come on," he said, his voice a quiet rasp.

"Where are we going?"

"To take a bath." He gently pulled her to her feet and began righting her bikini.

"I'm not going back."

"No, Angel, we're not."

Money talked, or so it appeared to Waverly, when the front desk clerk at the tiny inn barely batted an eye at her in Xavier's wet shirt while a shirtless Xavier handed over a credit card and spoke in broken Greek. The exchange lasted nearly a minute with both parties switching from Greek to English and back again. But the language barrier didn't seem to be a problem when the card was a black AmEx.

They'd walked half a mile down the beach in the opposite direction and into a bustling island town. Xavier had marched up a steep, cobblestone street and down several blocks as if he knew exactly where he was going. It turned out that he did when he led her up the stone steps of a white-washed building. It was a small, three-story hotel with each level boasting a slightly different design. An open-air hallway pierced the center of one level, dark, weather-worn wood accents adorned another, and a natural stone staircase led to a patio of columns and palms on the third.

There was a plunge pool in the courtyard, and the pocket-sized lobby was furnished with white couches and woven hassocks. Either the residents of Mykonos were incredibly discreet, or they had already seen it all. No one bothered to give the shivering half-naked blonde, nor her shirtless companion, a second look.

The clerk handed over a brass key and pointed toward the stairs before ducking back into the tiny office where his dinner cooled on the desk.

Xavier turned and held out his hand to her. She took it, and they began to climb the skinny staircase with its wrought iron scrollwork.

"How did you just happen to have a credit card on you?" she whispered.

Xavier smirked. "Boy Scout, remember? I'm always prepared."

"You dove off the deck of a yacht in the clothes you were wearing."

He patted the front left pocket of his still damp shorts. "Cash, credit card, pocket knife, and id."

"And I just thought you were happy to see me."

"I think I just proved to you that was definitely all me, baby," he reminded her. "One thing I didn't bother packing was a condom."

Waverly felt like she should have been stunned by their irresponsibility. She'd never not used a condom before. But in the heat of the moment with Xavier, she hadn't been thinking. And clearly, neither had he.

"Thank God I'm still on the pill," she said with relief.

Xavier paused at the last door in the hallway on the left and slid the key into the lock. "You make me forget all my rules, Waverly."

"Then what are we doing here?"

"I told you," he said, turning the handle. "We're taking a bath."

The room was small and simple, dominated almost entirely by a queen-sized bed draped in cloud-like linens and a mosquito netting more for fashion than function. The walls were white, the wood plank ceilings were white, and the rough hewn floors were rich and dark. There were two small tables flanking the bed and a rickety white-washed dresser opposite.

But the view, oh the view. Through two sets of patio doors, the Aegean sea winked back at her as the moon rose over the private postage stamp terrace.

It hit her then. The romance of it all. She stood at the open doors, overlooking the ancient town and its crescent of beach with Xavier's shirt draped over her. She heard bath water running and then he was behind her. He wrapped an arm around her shoulders and rested his chin on her head, and her shivers were suddenly no longer about being cold.

She turned her back on the sea. "Seriously, X, what are we doing here?"

He threaded his fingers through her damp hair, gently combing through it. "We're escaping. For tonight."

"Xavier, I can't go back after this." She wasn't talking about her parents or L.A. How could she go back to a life where Xavier Saint didn't touch her like this?

"We'll figure it out, Angel. I'm not giving you up, and I'm not leaving you unprotected."

"Where does that leave us?" she whispered the words as she lifted her mouth to his.

"Here." His lips met hers softly, warmly, and she felt his heat begin to spread through her.

He dipped his fingers to the buttons of the shirt she wore and worked them free one by one as he leisurely sampled her mouth. When the shirt fell to the floor, he abandoned her mouth and turned her away from him. He lifted her hair over her shoulder and trailed his fingertips down her spine to the tie of her bikini top. With a slow tug, it loosened. He kissed his way back up to her neck and, using his teeth, nipped at the tie there.

"Jesus, X, what are you doing to me?" she murmured as the fabric loosened, then tumbled to the floor.

"Everything I've wanted since I met you." His hands cupped the fullness of her breasts while his teeth nibbled at the spot where her shoulder and neck met. Stubble rubbed and abraded the sensitive skin, and Waverly dropped her head back against his chest in surrender.

He skimmed his hands lower and plucked both side ties

simultaneously. Her bottoms fell away leaving her naked except for the fine coat of sand on her back.

"Come with me," he said, leading her to the bathroom.

Here was another wow. The bathroom was the same size as the bedroom, but the level of luxury ratcheted up. The floor was tiled white with a thick pebble inlay that ran the length of the room. Rather than sinks, a long trough with two faucets was carved into the marble vanity. The cabinets were made of the same dark wood as the floor in the bedroom. A large free-standing tub took up the entire center of the room, riding the strip of decorative stone. Water steamed from the sleek faucet.

"Wow."

He shoved his thumbs in the waistband of his shorts, let them drop to the floor, and stepped out of them.

"Wow," she said again.

Xavier tested the water with a hand. Satisfied, he picked her up and plunked her down in the tub. He followed her and adjusted her so she reclined against his chest. The heat of the water and the feel of his naked body against hers sent the chill packing. Xavier lathered soap in a cloth in his hand and with lazy, circular strokes worked his way over her shoulders to her breasts.

Waverly arched against him as his palms plumped and caressed her flesh. "I can't believe this is happening," she whispered.

She felt his lips curve into a smile against her ear and then she lost all capacity for thought as his hands slipped over her belly and lower still. With the cloth, he gently stroked and played, arousing her as she never knew possible. Tenderly, he pressed his lips to her neck.

Xavier abandoned the washcloth and parted her delicate flesh. With whisper light touches, the pads of his fingers circled over that tiny bundle of nerves that demanded attention. Waverly whimpered and Xavier whispered dark words of praise, lips moving against her ear, while his fingers never ceased their exquisite torture. And then suddenly they were withdrawing.

He cut off her protest with a command. "Turn around and face me."

Waverly swirled around in the water, but instead of pulling her into him, Xavier grabbed her from the hips and lifted. She bowed back floating in the warm embrace of the water and let him support her with his rough palms under her buttocks.

"Don't drown," he warned her. "I've been wanting to do this for a long, long time. And it's not going to be over fast."

She wasn't concerned about drowning until his mouth lowered to feast on her wet flesh. Her muscles bunched with tension as she fought against the beautiful, languid pleasure that swirled through her core. His mouth was magic, and the spell he cast with masterful strokes of his tongue had her quivering.

After a long, deep stroke, Xavier deftly thrust his tongue into her. She gasped as her back bowed, and every muscle in her body tearfully begged for more. With one careful finger, he rimmed her opening until her legs trembled. And when she thought she could take no more, he slid that rigid finger into her.

In desperation, Waverly threw her arms over the sides of the tub to stay afloat. *Oh God, she was going to drown in the most salacious bathtub scandal Hollywood had ever witnessed. And she didn't care.*

He withdrew that one torturous finger and replaced it with two. Gently stroking her sex from the inside out, Xavier set a steady pace of thrust and withdraw, exquisitely full and devastatingly empty.

She was already rippling around those strong fingers, her

climax so near, when he again lifted her to his mouth. As his tongue laved her sensitive nub and his fingers played their magic inside her, she came in a glorious, molten flow that rolled on and on and on until she slipped beneath the surface of the water.

She was still trembling when she resurfaced. "What the hell was that?" she asked on a gasp.

"Preview of coming attractions," Xavier promised her. The glint in those whiskey eyes told her he was nowhere near finished with her.

"There can't be more than that," she said, shaking her head and wiping water from her face.

"Angel, I'm going to take you to heaven tonight," Xavier vowed

With a patience she'd never witnessed in him before, Xavier gently guided her hips down so she was straddling him. The head of his erection nestled against her still sensitive sex.

"Do you know how many ways I've fantasized about taking you?" he asked, trailing his fingers up her neck, into her hair. His thumbs brushed her jaw reverently. "How many times I've made you come in my dreams? How many times I've reached out to touch you but pulled back? Tonight, every fantasy I've ever had is going to come true."

He kissed her slowly, softly, taking his time until Waverly became the aggressor. She claimed his mouth with a fervor of need. When he opened for her, their tongues met and tangled, and his gentleness was momentarily forgotten as he fisted his hand into her hair and pulled.

"Damn it, Waverly. You make me forget everything," he said, easing back. She watched him gather his control again.

"What's so bad about that?" she asked, lips nibbling at his solid jaw.

"You wanted a memory of me jumping off a yacht with

you. I want to look back on tonight and remember every kiss." He brushed his lips over hers. "Every taste." His mouth moved lower to tempt the peak of her breast. "Every single thrust."

Waverly's lips parted with anticipation at the words, and Xavier lifted her so he could position himself at her waiting entrance. With her hips caught in his hands, he forced her down onto his shaft on a slick, slow slide. Waverly dropped her head back and reveled in the invasion. Xavier took it as an invitation to lean in and sample her breasts. He licked one taut tip and then the other, growling as Waverly began to move on top of him.

"Slow, Angel. Slow."

His mouth closed over one nipple, sucking in languid, deep pulls.

She rose up and on a long sigh, sank back down sheathing him fully inside her.

"My beautiful girl," Xavier whispered against her breast. "Just like that."

Waverly closed her eyes and tried to absorb it all. The sound of their labored breathing, the gentle caress of the now lukewarm water as it lapped against her, the smell of the sage soap. The feeling of Xavier filling her with decadent thrusts, carrying her up and up until there would be nothing to do but float back down.

It was unhurried ecstasy here in his arms. She rode him slowly, slowly until she felt her sex begin to ripple and quiver around him.

"Not yet, Waverly," he told her.

She tried to slow it down, but it was too late. And when he again took a nipple into the wonder of his mouth, she knew she wanted him wrecked with her. They could come apart together. She increased her pace, and he protested against her breast, but she held him there, fingers in his hair, and began to ride as if her life depended on it. Fast, hard strokes that had her wincing at the bottom. Always just past her limits, Xavier took her farther than she ever knew possible, and tonight she would do the same for him.

Clutching at his hair, his shoulders, Waverly rode. His hips answered her with forceful thrusts, and he murmured unintelligible words over her peaked nipples. His fingers dug into her hips hard enough that she cried out, but they were both too far gone to back down now. With his mouth at her breast, his cock impaling her once again with a desperate violence, Waverly gasped out his name.

Now. It had to be now.

On a low, thready cry, Waverly surrendered to the orgasm as it punched through her. It built from her toes and sang through her cells, and Xavier was there with her. His half-shout of triumph was muffled by the breast he worshipped. His hips thrust and froze in jerky shudders as he emptied his release into her. She felt him come explosively into her depths and cradled him against her as her body answered his, every wave of carnal fulfillment echoing the other's.

23

They both nearly drowned. And neither one cared. But when the water made the shift from tepid to downright cold, Xavier finally roused himself. He lifted Waverly out of the tub and patted every inch of her dry with one of the fluffy white towels stacked neatly on the shelf between vanities.

He took another for himself and briskly sluiced off the water before wrapping his arms around Waverly again.

"I'm never going to look at a bathtub the same way again," she said into his chest.

Xavier smiled, his lips grazing the top of her head. "It's my goal to ruin you for all other tubs."

"Consider your goal achieved," Waverly smirked. "I don't suppose you could try to find a way to ruin dinner for me, too?"

"Hungry?"

"I may waste away to nothing before your very eyes," she warned him.

"Well, we can't have that."

He wrapped her in one of the plush robes he found in the

closet and led her into the bedroom. There he pulled on his rumpled, damp clothing before dropping a kiss on her mouth. "Give me ten minutes."

Nine minutes later he returned to the room, shopping bags in hand. He felt a split second of panic when he realized she wasn't in the bedroom or bath, but panic turned to relief when he spotted her through the terrace door. Still in her robe, she was perched on a chair next to the table, her chin resting dreamily on her hand. Her hair had begun to dry in a riot of waves. She had the faintest smile of feminine satisfaction played across her lips as she stared into the Mykonos night.

He wished he could paint. He wanted to capture that moment on a canvas with paints as vibrant as the woman herself. But an artist he was not, so he settled for committing the moment to memory.

Drawn to her, as he had been since the first time, Xavier went to the terrace doorway.

She heard him approach, and that soft hint of a smile turned into the full wattage. The kind that reached her eyes and filled them with light. The kind of smile that made his heart turn over in his chest.

He held up the paper bag in his left hand. "Lobster spaghetti with garlic bread."

She made a noise that was uncomfortably close to how she sounded when he was inside of her, and he snatched the bag back as she reached for it. "That was close to your orgasm noise," he said with a mock frown.

Waverly wiggled her fingers toward the bag he dangled above her. "That was foodgasm, totally different from an orgasm. Now hand it over, and I won't hurt you."

He did as he was told, and while she unpacked the bag, he shucked off his damp clothes and traded them for the other robe in the closet.

"Nearly naked al fresco dining on a Greek island with a beautiful woman," he said, sinking down on the chair opposite her. "A man could get used to this."

Waverly took the first bite of her spaghetti, piling it high on warm, fresh garlic bread. "Oh. My. God. I love you."

His eyebrows shot up, and she laughed. "Spaghetti. I was talking to the spaghetti."

Xavier sampled a bite from his own plate and sighed in appreciation. "Okay, that is definitely not an overreaction. I think I'm in love with this spaghetti, too."

Waverly laughed and opened the bottle of Pellegrino she'd found in the bag. "Have you ever been in love before? With an actual person, I mean."

Xavier raised his gaze to her face. "I suppose I thought I was, once or twice."

"Is there a difference between thinking you are and actually being in love?"

He nodded. "I hope so. I've never had what my parents have with anyone. That's love. A partnership built on acceptance and appreciation and patience. That's what I hope to find someday."

"I've never been in love. I think it's impossible to fall in love in my world, you know? Everyone is always playing the game to get what they want. It's just not possible to fall in love in the game." She daintily wiped her lips with a paper napkin. "Want to hear a confession?"

"Almost as much as I want another piece of garlic bread."

She tossed him another piece of bread. "I've actually never told anyone that I loved them."

"Not even your parents?" He was shocked.

She shot him an amused look. "Especially not my parents. We're not a touchy-feely kind of family. We're more 'sweep it under a very expensive rug and hope it goes away' people."

Xavier watched her as she picked her fork up again and dug back in. She wasn't saddened by her admission. But he was devastated for her. Again he thought of that little girl abandoned and unprotected on the sidewalk. Despite all the fame, the lavish lifestyle, the shiny trinkets, Waverly Sinner deserved better than anyone had ever given her.

He thought of the hundreds and thousands of "I love yous" that had intersected his family.

"Speaking of your parents," Xavier began.

Waverly looked up from her plate warily.

"Do you want to talk about what happened today?"

"I take it you Saints are talkers?" she said, sidestepping his question.

"We've been known to discuss an issue here and there."

"Ah," she said, glancing out toward the night sea. "I've never found talking things through to be particularly helpful. Besides, talking about family issues makes me feel... disloyal."

"You've talked to me before about issues," he reminded her.

"That was different. I was amped up and frustrated, and you scared the hell out of me busting into Kate's garage like that. Tonight, you've already drained me of every ounce of tension I've ever held in my body. No tension?" She jabbed her fork in his direction. "No need to rehash events that can't be changed."

"That's very sexually Zen of you," he said dryly.

She winked at him and changed the subject. "I know this is thinking hours and hours ahead, but eventually I'm going to have to leave this room, and the only clothing I have is a bikini and this robe."

"Oh ye of little faith," Xavier said, pushing away from the table. He ducked into the room and stepped back out onto the terrace, a small shopping bag dangling from his finger.

"Too small to be an I Heart Mykonos sweatshirt," Waverly teased.

Xavier handed over the bag, and Waverly wasted no time digging through the tissue paper.

"Xavier!" her soft exclamation was filled with wonder. She pulled the dress out of the bag and oohed. It was airy, long, and white. Embellished with dark blue embroidery from the top of the simple halter to the ankle-length hem, the dress was perfectly Greek. The back was open except for a tie around the neck and another across the mid-back. "This is stunning! You were gone ten minutes. Where did you find it?"

"I sent Oberon—from the front desk—on a search for dinner while I called my men on the yacht to let them know that we were alive," he paused and looked at her pointedly. "And when I hung up, I saw the shop across the street was getting ready to close. This was in the window."

Waverly stood up and held it up to herself.

"It's beautiful, X."

"Don't put it on, yet," he told her, shoving his plate away. "I have more plans for your naked body."

"I hope you have a new pair of legs for me in that bag because if we keep this up, I'm not going to be able to walk," she warned him.

He glanced in the bag. "Hmm, no new legs. But I did see this." It was a tiny package wrapped in tissue paper. She greedily unwrapped it and her fingers paused.

"Oh, X."

He took it out for her. A small gold coin bearing Athena's wise face dangled on a long, delicate chain. "A new good luck charm for you."

She pressed her lips together and refused to meet his gaze for a moment. When she did, her eyes were glassy with unshed tears. She slid the chain over her head and patted the coin between her breasts. "Thank you, Xavier. I'm going to treasure this forever."

He was still thinking of her confession hours later while Waverly slept peacefully in his arms. He buried his face in her hair, and she snuggled closer against his chest.

She felt safe with him. That he knew. She trusted him—at least with her life—he was fairly certain. She liked him, sometimes. But he couldn't fathom going through life with the certainty that he'd never be in love. Never finding that partner that loved and challenged and supported him. No wonder she'd been so shut off from people. It wasn't just a necessary protection for her reputation and career. It was that she didn't see a point to letting anyone in. And why in the hell did it bother him so much that she was so certain she'd never love anyone? *Because it meant that she'd never love him.*

He shoved the thought aside. *It was dehydration and hormones from the four most soul-shredding orgasms he'd ever had,* he told himself. She'd had double that number and had promptly passed out after their last tangle between crisp white sheets with moonlight playing across the bed. She'd remember this night for as long as she lived, and he wasn't likely to forget it either.

His mind moved methodically on to the next area of concern. Ganim. The man had been in the wind for six days now and hadn't tried to communicate once with Waverly. Xavier knew because he checked in daily with Kate. What obsessed individual was able to go to ground and not give in to the impulses to reach out to the target of their unwanted affections? What was Ganim's next move? Xavier needed to be able to anticipate it, plan for it, and take him down.

Waverly wiggled against him in her sleep. Her lips whispered something softly against his neck. He held her a little tighter and brushed his lips across her forehead. It was time to put everything aside. He had a beautiful woman nestled in his arms who needed him to keep her safe.

No one would touch her, Xavier vowed.

~

Dawn was breaking when the tender bumped gently against the *Sea Goddess's* stern. Xavier got out first and lifted Waverly aboard as if she were precious cargo.

She was stunning in her new dress. Her hair hung long and loose, teased by the sea breeze. He took credit for the fresh glow on her cheeks, which came entirely from their predawn lovemaking rather than any palette of paint.

"Go pack your things, Angel. I'll break the news to your parents that we're heading to London early," he said, skimming his hands down her arms.

"I'll go with you," she told him with a reluctant sigh. "I'm not going to hide from them now. It'll just make going home more awkward in a few weeks."

He resisted the urge to talk her out of it. The last interaction he'd witnessed between Waverly and her parents had been unstable to say the least. Logically, he knew that Sylvia had a disease. She was a sick woman. It wasn't an excuse, but it was a "why." However, the why had ceased to matter when she'd struck Waverly. No one touched her. Not while he had anything to say about it. He didn't care that the Sinners were footing the bill for his services. That didn't give them the right to abuse their daughter.

Xavier couldn't let Waverly stay with them, not when his job was to protect her.

He planned to have a very blunt conversation with Robert to make sure the man understood the consequences of everything that had transpired.

Well, perhaps not everything.

Last night had been fantasy come to life. And there would be consequences there, as well. Professionally and personally. Maybe even spiritually. Loving every inch of Waverly Sinner had been like a religious experience, one that he wasn't ready to turn his back on.

He let her lead the way up the stairs to the salon on the main deck, doubting that anyone onboard was awake yet. After the amount of liquor Sylvia had managed to down by evening, she should need nearly a full day to sleep it off.

When Waverly slid the rear salon door open, he smelled it. Sickness and blood tangled with the breeze that played off the water.

"Oh my God," Waverly cried and rushed forward.

He made a grab for her arm intending to stop her, but then he too spotted Sylvia and let her go. The woman was sprawled between one of the overstuffed couches and heavy coffee table.

She'd bled into a sticky puddle from a wound on her forehead that was now dried on her skin and matted in her hair. There was vomit near the bar and again next to her head where she'd fallen.

Waverly was trying to move the coffee table, but it was bolted to the floor. He dragged her up, moved her out of the way. "Go call Cedric or Nestor," he told her. One of the guards would be able to help him pull Sylvia out.

"Is she okay?" Waverly asked, shoving her hands through her hair. Tears of worry clouded her eyes.

Xavier found a pulse, saw her chest rise and fall, and when

she gave an unladylike snore, raised an eyebrow at Waverly. "Barring any head trauma, she'll be fine."

Waverly ran to the phone and spoke quietly, she returned and knelt on the other side of the table. "Nestor's on his way up," she told Xavier.

Xavier called Sylvia's name. "Come on, Sylvia, wake up."

She frowned in her sleep, and lines furrowed her brow. She made a grumbling noise.

"That's right, come on now. Open your eyes."

When Sylvia's lashes fluttered, Xavier looked up at Waverly.

"Can you find me a flashlight, Angel? Check in that desk over there," he said, pointing.

Waverly scrambled up and dug through the drawers before triumphantly returning with a small flashlight.

"Good girl," he told her. "Sylvia, open your eyes."

She grumbled but slowly pried her mascara glued eyes open. "What?" she grumbled with iffy enunciation.

Xavier shined the light in first one eye and then the other. "Do you know what day it is, Sylvia?"

She squinted against the light, winced. "The first day of the rest of my life since my husband is a cheating swine."

Xavier looked wryly at Waverly. "Looks like a mild concussion, but I think she'll be okay."

Nestor hustled through the open deck door. He cut a swarthy figure in a pair of gym shorts and a gold chain around his thick neck. When he caught sight of Sylvia, he said something in rapid Greek that Xavier took for a long-winded, Mediterranean version of "fuck."

"I did a walk through in here at two this morning," he explained. "Both of them were in their rooms."

Xavier shook his head. "I don't think she was here too long.

She probably came down for something around three or four," he estimated.

Nestor approached and Xavier had him take Sylvia's feet. Together they lifted her from the floor to the sofa that Waverly quickly covered with a colorful throw. It would be easier replacing a blanket than an entire Fendi Casa silk sofa. Sylvia brought her hand to her head and winced. She focused in on Waverly and held out her other hand. "Darling, my pills, please? I've got a terrible headache."

"Hmm. I'll bet," Waverly said without sympathy. She dampened a towel from the bar and patted it to her mother's forehead gently cleaning away the dried blood. "She should probably see a doctor," she said quietly to Xavier.

He nodded and pulled Nestor aside. When they returned, Nestor approached Sylvia. "Miss Sylvia, I'm going to help you to your cabin, okay?" he asked in thickly accented English.

"Oh, darling. Don't trouble yourself. I'm perfectly comfortable… here…" She glanced around to determine where exactly here was. "Oh. Well, perhaps I should go to my cabin."

"You just hang on tight, and I'll get you there," Nestor promised. He scooped her up and carried her toward the elevator.

Waverly ignored the departure and set about filling an ice bucket with warm soapy water from the bar sink.

"What are you doing?" Xavier asked.

"Cleaning up," she said without looking at him. She grabbed a neat stack of white bar towels and carried everything over to the first mess.

She was shut down as she began what was clearly a ritual to her, and it pissed him off. It wasn't a daughter's job to clean up the sick and the blood of a parent who refused to get help. But it was someone's job.

"Angel," he waited until she lifted her gaze to look at him.

"I need to speak with your father. I'll be back in a few minutes, and we can pack."

She gave him a brief nod and turned back to her work. There was no hint of the happiness that had lit those eyes last night. Now they were empty.

By the time Xavier arrived at Robert's lower level stateroom, he was good and pissed. He pounded out a knock on the door and continued until a sleepy and confused Robert answered.

"What's going on?" he muttered groggily.

He wore rumpled silk pajamas, and there was an open bottle of scotch on his nightstand.

"Do you know where your daughter is?" Xavier's voice snapped out like a whip.

"Not at the moment. I thought she was with you? Someone said you went ashore last night?"

Xavier resisted the urge to plant his hand on Robert's face and give him a good shove back into the room. "Your daughter is upstairs in the salon cleaning up puddles of vomit and blood that your wife left seeping into the very nice carpets after she hit her head and passed out."

"Is she alright?"

"None of you are alright." Xavier let go of the reins. "Somehow you all think it's Waverly's job to clean up after the piss poor job you and your wife do of existing. She's twenty years old, and you have her scrubbing vomit like an underpaid maid."

"Now listen here—" Robert began to get his back up, but Xavier wasn't even close to done.

"No, you listen. You let that girl go live her life. Stop using her to babysit the wife you should be taking care of or divorcing. Make a fucking decision. Send her to rehab or call a divorce lawyer. Either way, leave Waverly out of it. She deserves better than being slapped around by a drunk and ignored by a man who's trying to fuck himself to relevance."

Robert opened his mouth and took a breath as if he were going to argue and then deflated like a balloon. He wiped a hand over his face. Exhaustion that went beyond interrupted sleep was evident in the way he held his shoulders.

"I don't know how to be who they want me to be."

"Be who they need you to be, not who they want you to be. Protect them, listen to them, support them."

"What if it's too late?"

"I can't speak for you and Sylvia, but your daughter could use a good man to lean on these days. You can start by taking some responsibility off of her shoulders." Xavier turned to leave. He wasn't going to let Waverly stay on this boat another five minutes. There was only so much a person could witness before the damage was permanent.

"You love her, don't you?" Robert asked quietly.

Xavier turned around but said nothing. He had no answer for the man or himself.

"It's okay. You don't have to say it. I can see it... now that I'm paying attention," Robert said with a sad smile. "It looks like she's already got a good man that she can lean on."

"There's always room for another," Xavier told him.

Xavier returned to the salon. Waverly was still scrubbing at the rug in the same spot. He crouched down next to her. "Come on, Angel. Let's go."

She shook her head, kept scrubbing. "I can't just leave this here like this. Someone has to clean it up." She lifted her gaze to him, and he saw the anguish in those beautiful sad eyes.

"It's not your mess to clean up," Xavier said softly. He tugged the soiled towel from her hand. She let him pull her to her feet.

Waverly crossed her arms over her chest and looked around the room. She looked lost without her purpose.

"Someone has to," she said again.

"I will." Robert stepped tentatively into the room. "I'm going to clean this up, and then I'm going to talk to your mother."

"You don't have to do that, Dad—" Waverly began.

"I need to," he said quietly. He shot a glance at Xavier, and Xavier nodded.

"Robert, I'm taking Waverly to London today."

Robert's face fell briefly. "Of course," he nodded. "I understand. I… uh," he cleared his throat. "I have some things that I need to take care of here."

"Dad, really, I can—"

But Robert shook his head and put his hands on her shoulders. "No, Waverly. It's long past time that I stepped up. Let me do this."

She took a shaky breath and Xavier put his hand on her back to steady her. Finally, she nodded at her father. "Thanks, Dad."

"Thank you, sweetheart. You too, Xavier. Have a safe trip, and be careful with my daughter."

24

Waverly and Kate met in a squealing hug in the foyer of Waverly's London hotel suite. "I missed you! How was your trip with your family?" Waverly demanded once the squealing had quelled.

Xavier enjoyed watching them chat animatedly as they moved into the suite's living room with its view of Kensington Gardens. Waverly may have never told anyone she loved them, but that didn't mean that she didn't feel it. With Kate, with Mari, even Louie the fashionista chef, Waverly's feelings were obvious.

The girls flopped down on the stuffy couch while Kate filled Waverly in on her trip to Boca for what sounded like a disastrous family reunion. Xavier checked his watch. He had a briefing with hotel security downstairs in a conference room in five.

"Can I trust you ladies not to do anything incredibly stupid for half an hour while I go downstairs?" he asked.

Waverly beamed at him. "If you hand me that room service menu on your way out, I'll order enough food to keep us all here for a week," she promised.

He handed over the leather bound menu and let his fingers linger on hers a little longer than necessary. If they'd been alone, he would have tilted her head back and kissed her senseless. But instead he just winked at her. He'd make sure to make it up to her when they were alone tonight.

Waverly seemed to sense his train of thought and flushed under his gaze.

"I'll be back soon. Good to have you back, Kate."

Kate grinned, "I missed you too, X-Man."

He left them with a stern order to behave themselves and Kate fanned herself.

"What was *that*?" she demanded as soon as the suite door clicked closed.

"What was what?" Waverly asked, all innocence.

"You guys are so molten I can't believe I still have my eyebrows," Kate announced.

Waverly laughed. "Oh, please. He handed me a menu not a marriage proposal."

"It was the way he handed you the menu. All lingery and smoldery. You guys are doing it!" Kate's voice was a squeal now. "Tell me *everything*, starting with penis size."

"Oh, my God! Why are you so excited?" Waverly wanted to know.

Kate clapped her hands and bounced on the cushion. "I can *finally* use your celebrity couple moniker. Ladies and gentlemen, please put your hands together for Xaverly!"

Waverly pulled a pillow over her face. "Kate, how long has it been since you've had sex?" Waverly demanded.

"Five months, two weeks, and four days. Why?"

"Well that explains why you're starved for details."

"Tell your sex-starved friend everything."

"You know that I don't orgasm and tell," Waverly chided Kate.

Kate heaved a disappointed sigh. "How about if I make a few educated guesses, and you can nod when I'm on the right track?"

Waverly gave a royal nod of acquiescence, and Kate clapped her hands. "Oh, goodie! Let's start with the most important stat. Average number of orgasms per twenty-four hour period. I'm going to guess three."

Waverly laughed, but didn't nod.

"Higher or lower?"

Waverly raised an eyebrow. "Definitely higher. In fact, double it."

Kate's head flopped back on the flat top of the sofa. "I so hate you right now."

"Xavier's amazingly attentive in areas beyond personal security," Waverly teased.

"Okay, this game isn't fun anymore," Kate groaned. "But seriously, Wave. I'm really happy for you. He has your back, like really has it. Not just physical protection, but he'll stand up for you, he'll challenge you."

Waverly bit her lip. Her tangle of feelings for Xavier went deeper than just physical. But they were complicated... and terrifying. Every time he walked into a room, she became hyper aware of his presence. She was drawn to him, orienting herself near him. Everything that passed between them, a smile, a look, a question—it all had layers of meaning... and heat. And when he touched her? The world ceased to exist. It was just him and the feelings he drew from her, the pleasure he fed her.

Was that a relationship? Was that love? Or was it the mind-clouding perfume of lust?

There was something between them. Something that strengthened and solidified more each day. Could she see a future with Xavier? If Stanford and normal were no longer an option, could she be happy where she was if she had Xavier?

"Earth to Wave." Kate snapped her fingers in front of Waverly's face.

Waverly flushed. "Sorry, what was that?"

"I was saying that maybe I'll meet some sexy British guy in line for the throne while we're here."

Waverly patted her friend's leg. "That's the spirit. Now let's order some food and catch up on all the gossip from home."

Over afternoon tea they caught up. Kate's sources told her the explosions at the premiere had the unintended side effect of creating quite the stir around the movie. Theaters around the country had sold out on opening night and continued to sell out prime show times. *The Dedication* was getting buzz that studios dreamed of.

"This could be *the* movie," Kate told her. "The one that lets you pick your projects and name your price from here on out."

Waverly sighed. She still didn't feel the rush of pride and excitement. "My mother must be over the moon. All her dreams are coming true," she said wryly.

"Speaking of, she's on her way to rehab now… or whenever tonight is back home."

"Mmm," Waverly made a non-committal noise. This would be her mother's third stint in rehab. She'd already used up all her hope on the first two stays.

"Xavier made the arrangements. It's some schmancy private place in Northern California that's part spa, part rehab. Very hush-hush, very hoity-toity."

"Sounds right up her alley," Waverly said. "What's the publicity plan?"

"Hush-hush there, too. Gwendolyn's going to anonymously

release some unused pictures of your mom driving around downtown to keep her visible. She also had me do an impromptu photoshoot around the house yesterday. Sylvia doing yoga, playing piano, sitting by the pool, blah blah blah. I'll be posting those every couple of days on Instagram to keep up the 'Sylvia's not in rehab' pretense."

"Think they'll hold up?" Waverly asked.

"They should. And if the natives get restless without a sighting, I dragged out that walking boot she had a few years ago from her skiing mishap and took a couple of pics of her in it. We can go with the whole, 'Poor Sylvia and her stress fracture' route."

"Uh-huh."

Kate shot her a sidelong glance. "In addition to the new talking points—stalker, fearful for your life, poor little rich girl—Media Barbie did give me a list of things you can do to help sell the whole thing."

"Yeah, I think you can tell Media Barbie that she shouldn't count on my help this time around," Waverly sighed.

"That bad, huh? I figured it must have been a shit storm for Xavier to drag you off of a yacht and go into hiding."

"Every time you think it can't get worse, they both toe over that line just a little further. But that doesn't mean that I have to be responsible for cleaning it up anymore."

Kate dropped her smoked salmon tea sandwich back on her plate. "I'm sorry," she said through the bite in her mouth.

"No one's fault but their own," Waverly said philosophically. Kate knew not to ask details. Waverly wouldn't give them, and Kate respected that boundary. There were areas in their friendship that remained off-limits, and it worked for them. "So Agent Travers called me when we got in yesterday."

"Still spinning their wheels?" Kate asked.

"He mentioned the fact that we need Ganim to make another move or the investigation is likely to stall out."

"Why was he telling you that?" Kate frowned.

"I think he was sending me a message."

"Oh, boy. Xavier's not going to like this," Kate predicted.

Waverly grinned. "But it's better than sitting around and hoping for the best. I'm tired of sitting on the sidelines of my own life."

"And that's why you wanted me to bring that sewing project with me." Kate slapped her forehead.

"Think you can find a tailor who'll provide emergency services?"

"You're diabolical."

Agent Travers and Xavier were comparing notes regularly these days. Xavier filled him in on precautions for the London premiere in two days. The press junket was tomorrow, and he was confident that no one was getting past the army of security the hotel and studio were ponying up for the event. It was the same with the premiere the following day. A security circus that was mostly for show. There had been no threats made, no contact from Ganim. But by reminding the world that Waverly Sinner was a target, it brought a new level of attention to the movie.

"Bottom line is—our best bet at bagging this asshole is having him stick his head out of whatever hole he's hiding in to wave hello to your girl again," Travers said from the screen of Xavier's laptop.

"We're not using her as bait," Xavier warned Travers.

"Yeah, I get that. Let's just keep that option in our back pocket as a last resort."

Xavier knew, if given the chance, the FBI would be waving Waverly all over L.A. like red in front of a rodeo bull. "Any headway on the electronic side of things?" Travers' team had been trying to track Ganim's whereabouts through his Facebook account.

"We left his account active in hopes of snagging some IP addresses, but the sneaky bastard's using Tor as a browser, which means we've got him bouncing all over Turkey and Argentina when we know he was in L.A."

"How about the email Plotts sent the investigating officer in El Plano?" Xavier asked.

Travers shook his head. "We're backed up here a good couple of months, and forensics wasn't too keen on bumping some of their big projects for a goose chase."

"I've got a team ready and waiting," Xavier reminded him. A team that was better equipped than any overworked FBI electronics forensics examiner.

Travers nodded. "Let me run it by my supervisor, and see if we can't get something moving there. I take it you've got some suspicions that Plotts didn't send that email?"

"Let's call it a working theory," Xavier said.

"Well, a theory's better than sitting on our asses waiting for something else in downtown L.A. to explode."

"We'll see if it gets us anywhere. Keep me posted, and I'll let you know if we hear anything on our end from Ganim."

"Have fun globetrotting," Travers said, without bothering to hide the envy.

Xavier grinned. "You track down Ganim and get him off the street, and I'm sure we could find some space for you at Invictus."

"I just might take you up on that."

Xavier disconnected the video chat and kicked back in the desk chair. Waverly exited the hotel's bathroom, hair still damp from her shower. "No good news?" she asked, tugging a brush through her hair. For the sake of appearances, Waverly and Xavier kept separate hotel rooms in the posh, five-star London high-rise. But for the sake of convenience, she stayed in his. To Xavier's thinking, it added another layer of security too in case someone on the hotel staff felt chatty about Waverly's room number. And it was damn convenient to have her all to himself every night.

"No news at all," he shook his head. "It doesn't make any sense. This guy is obsessed with you. He shouldn't be able to control his impulses to contact you."

"If he contacts me, will it give you something to work with?"

He gave her the eye. He knew where Waverly was going with this. "Have you been talking to Travers?"

Waverly crossed to him and stepped between his legs. She tugged at his tie. "He may have called yesterday." She pushed him back when he tried to come out of his chair. "Just think for a second. We're on radio silence right now. There's nothing externally tempting him to reach out again. Now, tomorrow? With about forty interviews exploding all over the media, I imagine he'll have a harder time controlling those impulses."

"Angel, are you saying you want to use your interviews to piss this guy off? Because you know what I'm going to say to that." Xavier tried not to let himself be distracted by the way her fingers were working his buttons free.

"I'm saying I can't control how an unstable person will react to what I say, even if it's all perfectly innocent. And, I'm half a world away. What's he going to do?"

Xavier dropped his forehead to her chest, tugged at the tie of her robe. "If I catch you doing anything reckless, I will stop the interview and throw you over my shoulder and lock you away."

Waverly pouted prettily. "Here I thought you were going to tie me naked to a bed."

Xavier pulled the tie of her robe through its loops until it came free in his hands. "Maybe I won't even let you make it to the junket tomorrow. Maybe you'll still be tied up, and I'll still be inside you."

~

"What are you wearing?" Xavier frowned at her as Waverly slid the backs on her earrings.

Waverly avoided Kate's gaze in the foyer mirror when she answered. Kate was a giggler under pressure, and she didn't need Xavier to be tipped off that they were up to something. "What? Every important inch of me is covered. You can't possibly have anything to complain about," she teased.

He studied her outfit again and continued to frown.

Kate's phone signaled a new text. "Oh, goodie. Looks like Media Barbie decided to fly in for this. She'll be here in two. X Factor, can you save me a headache and go down and meet her?"

Waverly waited until he'd left the suite before breathing a sigh of relief. "I was afraid we weren't going to squeak by on that one."

"How in the hell does he know to be suspicious of that shirt?" Kate demanded. "His instincts are ridiculous!"

Waverly ran her hand over the pintuck lace of the blouse. The illusion neckline and pleated front with its tiny satin covered buttons was intact. But the tailor had removed the long sleeves and the full satin skirt. She'd used part of the skirt to make an extra wide hem with a flirty bow on one side. Paired with skinny black leggings with leather accents and a pair of lipstick red Ferragamos, Waverly looked modern and chic.

No one would know, just by looking at the shirt, that twelve hours ago it had been a wedding dress. No one except for Les Ganim.

Waverly wasn't sure what reaction he'd have to seeing his mother's beloved dress, the dress he sent to Waverly, renovated into a casual top. But he would definitely have a reaction.

There was just one thing left to do to seal the deal. She sent Kate on an errand for water from the wet bar and snagged her friend's cell phone from the dresser. She opened up the social media messaging app and scrolled through the messages until she found him. Les Ganim. Her thumbs flew over the keyboard on the screen.

I hope you'll be watching today. I have a special message for you.

Just to let him know that it was definitely her, she took an unsmiling selfie of just her face and added it to the message.

"Let the games begin," she said grimly.

THE JUNKET BEGAN at precisely nine a.m. and was strikingly similar to the one in L.A. that Xavier had attended. Even the food had been Americanized to keep their Hollywood guests happy. The only real difference was the majority of the journalists here spoke with British accents.

The questions this time around were much different. No one cared whether or not Liam and Waverly had an affair on set or if the director made anyone cry. They wanted to know about Ganim and the L.A. premiere. *What happened after your bodyguard dragged you off of the carpet? When did you know everyone was okay? Where do you think he'll strike again?*

Gwendolyn gloated next to Xavier, a proper cup of tea balanced on a saucer in her hand. "God, the studio is eating this attention up," she said with a satisfied smile. "We've got Liam being a hero on the carpet, Waverly the damsel in distress, and a creepy bad guy waiting in the wings. Odds Maker is offering action on whether this premiere gets bombed, too."

"Wouldn't that be just great?" Xavier said, the sarcasm sharp enough to puncture Gwendolyn's bubble.

"Oh, now Xavier. Your business isn't hurting from this exposure either," she scoffed, then sipped. "I'm sure your calendar is booked with new client appointments."

It was. Micah was happily handling the influx and making noises about Xavier coming back to focus on hand-picking and training a new crop of executive protection agents. Invictus was already outgrowing its current model, three years ahead of their projections.

"My number one concern is Waverly's safety," he reminded her. "And yours should be, too. Something happens to her and you might go awhile between meals before you find a new ticket."

Gwendolyn laughed. "You haven't been in the industry long enough to get jaded like the rest of us, yet. But it looks like you've been around a certain client long enough to develop some overly protective feelings for her."

She shot him an amused look and headed over to call time of death on the interview.

25

The day passed in a blur of interviews and photos. Waverly felt like she'd answered the same questions a thousand times. But Gwendolyn hadn't complained about any robotic replies, so she figured she'd kept the answers natural enough. From where she sat, she and Liam had nailed the interviews. Excitement about the film seemed genuine even if it had initially been sparked by crisis, and though each interview focused heavily on the terrifying L.A. premiere, she'd been able to bring it all back around to talk about the film. Hopefully the studio would be happy.

After the last interview had been given, she said good night to Liam and let Xavier usher her and Kate into the elevator. She leaned against her friend on the back wall of the elevator. "I can't wait to take these shoes off," Waverly moaned.

"I can't wait to put on pajamas and eat something with the sodium content of a bottle of soy sauce," Kate agreed.

"I can't wait until you two quit complaining," Xavier teased. "You try standing around behind the scenes trying to look scary all day. It's exhausting."

"Poor wittle Xavier," Kate crooned. Waverly snickered.

The elevator doors opened, and they all plodded down the hall and piled into the suite where Waverly wasted no time peeling off her shoes.

"Uh-oh," Kate said, glancing up from her phone, her eyes wide.

Xavier's cell rang in his pocket. He fished it out and frowned at the readout on the screen. Kate clamped her hand over Waverly's wrist when he answered it and dragged her into the bathroom, locking the door behind her.

"What? What is it?" Waverly demanded.

Kate held up her phone. Waverly's Facebook page had a new message. From Les Ganim.

"I can't believe it actually worked," Waverly gasped. She grabbed the phone and opened the message.

The pounding on the bathroom door started then.

"Waverly if you don't open this door in two seconds, I'm kicking it down," Xavier threatened from the other side.

"Uh, just a second," Kate called out. "We're peeing."

"You are not peeing. Get your asses out here now!"

"I can't believe you messaged him! What were you thinking?" Kate hissed. She snatched her phone back from Waverly and ran to the window. "Okay listen. I think the ledge is wide enough for us to crawl out on. One of us will probably fall, but I'm willing to take that chance."

Waverly sighed. There was no use prolonging the foreplay of battle.

"We're coming out," she said to the door. "But on one condition."

"What?" he snapped out.

"You can't yell at us."

~

Xavier paced back and forth in front of the couch. Kate was slumped down looking like a kid who'd just gotten detention. Waverly on the other hand looked bored. Her chin rested on her palm

"You're wearing the man's dead mother's wedding dress." It was the third time he said it, yet each time he was more incredulous than the last.

Waverly examined her nails. "The FBI needed him to make contact, and he made contact."

It took all of his control not to pick her up and shake her, which technically he hadn't promised he wouldn't. He'd only promised he wouldn't yell.

Xavier took a deep breath, yet still felt the urge to yell. He gave up on the pacing and sat down on the hideous hammered gold foil coffee table and rubbed his temples. "Did I or did I not make myself perfectly clear when I said that I didn't want you doing anything reckless? Was I not speaking English? Perhaps you temporarily lost your hearing?"

She had the good grace to look the teeniest bit guilty.

"You would have said no if I told you what I wanted to do."

"And could you possibly think of a logical reason why I would say no to you wearing your stalker's dead mother's wedding dress to do thirty-five interviews that will be splashed all over every media outlet in the world?"

Waverly bit her lip, and he wanted to kill her. Or kiss her. It was a confusing urge.

"But it worked," she argued.

"To what end, Waverly? So far they haven't been able to trace his online activity. What's going to make this time any different?"

"He responded to me, X. He wants to talk to me. Maybe he wants to tell me where he is or at least why he's doing this. Any information we get out of him could help stop him."

"We?" Xavier shook his head. "Angel, there's no 'we.' There isn't even an I at this point. It's the FBI. They're running the investigation, and except for a handful of peon IT tasks that they're willing to delegate to us, they aren't going to let us take the lead here."

"So they're just going to let it go?" she cried.

"No. They've just assumed control of your Facebook page. From now on Ganim will be talking to an agent posing as you."

"Awh, man," Kate moaned. "What about all the stuff on the public side? We can't have some middle-aged suit posting shit on Waverly's page. We'll lose half our followers in a week."

"I just had a call from Agent Travers who, after informing me what you two walking migraines did, that you will be providing content to the agent running the page."

"Well, it's better than nothing."

"Isn't Ganim going to know it's not me? I mean, he's delusional, but he's not an idiot," Waverly asked.

"We will also be feeding the feds any information they deem necessary to sell the pretense," Xavier explained and rubbed a hand over his face.

"So, can I read his response? Kate took the phone away from me before I could get past the first line."

Xavier met her gaze coolly. "Let's just say Ganim's not too happy to see Mommy's wedding dress desecrated for the sake of modern fashion. He's looking forward to the opportunity to teach you some respect."

Waverly's shoulders lost some of their self-righteous defiance. "Oh."

Xavier's phone rang again.

He paced away into the foyer. "What?" he answered.

"Uh, yeah. Is this Xavier Saint?" The voice was vaguely familiar.

"Who's this?"

"This is Arnie. The photographer? We met at the Sinners and then at the premiere, before it blew up."

"Right, I remember. What's going on, Arnie?"

"Well, the guy who left the package for you at the Sinners was just here again."

"Where are you? And is he still there?"

"At the Sinners. He left something at the gate again and then walked away."

"Arnie, if you follow him I will personally punch Douchebag Joe in the face for you."

"Already in the car."

Xavier snapped his finger at Kate. "Call Travers now."

Kate sprang up and began frantically looking for the phone that was still clutched in her hand.

Xavier rolled his eyes and gestured to Waverly. She got up, yanked the phone out of Kate's hand, and dialed.

"Okay, where are you, Arnie?" Xavier asked.

"I'm on the Sinner's street heading down the hill."

"How long ago did he leave?"

"Like a minute. I was sitting in the car and don't think he saw me."

"Was he on foot or in a car?"

"Uh, he was walking."

"Okay, good. If you see him, try to keep a safe distance. I don't want him to know you're following him."

"He's the same guy who blew up the premiere, isn't he?" Arnie gulped.

"Yeah, which is why you can't lose him," Xavier said.

Waverly handed him Kate's phone.

"Travers?" Xavier snapped.

"What's up? You're interrupting my lunch."

"Put your PB and J down and get your men over to Lockwood Drive," Xavier snapped.

"You got something?"

"A photographer spotted Ganim at the Sinners'. He's tailing him now." Xavier switched to the other phone. "You still with me, Arnie?"

"Yeah. I got him. He's still on foot. Walking pretty fast. Oh! He's stopping at a car."

"What kind of car?"

"Blue? Like a darkish blue."

Xavier looked heavenward and prayed for patience. "Can you see the plates?"

"Uh-uh. Not from here. He got in. He's just sitting there."

"Wait until he pulls out onto the road and then start following him but not too close."

"Am I going to have to arrest him? Like what's involved in a citizen's arrest?"

"I don't think it's going to come to that," Xavier said dryly.

"His taillights came on! He's moving," Arnie announced.

"Okay, wait 'til he starts moving and then ease up on him." He switched phones again. "Travers, tell me you have people mobilizing."

"We're dispatching two teams. One for Ganim and one for the 'surprise' that he just messaged Waverly about leaving. Tell me what kind of car we're looking for?"

"A blue one."

Travers swore colorfully in his ear.

"Hang on," Xavier told him. "Arnie, what have you got?"

"So the car is still blue. I think it's a Honda. An older one. The rear passenger door is a different color, like primer or something." He rattled off the license plate number.

"Where is he headed now?"

"Out of the neighborhood. Turning onto Linda Flora."

"Which way?"

"Uh, right?"

Xavier repeated the description of the car and the plate number to Travers. He heard yelling and then swearing in the background.

"Uh, Mr. Saint?" Arnie said in his left ear.

"Yeah, Arnie."

"He's turning onto Bellagio. I think he's—"

"Heading for the 405," Xavier finished the thought for him. *Shit.* "Where's your team Travers, and why the fuck don't you have someone sitting on the house?"

"I don't have time to educate you on all the ways budget cuts have fucked our investigations. We're tapping the locals to keep up with everything."

"Well tap whoever you have to. He's headed for the 405."

"Christ," Travers muttered. Xavier heard him pick up his desk phone again and start yelling.

"Arnie, what's going on?"

"We're heading for the on ramp. What do I do?"

"Stay with him."

It took Arnie exactly forty-two seconds to lose Ganim in the early afternoon traffic. Xavier sank down on a thick-legged occasional chair with a dizzying floral upholstery. "It's okay, Arnie. You did good. Listen, I'm going to have an Agent Travers from the FBI call you, and unfortunately, I don't think he's going to want you to talk about this to anyone."

Arnie sighed in his ear. "No good deed goes unpunished."

"I'll still punch Douchebag Joe for you."

Arnie sounded more cheerful. "I'll hold you to it."

Xavier hung up with him and switched back to Travers on Kate's phone. "What have you got?"

"A steaming pile of shit. That's what I've got. Car's plates are bogus. A blue 2001 Honda with a primer gray rear door was reported stolen two days ago. I've got some of Detective Hansen's patrols sweeping the 405, but I can already tell you they won't find him. Bomb disposal unit should be arriving at the Sinner estate in the next two minutes to check out whatever present this asshat left."

"All right. Call me back when you know what it is, and I'll send you Arnie's number. You're going to want to talk to him soon. He's paparazzi."

"Well if that just doesn't make my day even better," Travers grumbled.

Xavier hung up and tossed both phones onto the rolling serving tray next to the chair. "Fuck," he muttered.

He felt the weight of two stares on him. Waverly and Kate were sitting side by side on the couch gaping at him like carnival goldfish.

"So..."

"So thanks to budget cuts, the FBI didn't have anyone watching your house, so they weren't there to catch Ganim dropping off a 'present' at the gates. Arnie, the neighborhood photog just happened to be there and gave me a call. He then proceeded to trail Ganim to his car and onto the freeway where he lost him before the FBI could even get their heads out of their asses."

Waverly got up and walked over to the bar. She opened a decanter, dumped some scotch in a glass, and brought it over to him.

"Thank you." But he didn't drink yet. He put the glass on the tray next to the phones.

"When you say a 'present,' do you mean another explosive device?" Waverly asked, chewing on her lip. "My father might be home or some of the staff might be there."

Xavier shook his head. "Your dad is out of town, wrapping

up a shoot. He gave the staff the week off. Micah's had some of our personnel do drive-bys and random property checks a couple times a day."

His phone rang again.

"Saint."

"If this is this guy's idea of a present, I'm glad he's not my Secret Santa."

"What is it?"

"Let's just say we now have conclusive evidence that Tiffani Plotts and Daisy Louchner are no longer among the living. It was a box of pictures with a note."

Xavier shoved a hand through his hair. "What's it say?"

"This is what happens when women disrespect their men."

26

They hit five more cities in ten days. Liam and his wife peeled off on their own to double the international coverage, and at every stop, the fans and the enthusiasm about the film were even better than the last. It was exhausting with long hours and non-stop travel, but it was clear that they had a massive hit on their hands, and the studio was bending over backwards to make the trip tolerable.

Waverly's entourage now included an additional three studio PR executives whose job it was to tweak the publicity of the film to match the local culture. Every stop had slightly different talking points and a different film trailer. Xavier managed the local security teams for the duration of each stop and kept up with the investigation at home. The FBI had found the stolen car Ganim used abandoned in a shopping center parking lot, but he was still sending messages to her Facebook page and Travers was confident they would be able to pull some information out of him soon.

Xavier was tireless, Waverly thought. Up every day before her, he remained by her side throughout the day. And at night, when Waverly's obligations were finally finished, and Kate had conspicuously wandered off to give them privacy, he took her upstairs where they tormented and pleasured each other until late into the night. They made love in cities around the world, carving out a corner just for themselves where nothing else mattered.

They both played a part during the day, trying not to stand too close or stare too long. But at night, they were free to explore each other. Every evening, the elevator ride in whatever hotel in whatever city was charged with anticipation.

They didn't touch inside the elevator. Instead, they stood side-by-side watching the floors tick up. And when the doors finally slid open, Xavier would guide her to the room with a hand on the small of her back. By the time the suite door was closed and locked behind them, she was trembling with need.

He knew her body better than she did. And no matter how slowly or sweetly they began, it always ended in a fiery race to a finish that decimated them both.

Tonight had been no different. As Waverly lay in his arms with Rome twinkling outside the window, she thought about tomorrow. Tomorrow they went home. Tomorrow everything would change. But at least they had tonight.

She stretched languidly on the rumpled sheets.

"Mmm. I feel like I just did an hour of hot yoga," she murmured.

"I think it was an hour of orgasms followed by a spontaneous nap," Xavier said, dragging her on top of him. He kissed the tips of her fingers one at a time.

"And to think I've been doing yoga wrong all this time." She traced her fingers over his bare chest in a gentle, swirling pattern. "I can't believe we go home tomorrow."

"You don't sound happy, Angel." Xavier twirled a silky strand of her hair around his finger.

She'd spent every night in his bed, wrapped in his arms.

But she only felt that they were close enough when he was inside her, driving her up. Nothing else was close enough. She felt safe with him—and not just from Ganim. For the first time in her life, she felt like she could put her faith in a man who wouldn't be tempted to betray her. That, in itself, was terrifying because there were no guarantees.

"Just dreading the return to 'normal.'" She picked her head up to look at him. "How strange is it that I consider having a stalker who plans to kill me and dealing with my mother in rehab as normal?"

He gave her one of those slow, belly-flopping smiles of amusement. "What do you wish your normal looked like?"

"I couldn't even begin to imagine," she sighed. But she could. A scrap of her still clung to the hope that Ganim would be behind bars before the end of the summer leaving her free to attend Stanford. A new path with new opportunities. But the likelihood of that dream coming true was even slimmer than the possibility that her mother's stay in rehab would stick this time.

"Maybe I can help you with normal...at least for tonight," he told her.

"I'd like to see that," Waverly said, arching an eyebrow.

He slapped her bare buttocks. "We'll start with dinner. Go get dressed."

"Xavier, it's after ten. That's late even for Rome."

"Trust me, Angel. Have I ever led you astray?"

"I'm sprawled naked across your spectacular body. If that isn't astray, I don't know what is."

He dumped her on her side on the mattress. "Prepare to be amazed and well fed."

She took a moment and watched him pad naked into the walk-in closet. There wasn't a city in the world better equipped to worship the flesh of a man like Xavier Saint.

Every statue here looked as if it had been carved in his honor.

He came back out and tossed a long skirt and a soft black t-shirt at her.

"Why do you have my clothes in your closet?" she asked rising to her knees on the bed.

He gave her a wolfish look. "You seem to lose a lot of your clothes in my room. I have more of your clothes than my own in my luggage."

She dressed quickly, looking forward to a meal that wasn't room service, and hurried back to Xavier. He'd pulled on a pair of jeans and left his white button down untucked. He looked her up and down and gave a mock frown.

"What?" Waverly looked down at her clothes.

"You're missing something," he said with a wink and plopped an Invictus ball cap on her head. "Now you're incognito."

They snuck out the hotel's side entrance and avoided the lobby altogether. On the street, Xavier took Waverly's hand in his and led her west. They walked along like just any other happy couple enjoying the warm summer night.

He tugged her to a stop just a few blocks from the hotel. Neon signs blinked "gelati" and "pizza" in the arched front windows of the old building. A scattering of tables and chairs flanked the front facade. Only a few of them were occupied by raucous Italians enjoying the night.

No one paid them the slightest bit of attention as Xavier led the way inside. The shop was long and skinny with most of the space dedicated to a brick pizza oven and mile-long case of gelato flavors. They ordered at the counter by choosing slices of pizza from the display case. She went for the *margherita* while Xavier ordered the *diavola*. They grabbed drinks from the greasy cooler and settled into the back corner of the shop.

The wobbly table was covered in a well-worn burgundy cloth that didn't match the wooden chairs with red vinyl seat cushions. The air was thick with garlic and warm from the oven.

He was watching her with an amused smile. "When's the last time you went out for pizza?" he asked.

Waverly leaned forward and took a big gulp of her soda. "I can't remember. I don't know if I ever have," she confessed. "My parents always had a chef, and if we were going out, it was to a cocktail party or Nobu to be seen."

"You poor deprived child," Xavier teased, taking her hand in his.

"I feel like this is a date," she told him, looking at their linked hands.

"When's the last time you went out on one of those?" he asked.

She thought back. "Probably three or four months ago. He was a baseball player, and his agent called mine. His contract was up for negotiation at the time. He picked me up in a McLaren, and we went to Spago."

Xavier stared at her for a beat.

A waitress in a flour coated black polo and green apron dumped steaming pizza on paper plates in front of them and bustled off.

"I'm afraid to ask how it went," Xavier said dryly.

"His contract was successfully renegotiated, and he didn't make it past my front door," Waverly said, picking up a slice from her plate. "How about you?"

"Two months ago... maybe three. An attorney I met at a conference. She called me at the office when she was back in town and asked me to dinner."

"You didn't fall in love over candlelight?" Waverly asked.

"She told me the never-ending saga of her last divorce over

mediocre Italian. I gave her some solid advice that she didn't like, and we didn't even order coffee."

"I'm not sure which of our stories is sadder," she commented.

"Mine didn't involve a McLaren."

"You're right. Yours was sadder."

They ate and laughed until the kitchen closed and the waitress booted them out. They took gelati to go, and tucked under Xavier's protective arm, Waverly enjoyed the late night quiet of Rome.

They wandered a circuitous route heading back in the direction of the hotel with neither of them in a hurry to arrive. The cobblestones beneath their feet were worn by centuries of feet. Here, ancient buildings were glued together on narrow laneways, rolling uphill and down. Bouquets of flowers spilled over window boxes on every floor. Most windows were dark now in this neighborhood. It felt like they had the world to themselves.

Waverly knew what neither of them was willing to say. This relationship that had bloomed between them was possible only because of the bubble they were enjoying. Temporarily safe from Ganim, on the other side of the world from her parents, and not chained to a movie set, Waverly and Xavier could just be. It was easy to fool a handful of studio execs who were more concerned about profits than personal relationships. But once at home, there would be others to consider and consequences to weigh.

This night might be the last one they could share.

He brought her to a halt and brought his finger to his lips. With a furtive glance around them, Xavier reached into a window box and nipped a freesia bloom from its stem. He tucked it into Waverly's hair behind her ear.

Charmed, she wrapped her arms around his waist and

smiled up at him. There was a look in his eyes, a softening, a warmth. He ran a thumb over her lower lip, then skimmed his hands through her hair. And when his mouth lowered to hers, it was magic. Softly, softly his lips moved over her, teasing her until she opened for him. His tongue swept in to claim new territory, mating with hers in the kind of gentle possession she'd never before known from him.

He kissed her under the inky night sky until she forgot everything. Nothing else existed beyond this postage stamp of cobblestones. Just Xavier offering her the gift of one more magical night.

As gentle as he was being, she still felt fierce need ripple through him. He was hard against her. She felt him straining against the denim and it made her ache. She broke free of the kiss, and when he moved to pull her back, Waverly shook her head.

She took his hand and pulled him into the skinny, arched alleyway carved out between two buildings. Three feet into it, the light from the street disappeared leaving them completely isolated in the dark.

When her fingers moved to the fly of his jeans, Xavier stiffened.

"Waverly, what are you doing?" his voice carried a warning.

She brought her mouth to his as she lowered the zipper. "What I want on our last night here," she whispered.

She felt his glorious abs tense when her fingers slipped inside, heard his intake of breath when they closed around him. Carefully, Waverly freed him from his jeans, and he fell heavily into her waiting palm. She realized she'd never seen him not hard. Their physical reaction to each other was so visceral and, it seemed, never-ending. Just as her desire to do this.

She sank down to kneel on the stone path in front of him.

"Angel." Any further words died on his lips when her tongue darted out to steal a taste of him.

He sucked in a sharp breath, and she felt the tension radiate off of him. She was going to take Xavier Saint's formidable control and shred it. Waverly gripped his shaft by the root and without preamble slid her mouth over the blunt head. His gasp turned to a groan of agony when he hit the back of her throat.

Waverly moaned, and the vibration of it had him fisting his hands in her hair. She drew back, stroking with one hand while her other palmed his balls, tugging and rolling.

Again, she slicked her mouth over him, and this time, his hips met her with a shallow thrust. His hands weren't gentle in her hair, and she matched his violence with her mouth. She slicked her tongue over him and dragged lightly with her teeth. The growl that escaped him was no longer human.

Again and again, Waverly took his steely length to the back of her throat, pumping him from root to tip with her hand. She could taste him, that salty sample of what was to come, and she moaned again. He was moving for her now, and he swelled, growing impossibly thicker when she sucked at him gently.

"God, yes, Angel. Just like that." His murmured words were labored, desperate, and nothing in her life had ever been such a turn on to Waverly.

She gripped him hard, stroked faster, and was rewarded with the low animal sound from deep within his chest.

"Angel, you're making me—"

She didn't even have time to prepare because he was coming with a violence that had his thighs trembling against her. She swallowed desperately over and over again, wanting to destroy him the way he so often destroyed her. Xavier was out of his mind with pleasure as he worked his cock in and out of her willing mouth. He didn't start breathing until she milked the last drops of his release from him. Then his breath came in shuddering groans.

His knees buckled, but he caught himself before dragging her to her feet. He rested his forehead on hers and struggled to get his breath back. Even spent, his penis remained hard against her belly.

"Jesus, Waverly. What did you do to me?"

"Destroyed you. Just a little bit. I wanted to make sure you knew what it felt like."

"Angel, you destroy me every time. Don't ever think that you don't."

He let his hands roam over her back and sides, and she felt him twitch against her.

"You can't be serious, X. You can't have anything left after that," she said in wonder.

"I'm never done with you, Angel. Remember that." And on that threat, his hand found its way under her skirt. When he found her bare, she heard the rumble of approval from deep in his chest. "I'll always want you again, Waverly. Always." His fingers dipped into the slick folds, and it was her turn to sag against the wall. He worked them in and out, gently at first and then building up to speed. He was driving her insane with need.

"Are you ready for me, baby?"

"God, yes, X. Please," she begged. Then he was lifting her in his arms and when he pressed her against the wall and entered her on one swift thrust, she was his.

There was no time or need for finesse. They were two joined as one racing to the finish. Racing to salvation. And as the stone bit into her back, and Xavier filled her from the front, Waverly felt a door in her fly open.

He gripped her hips and squeezed. With just the slightest shift in angle, she was coming on him, around him, over him. The orgasm raced up and detonated inside her. He covered her mouth with his, swallowing her screams, and on the next thrust, poured himself into her.

27

Their international honeymoon ended somewhere over Colorado.

"So what's new?" Waverly asked lazily as she flipped through the pages of a glossy magazine.

The drone of the plane's engines exacerbated the extended silence. She looked up and found Xavier staring at her over his laptop. His expression was unreadable. He'd been in a crappy mood the entire flight, spending most of it on his laptop or muttering into a phone. The closer they got to home, the stronger Waverly's sense of impending doom.

Even though her return was cloaked in secrecy, she felt like she was flying back into a trap. The studio was throwing a splashy party for the cast and crew tonight on the strip in L.A.: a kind of "thanks for making us a ton of money" thing to make up for the premiere and after party that hadn't happened. Waverly's presence had been very firmly required by the higher ups.

Xavier was pissed at her for not saying no, and he was pissed at the studio for not taking into consideration the logistical hell of protecting Waverly in a nightclub on a Friday night in downtown L.A.

He'd worked his very fine ass off to extract a promise from the studio that their publicity team would announce her much anticipated return for the following day and express Waverly's regrets for missing the festivities. If Ganim didn't know Waverly had returned, it should buy her a few precious hours. At least until all the gossip sites caught her at the club. Even so, the FBI and local cops would have undercovers stationed in the club to be on the safe side.

"You mean with the disaster that's waiting for us in L.A.?" Xavier asked, heavy on the sarcasm.

He was more pissed than she'd realized.

"Yes. What's happening in my life that I need to know about?" she asked pointedly.

"Gee, I'm sorry. I thought you going out clubbing tonight meant you didn't give a shit about your security."

She stared at him coolly, not ready to voice the fifteen snarky comments she had on the tip of her tongue.

"Well, we could start with the fact that Ganim is still spouting off threats about teaching you some respect to the agent running your page. Or maybe we should talk about the fact that my team proved that the email allegedly sent by Tiffani Plotts to the investigating officer came from the guest Wi-Fi network at the Rail Car Diner where Daisy Louchner worked—the diner that's two blocks from Ganim's house. And the convenient timestamp on the photos of the dead girls that Ganim sent to you proves that she was already dead when the email was sent."

Waverly took a deep, cleansing breath. Then another.

"Or maybe we should talk about how asinine it is to sneak you back into the country only to parade you around in a nightclub filled with assholes with cell phones begging Ganim to make a move on you? Or the fact that our internal investigation turned up nothing on the leak that told Ganim you were staying with me the night of the premiere. So we still have no idea how he found you there."

"X, relax," Waverly sighed.

"How about you relax? You're the one with the security ready to take bullets for you. You pay us to worry for you. I'm happy to serve my people up tonight so you can go out clubbing," he snapped.

Her control was fraying. "You know it's not my choice!"

"Everything is your choice," he snapped back. "Some decisions are just more complicated than others. You are willingly walking into a fucking trap and dragging me and my team along for the ride."

"Then don't go," she snapped.

"You're starting to piss me off," he warned.

"Starting to? You've been in dick mode since we took off," she argued. "You think I want to go out tonight? You think I'm happy about opening you up to the threat that sees you as an obstacle to me?"

"Then don't fucking go. Stay home and lay low. Don't put other people in harm's way so you can get your attention fix."

He wasn't playing fair. He was hitting her where it hurt on purpose.

"Xavier, I have a contract—"

"You have more fucking money than God. Fuck your contract. Stop being a doormat to these people who don't give a shit about you."

"Look, not everyone has the same freedom that you do. You can walk away from this easier than I can," she told him.

"Oh, yeah, because that would look great to potential clients. Invictus let Waverly Sinner go out clubbing all by herself, and then she got attacked by a fucking serial killer. That's a ringing endorsement for my business."

"So that's what you're worried about? Your business. Wow, for a second I thought it was me. My mistake." Sarcasm dripped from her words.

"Shut the fuck up, Waverly," he snapped.

"No, let's try it your way. Let's talk this out." She was fired up now. God, to think she'd forgotten that he could burn her like everyone else. It was a humiliation to realize she'd purposely let her guard down with him. He was just like everyone else. "I was feeling so dreamy-eyed from last night. I'm glad you're clearing the air before we hit the ground and I embarrass myself by professing my undying love for you."

Xavier leaned forward in his seat. "You've got me lined up as second prize to Stanford. I'm no one's second prize. And we both know you're not in love. You don't know what love is."

"Message received." She released her seatbelt and stood.

"Where are you going?" he demanded.

"Somewhere where I don't have to look at you," she snapped.

She strapped herself into a seat in the back facing away from him and closed her eyes. How had she let herself be so vulnerable to him? She tucked her ear buds into her ears and cued up her Pissed Off playlist. She'd almost let herself... care for him. Almost let him in. *Who was she kidding? She already did. She already had.* Tears burned at the back of her throat, but she'd be damned if she'd shed them in front of him. They could wait until she was home, alone, in her own bed tonight.

As the lump in her throat choked her, all she could think of was that maybe her mother was right. Her phone buzzed with her first domestic text in three weeks. It was from a blocked number.

Welcome home. I've been waiting for you.

She frowned at the screen. No one had this number. It was probably just spam or a mistake. It certainly wasn't anyone she knew. She decided not to mention the text to Xavier, mostly because the idea of broaching a conversation with him made her want to throw things.

The text couldn't have come from Ganim, she told herself. If he had her number he would have been contacting her for months. It was just some random mistake.

Bob Hope Airport was a decidedly different experience than landing at the paparazzi hive of LAX. Xavier snuck her in the country eighteen hours early under the radar by landing the jet in Burbank. Xavier and Waverly said nothing to each other as they exited the plane and headed into the terminal.

It was a matter of minutes before Waverly was transferred from the cream leather of the jet to the backseat of a black SUV with tinted windows.

With only Gwendolyn and a handful of studio execs aware of her return, she would be avoiding her house and was supposed to go straight to Xavier's for the night. It was the last place she wanted to be. At the moment, she'd rather walk down Sunset Boulevard wearing a sandwich board begging Ganim to take his best shot.

She sat against the door as far away from Xavier as possible and cursed her body for being so aware of his presence. She wanted to be immune to him. She wanted him to mean nothing to her. But he was everything, and that was terrifying. She'd welcomed him into her life, bared her soul and body to him, and had the naiveté to be surprised when he too turned on her.

She distracted herself from her mad when they pulled into the parking garage of an unfamiliar building. "Where are we?" she asked coolly.

"I decided it would be better to keep you at one of our other properties," he answered without looking at her.

"Good idea. Then I'm not putting anyone else at risk," she said flatly. She didn't wait for him to get out and open her door.

They rode the elevator with the driver to the fourth floor of the apartment building where Xavier led her to the first door on the left. It was a nicely appointed condo with a good view of Dodger Stadium.

Xavier ignored her and focused on setting up his laptop and files on the dining room table. Waverly wandered around until she found the one and only bedroom in the unit. She shut and locked the door behind her and lay down on the bed to cry.

She must have fallen asleep because she woke with a raging headache to a knock at her door.

"Ready to go in twenty," Xavier said from the other side of the door.

Shit. She groggily sat up and swiped a hand over her face.

"Waverly?"

She wondered how long it would take for her name on his lips to mean nothing to her.

SHE WORE FIRE ENGINE RED. The dress showed off miles of leg and had a strip of red translucent lace that wrapped around her midriff. Her hair was down and styled with loose waves.

She'd applied her make-up as if she was going to war. And in a way she was. She was going into that club ready to make fans swoon, investors worship at her feet, and tell Les Ganim it was time to make his move. She was tired. Tired of being a target. Tired of being a doormat. Tired of being hungry for someone to love her.

From now on, there was only one person she needed to look out for, and that was herself. It was about damn time that she started.

Thirteen was L.A.'s club of the moment. Waverly wasn't a club goer herself by any means, but even she knew that if you wanted to be seen, you showed up at Thirteen. They aimed for an eleven p.m. arrival through the downstairs kitchen to avoid being spotted outside. There wasn't much they could do about exposure once she was inside. Everyone had a phone with a camera, and the Celeb Spottings upload app. There were no secrets in L.A.

Xavier had stared hard at her when she came out of the condo's bedroom. But she'd ignored him, and he hadn't tried to start a conversation in the SUV on the way there. It had been a chilly ride.

But once inside, Waverly turned it on. She grinned and waved her way through the club's kitchen and was already moving to the beat as she climbed the back stairs to the VIP lounge.

The subterfuge must have worked because the place went dead silent for two whole seconds before erupting when she sauntered in through the service door. And for once, as the crowd closed in on her, she didn't feel Xavier's hand at her back. But tonight she didn't need it. She was determined to never need it again.

She was spun from person to person in a dizzying dance. Investors, producers, executives—each wanted a piece of her.

A promise for even more than what she'd already given. None of them could guess that her quiet acquiescence was over. *God help the suit that got in her way first*, she smiled to herself.

Waverly ignored the bottle service and ordered a club soda and settled on a white leather sofa. She talked the talk and laughed when appropriate but on the inside felt absolutely nothing. She took a moment to wonder if this was how her mother felt.

She avoided Xavier's gaze at all times, pretended he was nothing more than furniture, and lavished everyone else with attention. Sipping from her glass, Waverly could feel Xavier's frustration, feel the friction he put off, and she secretly relished it. She shouldn't be the only one hurting.

She was leaning in for a particularly juicy piece of gossip from a producer when the sudden wave of dizziness caught her off guard.

Xavier stood ten paces away from Waverly and watched every move she made. She was pretending he was invisible, and that was fine with him. He was a millimeter away from dragging her out of here. It was stupid for her to be here, like dangling a mouse in front of an alley cat. And her lack of concern about her own well-being or the others who could suffer from her ignorant decisions pissed him off. They'd have it out tonight. One way or another, she would hear him.

He watched her as Waverly brought a hand to her head. It looked like a casual move to the untrained observer, but Xavier felt the buzz in his gut. She looked pale to him. Off. Maybe it was exhaustion. She was certainly entitled to it having been on the move for three weeks straight.

Shit. He was going to have to talk to her. He approached her from behind and leaned over the couch.

"Everything okay?" Xavier asked in her ear.

Her spine went rigid at his voice. "Fine."

"You don't look fine."

"Gee, thanks for that assessment."

"Listen, smart ass, if you're not feeling well, we can go. Just say the word, and I'll call the car."

"I just have a headache." She took a shaky breath, and he wondered if she was about to lose her dinner. Then he realized he hadn't bothered to feed her and cursed himself. "How about another fifteen minutes and you call the car?" she decided.

"I'll have some food brought over to the condo for you," he said, his tone gruff. "Do you want anything here?"

She shook her head, shook him off, and ordered another club soda from the server, who looked annoyed that she wouldn't be seeing any tips from Waverly on the open bottles of Champagne and vodka that sat on the table in front of her.

He decided to follow the server so he could take the drink directly to Waverly. She didn't need to wait while Miss Attitude took her time plugging in a notebook full of orders. Xavier nodded at Darius, one of his undercovers, to take over on Angel Watch for him. He followed the server to the bar and watched her ring in the order. The ticket spit out instantaneously, and the bar back ripped it. He was pierced and tatted and wore his black Thirteen shirt a size too small. A furtive glance around was Xavier's first hint that there was trouble. The sweat beading on his forehead was the second.

He watched the bar back fill a fresh glass with ice, and then, a second before he reached for the soda gun, the guy pulled a small vial from his pocket. He poured a few drops of the clear liquid over the ice and then topped it with club soda.

He wrapped the ticket around the glass so there was no mistaking who it went to.

The fucker was drugging Waverly's drink, Xavier realized. He'd probably drugged the first one, too. It was his last coherent thought before his vision went red. There was no good reason that he could think of to control the rage that filled him.

The bar back looked around again, eyes skimming over Xavier and flashing through the crowd. Before he could set the glass on the service bar, Xavier was hauling him over the bar knocking over stools.

Two women in sequined dresses that barely covered their crotches screamed next to him, and the whole place erupted.

Xavier tossed the bar back down on the cement floor. His anger didn't dissipate with the first punch or the second. Someone grabbed his arm on the third, and he took a swing at them too. All hell broke loose. Someone got in a lucky shot to his ribs and another to his face, but Xavier wasn't going down. He swung with all his fury.

The other bartender jumped to the aide of his friend. The bouncer for the VIP section waded into the fray and called for backup. Five undercovers, guns in hand, jumped in from their respective spots around the club.

VIPs hid under tables or ran for the exits. Everyone was screaming over the beat of the music.

It took two precious minutes before Hansen and Travers' badges convinced club security to let Xavier up off the floor. And in those two minutes it had gone down. Waverly was gone.

28

Video surveillance showed Waverly slumping over at her table just as the fight broke out. While everyone else was distracted by the brawl, a man in a baseball cap slunk in, slipped her arm around his neck and half walked, half dragged her into the hallway near the restrooms. The fire exit's alarm had been disabled.

Ganim had her, and Xavier knew it was his fault. He'd allowed himself to be distracted. He should have stayed with Waverly and let someone else go to the bar. But he hadn't. They'd been pissed at each other, and he'd miscalculated.

The VIP section of the now-empty club had been turned into command central with Travers, Hansen, and fifteen men and women from their respective law enforcement branches and Invictus. People were yelling into phones everywhere.

The bar back, now with a broken nose, was sobbing in a booth as he answered questions.

His answers barely registered with Xavier. *He'd walked up to him in the parking lot before his shift. Just a skinny guy in a black cap. Showed him a gun and said if he didn't do what he was told, he'd shoot up the whole club.*

They needed video surveillance of the entire block. They needed the car.

Ganim had gotten through the net.

Xavier's head spun. Years of instinct and the need to act warred with the memories of what he'd said to her on the plane. Those wouldn't be his last words with her. Not what she meant to him. No, their last conversation would be him accusing her of selfishly putting his people in danger.

"I need to find her!" Xavier railed. He fisted his hands at his side, ignoring the zing of pain from his split knuckles.

"You need to calm down, Saint. You're no good to her like this," Micah said calmly, laying his hands on Xavier's shoulders. His partner had arrived just as the fight had broken out and had been the one to pull Xavier off the bar back.

Xavier knew Micah was right. It was his emotions that had put Waverly in danger in the first place. He hadn't seen it, hadn't felt it, until it was too late. That buzz of danger, he'd attributed it to something being off at the bar. Being pissed off at her, wanting her so fiercely, had dulled his instincts. And now his Angel was going to pay the price.

"Fuck." He tried to get a hold of himself. But standing around with his thumb up his ass wasn't going to save her. He had a window, a very small window, and he needed to find her. He needed to stop feeling and just think. *Think.*

He looked around them at the clumps of cops and agents who were following their painful, methodical protocols. "We need to be out there looking."

Micah looked him in the eye and nodded. "I'm with you. Let's go."

They started for the door, and Travers stopped them. "You leaving?" he demanded, disconnecting a call.

Xavier clenched his jaw. If the feds tried to keep him locked down here, he wasn't afraid to shoot his way out.

"We're no good to you here," Micah said diplomatically. "We're going to start driving. If you catch anything, maybe we can get lucky and get a jump on them."

Travers studied Xavier for a moment longer. "Here," he said finally. He fished a set of keys out of his pocket, handed them to Micah. "It's out back. Use the lights."

They hustled down the emergency exit stairs, just as Ganim had done. When they exited the building, they were in a narrow walkway between buildings. To the right was the street, to the left was the alley.

"He'd have taken her this way," Xavier said, moving toward the alley. She'd been drugged. She wouldn't be walking easily. And there's no way Ganim could have paraded her past the paparazzi out front without being seen.

In the alley, they found investigators taping off the scene. A strappy gold stiletto lay on its side, and he remembered watching her slip it on before they left. She'd glared at him when she caught him staring. Even angry, she still made him hard. Still made him crave her.

"Christ, her anklet! Tell me she's wearing her tracker." *Please.* Xavier yanked his phone out of his pocket, and his hands shook as he opened the app.

"She's on the move."

Micah hit the button on the fob, and the lights on a black Yukon lit up.

They sprinted down the cracked asphalt and jumped in. "Call Travers, let him know where we're going." Micah turned the key and fishtailed out of the alley. On the street, he hit the blue lights and the gas.

Ten minutes. Ganim had ten minutes on them, but they were going to narrow that gap. They were flying now, red lights be damned. Xavier dialed Travers and gave him the general direction of Waverly's blip on the screen.

Hollywood Boulevard. They were heading in the opposite direction that they should have been to escape.

"What do we know?" Xavier demanded from Micah.

Micah casually scanned his mirrors as he made an illegal left hand turn and floored it through a red light. "Ganim approached the bar back in the parking lot before his shift. Idiot has on his Facebook profile that he's the Friday night bartender for the VIP section so it didn't take much research. Ganim showed him a gun, made some threats. Had the guy drug Angel's drink. The lab's going to look into what he gave her, but my guess is some kind of sedative or roofie. The emergency exit alarm has been broken for weeks, and no one noticed that the outside lock had been busted open. It was intact last night when they locked up."

"How did he know she'd be there? Do we have a leak?"

Micah shrugged. "It's a possibility. So, talk to me, Saint," he said, calm as a Sunday morning from the driver seat.

"He's not trying to get out of the city. He's got the jump on all of us, but he's not running. He's heading somewhere specific."

"He's escalating," Micah agreed. "The flash bangs at the premiere, taking her in public with witnesses."

"His face has been splashed all over the screen for weeks now. He's finally somebody," Xavier thought out loud. Micah slowed for another red light before accelerating through it. "Daisy and Tiffani didn't think he was someone. They thought he was no one. So he had to prove it to them."

Micah shifted in his seat, and Xavier knew he'd come to the same conclusion. "You can't just take a girl off into the woods and kill her when you're a big deal. You need to make a statement."

"Fuck. I know where they're going," Xavier said.

WAVERLY WOKE, dizzy and sick, in the dark.

Her entire body tensed before she was even fully conscious of the danger. She was in a car, facedown on the backseat. Her hands were secured behind her back, but her feet were free. *Ganim.*

She remembered the club and the wave of dizziness that had swept over her. She wanted to call out to Xavier, but something happened. Some commotion, and then it was Ganim at her side. She couldn't scream, couldn't do anything but fall into unconsciousness. Now she was tethered and helpless.

And she was going to die.

A rush of visions hit her. All she could think about was all the things she'd never do. There'd be no college. No house of her own. No Xavier. She'd have no chance to tell him that she was sorry, that this was all her fault.

At least he'd get over her death. They all would. After all, wasn't this the price some paid for fame?

Ganim was whistling now. A cheerful, tuneless riff. Looking forward to killing her, she supposed. *God damn it.* She felt a hot tear streak down, sliding over her lips so she could taste the salt.

She had lived her life so carefully, and now she was going to end up as some grisly Hollywood story? *No. For once in her pathetic, charmed life, she was going to put up a fight.*

The car was moving but not at highway speeds. There were streetlights here and headlights from other cars. Maybe she hadn't been unconscious too long. If they were still downtown, there was a good chance Xavier would find her.

She just needed to hang on until then.

She worked through her options in her head. If she could open the backdoor with her foot, she could slide out. It wouldn't be a pretty exit or a fast one, and odds were he could catch her before she made it out. Her other option was to wait until he tried to get her out of the car. If he thought she was still unconscious, she might have a chance at surprising him and getting away. But if he didn't stop soon, if he took her out of the city, her chances for survival were zero.

"I bet you're wondering how I found you," Ganim said, and Waverly froze. Her breath stilled in her chest. His voice was thin, reedy, and oh so confident. "Come on. I know you're awake. I can hear your breathing."

She weighed her options. If she was going to die, she at least wanted some answers.

"Why are you doing this?" she asked, her voice a rasp of fear and sickness.

"Wrong question," he admonished. "Ask me how I found you."

Waverly took a shaky breath. "How did you find me?"

"Do you remember when we met?" he asked.

She closed her eyes and took another breath. "At the premiere."

"Good girl. What do you think I was trying to do there?"

Waverly squeezed her eyes shut tight against a new roll of nausea. "Get my attention?" she guessed.

"Well, that was secondary. Tell me, what did I do?"

"Besides the bombs? You got close to me."

"Exactly right. A-plus. I could have killed all those people, you know. I could have killed you. But I didn't."

"Th-thank you." Blackness lurked on the edge of her vision, and her heart thundered in an irregular rhythm.

"Don't be stupid. I didn't do it for you. I wanted witnesses. I wanted them to see what I was capable of and spread the word," he crowed.

And it's exactly what they had done. Les Ganim's name was currently synonymous with terror.

"Why did you want to get close to me?" Waverly asked. She debated sitting up but decided that appearing too weak to sit would play more in her favor. And she wasn't one-hundred percent sure that she was capable of sitting up.

"Well, you see, my dear. I have a bit of a flair for technology."

"You were a... a systems analyst. At home."

He scoffed. "I was a puppet to them. A speck of nothing. But in my own time, I developed some special skills. There wasn't much else to do while Mother was sick, you see. If I wasn't working, I was taking care of her. But I did carve out time to learn a bit about hacking and build an interesting little program."

Waverly's head was throbbing, and the urge to vomit was rapidly becoming a priority.

"What kind of program?" she whispered.

"All I had to do was get within ten feet of you, and my program could detect your phone."

"Detect?" Waverly felt the sick roll. "Oh my God. It was you. You texted me today."

Ganim laughed, a high-pitched snicker. "I did more than text you," he scoffed. "I tracked you. I knew the second you came home," he said proudly. "I knew where you went after the premiere. I knew how long you were there. As long as you were within a hundred miles of me, I knew where you were."

She hadn't told Xavier about the text, a mistake for which she would now pay dearly. Waverly groaned, making a noise that she hoped passed for admiration.

"Everyone always underestimates me," he said airily. "And they'll all pay in the end. Just like you."

"Why me?" she asked again.

"You know why. I was alone after I had disposed of Tiffani. Such a disappointment, that girl. She'd pretended to be special when she danced. Pretended that she saw that I was special, too," he tut-tutted. "I had a sick mother to care for and no one to care for me. And one night, I went to the movies, and there you were on the screen smiling at me with those green eyes. You saw me. You remember."

"We connected?" she guessed.

"Exactly!" Ganim slapped the wheel and Waverly flinched. "I came out here to bring you home. But what did you do?"

She prayed it was a rhetorical question.

"You disrespected me. Over and over again. I gave you chances to prove yourself to me, and you let me down every single time. First you couldn't bother to respond to me, then you openly taunt me, and then you let an imposter deal with me," he ticked off her faults one by one. "I knew it wasn't you. Because I know you, everything about you. But I played along until you came home. I was just toying with them. I gave you so many chances to prove yourself, to be worthy. And you failed."

He slowed the car and used the turn signal to pull over. "Are you ready for our destiny, Waverly?"

The excitement in his voice had her choking back a cry. Panic was closing in, and she was losing the fight.

"It's time." He put the car in park. "I'd tell you it will all be over in a minute, but that's only your part of the story. Mine will go on from here." He got out of the car and shut the door.

Waverly fought back against the short gasps of breath. She needed to keep it together. A panic attack would end it all here and now, and she wasn't ready to go yet. "Xavier, please hurry," she whispered to the night.

Ganim opened the door by her feet. She felt his hands on her bare legs, and her stomach lurched. "No!" she shrieked.

She tried kicking him, but the drugs swimming through her system left her weak.

He hauled her out and leaned her against the car. Waverly's knees buckled, and he let her crumple in the gutter.

"Do you know where we are? Look around."

They were on Hollywood Boulevard. The Walk of Fame. And her star was here.

"How poetic." he asked. "You'll die on your own star, and I'll become the famous one. Let's just hope we have an audience. Scream if you want. It'll only make it better."

Her hands were still tied, and her legs were shaky, but there was one thing she had reasonable control over. When Ganim hauled her up, Waverly staggered forward and connected with him forehead to nose.

She'd learned it from a stuntman years ago on set. "No one ever suspects a head butt," he'd explained. Well, if she lived through this, she was buying the man a steak dinner... and a mansion.

The night exploded in stars when she made contact, and she heard the satisfying crunch of Ganim's nose. He shrieked and backhanded her to the sidewalk. The blow had her tasting her own blood.

"Hey!" she heard it. Another voice in the dark, and there was the sound of running feet. "Hey, man! Stop!"

Ganim grabbed her by the hair and pulled her to her knees. She flinched as he raised his fist again. This blow caught her in the jaw and would have toppled her if he hadn't held her by the hair.

"Come closer," Ganim said, with a theatrical wave of his arm to the bystanders. He was a ringmaster, basking in the attention. "You're about to witness history. Do you know who this is?"

He twisted Waverly's head so she could look at them. "Tell them who they're about to see murdered."

When she refused, he slapped her again. Then she saw it. Streetlights reflecting on sharp metal. He waved the knife in front of her.

"Tell them who you are," he growled.

"Waverly Sinner," she whispered. Blood leaked onto her lips, but her eyes stayed dry. There were four of them, two men and two women, all young, all rapidly sobering up. One of the girls started to cry. "It's okay," Waverly told her. "It's okay."

"Don't hurt her," the tallest one, a guy wearing a shiny gray shirt unbuttoned almost to his waist, held up his hands.

"Oh, I don't want to hurt her," Ganim said. "I want to kill her." He held the knife up so they could all see it in its deadly glory.

Both girls were crying now. When the guy in the gray shirt and his friend both took a step forward, Ganim brought the knife down in a fast, shallow slice on Waverly's neck. She felt the blood well and spill, hot against her stinging skin. "Just run," she tried to yell, but her voice was so weak. "Run."

"Uh-uh-uh," he tutted. "Not another step, but I'll tell you what you can do."

"KATE?" Xavier answered his phone before the first ring finished.

"He has her. He has her, and he's making someone live stream it," Kate sobbed in his ear. "They're at her star. He's going to execute her! She's already bleeding, X. You have to do something."

"We're almost there," Micah said, putting the pedal all the way down.

One block to go, Xavier calculated.

"Kate, call Travers. We're here now."

He could see them from here. Waverly was kneeling on a star, her star, her head twisted at a funny angle.

"Go!" His voice broke on the command, and he unclasped his seatbelt. He and Micah had known each other long enough that they didn't need any other words to form the plan. This was life or death, and there was only one chance at making sure Waverly came out of this alive.

Ganim glanced in their direction as the roar of the engine caught his attention, but they were too fast. Xavier was already flinging his door open as Micah roared the Yukon up onto the sidewalk within inches of the man. When the knife flashed up, catching the light, Xavier fired three times into center mass and launched himself from the vehicle.

Ganim crumpled beneath him like a deck of cards. There was no resistance in his lifeless body. Xavier didn't bother checking for a pulse. He sprang to Waverly's side. Those beautiful eyes were closed, and there was so much blood. There were wounds on her face and her neck. His last strike had managed to connect, even as he died. The knife stuck in her chest, the handle angling out.

She was so pale. His Angel on concrete.

Xavier leaned over, framing her face with his hands. His lips hovered over her ear. "I'm here, Angel. I'm here. You're safe now. Don't leave me."

Micah was with him, kneeling at his side. But Xavier couldn't hear the words he was speaking. There were footsteps up close and sirens far away, but nothing registered with him. Not even the tears on his own cheeks. Her pulse was thready under his fingers.

"You can't leave me, Angel. Stay. Please stay, baby."

For the briefest moment, those gray-green eyes fluttered open. "I knew you'd come, X."

"Always, Angel. No matter where you are or what you need, I'll be there."

A ghost of a smile teased her pale lips. "I guess I can go to Stanford now."

"You can go anywhere you want, Angel." He pressed gentle kisses to her forehead and cheeks. "But I'm going with you."

Her eyes fluttered closed, but the smile remained.

"She's losing blood, Saint," Micah said grimly.

One of the bystanders jumped in with shaking hands. "I'm in nursing school," he said and set about assessing the stab wound. He and one of the girls applied pressure with makeshift bandages while Micah jumped on his cell phone.

The sirens grew louder, and Xavier could see red and blue lights reflecting in the store windows, but his gaze never left her face.

"I love you, my Angel," he murmured against her ear. "Since the moment you tossed me in that pool, I've been in love with you, and I'm not going to stop. So you need to stay with me."

29

Micah had to pull Xavier away from her when the EMTs arrived. His friend held him back in a bear hug while they went to work on her. A crowd, some hysterical and some ghoulishly excited, had begun to gather, and uniforms were putting up tape and pushing everyone back. Ganim's body lay crumpled where it had fallen, ignored as the energy of the scene focused on Waverly.

Xavier's gasp of pain ripped through him when he saw them lift her listless body onto the gurney. Micah held on to him for dear life, supporting his weight.

He didn't say anything. He didn't need to.

When they moved to load her into the ambulance, Micah shoved him after them. "Go."

Xavier was clamoring aboard before anyone could suggest otherwise. He didn't bother looking up as the doors closed, just held her hand and watched her face. Nothing existed to him beyond that beautiful face, frozen in time.

He couldn't have told anyone how long the ambulance ride was or how long he waited outside the trauma room. The only thing that he was able to recall was the nurse who pressed a cup of coffee into his trembling hands. He caught the words "lucky" and "recover," and it was enough to crack the dam inside him that had held back the fear, the remorse, the pain.

He followed along behind Waverly's gurney as they wheeled her into a private room with a host of IVs and monitors. The same nurse coaxed him into a chair next to her bed and suggested he talk to her while she slept.

He spent the next two hours doing just that.

IT WAS a wiggle of fingers that woke him. His head rested on the coarse cotton of hospital sheets, hand wrapped around Waverly's cold fingers. They were wiggling against his palm.

He lifted his head, foggy and too terrified to be hopeful. But those sea green eyes were watching him.

"Angel," he whispered it reverently.

"You found me. You saved me," she whispered back, her voice raspy and weak.

He rose up, bringing his forehead to hers. When she winced, he pulled back. "What is it, baby. What hurts? Tell me, and I'll call a nurse. A doctor. A team of doctors."

She gave him a pale-lipped smile. "I head-butted him."

"You remember what happened?" he asked, brushing his fingers whisper soft over her forehead.

Her eyes fluttered closed for a second before reopening. "I remember everything. I knew you'd come for me."

He leaned in, stroking her face and hair. "I told you I'd never be done with you."

"You told me you loved me."

He opened his mouth, closed it. And then nodded. "I may have said that. I thought you were unconscious."

Her eyes were heavy. She was having trouble keeping them open. "I won't hold you to it. You were under duress."

"I meant every word, Angel."

That ghost of a smile played on her lips again. "Good. Because I'm pretty sure I love you, too."

IT TOOK THREE DAYS, but Waverly was cleared by a team of doctors to go home. She cuddled up against Xavier's side in the back of an Invictus Tahoe. Xavier had shrugged off her attempts at conversation in the car but wouldn't let her wiggle out from under his arm. So she'd leaned against him and closed her eyes for the duration of the ride.

The foot of the driveway was a madhouse. There were twenty photographers waiting outside the gates, pushing back against the team Xavier and Micah had deployed to keep them off the property. She ignored the chaos on the other side of the tinted windows as the SUV slid through the gates.

He hadn't left her hospital bed for twenty-four straight hours until she'd begged him to go home to grab a shower and some sleep. It was the last she'd seen him until he arrived to take her home looking just as exhausted as he had when he left.

She hadn't been alone in his absence. Kate, Mari, Louie, and her father had taken turns guarding her bedside and driving her generally insane. Her mother had flown in, and, much to Waverly's shock, flew back to finish out her rehab. She would be home in another week, and after seeing her in the hospital, sharp, focused, and sober, Waverly felt the first sparks of hope for her mother that she'd felt in a long time.

But Xavier's absence made her nervous. She spent hours wondering if her confession of love scared him off. Perhaps he hadn't meant it when he'd whispered it to her over and over again when he thought he was losing her and again when he thought she was sleeping.

They would talk, she promised herself. Saints were talkers, and they could clear the air. She wasn't going to let him just drift away. Not now that she knew what love was and how precious life could be.

Her father had hired a private nurse for her for the next few days to help change Waverly's dressings and keep an eye on her. The plastic surgeon was thrilled with how she was healing and was confident that most of the scars would be practically invisible.

Her doctors had been thrilled with how quickly she'd bounced back. "It must be all the hot yoga I've been doing lately," she told them weakly, but Xavier hadn't been there to get the joke.

There had been a lot of her blood pooled on the Walk of Fame and she'd learned just how touch and go it had been for a while. She'd yet to see the video of the... incident. But she did get to meet the bystanders who'd been dragged into her near execution. And, as a special thank you for his hard work, she'd smuggled Arnie the photographer into her room and let him take a photo of her with them. With her permission, he sold the picture to a big-budgeted celebrity news magazine for six figures and immediately quit his job.

Rumor had it Douchebag Joe nearly had a heart attack when he got his autographed copy from Arnie in the mail.

Waverly sat up when the SUV came to a stop in the driveway, but Xavier anchored her to his side and carefully lifted her out.

"I can walk, X," she said, with a teasing smile. "I'm going to be hitting up barre class in a day or two."

But it didn't bring a smile to his handsome face. Nor did

the beautiful summer bouquet from Xavier's family that waited for her on the pool house's kitchen table.

She sank down on the couch and let Xavier fuss over a glass of water for her. She wasn't about to admit it, but even walking short distances exhausted her. The doctors assured her it was temporary but also warned her to take it sloth-like easy for a while. She closed her eyes and leaned her head against the couch cushion and listened to the blissful silence. No beeping monitors, no worried visitors, no vitals checks by the nurse.

Xavier set the glass down in front of her as well as a steaming bowl of chicken noodle soup and then just stood there looking at her. Nerves jittered out of him. He looked gaunt, haunted. Like a man who hadn't ate or slept in days.

She patted the cushion next to her, but he shook his head and shoved his hands in his pockets.

Waverly knew something was wrong. A queasy anxiety rolled through her stomach. "Where is everyone?" she asked, breaking the silence.

"I told them to give you some time to settle in. You haven't been alone in since… since before. I thought you'd like some time to yourself to get settled."

"Thank you," she said quietly. As distant as he was keeping himself, he still knew her. And knew she'd be suffocating under the constant watchfulness of others.

"So, I'm going to go," he said, briskly. But he made no move toward the door.

She took a settling breath. "Okay, while I'm settling, why don't we settle whatever's made you turn into the Invisible Man? What's going on?"

He must have been waiting for the question because the words rushed out of him.

"I almost got you killed." He said it flatly as if he'd felt every emotion in the gamut and was now empty. *God, she knew that feeling well.*

"Xavier," she said firmly. "You saved me."

"You trusted me, and I failed you. I let you down," he argued dispassionately. His mind was made up, but about what, she wasn't sure.

"You shot and killed the man who was trying to execute me," she said evenly.

Xavier unfroze from his spot and began to pace. "He never would have had the chance to get to you if I had been doing my job. But I wasn't. I let my personal feelings get in the way, and I missed the trap. I walked you right into it."

"You didn't want me to go to the club in the first place. You were worried that something like that would happen."

"And even expecting it, he still got past me." There was feeling now. A simmering anger.

Waverly carefully pushed to her feet, but Xavier stepped away from her. She crossed her arms against the chill that was settling over her.

"You saved my life. I'm alive because of you."

"Don't you get it?" he snapped. "You wouldn't have been in this situation if it weren't for me. I almost cost you your life because I was so blinded by lust and anger—"

"So it's lust now?" It was her turn for a cool, empty tone.

"You do things to me that I can't handle. You make it so I can't function," he said.

"Make up your mind, X. Is it your fault or mine?"

He was reaching. She recognized the fear and wished she could make it go away for him. He glared at her floor, still avoiding looking directly at her.

"Xavier, how many cops were there in that club? How many FBI agents? Yet it's your fault and your fault alone?" She reached for him, but he shrugged her off.

"You trusted me to keep you safe, and I failed."

"I am trusting you not to walk away, X. We have something here. You are the only person in my entire life who ever made decisions based on my best interests, Xavier."

"Don't guilt me into staying," he snapped. "Did it ever occur to you that maybe it's time you start making your own decisions?"

She winced at the anger and truth behind his words. "I thought you understood."

"I did. I do. But I'm not going to be your new jailer, the next person that you live your life for. When are you going to stand on your own two feet?"

"I love—"

He held up his hands cutting her off. "Don't say it. You can't say it."

"I can't tell you that I love you? That you're the only person I've ever said those words to? That even though you're backing down off of yours, I still love you?"

"It's not love!" He snapped the words out like a whip, but at least he was finally looking at her. "We are toxic together, Waverly. What I feel for you? It's not healthy. It's an obsession. I'm no better than Ganim."

"What are you talking about?" she felt the tears rising. "What are you telling me?"

"I've done *nothing* but obsess over you since I met you. Everything I've done since that first day has been about you. I go to sleep fantasizing about you and wake up more fixated with you every day than the last. I touch you, and it's never enough. I stay close to you, and it's never close enough unless I'm inside you, and even then, I'm wanting more of you."

He stopped, and she noted the tic in his jaw, the line between his eyes. This wasn't just a fight.

"I can't be around you anymore, Waverly."

"What?" Her gasp made her stitches sing. She shook her head. "No. No. Why are you doing this? We have a chance, Xavier. We survived. It wasn't for nothing. We have something—"

"We have nothing that we can build on," he argued. "We have sex, and we fight. That's not a relationship. But you wouldn't know that, would you? You're..." he trailed off, tucked the words back inside.

"What? Say it. I'm what? Damaged?"

Xavier looked away, and Waverly stepped in to face her worst fear. "Maybe so, Xavier. But I'm willing to fight. I'm willing to try." She hated the plea she heard in her voice, but damn it, for once in her life she was going to fight for what she wanted. "I'm alive because of you, and I want to see where this life will take us."

He looked sick and caged. She was standing between him and the door.

"Tell me how we can make this work, X," she said. A tear worked its way down her cheek.

"I can't fix you. I'm not your future. I'm just an extension of where you already are. You would just move from under your parents' thumb to mine. Trade a cage for a cage because that's what I would keep you in. I keep seeing you, bleeding out on a sidewalk." His voice cracked, shuddered.

"I'm not bleeding on a sidewalk. I'm standing in front of you asking you to give me a chance!"

"You're not hearing me, Waverly. I don't want to make this work. You're not good for me. You're damaged, and you'll damage me, too." His face was ashen, tortured. "You already have."

Waverly sank down on the couch as her knees buckled.

"Get out." She said the words quietly with a strength she didn't feel.

"I'm sorry—"

"Get out of my house. Save yourself before it's too late." Ice and fire went to war in her belly. She stood again and wobbled.

He reached for her on instinct, but she froze him with a look.

"Leave your key and get out of my house."

She held her head high as he slowly dug his keys from his pocket. He pulled two off and laid them on the coffee table.

"Can I call someone for you?" His voice was tight with emotion.

"Leave now," she said mechanically, using every ounce of her shaky will to hold back the tide of pain.

He nodded and walked, shoulders hunched, out of the room and out of her life.

She didn't care if he heard the crash as she upended the coffee table, sending bowl and glass and keys flying. She didn't care about anything anymore.

Her sneakers crunched through the debris, and she dragged herself into her bedroom. She lay face down clutching a pillow to her chest, grateful that this was one place she'd never made love to him.

She started to sob and was afraid she'd never stop.

30

Waverly wallowed in grief for another two days. Her heart bled worse than the knife wounds, and she wondered if this anguish was what would kill her. She loved him. For the first time in her life, she'd opened herself to someone, given him free rein with her heart and her body. And he'd betrayed her. And she was dumb enough to be surprised.

She couldn't think about it, about him. Couldn't think about the aftershocks that Xavier Saint would send through the rest of her life.

Her world had been reduced to her bed and the couch in the pool house. The usually outspoken Kate stood stoically by her side, a sentinel to Waverly's endless tears. Mari and Louie took their turns plying her with food she didn't eat. She knew they meant well but wished they would all leave her alone so she could let her grief swallow her.

Her body hurt, and her heart ached, and she didn't see an end to her pain. If this was what love did, her mother had been right to close off to it.

Waverly was wiping silent tears away when her father

knocked on her bedroom door. She didn't even try to paste on a smile. What was the point? "Hi, Dad," she offered flatly.

Robert entered holding a brown paper bag with twine handles. "I brought you something, sweetheart." He settled on the edge of her bed and handed her the bag. When she didn't make a move, he dumped the contents on her duvet.

"Hot dogs?" Waverly asked listlessly.

"Do you remember when you were little and thought it was the biggest deal to roast hot dogs outside in the fireplace?"

She did. The memory hit her like a warm embrace. Her mother and the chef before Louie had made them all vegan for a few weeks. Robert and Waverly would sneak out onto the patio and fire up the massive stone fireplace and roast hot dogs.

It had felt... normal.

"You want to roast hot dogs?" she asked him.

Her father nodded. "I want to roast hot dogs and talk. Also, just in case you're wondering, I'm not taking no for an answer."

Waverly raised her eyebrows. Her father being firm? What had the world come to?

"Well, then. Let's go," Waverly said. He helped her out of the room, Marisol was in the kitchen and gave Robert an approving nod when he opened the front door for Waverly.

It hurt to move, and she realized that it wasn't necessarily the wounds that hurt the most, it was the rest of her body that had atrophied. *When had Waverly Sinner turned into a woman who could be destroyed by the capriciousness of a man?* she wondered with the first flush of embarrassment. Feeling anything besides pain was a relief.

Robert pulled two loungers up in front of the massive outdoor fireplace and produced a pair of brand-new roasting sticks. He glanced at her, studying, and then nodded. "You look hungry," he decided and speared two hot dogs on both sticks.

She offered him a sad smile.

On the side table between them was a bag of rolls and a collection of mismatched bowls and spoons. Ketchup, mustard, chili, irregularly diced onions. "Did you do all this?" Waverly asked incredulously.

Her father glanced at the hodgepodge of toppings. "I hope I didn't forget anything important."

She looked at him for what felt like the first time. He was dressed in casual shorts and a three-hundred dollar polo that was going to end up with ketchup on it. And he was present. His phone wasn't clutched in his hand. There wasn't a beautiful girl he was making eyes at. He was sitting with her, being present. He handed her one of the sticks and sat next to her. They stuck the sticks into the gas flames and Waverly focused her attention on slowly rotating her hot dogs.

"We're overdue for a conversation," Robert began.

"Sinners aren't big on talking," Waverly said evasively.

"I think we should consider changing that," he said. "Your mother is coming home this weekend. And there are a lot of things that are going to change."

"I'm glad you're feeling hopeful, Dad. But you can't count on her recovery," Waverly reminded him.

"I know that. And I'm going to support your mother in her ongoing treatment, but I can't control the outcome and neither can you. What we can do is be more honest with each other."

Waverly spared her dad a glance. "Uh, Dad? You sound like a therapy session."

"Good. That means it's working."

She bobbled her hotdogs and barely rescued them from the marble of the patio. "You're in therapy?"

"I started after Greece."

"Wow." Waverly didn't know what to think. Her mother in rehab, her father in therapy. What was her world coming to? "Uh, how's it going?"

"Good. Painful, but good," he admitted. "And speaking of painful, I have to tell you something."

Waverly closed her eyes. More pain. There was always more, a never-empty well of it in this lifetime.

"I went to see Xavier."

"What?" This time she did drop her hot dogs. Her father picked them up for her.

"The fire will sterilize them," he predicted.

Still in shock, she took the stick back from him.

Robert cleared his throat and pressed on. "When we were in Greece, he—shall we say—encouraged me to step up and be a better man."

"Oh, God."

"I went there with the intention of doing the right thing by my daughter, threatening him with bodily harm if he ever so much as thought about you again."

Of course this was the moment her father chose to stand up for her. When a father's interference would add to the humiliation.

"How did you know we were... he and I were..." she couldn't find a way to end the sentence without tears or awkwardness.

"After he got done putting me in my place on the yacht, I could see how much he cared about you," Robert told her.

"And so you went to return the favor." Waverly heaved a heavy sigh.

"That was my intention. Until I saw him. I've seen men destroyed before, but nothing like that." Robert shot her a glance. "He looks worse than you, and you nearly died."

For some reason it made her want to laugh. The absurdity

of it all. She'd almost died, and when she knew she was finally safe, that she once again had that gift of life, she'd lost her will to want it. *Could she find it again? Could she grab onto that gift and run with it, finally? Even without Xavier?*

"How was he?" she asked, hoping she sounded casual. She wanted to know the details of his suffering, wanted to know that he hurt like she hurt.

"He was so drunk I had to help him to the sofa," Robert told her. "He hasn't left his condo since he left you here the day you came home. And, from the smell of it, hasn't showered either."

"He's probably just mourning a near miss with his perfect record. Almost lost a client," Waverly muttered.

"Oh, he talked about you—well, slurred. But it wasn't about you being a client. It was about how he wasn't good enough for you and that you deserved a man who could keep you safe from danger. Someone who wouldn't fail you like he had."

"Why is he such an idiot?" Waverly wondered.

"I know how he feels, Waverly," Robert confessed. "I've felt that way about you and your mother for a very long time. I wasn't good enough, and I did my best to prove just that to both of you."

"I wasn't looking for perfect, Dad. I was looking for real."

"I'm starting to understand that. And maybe someday, so will Xavier," he sighed. "You have to understand, I owe him. He kept you safe when I couldn't and wouldn't. You're here with me because Xavier Saint was a good man."

"Whose side are you on here?" Waverly asked him.

"Always yours. From now on, always yours," Robert told her.

Waverly pulled her hot dogs out of the flames. She tucked them into buns and handed two more to her father.

"I'm going to need you to be on my side for something."

"Name it," he said, adding onions to his dogs.

"I'm going to college."

THE MORNING SUN was promising a sultry L.A. day when Micah made his way out to the Sinner's pool. Waverly greeted him from her seat on a wide wicker chair. She wore gym shorts and a t-shirt that mostly covered her bandages. Her eyes were still red from days of crying, but now they held something new. Determination.

"Thanks for coming, Micah," she said, shaking the hand that he offered. She pointed to the chair across from her. "Have a seat."

Micah folded his long legs under the table and looked around the patio while Waverly poured him coffee into a sturdy mug. "Thanks," he said, accepting the caffeine. "So what do I owe the pleasure of this meeting?"

Waverly hugged her knee into her chest. "I have a delicate situation that I'd like to address with you."

At Micah's uncomfortable throat clear, she knew he was keenly aware of what needed to be discussed.

"As I'm sure you know, Xavier and I are no longer able to work together."

Micah nodded slowly and chose his words carefully. "I am aware of the situation."

"However, I see no reason why the reputation of Invictus should suffer based on personal issues. I don't want anyone to think that after last week's incident that I am anything but eternally grateful to you and your staff. I'm alive because of... all of you."

She saw Micah's broad shoulders relax fractionally. "I'm grateful that you think so," he said diplomatically.

"So if you wouldn't see it as a disloyalty to your partner, I've discussed this with my father, and we'd like to keep Invictus on board for the remainder of the summer. A driver, alarm system monitoring, and personal protection when I do media events."

"Of course. We'd be happy to continue working with you," Micah agreed.

Waverly nodded. "Excellent. The official line will be that Invictus saved my life and, should the question arise, there is and was no personal relationship between myself and Xavier Saint."

Micah cleared his throat again. "I believe you'll be fielding that question often. Have you seen the video?"

Waverly shook her head. If she didn't enjoy watching herself acting on the big screen, she was fairly certain she wouldn't like watching herself beg for her life before nearly losing it.

"The video is very... emotional," Micah told her. "We've been bombarded with interview requests, and they all want to know if you and Xavier were... involved."

"I see," Waverly sighed.

"If you'll forgive me for saying this, if you can stomach watching the video, maybe you'll have a better understanding for the reaction that my partner had after the fact."

"Can we just ditch the politically correct bullshit?" Waverly asked. She was a newly impatient woman who didn't want to waste time tip-toeing around.

"He's a fucking mess, Waverly. He thought he lost you, and it nearly killed him. He thought it was his fault that you almost died in front of the entire Internet. I don't know if he's going to come back from this."

She took a steadying breath, forcing the impending storm of tears back. "I can't do anything to change what happened or how he reacted."

"I thought we were ditching the bullshit," Micah said politely.

"I told him I loved him, and he said I was too damaged to love anyone."

Micah swiped a hand over his face. "He's an idiot."

"No argument."

Micah sat back up. "I'm sorry that he didn't handle it even remotely well."

"Me too," Waverly said, masking the bitterness she felt. Even if what Micah was saying was true, that Xavier did have feelings for her and that he was devastated over ending things, it would only add him to the long list of people who had worked their own agenda on her. And those days of allowing it to happen were over.

"I do have a personal request," she said, taking a sip of coffee. "I don't want Xavier to be briefed on anything concerning me or my family."

Micah nodded. "I understand, and that won't be a problem. If I can get him sobered up, he's going to New York. We've been kicking around opening an office there and now is probably a good time to get him out of town."

Waverly nodded and stared into her coffee. A fresh start for both of them—on opposite sides of the country. She hoped it would be enough to eventually numb the pain, for her at least. Xavier deserved to suffer for a while. A long while. She was done forgiving and forgetting.

"Thank you for meeting with me, Micah," she said, declaring the meeting over.

Micah rose and buttoned his jacket. "Thanks for all of this. I appreciate your professionalism."

"Thank you for keeping me alive," she said.

Micah smiled, bright and toothy. "Take care of yourself, Waverly."

She felt the smile play at the corner of her lips. For once, she was going to do just that.

"Watch the video," Micah called over his shoulder as he walked toward the drive.

Waverly sat quietly for a few minutes, staring out over the pool, over the hills, over the only world she'd ever known. She pulled out her phone.

"Kate? I need you to set up a meeting with Gwendolyn for today. And how do you feel about doing some house hunting with me in Palo Alto?"

It was time for a new life. One that she chose for herself. One where she would never again allow herself to be blinded by love.

AUTHOR'S NOTE TO THE READER

Dear Reader,

I hate cliffhangers. The Harry Potter books tortured my reader's soul for years, which is why I was angry, terrified, frustrated, and hungry when Sinner & Saint was too girthy to fit into one book.

Please consider this my personal apology for the cliffhanger. It was unintentional, but once Xavier Saint got started he was impossible to tame. I swear to you that the conclusion of their story, Breaking the Rules, will make up for it.

Think of the groveling grumpy Xavier is going to have to perform! Wink! Thank you for sticking it out for this couple. They're one of my all-time favorites.

Yours apologetically,

Lucy Score

ABOUT THE AUTHOR

Lucy Score is a *Wall Street Journal* and #1 Amazon bestselling author. She grew up in a literary family who insisted that the dinner table was for reading and earned a degree in journalism. She writes full-time from the Pennsylvania home she and Mr. Lucy share with their obnoxious cat, Cleo. When not spending hours crafting heartbreaker heroes and kick-ass heroines, Lucy can be found on the couch, in the kitchen, or at the gym. She hopes to someday write from a sailboat, or oceanfront condo, or tropical island with reliable Wi-Fi.

Sign up for her newsletter and stay up on all the latest Lucy book news.
And follow her on:
Website: Lucyscore.com
Facebook at: lucyscorewrites
Instagram at: scorelucy
Readers Group at: Lucy Score's Binge Readers Anonymous

LUCY'S TITLES

Standalone Titles

Undercover Love

Pretend You're Mine

Finally Mine

Protecting What's Mine

Mr. Fixer Upper

The Christmas Fix

Heart of Hope

The Worst Best Man

Rock Bottom Girl

The Price of Scandal

By a Thread

Riley Thorn and the Dead Guy Next Door

Forever Never

The Blue Moon Small Town Romance Series

No More Secrets

Fall into Temptation

The Last Second Chance

Not Part of the Plan

Holding on to Chaos

The Fine Art of Faking It

Where It All Began

The Mistletoe Kisser

Bootleg Springs Series

Whiskey Chaser

Sidecar Crush

Moonshine Kiss

Bourbon Bliss

Gin Fling

Highball Rush

Sinner and Saint

Crossing the Line

Breaking the Rules

Made in United States
Troutdale, OR
02/24/2024

17953346R00249